GIRLS OF JULY

ALEX FLINN

GIRLS OF JULY

HARPERTEEN
An Imprint of HarperCollinsPublishers

HarperTeen is an imprint of HarperCollins Publishers.

Girls of July

Copyright © 2019 by Alex Flinn

All rights reserved. Printed in the United States of America.

No part of this book may be used or reproduced in any manner whatsoever
without written permission except in the case of brief quotations embodied
in critical articles and reviews. For information address HarperCollins
Children's Books, a division of HarperCollins Publishers, 195 Broadway,
New York, NY 10007.

www.epicreads.com

ISBN 978-0-06-244783-8

Typography by Laura Eckes

19 20 21 22 23   PC/LSCH   10 9 8 7 6 5 4 3 2 1

❖

First Edition

In memory of Richard Peck, whose advice I still take (and pass on)
twenty years after we first met

1

Britta

TO THOSE WHO APPRECIATE STARLIGHT AND FRESH AIR: three rooms for rent in secluded cabin in the Adirondacks, July 1–31. Teen girl and grandmother seeking teen female housemates. Private lake with canoes and kayaks available. Come see our deer! Pick wildflowers and blackberries! Dip a toe in our icy lake! Hike our mountains! Stargaze in a sky devoid of city light bleed! Responsible renters only! NO PARTIERS! Also, no cell phone reception. Get away from it all! Interview required. Contact Alicia Webster alicia@spiderwebster.com

BRITTA'S DAY COULDN'T have been worse, and it was only half over. If you could even count lunch as half when it began at 10:40. The meal you ate at 10:40 was called brunch.

It had started with rain, pouring-down Miami rain that began right at 6:20, when Britta had to leave for the bus. Her mother had taken away her car. Then, first period, she got back her Algebra II test with a big red *F* across the top. And third period, she'd argued with Ms. Barfield, her drama teacher, about the pukey-yellow costume she had to wear for her second act duet. It made her look like a summer squash. Unfortunately, she'd been impulsive enough to say just that. Now her favorite teacher thought she was a brat. Why couldn't she control herself sometimes?

Enough with people. At lunchtime, instead of meeting her friends, Britta ducked into the library. She settled onto a beige plastic couch under a "Read" poster of some basketball player reading *Harry Potter* and took out her iPad. She scrolled, clicking on posts about "9 Actors You Didn't Know Almost Played Batman" and a gif of two cats fighting with lightsabers.

Scroll, scroll, scroll. Then she saw the ad.

It had been shared by a friend of a friend of a mutual's cousin or something, as such things were. Or such things would be, if people usually posted ads for summer vacation properties on social media instead of Airbnb. Which, of course, they didn't.

Starlight and fresh air.

The accompanying picture showed a peaceful lake mirroring pine trees. She clicked on it. Then, one of a house with a porch going all around.

It was like a sign, like someone was saying, "Relax, Britta! Get away from Mom and her skeezy boyfriend and relaaaaax."

She wondered what city light bleed was.

Britta noticed Meredith Daly, sitting under a poster of Taylor Swift reading *The Giver*. Meredith wore khaki shorts that were longer than any teenager should wear and a white polo that said "German Honor Society." Because of course she did. She crouched over a stack of homemade flash cards, her reddish hair covering her eyes. She sort of rocked back and forth, flipping over first one, then another pink card.

"Wagner Act." Meredith turned the card over and pumped her fist in victory. Britta bet Meredith knew what light bleed was. She switched sofas and tapped her shoulder.

Meredith started. "What? Huh?" She pulled away her noise-canceling headphones.

"Do you know what city light bleed is?" Britta asked.

Meredith looked at Britta like she was on bath salts. "What?"

"City light bleed. 'Devoid of city light bleed.' What does that mean?"

Meredith shook her head. "No idea." She replaced the headphones.

Britta googled "city light bleed," which she should have done in the first place. It had to do with astronomy. With less city light bleed, you could see way more stars.

Once Britta's family had gone camping, and she remembered the stars, millions of them, spread like a lace overlay on a black velvet dress. Dad had held her hand and shown her the Big Dipper and her own constellation, Libra. That was when Dad had been around.

Now Dad was gone, and there was her mother's new boyfriend, Rick, who was always "joking" about her tight shorts or how many boys she must be dating or asking if she wanted a ride in his Lamborghini. And who was the reason she didn't have a car anymore. She needed to get away to someplace Rick-free for the summer.

In the past, her mother would never have let her. Britta hadn't been allowed to sleep over at a friend's house until ninth grade, and even then, her mother had called five times.

But now that Rick was in the picture, it might be different. Her friend Teghan had suggested they be CITs together at a Girl Scout camp in North Florida. Yeah, no. Being in a cabin with fifteen eight-year-olds was not Britta's idea of a summer vacation. And what if she misplaced one or something? It could happen.

Britta looked back at the photo of the lake. This! This was what she wanted—to hike and kayak and stargaze. Not use chopsticks to check little kids' scalps for lice.

Beside her, Meredith said, "Works Progress Administration."

Britta looked Meredith over, since Meredith was plainly oblivious. Meredith would be pretty if she'd lighten up. They had no classes together, Meredith being a genius who only took AP think-tank classes. But they'd sort of been friendly in grade school, when Meredith, skinny and sad-looking, had transferred in second semester of fourth grade. Every day at lunch, she sat alone, reading. So weird. But Britta felt sorry for her, sorry enough that once, she'd asked her about her book.

Meredith's eyes had lit up. "It's called *Inkdeath*," she'd said. "It's the last book in the Inkheart trilogy. Have you read them?"

Britta had shaken her head no, sorry she'd said anything. Now Meredith would think she was dumb. But Meredith had said, "Well, you should. They changed my life."

That was sort of a funny thing to say, but the next time the class went to the library, Britta had checked out the first book, which had a picture of a lizard on the cover. Meredith had smiled when she saw her doing so. And, while Britta wouldn't say the book was life changing, it was a pretty good story, and Britta had actually finished it, instead of losing it under the debris on her nightstand and returning it unread, her usual habit with library books.

Meredith flipped through the cards, furrowing her brow so much Britta's mother would say she'd have crow's-feet at twenty. Man, if anyone needed to relax, it was Meredith. Suddenly, it struck Britta that someone smart like Meredith might make a good partner in crime.

So, like in fourth grade, Britta decided to suck it up. She held her iPad out. "Meredith?"

Meredith didn't respond, flipping a yellow card. Britta rolled her eyes and stuck her iPad between Meredith's face and the flash cards.

Meredith jumped. "Excuse me! Do you have no concept of personal space?"

Now that she had Meredith's attention, Britta pointed at her own ears, hoping Meredith would figure out she should take off the headphones.

She did. "What?"

"It's silly."

"Probably," Meredith agreed, replacing her headphones.

"Wait!" Britta pointed to the ad. "Just look. Isn't it heavenly?"

Meredith glanced at it. "Nice." She went back to the card that said "Act passed by Congress in 1933 to stabilize the banks."

Meredith said, "Emergency Banking Act."

But Britta persisted. "It says they have three rooms to rent for July."

"Uh-huh." Meredith reached for the headphones again.

Britta talked faster, competing with the headphones. "And a private lake! And kayaks and stars and . . . deer! And no light bleed! I looked it up, and it means it's so dark you can really see the stars, all of them." She had to stop to breathe, but Meredith had paused anyway. "Don't you ever wish you could go someplace where no one knows you, where you can't be reached? Where there's not so much stress?"

"Why are you asking me this? We're not friends." Meredith looked back at the cards.

"We're not enemies. And they have three rooms. We could take two of them. I want to get away from my mom's boyfriend, and . . . everything." She tried to decide whether to say what she was thinking, about the real reason she'd thought Meredith should go. "I heard about what happened last week."

Meredith's head jerked up. "What? Does the whole school know?" The unspoken words, *even you*, hung there like Taylor Swift's poster.

Britta shrugged apologetically. "Word gets around. And everyone looks up to you."

Meredith hung her head. "God. I'm so embarrassed."

"Don't be." Britta's hand hovered over Meredith's shoulder. She wanted to pat her or something. "People freak out sometimes. You just need a vacation. We could go up there."

Sighing, Meredith scrolled through the photographs again. This time, Britta could tell she was really looking, because she glanced away from the flash cards.

"I know it's weird, asking you," Britta said. "But if I asked any of my actual friends, they'd laugh. And if you asked any of your actual friends, same thing, right?"

Meredith tried to hand back the iPad. "I can't take a vacation. I need to do something important over the summer, pad my resume for college."

"Aren't you in a bunch of activities?" Britta said. "Isn't that why you're stressed out?"

Meredith laughed. "Yeah. I'm in all the activities. That's why I can't just take off. I'm president of the National Honor Society and the Key Club, and I built Habitat homes, and I organized a walk for cancer, and I'm on the bowling team."

"The bowling team?" Britta said. "You bowl? Like, on a regular basis?"

"You have to have a sport—to show you're well-rounded."

"Okay, so you're president of all these clubs and on the bowling team, and—"

"I'm the captain of the bowling team."

"Captain of the bowling team. But you're not going to get into college because you took a month off to go to the mountains when you're obviously stressed out?"

"Maybe not the right college. My mother went to Princeton." But Meredith looked at the ad again, expanding the photograph of the house with her finger.

"I bet it smells like pine trees," Britta singsonged. "Like Christmas all year-round."

Meredith nodded. "My mother would say I have time for this after I get into college."

"So don't tell your mother. Tell her you're taking a college class. At Princeton."

The bell rang then. Meredith handed the iPad back to Britta.

Britta packed her stuff up slowly. Her next class was close to the library, and she wanted to give Meredith more time to change her mind. "You could write your college essays in peace."

Nothing.

"It could change our lives," Britta said.

Meredith laughed. Still, Britta's patience was rewarded when Meredith called after her. "Britta?"

Britta smiled. So she remembered her name, at least. "Yeah?"

"Call me later." She gave Britta her phone number.

2

Kate

Three months later

"HURRY, KATY, YOU don't want to miss the flight," Kate's father called across the clockwork craziness of Hartsfield Airport at ten o'clock, when the travelers swarmed like ants on a doughnut.

What if I do want to miss it? "I'm tying my shoe."

"Well, giddyap." Her father wore a suit, scanning the crowd as he always did when they went anywhere, to see if there was anyone he knew, the consummate politician.

"I don't think I should go." Kate rose and started down the concourse. "Mother's having a fit that I won't be able to go to twenty-seven debutante events, and—"

"It's for the best. I don't want you and Blake here if this hits the papers."

Kate nodded, eyes on the gate numbers. Kate didn't want to think about what "this" was, that he might get arrested. It made her stomach jump to think about it. Her father was kind and gentle and wanted to help people. How could he go to jail?

"I'll talk to your mother." Her father walked faster. "Come on. If you miss the plane, you won't make the bus either."

"Right. The bus." She'd never taken the bus, even to school. The Covingtons didn't take buses. No one she knew did. She wondered if it would be dirty. She shuddered, imagining it.

People at the gate were lining up to board. She noticed two girls her own age, a redhead and a petite brunette with French braids. The brunette might have been younger than her, judging from the pink camouflage duffel bag she carried. She wondered where they were going.

"Will you call and tell me what happens?" she asked her father.

"Not sure. Cell phone reception's pretty bad there. And internet. It's for the best."

"Oh. Right." She remembered that from when she had spoken to the girl who was renting the place—Spider was her very odd name. She had interviewed Kate to make sure they were compatible, and she'd said, not apologetically, that reception was spotty. "Sometimes, when the wind blows right or you're on a hill, you get a text." So there would be no calls from her mother about debutante party themes or the perfect white dress or what kind of flowers wouldn't make her father feel ill or matching bow ties for the dog. No Snapchat or Twitter or Instagram with gossip about her family, no updates from Daddy.

And no calls from Colin.

Kate felt her phone vibrating inside her purse. Mother. Or maybe Colin. He'd called several times since she'd broken up with him by text the night before. She knew that was cruel, but it was for the best. She didn't want him embroiled in her family scandal either, or to feel like he had to stick by her to avoid looking bad. Better to think she was a bitch.

The airline was calling the first class, gold, platinum, emerald, titanium, tin, copper, bloodstone, and all the other levels that came before boarding group one. She remembered her mother's face the last time she saw her.

"Katy!" Her father held out her carry-on, a Louis Vuitton that would look ridiculous out in the wilderness.

"Now boarding group one."

"So you're just going to dump me in the woods? Like I'm Snow White or something?"

He handed her the bag. "I'm protecting you."

"What if I don't want to be protected?"

"It will be peaceful there. You can hike." His voice went down at the end, like when she was little and he used to say something and you just knew it wasn't open for discussion.

"Now boarding group two."

"Is that your group?" her father said.

"Yeah." Kate felt the incredible urge to hug her father, throw herself into his arms like she had when he'd come home from business trips when she was little. But the Covingtons didn't hug, not as adults, anyway, except maybe at funerals. That was why she was surprised to see that he had his arms out, right there in the airport. She moved closer, and he drew her in.

"Have a good time, Katy. Don't worry about me. Don't worry about me."

Finally, he released her, and she started toward the gate.

"Now boarding group three."

The two girls from before were in group three. She got in line behind them. Lucky girls! They probably went on adventures like this all the time.

That was silly, Kate knew. They might be cousins, visiting their sick grandmother or on their way to some boring church camp, and the only reason their parents hadn't insisted on getting a special pass to walk them to the gate was because they were just changing planes in Atlanta.

She looked back to tell Daddy she'd call when she arrived, but he was already gone. She trudged forward. Then, somehow, she was on the plane. A man looked annoyed when she brushed past him. But when he saw Kate's face, he smiled. People always did that. It was the blessing and the curse of being beautiful. It was impossible to pass unnoticed.

But people thought they owned you, like they had the right to stare just because of an accident of birth of having blond hair and symmetrical features.

"Do you need help with that?" He gestured toward her bag.

"Oh, that's all . . ." She glanced at the tiny space left in the overhead bin. It was going to take some shoving. "Yes. Please."

He hoisted it up. "There you go!"

"Thank you." Kate took her seat. Her phone buzzed inside her purse. She didn't want to answer it. It was probably Mother, as close to hysterics as when the maid had used Carpet Fresh on the Persian rug from Sotheby's. But she knew she should pick it up.

"I'm about to take off," she said.

"You finally answered."

Not Mother. Not Mother at all. Colin's deep, sweet voice.

"I can't talk to you," Kate whispered, even though she wanted to.

"Just one minute. Where are you going?"

She felt the resolve draining from her like blood from a wound.

"I can't, Colin. There's no point."

"No point to us? But why? I thought—"

"Please. I don't want to hang up on you."

"Then don't. Don't. We can work out . . . whatever it is."

"No, we can't. It isn't fair to you." As she said this, she realized she sounded like her father, trying to protect her. "I can't anymore. I'm sorry. Goodbye."

Before she changed her mind, she ended the call, then switched the phone to airplane mode. She stuck in her earbuds.

The boy in the next seat, who wore a T-shirt from a college she'd never heard of, looked at her. "Boyfriend trouble, huh?"

Kate drew in a deep breath and pretended not to hear, even though he could probably tell she didn't have any music on.

Music would drown out the only sound she wanted to hear, Colin's voice, saying, "No point to us?" When he'd said it, she could see his face before her, sweet, shy Colin.

She leaned her forehead against the cool, smooth window.

3

Spider

FADE IN:

INT. CHARMING CABIN, BEDROOM — DAY

RUTHIE WEBSTER, 72, an elderly former
flower child and SPIDER WEBSTER, 17, her
bespectacled beanpole of a granddaughter
are making up a bed. We see them talking
from behind. Both move similarly. It is not
until Spider turns toward the camera that
we realize that she is younger.

SPIDER SAW HER life as a movie. She planned to write and
direct someday, to make an impact with her brain, since she

obviously wasn't going to be competing in the Olympics any-time soon. Everything that happened to her would end up on screen, including this summer.

"We'll put Meredith and Kate in the rooms up here," she told Ruthie as she smoothed down a yellow-and-white double-wedding-ring quilt. "Britta can sleep downstairs."

"The two girls are friends," Ruthie said. "They'll probably want adjoining rooms."

Spider shuddered to think about that. Two girls giggling all night and running in the halls. They might even sneak out for beer or boys.

"I don't know. That Britta seemed kind of loud, and the walls are thin." Spider knew this from hard experience. Her sister, Emily, had been in the room adjoining hers every summer. Em could even do yoga loudly, thumping her feet against the wall while Spider tried to write. But at least she was familiar with her sister's brand of annoying. A stranger would be worse.

"The walls are made of logs," Ruthie said. "I saw that ad you placed, and it sounded like you were looking for three monks."

"I was not." Spider folded the sheet over the top of the quilt. "I specified female roommates, so they couldn't be monks . . . though a vow of silence would be a plus."

"And what did poor Britta say to make you think she might be"—Ruthie pretended to cringe—"loud?"

Spider thought back to the phone call. It wasn't anything specific the girl had said, just her energy level, which could be described as a shih tzu on Adderall. But she and the other girl,

16

Meredith, had answered the ad together, so they were a package deal. Also, they hadn't gotten many responses. Apparently, teenage girls weren't all that interested in relaxing.

Spider was not a typical teenage girl, as people in her life loved to remind her. Extroverts frightened her.

"Alicia?" Her grandmother still called her Alicia. The nickname Spider had started when a middle school bully had seen her struggling up stairs, all long arms and legs, and yelled, "Hey, look at the spider!" But Spider had taken ownership of it. After all, spiders were pretty smart about things like spinning webs and trapping their prey. Lately, she'd taken to wearing a lot of black too. It was like her superhero name.

Spider pushed her glasses up the bridge of her nose. "She mentioned being into theater. She'll probably go around singing show tunes all day."

"*I* was in theater," Ruthie said.

"Well, sure. But that was, you know . . ." Spider bent, then flexed, her aching fingers.

"The dark ages?"

"I was going to say when Shakespeare was alive."

"Ha ha ha." Ruthie picked up another quilt and walked to the door. "Well, I, for one, think it would be nice to have some young voices here."

"What am I?"

"You're an old soul. I miss when your whole family used to come."

"Me too." She hadn't always gotten along with her siblings,

17

but at least when they were little, they'd gone frog hunting or out for ice cream together. Spider guessed she understood that they had other things to do, but she would miss this place if she couldn't go here. It was like summers fortified her, so she could stand the rest of the year.

"It was a good idea you had, renting out the other rooms," Ruthie said.

"It was the only way to keep Dad and Aunt Laura from renting out the whole place. Or worse, trying to get you to sell it." Spider started toward the room that had belonged to her brother, Ben. The sheets there were blue and comfortable-looking. She wouldn't have minded nestling down on them, smelling the mountain air through the window, listening to the leaves fluttering in the breeze. But she'd promised to go with Ruthie to the bus station. Spider herself had never taken a long bus trip. She probably should, as part of a filmmaker's experience, but it looked pretty bad in movies, like *Planes, Trains and Automobiles*, and even worse in the movie *Speed*, which was about a bus where a bomb would go off if the driver didn't go fast enough.

"You keep drifting off," Ruthie said. "Are you thinking about movie plots again?"

Spider laughed. "Movie plots are my life. I actually got the idea of renting out the rooms from *Enchanted April*, you know?"

"Was Maggie Smith in that?"

"It was Joan Plowright." Spider fluffed the quilt and let it fall over the bed.

"No one your age has heard of Joan Plowright."

Spider surveyed the room a final time. "So Meredith will be in here. And Kate in Em's, and that Britta can sleep downstairs in my parents' room."

"You could take the downstairs room if you wanted. It would be fewer stairs."

"Nah." Spider had already considered and rejected this idea. Much as she hated noise and stairs, she didn't want to be the one left out. "I want my old room."

Ruthie glanced at her watch. "We should go."

Spider took one last look. "Okay, let's go get Katherine and Meredith and that Britta."

"You might not want to call her 'that Britta' to her face," Ruthie added.

"I'll say it a few times in the car, get it out of my system."

They started downstairs, Spider running her hand against the exposed-log walls, smooth from years of children's fingers, her family's fingers. She hoped this summer would be the start of a new adventure. She hoped she could be friends with these girls, at least one of them, since she was stuck with them. She hoped at least one of them would know how special the place was.

4

Meredith

Essay topic: What would you want your future college roommate to know about you?

I'D WANT HER to know that silence is a virtue, especially on a bus.

"Can you believe we're doing this?" Britta said for the fourteenth time.

Britta was like a bird. Or a small dog. Meredith had regretted her decision to travel with her about three minutes into the flight. For four hours, she'd talked about trees. What were Meredith's thoughts on pine trees? Did Meredith think there'd be deer? And were kayaks the same as canoes? If not, what was the difference?

"What did you say to get your mother to let you go?" Britta asked now.

Deep breaths. Meredith thought about the Universal College Application essay prompts. It calmed her. According to them, an essay should "demonstrate your ability to develop and communicate your thoughts," whatever that meant. Suggested topics were a current event or a life-changing personal experience. This was where she was supposed to write about how she'd discovered a way to build landfills on the moon or how her father had died when she was nine, only one of which was true. And then, there were supplemental essays for each college, like Dartmouth's: *It's not easy being green" was a frequent lament of Kermit the Frog. Discuss.*

Only a few problems with that.

1. That prompt made no sense.
2. The seat wasn't comfortable with her lap desk.
3. Britta, who wouldn't be quiet.

"Meredith, did you hear me? I asked you—"

"I told her the truth, that I was stressed out."

"That worked?" Britta's giant, brown eyes opened wide. "I thought you were going to say you were saving the rain forests in Africa or something."

"Costa Rica. I was going to say Costa Rica."

"Whatever."

"You know Costa Rica's not in Africa, right?"

"Duh. It's in South America. I'm not dumb. I just forgot what you said. So you told her the truth, and she said yes?"

Central America. "Yeah. She knew I flipped out in class that time, so I told her I was stressed out and needed a vacation.

She wasn't happy about it, but she let me go, after I promised to write my college essays on the trip."

"What happened that day, exactly?"

Meredith pretended not to hear Britta. Maybe she'd move on to the next subject, as usual. But no. "Meredith? What happened that day in class?"

"It was nothing, just a panic attack." Though, at the time, it felt like being trampled.

"What was that like?" Britta asked.

Meredith breathed in, feeling a little short of breath thinking about it. "I thought you heard all about it." Her voice was a whisper.

"I just heard you freaked out in class."

"That's what happened. I got a C on an AP Chem test, and I thought, what if I get a C in the whole class? Then I won't get into college, and I'll have to explain to my mother. I started hyperventilating and my vision blurred like it did when I fainted at the doctor's office once when they were taking blood. I felt the walls closing in, and I got chills. And then, I don't remember. A minute later, Mrs. Mateu's standing by me, looking actually concerned, which if you knew her, you'd know is a sign of the apocalypse."

"I've heard that about her. Was that the first time it happened?"

Meredith shook her head. "Just the first time anyone knows about." She wanted to change the subject away from how messed up she was. "Here, let's take a selfie."

That worked. Britta immediately scooted closer and made a duck face. "Send it to me."

Meredith did and then looked at the list of supplemental prompts.

You are teaching a Yale course. What is it called? (35 words or fewer)

Surely Britta could be quiet long enough for her to write thirty-five words.

Why she was traveling with Britta would be a good essay topic. It had been sort of an alternate universe. One moment, Meredith had been sitting in the library, studying for a test. Then, somehow, she'd gotten drawn into this fantasy of going to the mountains with Britta, whom she barely knew, but who had—she remembered—asked her to be in a group for a project once in fourth grade. She doubted Britta remembered, but it had saved Meredith the humiliation of telling the teacher she had no group and having to be foisted on one. Meredith had never understood why kids didn't want her in their group when she was smart and would do all the work. Her mother said they were jealous, but Meredith knew that wasn't it.

"I feel so guilty!" Britta was saying now.

So much for the essay. "Why do you feel guilty?" Meredith asked.

"You know why. I lied to my mother. I abandoned her in her time of need."

Meredith tried to look out the window. "You didn't abandon her in her time of need. You left her with her boyfriend."

"But a *bad* boyfriend. He's so skeezy, Meredith. He's always staring at me."

"That seems like a good reason to get away for the summer."

"It is. But my mother wanted me at camp, not running wild somewhere."

"You're not running wild."

"I just had to get away from it."

Meredith sighed. She didn't really want to be responsible for Britta. That was the advantage of going away with someone she wasn't really friends with.

Though, come to think of it, none of her friends would have gone. She thought of Eva, her best friend from bowling, or Lindsay, who ran German Honor Society with her. Her friends never felt stressed out or overwhelmed or needed a break.

It's not easy being green. Discuss. Should she talk about the environment? Or envy? Green was Dartmouth's color. Did they just mean it was hard to get into Dartmouth?

"God!" Britta was saying by the window. "I am so awful!"

"Shh. Would you?" Meredith noticed the blonde in the seat in front of them giving them side-eye. "Can you please be quieter?"

"I'm awful," Britta whispered.

"You're not. You're nice," Meredith whispered, patting Britta's shoulder in what she hoped was a comforting way. "But I'm trying to think."

"Sorry," Britta whispered. Loudly. "I'm a bad person."

"You're not a bad person," Meredith said, even though she didn't really know. But word usually got around, even in a big school, so you knew who the cheaters were, the potheads, the general screwups. Meredith guessed if Britta had done something more subtly bad, she wouldn't know, but Britta didn't strike her as subtle. "If you were a bad person just for lying to your mother, then everyone's a bad person. Everyone lies to their parents."

"You don't. You're, like, a total Girl Scout with perfect grades, and if you're not washing lepers' feet on weekends, it's just because you can't find any lepers in Miami."

Meredith laughed, then noticed Blondie looking back again. She lowered her voice. "Actually, washing lepers' feet sounds really gross. I mean, what if a toe fell off?"

Britta giggled, sort of a sniff-giggle.

"I wasn't joking," Meredith said.

"I know. You're never joking. That's what makes you so funny, Meredith."

Meredith blew out a puff of air. She could see the blonde's piercing blue eyes and disapproving frown. On the other hand, this was a bus, not the library. People talked on a bus. Maybe the blonde should get some noise-canceling headphones.

"What did you do," she said to Britta, "that was so awful?"

"I crashed Rick's car."

This was new. And kind of hilarious. "Really? Rick's the skeezy boyfriend?"

"He has a Lamborghini. He's obsessed with it. It has these doors." She mimed up-and-down car doors. "Scissor doors, *Lambo* doors. I'm so sick of hearing about the stupid doors. He thinks girls my age are going to think he's hot because of it. Yeah, no."

Meredith bit back the urge to tell Britta to please be quieter. She was trying to be more zen, so she said, "What a weirdo." She imagined that was what one of Britta's friends would say.

"I know. Anyway, he moved in, and of course, he needs to park in the garage because his car's so fancy, so I get stuck in the driveway even though it's my house."

"That sucks." Again, what she figured Britta's friends would say.

"So my friend Nikolai— Do you know Nikolai?" When Meredith shook her head, Britta went on. "He had this party at his house, and he dared me to drive the car over there."

"You didn't?" Of course she did.

"Obviously I did. It was one in the morning, so I figured no one would be on the road, and no one was. Except this possum."

"Oh no." Meredith wondered if Britta had been drinking at this party.

"Yeah. I swerved to avoid hitting the cute little possum, and this huge mailbox just sort of jumped in front of the car. Totally killed the door on the passenger side. It wouldn't . . ." She mimed the doors again, but this time, one of them was frozen in motion. "Scissor anymore."

Meredith bit her lip, picturing it. "That sucks," she repeated.

"I'm just so stupid," Britta said.

"You're not stupid," Meredith said. "You're good at drama. I saw you in a play last year."

Britta scoffed. "Yeah, I'm great at drama. My mom says I'm good at *causing* drama. Anyway, after I crashed and she took away my car, I told her I wanted to be a CIT at this sleepaway camp so I could learn responsibility or something by teaching eight-year-olds to make lanyards. But I told the camp I broke my leg, and spent all the money my *abuelo* left me on this trip."

Meredith hated to ask the obvious question. "Why didn't you just go to the camp?"

"Because I'm *not* responsible. I can't be in charge of a bunch of kids. I'd screw up, and they'd send me home, and I'd have to spend the whole summer in shame watching my mom make out with Rick or sitting in my room so he won't stare at me in my shorts."

Meredith didn't know what to say. Comforting people who'd screwed up wasn't really in her wheelhouse. So she said, "That sucks," again.

"It sucks that I'm a screw-up," Britta agreed.

"That wasn't what I meant," Meredith said.

"But I am. I am!" Britta's voice was getting louder or, rather, higher. "I always do this. I don't face up to things, and I just make everything worse."

"Oh my goodness!" A voice came from the seat in front of them. "Am I going to have to listen to you whine about this Rick the whole way upstate?"

Meredith looked at Britta. Britta looked back at her. Meredith said, "Excuse me?"

The blond girl raised herself up to see over the seat. She was beautiful, with cheekbones like knives, and generally looked the way Meredith had always imagined Blanche Ingram, Jane's gorgeous and upper-class rival in *Jane Eyre*, looked. "You were on the plane with me. And I thought, 'The plane ride won't be that long. It will be over soon.' But now, here you are on the bus. People are trying to read, sleep, think. But instead of being able to do so, we are all being treated to your conversation. I have tried to ignore it, but I keep being drawn in. So I am asking you as politely as possible, could you please be a little quieter?"

That was as politely as possible? Meredith looked around to see if others were going to say something, but no eyes met hers. They probably also agreed that Britta was super loud.

This was so unfair. She, Meredith, was never loud. If anything, people told her to speak up more. Yet now, she was loud by association. Besides, Britta was just being friendly. Now that it was being challenged, she saw that.

Beside her, Britta sniffed. "I'm sorry. It was me, not Meredith. Meredith never talks. She's, literally, like a mute."

"I'm not *literally* a mute," Meredith whispered.

The blond girl looked down like she couldn't believe Meredith had spoken. Finally, she said, "Well, okay then," and turned away.

Meredith didn't say anything from that point on. She turned on her music and thought about being green. Then, she stared out the window. The traffic of the city, with its crowded bridges, soon gave way to road, so much road, all the same and hours more to go.

Finally, she must have fallen asleep.

She woke with Britta shaking her shoulder.

"What?" she said.

Britta held her finger to her lips and pointed out the window. It was a bridge, two bridges actually, side-by-side, steel bridges spanning a blue river. On each side were high mountains, tall pines, and so much green, green trees, green mountains, red with the setting sun, white with clouds that moved like living things.

Britta smiled.

Meredith smiled back.

They both gazed out the window, their breath synchronized with their wonder at it all, the mountains, the trees, the wild-flowers, purple like silk, white like lace, covering the ground. They passed towns with names like Crescent, Burnt Hills, Glens Falls.

Finally, they reached their stop. Meredith started to gather her things, then stopped.

"Oh no," Britta said.

The blond girl was also getting off the bus. Meredith touched Britta's arm.

"I'm sure we'll never see her again," Meredith said. "There's miles of wilderness here."

"Still," Britta said.

Both hung back, letting another person get between them and the blonde. Finally, they had to disembark.

"How are we supposed to find Spider?" Britta asked.

Meredith was starting to shrug when she saw a gangly brunette in black jeans and combat boots and an old lady in a flowing dress. The girl held a sign that said:

KATHERINE LYONS COVINGTON
MEREDITH DALY
BRITTA RODRIGUEZ

Meredith realized with a sinking stomach that only one other girl had gotten off the bus.

"Oh no," she said.

But Britta was already tugging at Meredith's arm. She started to run toward them.

The blonde reached them first. "Hello," she said. "You must be Spider. I'm Kate. I've come to spend the month."

5

Britta

FFS.

When Britta was little, she used to think that God was watching her, personally, following her like a drone, ready to punish her if she said something mean, stole someone's pencil, or ate all the Oreos and blamed her brother.

Or lied to her mother.

That belief went a long way in shaping Britta's personality. She was nice because she feared consequences. She knew God would strike her down for copying her neighbor's paper, even if the teacher didn't see. So she didn't cheat, lie, didn't even talk back. It wasn't worth the risk.

Then, one day she realized that was dumb. God didn't personally intercede in people's lives. If he did, there'd be no poverty, no hunger, and only mean girls would have their period in white skinny jeans. From then on, she was nice because she was *nice*, not because she believed God would give her bacne if she wasn't. She still believed in God, but not in his vengeance.

But lately, she'd had doubts.

Ever since she'd lied to her mother, things had gone wrong, horribly wrong.

Things like failing math when she had a C first semester.

Or like breaking three nails on the day of prom.

Or Maleficent herself being the third roommate.

Britta stared at the sign, the names, the blond girl who'd just introduced herself.

"You're . . . the other roommate?"

The blonde turned to face her. Britta tried not to stare. She was taller than Britta and had one of those high-class Anglo faces that looked like it belonged on the cover of *Town & Country*, this society magazine her mother started reading when she met Rick (about the same time she started telling people they were "Spanish" instead of Cuban). Britta could almost picture this girl, Katherine, in one of those pictures of girls riding horses while wearing pearls. Even her name, Katherine Lyons Covington. Who had two last names?

The blonde's nostrils flared. "Other roommate?"

"Surprise!" Britta said.

Awkward silence. And Meredith ditched her to get her suitcase.

Sometimes, it helped to pretend she was in a play, a comedy by someone like Oscar Wilde or Noël Coward. Those characters always knew the exact right thing to say.

Britta straightened her shoulders, smiled, tilted her head (vivaciously) to one side, and stuck out her hand. "I don't believe we've been properly introduced. I'm Britta. From the bus?"

There was nothing the blonde could do but take her hand. "Kate."

"Pleased to make your acquaintance." Another line from a play. She shook the blonde's icy hand. Then she turned to the other girl, who had on a T-shirt that said "I shoot people . . ." with a graphic of a movie camera. "And you must be Spider. I'm so excited about this!" She stood on tiptoes to kiss Spider on the cheek, which was the expected greeting in Miami. Not in New York, apparently, because Spider stepped back, shocked, then recovered. They air-kissed.

The older lady who was with her, on the other hand, folded Britta into her embrace. "Britta. I've heard so much about you! I'm Ruthie, Alicia's grandmother."

"It's so nice to meet you." Old ladies loved her!

"I heard you're a theater aficionada."

"I am," Britta said. She loved old ladies! This was like having a vacation *abuela*!

"We should get our suitcases." Britta started to walk away, then turned back to Kate. "Please. Come, and I'll introduce you to Meredith. I'm sure we'll all be good friends!"

Shit. This girl knew about Rick's car. Why had she said that? Catholic guilt definitely had a point. But, because there was not much else to do in the face of Britta's incredible acting

33

ability, Kate went with her.

"Are you from Atlanta? Or were you just switching planes like we were? Me and Meredith are from Miami." Or was it *Meredith and I?* Britta just kept going on, filling the silence, though pausing after every sentence in case Kate decided to speak instead of acting like a snob. "I'm sorry. Did you say something?"

"I'm from Atlanta," Katherine said. "I mean, it's a suburb near Atlanta."

Britta waited to see if she would go on, but she didn't, so Britta said, "Oh, that's exciting. I've only been to Atlanta once. We went to the Coca-Cola museum." Nothing from Katherine. They'd reached the bus. The driver was pulling out all the suit-cases. "There's Meredith! Meredith!" *God, Meredith. Save me.*

Meredith turned around. She saw Britta and Kate and drew in her breath. "Oh. Hi."

"Meredith, this is Katherine. She's staying at the house with us."

"Hi." Meredith shifted from foot to foot. "We met on the bus."

Katherine smiled. "So nice to meet you, both of you. I'm Kate."

"Kate's from Atlanta," Britta said.

"There's mine." The driver took out a ginormous Louis Vuitton suitcase. Kate grabbed it with a little grunt, like it was super heavy despite the wheels. Britta noticed the "Overweight" tag on it. Kate stumbled a bit. "Tennis elbow," she said.

"Hey, I play tennis," Britta said. "We should play together. Meredith bowls."

"I didn't pack a bowling ball," Meredith said.

"I might have one in here . . . somewhere," Kate said, gesturing at the huge suitcase.

At first, Britta thought she was serious. Then Kate laughed. It sounded like a wind chime.

"Oh! Ha!" Britta said. Scary Girl was trying to be funny. Points for Scary Girl!

Kate grabbed a matching Louis Vuitton bag. "Oh, this one's mine too."

It was also overweight. Britta hoped they had an SUV. Or maybe a U-Haul. "Do you need help with that? Because of your elbow?"

"Oh, no, um. I mean, I guess I overpacked."

"Be prepared."

"That's me, prepared for anything." Princess Kate pulled the bag over. "I'll bring this one to the car. Can you watch that one? Please?"

"Sure!" Britta stood closer to Kate's mountain of a suitcase. She noticed Kate checked her phone, then put it back into her purse, frowning. Finally, Britta's own red bag came out. As she stood there, waiting for Kate to return, the driver took out a Louis Vuitton carry-on. Not. Possible. It must be someone else's. Surely many people had thousand-dollar French suitcases out here in the boonies.

"This yours?" the driver asked.

God. "Not mine, but . . ." She looked around. Kate was hoisting the first bag into the back of a green Subaru SUV, where it was taking up half the trunk space. "Maybe it's hers?"

The driver looked over at Kate. "Yeah, she had three." He smiled fakely.

Jeez. Britta grabbed the carry-on from the impatient driver.

"Let me help you with those." Ruthie went for the big one.

Britta took her own bag and left the carry-on for Ruthie. It wasn't that heavy. "So you were in theater?"

"I was in *Camelot* on Broadway, just the chorus, but I understudied Nimue."

"Really? Wow."

"Yes." Ruthie sighed. "Unfortunately, that witch never got sick."

Britta laughed. "Still. Great history."

"I know. My big break was when I was cast in *Hair* off-Broadway."

They approached the SUV, where there was still a little bit of space carved out. "You're not talking about *Hair* already, are you?" Spider said. "Please don't tell them about—"

"It was a very poignant and respectful nude scene," Ruthie said. "It was about the Vietnam War."

". . . the nude scene," Spider said. "Don't talk about the nude scene."

Britta felt her hand rise to her mouth. "You were naked? Onstage?" Her mother would die if she did that. Well, disown her, then die.

"Unfortunately, no. That was when I got pregnant with Alicia's aunt, so I had to quit."

"I'm sure Aunt Laura loves hearing about the tragedy of her birth," Spider said.

Spider and Kate hoisted Kate's mega-suitcase into the trunk. Spider gestured for Britta to stow her second bag. There was a spot for it, assuming no one wanted to use the rearview.

"It *was* a tragedy," Ruthie said. "I could have been part of theater history."

"Yeah." Spider stepped back, rubbing her shoulder.

"It's still . . . wow," Britta said, taking Kate's carry-on from Ruthie. "Do you have any clippings or albums or anything like that?"

"I just might have a few lying around," Ruthie said. "I'll show you."

Britta looked from the trunk to the carry-on. "There's no way that's fitting. I can hold mine in my lap. I hope it's not far."

It was far. Almost an hour, and Britta ended up with her carry-on in her lap and Kate's carry-on at her knees. She hoped Kate realized the sacrifice she was making, which more than made up for talking too loudly on the bus. Kate sat in front. Because of course she did.

"I am so sorry," Kate said. "You are so, so sweet to sit in back. My legs are so long."

"No big deal," Britta said. "This is going to be fun."

"It will be," Ruthie agreed. "I have photos of me playing a stripper, in summer stock."

"Ruthie!" Spider said, laughing.

"I wasn't nude in that one," Ruthie said. "Though I could have carried it off."

6

Spider

INT. CHARMING CABIN — EVENING

Spider and Ruthie enter the house, now
joined by KATE, 17, blond Disney princess
who packed for a tour of Europe, MEREDITH,
17, a studious redhead, the only reasonable
one in the bunch, and THAT BRITTA, 16,
and every bit as perkily awful as Spider
had envisioned. To call this part the
"Call to Adventure" might be a bit of an
exaggeration.

"WHY DON'T YOU take the downstairs room, Katherine?"
Ruthie said. "You shouldn't have to lug those heavy suitcases
upstairs."

Ruthie probably hadn't done that on purpose. Oh, who was Spider kidding? Of course she had.

"I can help you lug that up," Spider said, even though her shoulder still hurt from picking it up earlier.

"It's Kate, and don't be silly," Kate said, turning in to the peach-and-white bedroom near the door. "Your grandmother's right. This will be easier."

"It's no big deal," Spider said.

But she knew she was defeated when Ruthie grasped Britta's elbow and said, "And you, my rising star, will take the room by mine. We can stay up all night and giggle like schoolgirls."

Ruthie was definitely messing with her. She always thought Spider should be more outgoing, more like Britta. At least Britta would be across the hall, not in the room that shared a wall. Spider wouldn't put it past her to have brought tap shoes.

Later, when they were all settled, Spider lay in bed, watching *Eternal Sunshine of the Spotless Mind* on her laptop. It was one of her favorites, about a couple who erase one another from their memories. She'd found it on a list, "15 Essential Films Every Aspiring Screenwriter Should Watch." She'd watched those fifteen movies so often she'd memorized them. Like the part she was watching right now, where Mary, the character played by Kirsten Dunst, says, "Adults . . . they're like this messy tangle of anger and phobias and sadness . . . hopelessness." She said the line with her. It was so true. She realized she missed Emily's loud yoga. From Ruthie's room, she heard the clack of tiles on a table, a sound she remembered from when they all used to play board games together. Now Ruthie was playing with

Britta. They hadn't invited her. But why would they, when she was being such a jerk?

There was a knock on the door.

"Yeah?" Spider pulled the quilt over her laptop.

Britta opened the door. "Hey, we're playing this game, Rummikub. Your grandmother said you're really good." Spider saw Britta notice the movie. Fortunately, she didn't comment.

"Oh." They probably didn't really want her. "That's okay. I'm tired."

Britta shrugged. "Another time, then." She shut the door. A moment later, Spider heard them gathering tiles. She couldn't sleep now. Maybe she should join them after all. No, better to go outside.

She didn't turn on the porch light. She knew the way in the cool, silent night. At first, it always seemed dark, but the farther out she walked, the more stars appeared until the sky went from being a scattering of diamonds to an Oscar nominee's sequined dress. Then, she could see clearly, each tree, each fence post. She stared up at the round, endless sky, hearing the chirp of crickets, the singing of frogs down at the lake, and maybe the deep whisper-breathing of birds she couldn't see.

No people, though. Sometimes there were lights. Or conversation, carrying up, up from the lake. But tonight was gloriously quiet. Spider made her way across the grass to the lounge chairs. They were called Adirondack chairs because they were popular up here, half-reclining wooden chairs with generous arms. She started to sink down into one.

"Oh!"

At the shriek, she jumped up. "What? Who's there?"

"It's me!" a voice said, not Britta's or Kate's southern accent. Meredith.

"God, I'm . . . I didn't realize anyone was out here!" How embarrassing.

Meredith laughed, though her breathing still sounded surprised. "I guess I should have turned on the porch light. I left it off because of what you said about city light bleed."

"Me too." She settled into a different chair, carefully this time.

Meredith said, "It's beautiful here."

"Yes," Spider said, hoping Meredith would stop talking.

She did, not even to question the origin of the noises that, again, became evident, like a night bird's faraway shriek. Sounds carried for miles here. Spider leaned her head back and gazed at the sky. After a few minutes of looking, what seemed like clouds were revealed as stars, continuous white like a puddle of spilled milk, the Milky Way.

Meredith was still quiet, almost as if she'd fallen asleep. But no. She shifted. Spider quite liked her. She could be friends with someone like her, someone quiet. Most people wouldn't see the point of a friendship with someone who didn't talk incessantly. Even Ruthie (whom Spider considered to be her best friend) sometimes felt the need to ask questions. How was she feeling? Did she like her book? Questions to try to make her talk. It wasn't people Spider disliked so much as talking. That was why

41

she dreamed of living here year-round. When the summer people left, she could come out here in the cold evening and look at the sky and not have to have an opinion about it.

That would be lonely. Spider was used to loneliness, though.

Against the background of crickets, Spider heard Meredith's sigh.

Yes, yes, I know how you feel. But she didn't speak. She wished she could capture the feeling of this night in words, so others could experience the airy peacefulness. But the absence of words, of human speech, was the essence of it. Finally, she began to shiver. She had no sweater. Her legs ached from her awkward position. She rose but didn't say anything. She wondered if she should.

When she opened the front door, she heard someone crying. Was it Kate? And was Spider supposed to do something about it? Ask what was wrong? No. Surely not. Surely Kate had waited until she thought no one was around. It would be rude to bother her. She didn't want some stranger intruding. Spider closed the door without a sound, then tiptoed up to bed.

Britta and Ruthie seemed to be finished talking. Maybe it wouldn't be that bad. Outside, she heard an owl shrieking. She'd never heard one so close to the house.

Spider wondered if she had done the right thing, ignoring Kate. It wasn't until she was cuddled under her soft, old periwinkle-and-white quilt in the silent darkness that she wondered what rich, beautiful Kate had to cry about.

7

Kate

KATE STARED AT the texts, bubble after depressing bubble.

She'd been asleep on the bus when they'd come in. Fortunately, she'd awakened, by some instinct, at the right stop, or she might have ended up in Canada somewhere, hunting caribou. Then, when she finally reached the bus station, she hadn't been able to look at her phone because she was listening to Britta, being polite because, possibly, she'd overreacted on the bus. Okay, she had overreacted. Britta kept talking, trying to be her BFF. Bless her heart.

To be fair, had she been in a better mood, she might have liked Britta. But she was not. In. A. Good. Mood. They probably thought she was a snob. Maybe she was one.

Only when she'd reached the privacy of her own room had she looked at her phone. Most of the texts were from her mother.

Your father's in trouble.

I don't know what to do.

Please call me.

Did you know?

And on it went. And on. Why had her father warned Kate but not his wife?

And one text from Colin, just one:

Is this why you broke up with me?

Yes. She had known. And yes, that was why she'd broken up with Colin. But it was too late to answer either message. She had no bars. They were out in the wilderness.

It was better that way. That was what she'd wanted. No need to drag Colin into this mess. She couldn't stand the idea of his family judging hers, of them telling him to break up with her. She had her pride.

She noticed that there were no texts from her friends at home. Not one.

Not that she was expecting some outpouring of sympathy from Marlowe and Greer, certainly not from Lacey, who'd probably be thrilled to get her spot for Extemporaneous on debate team if Kate had to transfer schools. But there wasn't even a normal text, like a cat meme. Which meant they were all probably texting one another about her.

She heard laughter drifting down the stairway, Ruthie's old laughter, then Britta's younger voice. She would be especially nice to Britta tomorrow, to make up with her.

She scrolled through Colin's old messages, months of them, pictures of them together, at homecoming, on a spring break ski trip, at a charity white elephant sale, Colin wearing an old Mexican sombrero someone had donated, Kate with an aqua belly-dancing skirt over her jeans. Mrs. Bader had yelled at them not to wear the merchandise.

"I think you look hot in it," he'd said, and he bought it for her. "Wear it without the jeans next time."

She had never put it all the way on, though. As soon as she'd tried, that night after they'd counted the cashbox, he had kissed her. Kissing Colin was like skiing down a perfect, powdery slope. It was her first time being in love, and her mother had assured her it wouldn't last forever. But God, she'd wanted it to.

Her fingers kept scrolling to a photo of them in the park. They'd spoken Latin all day, Colin consulting his Latin dictionary, and someone had yelled at them to speak English; this was America. Kate had yelled back, *"Ignorantia non excusat nam odium,"* which she thought meant "ignorance doesn't excuse hatefulness," but she might have been wrong. It was at least close enough to make Colin laugh as the woman shooed them off.

"You told her," he had said.

"I don't think she knows *what* I told her," Kate had replied.

"Sometimes it's only important that you know."

How she wanted to answer Colin's texts. Fortunately, the Gods of Cell Phone Reception prevented it even if her own conscience didn't. But had Spider said something about a hill? Being able to get service on a hill?

Now it was too dark. Her hand ached from clutching the phone so hard. She lay down on the bed and sobbed, sobbed for Mother and Daddy and Colin and her stupid spot on the debate team, for not being able to take in the beauty of this new place because of all the old thoughts crowding it out.

8

Meredith

Essay topic: "One of the great challenges of our time is that the disparities we face today have more complex causes and point less straightforwardly to solutions."

—Omar Wasow, assistant professor of politics, Princeton University, and cofounder of Blackplanet .com. This quote is taken from Professor Wasow's January 2014 speech at the Martin Luther King Day celebration at Princeton University.

WHAT DID THAT even mean?

She decided not to think about it. After Spider left, Meredith spread out and put her feet up on the second Adirondack chair.

She was alone! Blessedly alone, with the stars! Now she could start relaxing. She'd promised her guidance counselor, if not her mother, she would.

She had to admit, though, that she was weirdly impressed with Spider. Never before had she met someone so untroubled by the obligation of appearing friendly, even to paying guests. From the time she'd picked them up at the bus stop until now, she hadn't said one extraneous word. She hadn't even apologized very much when she'd actually sat on Meredith.

But that was what Meredith had wanted. Absolute silence.

And stars.

Meredith leaned back and breathed deeply. *Look at me now, Ms. Gayton! I'm relaxing in a chair! I'm taking deep, cleansing breaths!*

So many stars. At home, you could see the basics, the Big Dipper and Jupiter. Now, Meredith didn't even know where to look first. She'd consult her astronomy book, but it seemed like every constellation was there. In the silence, they almost sang.

There were no cars, televisions, lawn mowers. Even the crickets seemed muted.

Then, a sound rose from the trees.

"Whoo-whoo-whoo-whoo. Whoo-whoo-whoo-whoo!"

What was it? A mournful song, or a ghost.

Or was it someone crying?

The house was way off the road and separated from the next closest house by acres of woods that went far back and down a hill. It was from these woods that the cry came.

"Whoo-whoo-whoo-whoo. Whoo-whoo-whoo-whoo!"

An owl. Was it hunting? Meredith stood slowly on the pine needle–dappled dirt. She placed first one careful foot, then the other, on the ground. She tried to follow the sound. In the silence, her every step sounded like the crunch of a bag of potato chips.

Could the owl hear her? She shivered. The night was actually cool, though it was July.

"Whoo-whoo-whoo-whoo. Whoo-whoo-whoo-whoo!"

It sounded closer. Meredith walked farther into the woods, holding her arms out to fend off the trees, like Red Riding Hood about to confront a wolf. Meredith felt the soft ground underneath her sneakers, the wind between her fingers.

She touched something.

It did not feel like a tree.

She jumped back. The owl? Had she actually touched the owl?

"Eek!" she screamed, sure she had, sure it was going to attack her with sharp talons as if she were a helpless mouse.

She dived to the ground, shielding her face.

Only then did she realize the thing she had touched did not have feathers.

Hope is the thing with feathers. Emily Dickinson had said that. But, though the thing she had touched wasn't feathered, she was pretty sure it was living. A person. A person taller than she was.

Meredith screamed for real, her shrieks piercing the quiet night.

"God! Stop it!"

It was a guy's voice, and his words did nothing to silence her.

"They're right there!" she yelled, gesturing wildly in the direction she assumed the house was in, even though she could just barely see one lit window through the trees.

"Who's there?" The voice was laughing, laughing the way killers do in books when they have their victims cornered. Why had she come here? Why hadn't she stayed in Miami?

"My . . . friends . . . ," she stammered out. "Four of them. They'll hear me. They'll know if something happens to me. They'll call the police."

Another laugh. "And the police will come in a few days, I guess."

Meredith felt her heart hammering away. But, she realized, he wasn't attacking her. Instead, she heard him fumbling, maybe looking for rope to tie her up. She'd never thought about how scary it was to be alone. At home, there was the safety of crowds. She tried to scramble to her feet, but the pine needle–covered ground was silk-slick beneath her feet. She started to slide downhill.

He grabbed her. "Whoa!"

She stopped sliding. She saw what he'd been fumbling for, a flashlight. It illuminated her face, and she struggled to get away. No one was coming to help her. There was no one.

The guy let go of her, still laughing. Meredith stumbled back, heart pounding more and more furiously. "Who are you?" The flashlight raked her from head to toe. "Not a Webster."

Meredith breathed in, saying nothing. Deep breaths. Deep breaths.

"I know all of them," he continued. "They're not here this summer except the old lady and Spider, and Spider doesn't leave the house much."

Gradually, it dawned on Meredith that, just maybe, she wasn't going to die.

"Who are you?" she gasped out.

"Oh!" He laughed and shone the flashlight on his own face. "I'm Harmon Dickinson."

Hope is the thing with feathers.

In the flashlight beam, his face looked skeleton-like, a campfire nightmare image. Still, she could make out that he was not a man. Rather, he was a guy about her age, tall, with brown, curly hair and broad shoulders. He had something strapped around his neck. Camera.

Who took pictures in the woods at night?

Pervs, that was who. Stalkers. Had he been going to their house to take pictures through the window? Was that how he knew so much about the Websters? Was he a Peeping Tom?

Still, she said, "Dickinson, like the poet?"

He shrugged. "Dickinson like the Dickinson family, my family. We've lived here forever."

"I haven't been here forever. I'm from Miami." Meredith eyed the camera.

"Ooh, Miami. *¡Muy caliente!* I learned that in Spanish class."

"I take German." She tried to stand, but her foot slid out beneath her. "Oh!"

His hand was on her back, steadying her. She planted her

feet and tried to right herself. Who knew pine needles were so slippery?

"Want a hand?" He held out his arm. "Grab it."

She did. His grip was firm. She pulled herself up with a minimum of slippage this time.

"Thank you."

She stood a moment, unsure what to say. She couldn't very well go back to sitting on the lawn looking at the stars like she was alone, now that she knew she wasn't.

"You know," he said, "just for the record, *you* mauled me."

"What?" Meredith brushed her butt, which she suspected was covered in pine needles.

"You screamed like I was an ax murderer, but I'm actually the injured party here. I went innocently out into the woods, and you mauled me. To my great humiliation, I might add. What were you doing here?"

He had the light back on her, like she was under interrogation. Still, she guessed he was somewhat right.

"I thought I heard an owl. I've never seen an owl before." She moved to the side a little, out of the light. "What were *you* doing there?" Giving him a chance to make it something other than peeping.

Sensing her discomfort, maybe, he shone the light back on himself. "Like this?" He called, "Whoo-whoo-whoo-whoo. Whoo-whoo-whoo-whoo!"

"Yeah."

He gestured toward his camera. "I was looking for an owl."

"Oh." Meredith looked down, glad he couldn't see her face, which she suspected was getting red. "So much for nature."

And then, because she couldn't think of anything intelligent to say, and she hated situations where she couldn't think of anything intelligent to say, she started to walk away. "Good night."

A moment later, his voice followed her. "Do you like nature?"

She turned back. "Who doesn't like nature?"

"Lots of people. Everyone in New York City, I'm guessing. There's plenty of nature around here, birds, flowers, butterflies. I could show it to you sometime."

She didn't answer. Was he asking her to hang with him? *Her?*

"I'm mostly harmless. We live in the white house down the road. You could ask my mother, if you don't believe me."

She laughed. "You're giving your mother as a reference?" It occurred to her that, up here, people didn't know she was a huge nerd.

"Not too many people around here. You could ask my math teacher, Mrs. Campanella, but I think she's on vacation. I know every inch of these woods. Lived here all my life."

She was almost back to the house when she yelled back, "Maybe!"

He didn't answer, probably hadn't heard her. Still, it made her smile.

9

Britta

QUIET. BRITTA HAD never thought about how *quiet* quiet could be. She'd imagined a lack of actual noise, like people talking or music, but she hadn't thought of all the noise you didn't consider. Like airplanes. Cars off in the distance. The stop-start of the air conditioner in the neighbors' yards as she walked by their houses. Dogs barking at dogs barking at dogs in an endless procession. She realized she'd never been in an actually quiet place before.

Until now. This place was silently silent, so silent that, when she moved the little Rummikub tiles around the table she shared with Ruthie, the sound was deafening.

She picked a tile. Black six! She'd needed that one. At least, she thought she did. She wasn't completely sure. Ruthie was just teaching her the game.

"Is it a little like dominoes?" she asked Ruthie.

"You play dominoes?" Ruthie asked, surprised.

"I used to play with my grandfather. Old Cuban people play it."

"Used to?" Ruthie put down her tiles. Three eights and a red six, seven, eight, and nine.

"He died." Britta examined the tiles Ruthie had placed. "When I was little, he'd let me sit on the chair beside him and help him choose which *fichas*—that's what he called the tiles— to play. And he gave me tips—like always set down the doubles first and keep track of what numbers are showing when your opponent passes. By the time I was nine, I could even beat him sometimes." She remembered Abuelo asking her advice even. She missed that.

"Interesting. You'll have to teach me."

"I'd love to. So how does this work? Can I take one of your tiles? Like if I need the nine?"

Ruthie nodded. "But only after you put down fifty points on your own."

Britta sighed and took a tile. A nine, but yellow. She already had one.

"So what brought you here this summer?" Ruthie removed the nine from the board and placed it with two other nines from her hand.

Britta selected another tile. "Just . . . wanted to relax."

Ruthie raised an eyebrow. "You don't seem like a relaxing kind of girl."

"What's that supposed to mean?" Not that this wasn't true.

"You remind me a great deal of myself at your age, a bundle of energy." Ruthie placed a tile down. "I couldn't wait for something interesting to happen in my life. I wouldn't have wanted to spend a month lying on a hammock."

Britta said nothing, putting down a blue four, five, six, and seven, then three tens. "That's fifty-two, right?"

"Yes."

As Ruthie made her move, Britta took in the bright-yellow walls. The other rooms in the house were decorated like the vacation places her friends had in the Keys, only more mountainy. Antique quilts, rustic furniture, lamps made out of antlers, pillows and hangings with sayings like "Heaven is a little closer in the mountains," homey decor her mother would find tacky if she knew about it. Ruthie's room was alive with posters and memorabilia. Britta noticed one from Shakespeare in the Park and another from the production of *Hair*.

"I don't know," she said, putting down a seven. "I just wanted to get away from home. Didn't you ever feel like that when you were young?"

Ruthie smiled. "I feel like that now sometimes. But of course, when you're a teenager, you think no one can understand you. Maybe they can't."

"It's not like that." Britta hated being characterized as just another stressed teenager.

"What's it like?"

Britta took a tile. It would be weird to unburden herself to a stranger—even her vacation *abuela*—about her life, Mom, Rick, how icky it was when he said she was pretty or brought her presents like an expensive Body Glove bikini. Ruthie would probably think he was just being nice, which is what her mother had said. "How do jokers work?"

"They can substitute for any tile, and if you have the tile it's substituting for, you can take it and use it yourself." Ruthie took a tile.

"Got it." The joker smiled up at her from between a red two and four. Britta had a red three, so she substituted it. Her eyes fell on Ruthie's nightstand. In one photo, two girls stood arm in arm, wearing costumes of the type you'd expect in a production of *Oklahoma!* Instead of looking at the camera, they stared at one another. The shorter girl was obviously Ruthie. The other girl was tall, with brown hair. The expressions on their faces were almost dreamy.

Britta looked around and noticed a few other photos of the brown-haired girl. In one picture, she was part of a group wearing 1920s flapper costumes. There was another of the same girl, all alone. She must have been someone special. Britta wondered who she was.

"Are you finished?" Ruthie reminded her.

"Oh." Britta looked away from the photo and at the tiles. She added an eleven to a group. "So that's Spider?" She pointed to a photo of a girl with braces, smiling gummily at the camera.

"Yes. She was at an awkward phase when that was taken." Ruthie contemplated her tiles.

"And those are your other grandchildren?"

Ruthie looked at the photo again. "Yes. That's Ben, Alicia's brother, and the girl is her sister, Emily. Her cousins Zoe and Zack are in this photo."

Britta pointed to the photo of the two girls. "And that's you?"

"Yes. It was a summer stock production of *Oklahoma!* I played Gertie, that annoying girl. I was good at playing annoying girls."

"I played Gertie in middle school too. I thought it was *Oklahoma!* And who's the other girl? The one in the picture?"

Ruthie's old mouth twisted into a smile as she placed four fives. "That's Janet. She was in the chorus, and we were . . . best friends. It was my first summer stock, and I was so frightened, but Janet was my rock. She taught me to meditate before performances to relax. And sometimes, I'd pass her backstage, and she'd say, 'Deep breaths.'"

Britta put down a blue six and a seven. "Do you still see her ever?" She clapped her hand over her mouth. What if the answer was no because Janet was dead? That would be a typical Britta screwup.

But Ruthie said, "You're getting the hang of it." She added an eight to Britta's tiles. "No, it's been a long time."

Britta wondered again if Janet had died, but there was no polite way to ask, so she took a tile. Ruthie said, "We just lost touch." She started to make an elaborate move that involved taking a tile off the beginning of one run, another off another group, and adding them to two of hers. Britta heard footsteps on the stairs, heavy ones that sounded like army boots. Spider must have gotten up after all.

"Did you ever try to find her, like on Facebook?"

"I looked once. She had an unusual name, Janet Calisti. But the only Janet Calisti I found was younger and lived in Minnesota. She wasn't my Janet." She moved some more tiles around and added them to another of her own.

"Maybe she got married and changed her name."

Ruthie smiled and shook her head slightly, but then said, "Probably." She added a last tile to a group of four, then turned over her tile rack. "Done."

"Oh," Britta said. "Wow, that was quick."

Ruthie shrugged. "Luck of the draw."

Britta yawned. "I was tired anyway." She helped put away the tiles.

"We can play again tomorrow, if you want. I'll teach you some moves. And maybe we'll buy a set of dominoes at the drugstore."

"I'd beat you for sure." Britta swept the last of the tiles in. "Good night."

She took a final look at the photo of Ruthie and Janet Calisti. It was weird to think about it, that people who were her close friends now might be completely out of her life. Sad.

She had to wait for Spider to come out of the bathroom. Princess Kate had a whole bathroom downstairs. She wished she'd gotten the downstairs room. What was Spider doing, flossing each tooth? Finally, she finished.

A minute later, Britta was in bed. The quilt was yellow and white, with a ring pattern, like she imagined ladies made in simpler times. All thoughts of home and lying to her mother and skeezy Rick were gone or, at least, pushed to the side. It was so beautiful here! It would be all right—she was sure of it. The window was open, allowing a breeze, and life was good. She heard the screech of a bird, maybe an owl, in the distance.

Britta burrowed into the nest of quilts and pillows and blankets. It was her first night in the mountains, and she was going to have thirty more! Thirty nights to uncover the house's secrets, everyone's secrets, even her own secrets.

Finally, she drifted off to sleep.

10

Kate

WHEN YOU WALKED among tall trees, the sky seemed higher.

Or maybe she just felt smaller.

It was morning. Kate trudged uphill, close to a mile from the house. Coming here had seemed like such a good idea. Fresh air! Sunshine! Peace on earth, good will to all! No mother or father or debutante balls . . . or soon-to-be-revealed political scandal.

And no Colin.

Now she wasn't sure. The cell phone reception here was weird. It wasn't nonexistent, as Daddy believed, but, as Spider had said, spotty. Random. If the wind was blowing right, she could get a text. But when she tried to respond, it wouldn't send.

She had not expected this to be a problem. But, apparently,

she wasn't as heartless as she had led herself to believe. She thought about her mother's last text: *Did you know?*

And the thing was, she had, since dinner a month ago.

They'd been having tilapia. Daddy often joked that the fish hadn't existed when he was a kid. "My brother and I, we'd sneak onto someone's dock and get a rainbow trout or maybe even a tarpon. We'd never heard of tilapia. They created it in a lab in 1995." Mother hated when Daddy talked about fishing. She said it made him sound so low-class. That day, he was silent, cutting off a burned portion of skin.

"Did you know that there was tilapia in ancient Egyptian art?" Kate's brother said.

Her father didn't seem to hear. Kate said, "So we're eating Egyptian fish?"

Blake looked at Daddy. Still nothing. He said, "Yeah. They were a symbol of rebirth. So they've been around a while." Blake met Dad's eyes like he thought he was smart.

The sound of forks on a plate, then chewing.

"I saw Patty Lind at the grocery store," Mother said. "She was wearing a scarf and pretended she didn't see me. But I knew it was her."

Nothing.

Blake said, "So, with the tilapia, it's aquaculture that's made them more—"

"Did you say hello to her?" Kate asked.

"Well, I . . . no. I didn't think she'd want that, what with her husband's disgrace and all."

More silence. Her father stopped eating. Then, her mother added in a low, conspiratorial voice, "I wonder if she'll quit the club now."

Daddy's knife clattered to his plate. "Probably the club that got him into this mess."

"What?" Mother scoffed. "He's in this mess because—"

"Because he had to pay for club dues and charity balls and private schools, and ski trips. Every small-town politician isn't a Bush or a Kennedy, even if y'all spend like we are."

That had shut Mother up. Kate knew Daddy didn't come from money, the way Mother did. He didn't really care about things like country clubs and debutantes. That was Mother.

That night, she'd heard her father downstairs, pacing. She went to his study.

"Oh, Katy. I was just thinking about you." He showed her the ad for the cabin. Kate didn't know how he'd found it, but it wasn't open to argument. Kate was to tell her mother it had been her idea, that she needed to rest up for her debutante year. Her brother was off to some college science program. "At least you'll miss the worst of it," Daddy said.

"The worst of what?"

He looked at her, surprised she hadn't figured it out. "Edwin Hamilton, he's going to tell the feds I took a bribe from him."

Edwin Hamilton was one of her father's best friends. His daughter, Lacey, was a classmate of Kate's. They were on debate team together. "So you're being . . . ?" Arrested? Put in jail? She pictured something like *Orange Is the New Black*, only worse because it would involve big, tough men. Kate didn't even ask if it was true.

"I don't know, Katy." Daddy handed her a thick envelope. "Pack this with your things."

When she reached her bedroom, she opened the envelope. There was five thousand dollars cash inside. Kate hid it in her carry-on. Before the trip, she broke up with Colin. No need for him to be involved in a scandal. They probably wouldn't even be in school together in the fall. She'd get kicked out of Bradley Prep. Or they wouldn't be able to afford it.

Now Kate squinted to see her mother's text in the brightening light.

Did you know?

She wondered if it was in the papers yet, or on the news.

Kate saw the little road going uphill. Service Hill, Spider had called it. Ruthie had said she could call home when they went to the grocery store. But Kate wanted to talk in private, in case she cried. The climb was long, steep, but she couldn't help noticing it was also beautiful. She heard a bird's mournful cry. Kate gazed at the blue-green pines but saw nothing. She hadn't ever spent much time in nature. A few summers, she'd gone to camp, but the cabins had been air-conditioned. Other years, they'd traveled to Europe. This year, though, she'd wanted to stay home, to be with Colin.

But here she was, walking a strange road she didn't know, a road lined with flowers, white lace and fluffy purple and gold. It would be so beautiful if she weren't so perturbed. Even the ache starting in her calves was freeing, invigorating, normal.

Her steps quickened, not, she realized, because she wanted to reach the top sooner but because she wanted to see how fast she could go. Though it was July, the temperature had been below sixty when she left, and she felt the cold, persistent breeze against her skin. She climbed faster. Only when she reached the top, did she stop and check her phone.

It was as Spider had said. Three bars even though her phone had flashed "No Service" since they'd entered Adirondack Park. Her legs throbbed, but in a good way. She felt strong enough to take whatever happened. As she watched, more texts from Mother loaded up. She didn't want to talk to her mother. It was too early anyway. Let her sleep.

Instead, she dialed her father's number. She knew he'd be up though it was barely past five. As predicted, he answered immediately.

"Kate?"

"Were you arrested?"

"I got bail. Apparently, I'm not a flight risk."

A flight risk. That made him sound guilty. She knew, somehow, that he was. Still, the thought of him in jail was too disturbing. Needing bail wasn't much better. "I am."

"What?" He sounded confused.

"A flight risk."

"Katy, I don't want you to worry about me. I sent you away for a reason."

"Mother's hysterical. She texted me fifty times."

"I'll tell her to stop. She can't get much madder at me."

Out of the corner of her eye, Kate saw something moving. There, at the side of the road, among the black-eyed Susans and goldenrod, were a doe and her fawn. For a moment, her eyes met the mother deer's. Then, as if connected, the pair trotted off.

Kate sighed. She missed home.

"Kate? Kate?" Her father's voice over the phone.

"Reception's bad here. I climbed a hill." The sky was pink and red behind dark trees.

"I know. I wanted it that way, so you wouldn't have to hear—"

"But I was worried about you. Is it bad, the news coverage?" She wanted to ask if Colin had called. Even though she'd broken up with him, she wanted to hope she was wrong about him, that he really loved her.

"It's not that bad," her father was saying. "I'm just a small-town councilman. Some rock star will lick a doughnut, and I'll be old news soon."

"And . . ." *Colin?* "Mother?"

"Don't call your mother. I'll tell her you had nothing to do with it. Enjoy yourself. Try not to think about us too much."

Like that was possible.

"That boyfriend of yours came by," he said. "What was his name, Caleb?"

"Colin." He had come to look for her.

"I told Marjana to say you were away."

Kate shivered.

"Katy?"

"Okay. I love you, Daddy."

"Love you too, Katy. Goodbye." He hung up.

She started to walk back downhill. It was cold, and though she had brought several sweaters and hoodies, she hadn't thought to wear one.

But some instinct or muscle memory made her call Colin, just this one last time. Probably he wouldn't even answer. Probably he was asleep.

"Kate?"

He wasn't asleep. She pictured him lying in bed, phone in hand, waiting for her call.

"Now you know," she said.

"I don't know. That's why you broke up with me? Because of your father?"

Kate laughed even though nothing was amusing. She thought of admitting it. It would be easier on her, not having to lie. She could tell Colin the truth, that she still loved him but she didn't want him to have to deal with her family's disgrace.

He, of course, would say it didn't matter. But then, after a week of everyone talking about them the way her mother had talked about the Linds, he'd see she was damaged goods.

"Kate? Kate, what's wrong?"

What's wrong? He'd said that to her the first time they met, at cotillion classes at the club, a bunch of thirteen-year-olds learning the cha-cha. She'd been on the side, wishing she was home. The others had probably assumed she was a snob, but he'd drawn her out, imitating a French dance teacher talking about how "zee cha-cha dancing will be a zignificant asset in zociety." He'd made her laugh. He took her hand and cha-cha'd her across the floor.

But he wasn't laughing now. "Kate?"

Better to rip the Band-Aid off the open, festering wound.

"What?" she said. "Bad service around here. I'm in the mountains."

"In the mountains? What mountains?"

"I'm . . . visiting a friend. It's out in the sticks with barely any coverage. I had to walk a mile uphill to make this call." Be strong. She was strong, strong from the exercise.

"You have mountain-man friends suddenly? You're going on a pleasure trip when your dad's . . . your family's . . . ?"

"I came here to get away." Her own voice sounded unreal to her.

"Get away?" His tone was incredulous. A black bird landed before her. It was such a big bird, with a bright-yellow bill. She wished he could see it. That was stupid—why would he want to see a bird? Kate always wished Colin was with her.

"Yes. Get away from everything, my parents and . . ."

"Me?"

"Yes! Yes! I needed to get away from you. We can't be together anymore. I don't love you." She loved him. "Why is that so hard to understand?"

"I just can't believe you're saying this." Colin's voice sounded different now, husky.

"Look, I have to go. They're expecting me for breakfast." They probably were.

"Your mountain friends?"

Kate didn't want to hang up on him. It was too cruel. Suddenly, she realized that, if she walked downhill, the call would drop. Then, it wouldn't be her that hung up. She took a step forward. It was like walking into sludge. The bird, startled, flew off in a flurry of wings.

"Colin, the service is really bad here. I'm losing you." She wasn't, but she took another step down the hill, away from him.

It worked. His voice was missing in pieces. "Don't I . . . choice?"

She remembered the feeling of his hand on her cheek, when they'd kissed in the school library stacks. She wanted to walk back up the hill, walk back up to Colin. But it was no use.

"I'm losing you, Colin." *I'm losing everything.*

"Can you . . . ?"

Then nothing.

"Colin?" She couldn't stop herself from asking. "Colin?" But the call had dropped.

She walked back down, trying not to imagine him calling her name on the other end. She looked around, taking in the mint blue of the sky, the whiteness of clouds. She drew a shaky breath in, let a shakier one out. Breathe in, breathe out. If she did it a million times, the summer would end.

She kept walking. Her father was right. She should try not to think about it. First, she needed to make her lie true by going back and talking to her newfound friends.

If she could just get back to the cabin without seeing anyone, she'd be okay. She could calm down.

So, of course, someone was coming up the hill. Meredith. She'd pretend to be taking pictures, so she wouldn't have to talk.

11

Meredith

Essay topic: What historical moment or event do you wish you could have witnessed?

MEREDITH WAS UP at dawn, wondering if people really recognized history while it was being made, or if they figured it out later. Dawn turned out to be four thirty a.m. here. The sun had set at nine. Everyone else was still sleeping, so it was the perfect time for college essays. Except she couldn't think of anything to write. She decided to take a walk.

If there were woods in Florida, Meredith had never seen them. Probably she wouldn't want to because they'd be in the boiling red-hot, mosquito-filled center of the state.

These woods were cool, with a breeze the color of the sky. She walked faster, pushing herself against the wind. The ground beneath her felt rough and slippery with pine needles, and she remembered the boy, Harmon? Harlan? He'd taken her hand when she slipped. She'd barely seen him, but she'd know his face if she saw it again. She reached the place where she'd fallen the night before (recognizable because of the embarrassing butt print in the dirt). There was a rustling in the brush. She whirled. Was it him?

No, just a chipmunk, a tiny, adorable creature. She had brought her phone this time. She moved closer to take a picture, but it scurried up the closest tree, spiraling around in a circle.

It stopped. About ten feet up the tree was a platform, like a treehouse, but for wildlife. A few sticks protruded from it like bits of a nest. Meredith couldn't see inside. It was too high.

She wondered who had put it there. No, she didn't wonder. She knew.

No more animals. Finally, admitting to herself that she would find neither wildlife nor the mystery boy, she started back toward the road.

He'd said he lived close by, but she didn't see a house. After Meredith walked a good half mile, maybe more, she saw a road sign. It said "Abel Dickinson Way." It was surrounded by wildflowers, black-eyed Susans, and Queen Anne's lace, bowing in the summer wind.

Just as she did, she saw the other girl, Kate, coming from the opposite direction down the road. She glanced at her watch, five thirty. Kate clutched her phone.

There was a strange, mournful wail in the distance, not an

owl, another bird. It came from the direction where Spider had said the lake was. She hoped to go there today.

She looked back at Kate. Kate wasn't taking pictures, and her mouth was a thin line. Meredith remembered that Kate had asked about cell phone reception. Meredith hadn't really cared, since she was trying to get away. But it had been the only thing Kate had said the entire ride. Meredith wondered if something was wrong.

They kept walking until it became inevitable that their paths would cross, until it would be rude not to speak to one another. And yet, she didn't know if Kate wanted to talk to her. Kate was sort of unapproachable, so pretty and rich. She was wearing actual hiking boots, adorable ones that were probably from some fancy designer, with cute blue-and-white socks sticking out of the top. She was the kind of pretty, popular girl who never wanted to be friends with Meredith.

Kate was, at most, ten feet away, which gave her about five seconds to say something. But what?

Lovely day.

Was something her grandmother would say.

Hey. How's it going?

Said nobody interesting ever.

Five feet.

Just as Meredith opened her mouth to say "Hello," Kate turned, aiming her phone at . . . something, something Meredith was pretty sure wasn't there. What a snob.

Meredith passed without speaking.

12

Spider

INT. CABIN DINING AREA — MORNING

Britta and Spider are setting the table
under a chandelier made of antlers. Spider
is trying to avoid eye contact or anything
that might encourage Britta to converse
with her. We can see her failure haunting
her eyes.

"IT'S SO COLD here in the morning!" Britta said for about
the third time.

"Uh-huh." Spider added a napkin to a place setting without
bothering to fold it.

"I mean, maybe you don't think so, but I'm from Miami and sixty degrees is pretty cold." She pretended to shiver. Or maybe she actually shivered. Spider didn't know. Or care.

Strangers. When she and Ruthie had hatched the idea of renting the rooms, it had seemed like a good idea. Her parents would stop pressuring Ruthie to sell the place. Then, Spider would be able to come here forever. But she'd forgotten one important aspect of the plan. She, Spider, would have to spend a month "relaxing" in a houseful of strangers.

Ruthie probably hadn't forgotten. It would be just like her to think it was good for Spider to be more social. Ruthie believed the old saw about strangers just being friends she'd never met. She talked to everyone. Everyone. Driving up, Ruthie had held some woman's baby at a rest stop while the woman fixed her makeup. She knew every shopkeeper in town, from the boy at the meat market, who wanted to be an actor, to the antique store owner, who had three dogs. She even knew the dogs' names.

Spider didn't know the dogs' names; she didn't care about the people's names.

So now Ruthie was scrambling eggs and Spider was setting the table with some perky girl from Miami. "You do the plates," she told Britta after she almost dropped one because sometimes her hands didn't work right first thing in the morning. "I'll do silverware and napkins."

Britta took the plates. "Has your family been coming here long?"

"Yes." Spider went to find the silverware.

75

When the others returned, Ruthie served breakfast. Spider sat next to Kate and tried to be nice. She even passed the toast. Then, they sat in silence, chewing.

"Mmm," Kate said, trying the potatoes. "Good!"

Spider could tell Kate was also trying to be friendly. Ruthie smiled. "Do you like it?"

"I do."

"It was my grandmother's recipe," Ruthie said. "They had a deli in Borough Park when I was growing up. People came from all over for her hash browns."

"I guess you're used to grits," Spider said. Why had she said that?

But Kate smiled. "I do like my grits, but these are wonderful." She took another bite.

The table fell silent.

"Why don't you tell us more about your theater career?" Britta said to Ruthie, and Spider smiled because Ruthie talking for an hour about *Hair* would take the onus off her.

But Ruthie shook her head. "Enough about me for now. We should get to know one another, all of us. I think your parents' generation calls it bonding."

Spider noticed Kate looked dubious. Maybe she was shy too. But Britta said, "Good idea," because of course she would. "Does anyone know any, like, icebreaker games?"

Spider stifled a groan, and Kate looked down, but Meredith said, "Last fall, when I was president of Key Club, or maybe it was German Club, the vice president suggested a getting-to-know-you activity. We divided into groups, and each group had to come up with one thing they all had in common, and then each person in the group had to come up with one unique thing, something no one else in the group could say."

"Like what?" Britta asked.

"Well, like this one girl said she had a pet sugar glider. And there was this boy who had lived in Thailand until he was five. So different stuff."

Spider thought there was nothing interesting about her, at least nothing she wanted to share.

But Ruthie said, "Oh, that's a splendid idea!" Spider knew better than to mess with Ruthie when she was using words like *splendid*. "What a clever girl you are, Meredith."

Meredith smiled, chin raised, like she knew she was clever. Spider resolved to go last, to see what the others said.

"So how do we start?" Britta asked.

"In Key Club, we all said things about ourselves and saw whether other people had them in common." Meredith looked around the table, to see who would go first. Spider knew she should volunteer, as hostess. But maybe Meredith should go first, since this was her idea.

"I'll go." Britta smiled. She'd taken out her braids, and her dark hair hung in silken curls that reached just past her shoulders. "Okay, so I'll say stuff, and if you have it in common, raise your hand." When they all nodded, she said, "I'm sixteen years old."

No one raised their hand. The others must all be seventeen already. Except Ruthie.

"I'm going to be a senior in the fall." Britta looked at Ruthie and said, "Oh, wait. You definitely aren't," and laughed.

"Um," Britta went on. "I love musical theater."

Only Ruthie raised her hand for that. Kate said, "I mean, it's okay. We went to New York last year and saw a play, *Harry Potter and the Cursed Child*. It was pretty good."

"Lucky! Tickets to *Harry Potter* are really hard to get!" When Kate didn't respond, Britta continued, "Okay, more things, more things. I love mint chocolate chip ice cream."

Meredith raised her hand for that, but no one else.

"And *Marvelous Mrs. Maisel*."

Spider knew it was an Amazon Prime show, but she hadn't watched it. The others hadn't either.

"No one?" Britta said. "Guys, you have to watch this show. Okay, and I have a cat named Scooby." She rolled her eyes. "I mean, no one else is going to have a cat named Scooby, but I have a cat. I like cats in general. That's what I meant to say."

Everyone but Meredith liked cats. "Sorry, they seem sneaky," she said.

"And I like dogs too, but my mother won't let me have one. She thinks they're messy."

"I think she's right," Spider said.

"Um, and I like pizza, online shopping, and watching makeup videos on YouTube."

Spider noticed Meredith grimaced at this last, probably mirroring her own expression. Kate had started to raise her hand but put it down.

Britta turned to her. "You look like you've watched a few videos," she said.

It was true. Kate had a face full of perfect makeup in the middle of the woods.

Kate sighed. "Okay, okay, I have been known to study up on the intricacies of the smoky eye. But y'all don't have consensus on that."

"Thank you for your honesty." Britta looked around. "Pizza? You guys don't like pizza?"

All but Ruthie raised their hands.

"Lactose intolerant," she said. "I like pizza, but it doesn't like me."

Britta giggled. "I'm right-handed?"

Spider was left-handed.

"Well, I give up," Britta said, "not because you're left-handed or you're lactose intolerant," she assured Spider and Ruthie. "Maybe we should try the different things first."

"That might be a better idea," Ruthie agreed, and they all nodded, though Spider had been dreading this. She could only think of three different things about herself, and they'd all make people think she was weird. "Though we have seen several commonalities, so that's helpful. What's your different thing, Britta?"

Britta thought for a second, then said, "I can perform *Wicked* by heart. It's a musical," she added, in case any of them had been in a cave in France the past ten years. "The whole thing, start to finish. I first saw it when I was eight, and I loved it. I loved the friendship Glinda and Elphaba had, even though they were so different, and I loved how heroic Elphaba was, even though she was weird, or maybe *because* she was weird."

Had Britta glanced at Spider when she'd said "weird"? No, it was just her imagination.

Britta continued. "The first time I saw Elphaba flying at the end of the first act, singing 'Defying Gravity,' I turned to my mother and said, 'I want to do that.' I saw the play four more times onstage, and then I watched it online even more times and read the book. So, anyway, if you all ever have two and a half hours to kill, I can do *Wicked* for you. The whole entire thing."

She laughed a little awkwardly. They all did.

"Is that the kind of thing you mean?" Britta looked at Meredith. "Or should it be something more unusual, like having absorbed a twin before birth?"

"Oh, I did that," Spider said, then laughed. "Kidding."

Meredith said, "No, that's good. That's what I meant, a special talent or experience."

"Bless your heart. I feel like I know absolutely everything about you now," Kate said. Was that sarcasm? Spider looked up at her.

But Britta said, "I'm glad," like she was oblivious to Kate's tartness. Or maybe she was trying to deflect it? Or trying not to care?

"So, I'm next?" Meredith said. Spider was sitting to Britta's left, and that would make her next. But Ruthie gestured for Meredith to go ahead.

"Okay, um, when I was a kid, I was really smart."

Spider tried not to raise her eyebrow. Sometimes the left one just raised involuntarily when people said things like *I'm really smart*. "So that's your thing? Being really smart?"

"She *was* really smart," Britta said.

Meredith nodded. "Thanks, Britta. But, no, that's not it. My mother always pushed me. Like, I could never just dress as a Disney princess for Halloween. Instead, it was like Career Day. One year, I was a doctor, the next year, a lawyer. One year, a famous author came to our school and mentioned her editor. That year, I was an editor for Halloween."

"How do you dress up like an editor?" Kate asked.

"My mom did some research, and after some serious thought, I wore black pants and a fashionable sweater with some chunky jewelry, and I carried a cardboard cutout of a laptop." She laughed at her patheticness. "Even when we read stories, my mother changed the endings. Like when Snow White went to sleep, she woke up not to a prince but to a recruiter from Princeton. She said a duke would also be acceptable, as long as it was Duke University."

"That's a lot of pressure," Kate said.

"Tell me about it. Anyway, my thing is, since I was so smart in school, my mom had me take the online test to go on *Jeopardy*. I guess I passed because I got to audition in person."

"So you were on *Jeopardy*?" Britta said.

"Nooooo. There was a test first, where you read the answers off TV monitors and wrote the questions. Then, they had us play a practice game. That was when I completely freaked. I couldn't remember any of the answers, even easy ones like R.L. Stine or the capital of Australia. All I could think about was how disappointed my mother would be. I sort of forgot how to form words. Needless to say, I did not get chosen. My mother said it was fine, but a few months later, when it was the *Jeopardy* Teen Tournament, she made some comment—several comments, actually—about 'what might have been.' But, anyway, I got to audition," she finished with a shrug.

"Did you meet Alex Trebek?" Ruthie asked. "Is he very wise?"

"I wish," Meredith said. "But I guess I got further than most people."

"Definitely further than I would have," Britta said, and they all agreed, but Spider wondered if Meredith was really that boring. Surely there was something more interesting about her than having failed at *Jeopardy*. What was her deep, dark secret?

No, that was silly. She had said she was president of two clubs at school. Spider knew kids like that, resume builders. The story had been an attempt to humanize herself.

Meredith said, "Well, I can't perform a Broadway musical or, really, perform anything. So we all have our special things, I guess."

Spider wondered what her special thing was—that she liked to read a lot? That sometimes, her legs hurt so much she couldn't get out of bed, and that she missed so much school that they'd yelled at her mother about all her absences? Spider looked around at the cute, dark-haired Hispanic girl, the serious redhead, and the ridiculously beautiful blonde. She wondered how she looked to these girls, what they thought of her. She wasn't sure she wanted to be friends with them, not yet. But she didn't want them all to reject her either.

Or, worse yet, be nice because they felt sorry for her. There were girls like that at school too. She didn't want to be a charity case.

She noticed Kate looking at her hands, her red knuckles, and she stuck them under the table. No, Kate wasn't looking at them. She was just looking ahead. Still, Spider kept them in her lap. Her hands were so ugly.

They'd figure out sooner or later that there was something wrong with her. Eventually, she wouldn't be able to keep up with them, run down to the lake or carry a heavy cooler, and it would look weird. Girls her age didn't stay home like old ladies. But, for a while, she could explain these things away as a sprained ankle or an old PE class injury or a cold. For a while. Maybe, once they got to know her better, they'd understand.

"Um . . ." Kate was speaking now, and Spider realized she'd been looking at her because she thought it was Spider's turn. Which it had been. Oops.

"Um, I'm from Georgia," Kate said. She looked at them, as if trying to decide whether that was enough. Technically, by the rules of the game, it was. No one else was from Georgia. Spider wished she could pull something like that, but Ruthie and she both lived in the same town on Long Island. So nothing geographical would work.

But Britta said, "And?"

Kate must have decided she was busted. "I'm on the debate team?" she said.

"Really?" Meredith said. "I'm in debate. What events do you do?"

"Oh, wow. Extemporaneous and Lincoln-Douglas. Guess that can't be my thing then."

"Maybe it could. I do Original Oratory because I don't like to think on my feet," Meredith said. "I'm not very good at it."

"Meaning she didn't win state competition," Britta said.

"Oh, I didn't either," Kate said. "Maybe next year, though. Let's see . . ."

"Any unusual hobbies, interests, pets?" Britta asked.

"In middle school, I had a horse," Kate admitted, looking down like she was sort of ashamed of it. "I used to think I'd like to do dressage in the Olympics."

Rich girl has pony. Hardly a surprise.

Kate looked around, like she was expecting someone else to say they had a fancy show horse, but no one did. In fact, Britta said, "You had a horse? That's so cool."

"Why don't you still have it?" Meredith asked.

"I didn't really have time anymore. I started doing other stuff, and the horse was probably lonely, so my dad said if I couldn't spend more time with him, he'd sell him." She pursed her lips. "I really miss Shalimar."

Spider stifled the urge to yawn, barely.

Britta looked like she was about to ask a follow-up question, but thought better of it.

"Oh!" Kate said, like something had startled her. "I just thought of something, something way more interesting."

That wouldn't be hard. Still everyone leaned forward.

"When I was younger, I used to sleepwalk." She looked around, like she was trying to see if they believed her.

"Like, you just walked around in your sleep?" Spider had heard of people doing that, but she wasn't sure she believed it was true. It would make a good plot for a movie.

"Apparently. I don't remember it, but I would get out of bed, walk around. I even ate in my sleep. At least, my mother said I did. Once, she bought some Thin Mints, which was a big deal because she thought the Girl Scouts were too feminist. She told my brother and me we could have four each. But the next day, they were all gone, two whole boxes. I accused my brother, and he accused me, but when I went upstairs, I found smudges of chocolate on my sheets. I had no memory of it."

"Weird," Britta said.

"Another time, I cut my hair. My mother took me to the doctor then. He said it could be caused by stress. My mother said I wasn't under any stress, but after that, she tried to be super nice to me and made my brother be nice and locked up the scissors and knives."

"Knives!" Spider said. "Good you didn't stab anyone."

Kate laughed. "I know, right? My mom was so mad about

my hair, though. I was starting cotillion, which are these dance and etiquette classes at our country club. My mother cleaned up my haircut, but I still looked like I was going for the lead in a production of *Peter Pan*."

"Maybe you were stressed out over the etiquette classes," Meredith said.

Kate's face darkened. "Probably. I still had to go, though, and wear white gloves and learn to fox-trot. There was this awful boy, Charleton Atherton, who picked on me for being the tallest girl, and I had to dance the rumba with him. He teased me twice as hard with no hair."

"Maybe you cut your hair off because you didn't want to go," Ruthie said.

Kate shrugged. "If so, it didn't work. But I did eventually stop sleepwalking."

Spider shrunk back. She still hadn't thought of anything. Fortunately, Ruthie said, "I think I have a few different things, other than just being older than dirt. I was a professional actress, as you may have heard. I was once in a commercial for Coca-Cola."

"Really?" Britta said.

Spider had known that. She'd seen the commercial.

Ruthie nodded. "I was Girl Drinking a Coke. People said I'd take Broadway by storm. But I gave it up to have two beautiful children and five grandchildren, one of whom you have met."

"The most beautiful," Spider said.

"Nice try," Ruthie said. "Another thing that's special about me is that, when I was a teenager, I drove down with two of my girlfriends to the March on Washington."

"Wow," Meredith said. "So you heard the 'I Have a Dream' speech in person? That's one of the best Original Oratories ever."

"It was difficult to hear," Ruthie said. "There was a problem with the sound system, and there were over two hundred thousand people there. But you could feel the energy. We each had lied to our parents about where we were going. My friend Janet said she was staying at my house, and I said I was staying at Rhoda's, and Rhoda said she was staying at Janet's. It was quite a house of cards."

"But worth it, right?" Meredith asked.

"Absolutely."

"I have such a cool grandma." Spider felt really proud as she said it.

"So what's your thing?" Kate asked Spider. "I noticed we skipped you."

"Oh, uh." Spider looked at her hands under the table, then at Ruthie. "Um, I love old movies, movies like *Casablanca* and *Rebecca*. I have dozens on my computer, and I watch them every night before I go to sleep. I want to be a screenwriter someday."

That was enough. No one had said it was supposed to be a deep, dark secret, and Spider hated talking about herself, especially to strangers. Most people were strangers to Spider.

"Is that what you were doing when I came in last night?" Britta said. When Spider nodded, she said, "I wanted to ask you about it, but you hid it."

"Yeah, it's sort of nerdy. I was watching *Eternal Sunshine of the Spotless Mind.*"

"Okay. I thought of something we all have in common," Britta said. "Two things. One is that we all wanted to come here to take a break from our lives, for whatever reason."

Spider noticed that Kate looked down, her long finger tracing the whorls in the wooden table. She was hiding something, same as Spider. Spider knew it.

"The other," Britta said, "is we all have pierced ears."

Spider's hand flew to her own ears. It was true. She was wearing two different earrings. One was the Big Dipper, the other, a star. Britta had on little earrings with heart-shaped pink stones. Kate wore small, flower-shaped silver earrings, and Meredith and Ruthie had no earrings, but they did have a hole where an earring would go, so they'd been through that same third-grade ritual. Spider remembered when her friend Lauren had gotten pierced ears, and she'd had to have them too. She always wanted to be exactly like Lauren. Lauren had dumped her in fifth grade to hang with the cooler girls, the ones who took dance lessons or horseback riding or, at least, didn't stay in bed all day Saturday.

But she said, "Good catch, Britta." Then she smiled at Ruthie to say, *See? I'm being nice.*

She wondered about the other thing Britta had said, about them all wanting to take a break from their lives. No one had objected to that, so it must be true. But normal teenage girls didn't want to go to the mountains to relax. Normal teenage girls were like her sister. They wanted to have fun, go to the beach, party.

Maybe the four of them had more in common than she'd thought.

13

Kate

KATE WAS SO happy when they moved off "getting to know you" and on to another subject—a cooking schedule for meals—that she momentarily forgot an important fact: she couldn't cook, not at all.

In the emails they'd exchanged, there'd been something about sharing cooking. It hadn't really hit her that it meant other people would be eating dishes she had cooked.

This was not a reasonable thing to expect, assuming people had functioning taste buds.

Kate couldn't cook. She could make sandwiches, but they'd always had a maid. Even her mother didn't cook, and she'd certainly never taught Kate.

Maybe she could make something frozen on her day. Or, when she'd visited her friend Hadley at college, she'd had something called ramen noodles. That seemed easy enough.

She felt this weird, sick feeling in her stomach, like it was about to give way. All these girls would think she was an idiot, a sheltered, spoiled idiot. Maybe she should go home.

"Um, as you may know, Ruthie . . ."

Kate became dimly aware that Spider was talking. Strange girl. She had on a black T-shirt probably for some movie, a scary alien with "Obey" written over his head. Her voice was slow and husky, almost the way Kate imagined an actual spider speaking. *"Will you walk into my parlor?" said the spider to the fly.*

Stupid. What was she saying?

"Ruthie, um, you know I'd probably poison people if I cooked." Spider turned her eyes on Ruthie, like she was trying to butter her up. "Would you maybe want to take my day?"

Silence. Spider added, "Pleeeeeze."

"Ha!" Ruthie said. "What utter nonsense! I'm taking my own days and no others. And no ramen noodles either. Any idiot can follow a recipe, and you are no idiot. We have cookbooks. If you haven't learned to cook in seventeen years, it's time you did."

So much for ramen!

"I can cook," Britta volunteered. "Maybe we can pair up, at least at first. I can help you." She smiled at Spider, who suppressed a scowl.

"Splendid!" Ruthie said. "Spider can be your *sous* chef for tomorrow's dinner."

"What's a sous chef?" Britta asked.

Kate said, "It's the person who does all the prep work, like chopping onions."

"Oh, goody! The boring stuff." Britta clapped her hands. "I make this great roast chicken, and I need onions, garlic, and two kinds of peppers. You have to chop the garlic real fine, like mince it. Otherwise, it's not as garlicky and . . ."

She kept going and going. Kate glanced at Spider. Her hands were folded atop the quilted place mat. When she noticed Kate looking at her, she snatched them away. So weird.

Britta must have noticed the movement too. She stopped midstory. "Um, but if you'd rather do something different, that's fine too. Like, I could show you how to—"

"I'm fine," Spider snapped. "I can chop garlic. I'm not an idiot." She smiled at Ruthie.

Kate decided it was only fair to admit she was in the same boat—or maybe the same kitchen. "Y'all don't want to eat my cooking either. I'm sure I can manage something, though, maybe heat something up, canned soup or . . ."

"I can show you," Meredith said. "I cook at home when my mom's working."

"Oh, wow. My mom doesn't work or cook."

"I mean, not that I'm a chef or anything," Meredith said. "I get most of my recipes off websites, or boxes of stuff. Like I make this meat loaf with Stove Top stuffing in it."

"I'm sure Stove Top stuffing is delicious," Kate said, even though she was sure of no such thing. She'd never had it.

They decided that each team of girls would take two nights a week, with Ruthie taking two because, she said, "I'm a generous soul." Wednesdays would be what she called Fend for Yourself Night, to eat leftovers. If they decided to go out one night, that would be taken off Ruthie's nights, which was only fair since she had two.

Britta and Spider went to consult Ruthie's stack of recipe books. Meredith said, "I have the meat loaf recipe in my head. It's just two pounds of ground beef, two eggs, stuffing, and barbecue sauce, and that makes two meat loaves." She entered these ingredients into her phone's memo feature. "Good to know the phone's still useful for something."

"Uh-huh." Kate wondered if Meredith had thought she was rude earlier.

"We can make a salad," Meredith continued, "and I'll teach you to mash potatoes."

"Sounds easy." Kate had never done anything as useful sounding as mashing potatoes.

"Not so much when I was ten. It really develops the pronators and supinators. Those are the arm muscles that turn your hand."

"I think I remember that from anatomy class."

"So how did you manage to eat," Meredith asked, "if your mother doesn't cook and you don't either?"

Kate looked down, turning her hand over, using her pronators and supinators. "Oh, um, someone came in."

"Like a cook? You had a cook?"

Meredith was looking at her like she was some member of

the British royalty—but in a bad way. Kate wondered if they'd still have Marjana when she got back. Probably not. Probably good if she learned to cook.

"More like a maid," she said. Then, to change the subject away from her family and their maid, she said, "Maybe we could make fish another day." Not that she knew how to cook fish.

"I want to see this supermarket before I commit to fish," Meredith said.

"Good point. Chicken then."

Meredith had a chicken recipe in her head too, baked breasts with parmesan cheese and mayonnaise. "From the parmesan cheese container. Or maybe the mayonnaise container—I'm not sure. We can make rice and some kind of vegetable. Let's see if they have a steamer." Meredith gestured for Kate to follow her into the pantry, a little room attached to the kitchen.

Kate followed, though she was unsure what a steamer even looked like.

"Check that cabinet," Meredith said, pointing.

Kate rummaged around. There was a metal globe-like thing that she was pretty sure was for draining pasta and a wooden thing with slats. That might be for steaming. She put them both on the counter.

"Oh, good! You found one." Meredith picked up the wooden thing. "Cool. This is different from ours. What kind of vegetables do you like?"

Kate did know the names of vegetables, and Meredith added them to her list, then instructed Kate to check the cupboard for what she called "staples," oil and rice and a couple of different spices.

"Hey, so they have the olive oil and the pepper and some kind of spice blend, but I don't see . . ." Kate stopped talking. Meredith wasn't listening. She stood, stock-still, staring at something in the corner.

"Meredith?" Kate said.

Meredith didn't speak but gestured with her head at . . . something.

"What is it?" The bottle of olive oil Kate was holding felt heavy.

"Shh." Kate noticed Meredith's gaze travel upward.

Where there was something hanging.

It was about as big as one of the gardener's old, dirty brown leather gloves, but it was hanging way too high to be one, attached to the wall above their heads.

Kate inhaled. Nothing to worry about. It was just dirt. Or dust. Or . . .

Kate's eyes focused sharply on the membranous folded wings, the small, pointed ears hanging underneath.

A bat.

It was a bat.

"Oh!" Kate backed up until she hit the cabinets. She wanted to bolt, but she didn't want Meredith to see she was scared. *Deep breaths.* Bats were nocturnal. It was probably just sleeping. Or dead. *Inhale. Exhale.*

Even if it was dead, she didn't want to touch a dead bat.

Just the words "dead bat" made her shudder. She imagined it flying around above her head. Her hand rose to her hair. The bat must have been awake last night when they'd come in. How close had it been? Had Meredith and Spider let it in when she was outside? Could it have nested in their hair?

But now it was motionless. Meredith glanced at Kate, then backed away. When she reached the pantry door, they instinctively linked arms and slid out of the pantry.

Once out, they kept backing, backing, backing, like participants in some kind of backward three-legged race, through the kitchen and into the dining room, where the other three stared at them, at Kate with her bottle of oil, thinking they were crazy. They exchanged glances. Kate nodded.

Meredith whispered, "There is a bat in the pantry."

They had hoped, of course, that one of them, maybe Spider, who loved arachnids so much that she didn't mind being called that, would say, "Oh, that's no big deal! We see those all the time—let me get this one with my bare hands!"

Instead, they had the following reactions:

Ruthie shuddered. "A bat? In the house?"

Britta ran for the front door. "Tell me when it's out of here." Then she scrambled outside.

"How are we going to get it out?" Meredith asked.

Kate and Meredith glanced at one another, then at Ruthie and Spider, then at one another again. Kate knew Meredith was having the same thought she was: as landlords, Spider and Ruthie should definitely be in charge of pest removal. Still, it was ridiculous to expect of an old woman and a girl who clearly couldn't chase down a bat.

"Is there someone we could call?" Meredith said. "A bat-catching service?"

Ruthie raised, then lowered her shoulders. "If we were home on Long Island, most definitely. But here, it could take days to get someone to come out. Can we wait days?"

They all glanced at the open pantry door.

"I guess we could close it?" Meredith said.

"And go out for meals," Kate added. Were there even restaurants here?

"Yeah, no." Britta's voice came through the door. "I am not sleeping for even one night in a house with that creature. Have you ever seen a bat house? I have, and they're skinny. He could just sneak out in the middle of the night, out the door, through the tiniest crack."

Apparently, in her terror, Britta became a zoologist.

"She's not wrong," Meredith said.

"So what do you suggest?" Kate asked.

"Someone needs to get it," Britta said through the door.

They all looked at one another, then at the pantry.

No one was really looking at Kate, she noticed. They were looking at the old lady more than at her. They probably thought she was too much of a privileged princess to catch a bat.

Well, they were right, weren't they?

Meredith spoke loudly enough for Britta to hear. "I think two of us should throw a blanket over it. And the rest—including

Britta—should stick around to close the door."

"That's a lot of people," Britta said. "Maybe some of us should get out of the way."

She was talking about herself. At least, Kate thought she was. Or was she talking about Kate? Was she assuming Kate would be more of a hindrance than a help?

Silly. She wasn't the weakest person here. She shouldn't be, anyway.

Kate straightened her head, causing her blond curls to fall backward. She thought of every brave heroine in every movie she'd seen, not the shrinking princesses, but the warriors. This was her chance to be one, to show them who Kate Covington really was. She was going to have to be brave in the future. A bat was an easy place to start.

"I volunteer as tribute," she said, channeling Jennifer Lawrence.

Wow. She sounded like sort of a badass. She looked around.

They were staring at her like she'd grown a third eye.

"I mean, I'll do it. I'll be one of the two, with the blanket."

"I'll help you," Meredith said.

"I'll open the door," Spider said.

"And I'll stay here, out of solidarity," Ruthie said.

"I guess that means you don't need me," Britta said through the door.

"You can go upstairs," Meredith said. "But first, stand here while we get the blanket."

"Maybe we should get a net. There's one in the closet," Spider said.

"And put up our hair." Kate gathered her hair into a band.

"Wait!" Britta stopped them. "Why am I standing here again?"

"To make sure the bat doesn't come out before we get back," Meredith said.

"Oh, okay. Wait. Do you think that will happen?"

"No. Bats are nocturnal. It's sleeping. This is just in case."

"Oh. Okay."

They all started to leave again on their various errands.

"Wait!" Britta interrupted them. "What am I supposed to do if it comes out?"

"Scream and run away," Meredith said.

Britta nodded. "I can do that." She fixed her eyes on the pantry door. They scrambled before she could ask any more questions.

"Come on," Kate said. "This bat isn't going to catch itself."

14

Meredith

Essay topic: What is courage?

BAT-CATCHING HADN'T BEEN on Meredith's list of
Relaxing Things to Do. Not at all. In fact, preparing to retake
the SAT might have been more relaxing.

But Kate, who had seemed like a spoiled rich girl with her
perfectly streaked blond hair, was walking downstairs with
an Eiffel Tower souvenir blanket and an expression that said,
"Bring it on." She wasn't about to be the crybaby. She'd leave
that to Britta.

She followed Kate, brandishing a fishing net. They both
wore plastic shower caps. "Get that bat!" Meredith felt weirdly
energized as they tromped toward the pantry.

Britta stood by the door, a pensive look on her face.

"Anything?" Meredith whispered.

Britta jumped, then whispered, "Oh! You scared me. But yeah, no. Nothing. Can I go hide in my room now?" She was already backing away.

"Sure." They were better off without her. "We've got this." Even though she wasn't absolutely sure they did.

In the pantry, the bat hung, motionless.

Kate backed out. "We need a ladder."

"That sounds dangerous," Meredith reasoned, following her.

"Maybe we should use the silly net after all," Kate said.

"Maybe so." Meredith sighed. "Okay, new plan. I'll try to get the net over it and gradually coax it down the wall where you can reach it. Then, you throw the blanket when it's low enough."

Kate unfurled the cedar-scented blanket. They marched back into the pantry.

The bat looked like a baseball glove, except with a face. This wasn't going to be a big deal. It wasn't. Meredith tiptoed toward it, net aloft. It was asleep, after all. She'd just sneak the net up the wall. That's what she would do. Nothing to worry about.

She raised the net, slowly, carefully, trying to ignore her pounding heart.

She slid the net up the wall and positioned it over the bat's small, brown body until she barely nudged it.

"Oh!" She screamed. Suddenly, it was in her face, wings flapping, air against her ears. She stumbled back, dropping the net with a clatter. She staggered from the pantry, ducking. She hoped that shriek was Kate, not her, but her throat hurt from it.

"Run!" Kate snatched up the blanket and ran. Meredith grabbed the net and fled too.

Once safely in the kitchen, they stopped, glancing around, shielding their heads against an unseen onslaught. Meredith had a horrible thought. What if it was *on* her? She shuddered. Stop it! Stop being a baby! But she couldn't help it. She noticed Kate was shuddering too.

Just as Meredith was about to peek around to try to look at her shoulder, there was a shriek from the living room. Spider! And a cry, "My goodness!" from Ruthie.

"Guess we know where the bat is," Kate said.

"Don't suppose we can just stay here and let them deal with it?" Meredith said.

"Good idea, except they won't. Ruthie will probably invite it in for pancakes."

"Good point."

Another shriek from the living room. They both scrambled to their feet, took up arms again, and clambered out the kitchen door and into the living room.

The scream had been Ruthie. She was on the floor in the fetal position, head in hands, with the bat swooping around her. Spider ran around, trying to chase the bat out the open door with a sofa pillow. When she saw Meredith, she yelled, "Get it! Get it with the net!"

Without thinking, Meredith started chasing the thing too. Kate put up the blanket to shield herself against the swooping, diving creature.

No luck. Once, she had it almost against the wall. She threw the blanket at it, her own body following. She shuddered, and dropped it. The bat flew up at her. Meredith screamed. Kate screamed. Ruthie (for she had risen too) screamed and dashed for the door and onto the front lawn. They all ran after her, and Spider slammed the door behind them.

They stood in the sunlight, panting. Meredith could feel the bright, sticky sweat on her brow, her heart beating heavily. She almost felt like she might have had a heart attack, were she only old enough to have the necessary plaque buildup in her arteries.

But she wasn't, and she didn't. She'd survive today at least.

She looked at the other three girls, women. They all glanced toward the house, perhaps all thinking the same thing she was: Could they camp out here?

Maybe they would.

Then, she heard laughter.

She looked out toward the road and saw a guy in a red-checked flannel shirt. Harmon Dickinson. The guy from last night. He laughed long, and he laughed hard, then looked at Meredith and Kate, who were standing side by side, holding the net and blanket.

"Going fishing?" he asked.

Then, he laughed again. Meredith pulled off the shower cap.

Meredith did not like being laughed at. She'd arranged her life in such a way that no one would ever—ever—have any reason to laugh at her. His laughter made her want to stomp her foot, but that would be even more laughable. And she couldn't go inside. The bat was there.

"Harmon Dickinson, were you spying on us?" Spider's hands were on her hips, and she pointed to the camera around Harmon's neck. "Pervert! Don't you dare trespass here!"

He shrugged and walked closer. "No one's spying *or* trespassing. I heard screaming, and I showed up—bravely, I might add—to make sure you weren't being murdered. Who said chivalry was dead?" He smiled. Meredith noticed he had a dimple.

And hazel eyes that shone when he laughed.

She found her voice. "We're fine." She turned away. It did not escape her attention that this boy had seen her scream twice in the past twenty-four hours. Something she never did otherwise. "We're fine," she repeated, maybe more adamantly than necessary.

"As long as you're fine." Harmon chuckled.

"Y'all speak for yourselves." Kate shook her golden tresses from her ponytail. "I, for one, am not fine, not fine at all. I came here all the way from Georgia, based upon the promise of rest and relaxation. But I have had neither, due to the presence of vermin in this cabin."

Harmon's mouth twisted into an obnoxious little smile, not the cute, dimpled one from before. Yes, Meredith had looked back at him. "Vermin?" He laughed.

The boy laughed too much.

"Stop laughing!" Spider said. To Kate, she said, "We can get the bat ourselves."

"A bat? You've got a bat flying around in there?" Harmon looked interested.

"I assume it has landed by now," Ruthie said.

"And you were trying to catch it with that?" Harmon gestured toward the net, his expression becoming a grimace. He looked at Meredith.

Boys who thought they were smart were truly annoying. The net had obviously been a dumb idea, but it hadn't been Meredith's dumb idea. Spider had been coming here her entire life—you'd think she'd know something about bat extermination.

"We chased it with the net," she said. "Kate was supposed to get it with the blanket."

"That sounds way more sensible." Harmon nodded approvingly at Kate.

"Well, thank you." Kate tossed her hair. Was she flirting with him?

"I can help you get it." Harmon started toward the house.

"No!" Meredith and Spider chorused just as Ruthie and Kate said, "Yes, please."

Harmon frowned at Meredith. "Aw, don't let pride get in the way of asking for help."

"I want the satisfaction of vanquishing it on my own."

"Then you're going to have to do it yourself," Kate said, "because that thing was gross, and if someone is offering to take it out, I will politely say yes!"

Meredith shook her head but didn't speak. Harmon coaxed, "Come on. I really just want to see it." He gestured to the camera hanging around his neck. "It's hard to find them by day."

Meredith didn't reply, but she thought, well, maybe.

"You can help, since your friend doesn't want to." Harmon had reached the porch by now. "It's a two-person job, and I'll need someone to release it so I can take photos of it in flight. And I know Spider won't help me."

"Release it?" Meredith asked. "Like, I'd have to hold on to it first?"

"With a blanket."

Meredith swallowed hard and stifled a shudder. "Okay," she finally agreed.

Harmon started up the stairs. "Leave the net." He called back to Spider and Kate, "Can one of you ladies man the door?" Kate had moved farther from the house.

"I guess," Spider grumbled. Meredith could tell she didn't like being referred to as "you ladies," or maybe just didn't like Harmon.

"We'll just stay out here and watch," Kate said.

"Good idea." Harmon turned to Meredith. "Into battle!"

"We aren't going to hurt it, are we?"

Harmon laughed. "A minute ago, you just wanted to get rid of it."

"That's not true. I am a very kind-to-animals person." Was there a word for that?

"I'm sure you are. No, we are not going to hurt the poor, sweet little ol' bat. We are going to gently reunite him with his extended family who, hopefully, don't all live in your attic."

106

"Ugh." Now they were inside the house again. Meredith glanced around, instinctively putting her hands over her hair. It probably wasn't a terrible idea to have Harmon's help, as long as she appeared not to need it.

"So, do you have much bat-catching experience?" she asked, hoping he did.

"Ooh, yeah!" Harmon made his voice an exaggerated hillbilly drawl. "I been catching varmints since I was knee-high to a toadstool."

"Really?"

"No, not really. You city slickers don't know sarcasm when you hear it? I also hardly ever say 'knee-high to a toadstool' in my everyday life. Or 'varmint.'"

"You country folk don't know an innocent question when you hear it."

"I prefer 'mountain folk.'" Harmon grinned. He really was handsome when he smiled. *Stop it!* Handsome boys never noticed Meredith. She didn't wear makeup or dress to impress. He was probably messing with her.

Meredith pursed her lips. She looked around the living room. The bat wasn't there.

Harmon glanced back at her and pointed toward the kitchen. "This way?" When Meredith nodded, he headed for the kitchen. He turned on the light and glanced around.

"Ah, here's the cute little guy!" Harmon said. "He wants to cuddle."

Meredith tiptoed behind him. The bat clung to the corner

between the cabinet and the wall, at her eye level. Harmon was right, it was tiny. Still, she backed up.

"Don't be scared of it. It's probably been living here for months with no one noticing."

"That is not a comforting thought."

"Okay, I'll get it," he said. "But don't you want to take a look first?"

Not really, but Meredith didn't want to look prissy either. It didn't do anything to advance the cause of feminism to go around acting like you needed a boy to do everything. "You're sure it won't fly up again?"

"I think he was provoked last time." He smiled. That dimple again. "He doesn't want to mess with you any more than you want to be messed with."

"Okay." Meredith stepped closer. She leaned in. At first, it looked like a crumpled bit of paper bag, but as her eyes got used to looking, she saw that its pointy hands (paws?) were covered with purple-black leathery skin. Up close, the rest of its body looked like a wooly stuffed teddy bear. She almost wanted to touch it. Bad idea. It might get scared and take it out on her by giving her rabies. Still, she found herself reaching out.

Click! And a blinding flash. Harmon's camera. Meredith jumped.

"Oh!"

"Sorry. Did I scare you?"

"What do you think? Are you always creeping around behind people?"

"Hey, you invited me in this time."

"*This* time. What if the light had startled him?"

"Do you want me to just get it?"

Meredith looked back. "No, it's harmless. It's not the bat's fault you're creepy."

"Thanks."

"Truth hurts. So I just throw the blanket over it?" she asked.

"Yeah, and, um, bunch it up a little so it won't fly back in your face."

"I don't want to hurt him."

"You won't. You're going to be gentle."

"Okay." Meredith took a deep breath. "Maybe back up a little."

Harmon did. Meredith drew back, then pounced, gently as she could, covering the bat with the blanket. She had it. She felt its bony little body struggling in her hands, its wings fluttering. She tried to hold it tight enough not to lose it, loose enough not to harm it.

She backed toward the door.

"Got it," she whispered.

"Good job." Harmon held up his camera. "Let me get ready before you release it."

Meredith sidled toward the door. The bat was struggling less now.

Harmon beat her to the door. Meredith improved her grip on the ball of blanket and followed. When she got there, Harmon was outside, camera raised. "Ready?" she asked.

"When you are."

Meredith pushed aside the momentary worry that the bat would land on her. Or that she'd hurt it. What if it just fell to the ground when she released it? She felt it in the blanket, moving. It was still alive. Of course it was.

She went back to worrying that the bat would land on her.

Harmon was in place with his camera. She noticed it had a real lens, like old cameras, but she could tell it was digital. She raised the bundle high and let it unfurl. At first, the bat didn't come out. She gave the blanket a shake. Finally, the bat emerged, tentative at first. It fluttered down, then up toward the trees and the noonday sun. She heard the shutter of Harmon's camera, following it as it disappeared into the forest.

She looked at Harmon. He met her eyes.

"Thanks," she said, "um, for helping. And . . ."

"Yeah, don't mention it." He looked down, like he was suddenly shy.

Meredith couldn't wait to talk to Britta. This would make a great college essay. For the first time in her life, she'd actually done something brave, something that didn't take the good, boring route but involved some risk. Maybe this whole trip was a risk.

Harmon said something else, but Meredith didn't hear it because she was so lost in her thoughts. She turned back to ask what he'd said. But just then, Spider approached them.

"So let me get this straight. Big Mountain Man made the little girl get the bat?"

Harmon scowled. "She did better than you could, City Girl."

Harmon started flipping through the photos on his camera. There were dozens, even though he'd only been snapping for a few seconds. He paused on one, the bat silhouetted against the sun, black wings spread like an angel.

"That one's good," Meredith said. When Harmon saw her looking, he snatched the camera away.

"I wish you'd leave us alone," Spider said.

"Fine. I will. Don't call me next time you're in trouble."

"Ooh, I'm so scared!" Spider sounded like a six-year-old.

And he turned his back and stomped away before Meredith could ask him for a closer look. She wanted to see the photo. She doubted he'd have let her, though, because when he'd been scrolling, she had noticed another one on the roll.

Meredith walked away, remembering the feel of the bat's body in her hands, the thrill of seeing it take flight, the gleam in Harmon's hazel eyes when they'd met hers.

And the photo Harmon had undoubtedly been hiding from her, the photo of her own breathless, fascinated face as she'd watched the bat take wing.

15

Spider

EXT. CHARMING CABIN, DOORSTEP — DAY

Meredith, Spider, Ruthie, and Kate are
outside, having just released a bat.
Picture the Three Stooges meet the cast of
Clueless. Spider is justifiably perturbed,
having just discovered that the only
normal girl in her cabin group is secretly
fraternizing with the enemy.

SPIDER'S THOUGHTS WERE whirling like an old-
fashioned film reel. Harmon Dickinson. The girl was talking
to—flirting with, really—Harmon Dickinson. In their house!

Spider loved just about everything about the mountains—

the weather, the trees, the birds' songs, even the crows' caws. Mostly, she loved the fact that they were far, far away from everyone else's annoying noise, from boys on skateboards, girls obsessing over their makeup, neighbors bragging about a new Lexus.

One thing she didn't like about the mountains were the Dickinsons.

The Dickinsons were a townie family who lived there year-round. Their house was covered in peeling once-white paint and Keep Out signs and filled with dirty, barefoot boys, maybe five or six of them, running around, climbing trees, and splashing in the lake like the Lost Boys in *Peter Pan*, no parents in sight, and always with at least one, but sometimes as many as three, dirty, smelly dogs. Spider hated those dogs almost as much as she hated their owners.

Once, when she was eight or so, she'd been walking with her brother, Ben, to the lake, wearing a new cover-up, of which she was especially proud. It had a picture of Ariel on it. One of their awful dogs, a spotted one, had come up behind her, and she'd run, screaming. When she'd stumbled, the dog had grabbed the back of the cover-up. Spider heard the R-I-I-I-I-P of the cloth. Then, she saw the swatch of teal fabric in the beast's snaggletoothed mouth. She ran home and pounded on the door until Ruthie answered. Harmon—yes, it was definitely Harmon, with his curly hair and greenish-brown eyes—had explained, "He wouldn't of chased her if she hadn't of run." Even Ben had laughed. Talk about blaming the victim! From then on, the Dickinsons had always treated her like a spoiled, prissy rich kid. But was it really prissy not to want dog spit all over your things?

The Dickinsons thought they were better than Spider's family because they'd lived here for generations. After all, they had their family name on a street and more than a few tombstones in the local cemetery. In Harmon's eyes, that made them special.

In Spider's eyes too. She'd love to live here year-round and never have to leave. Love to die here too and be buried in the peaceful little cemetery with its crumbling tombstones that went back to the Revolutionary War.

"So that was the meet-cute?" Spider said, following Meredith into the house.

"What?" Meredith said.

"The meet-cute," Spider said. "In romantic movies, the main couple should meet in some adorable way, like getting stuck in an elevator, or the guy's a cop and pulls the woman over, or they're shopping for pajamas, and one only wants the top while the other wants the bottoms." This last was from a 1938 movie, *Bluebeard's Eighth Wife*, which Spider had watched as part of an online film course she took. She was proud to know such an obscure reference.

"Oh, I don't watch movies like that." Then, maybe realizing she sounded completely condescending, Meredith added, "I mean, I don't ever get a chance to watch movies. I study too much."

A humblebrag. She thought Spider was lazy. "I don't watch

movies for entertainment," Spider replied, loftily.

"Right, you want to study screenwriting." Meredith smiled. "Are you applying to film schools in New York, or do you want to go to California?"

Spider pressed her lips together. "Not sure yet. But I took an online course last year through Columbia. There's all these free online college courses you can take."

"That sounds cool. I wish I had time for that, but I'm . . ." She stopped.

"Too busy studying for school," Spider finished for her.

"Right." Meredith sighed. "Hey, maybe we can watch some movies while I'm here. You said you have some?"

"Yeah." Spider knew Meredith didn't mean it. She was just being nice, and it would be forgotten. Spider could be nice too. "Let's do that."

Just then, Britta appeared at the landing. "Is it safe to come out?" she whispered.

"Oh, wow!" Meredith said. "We forgot you in the excitement."

Spider hadn't forgotten. She was enjoying the quiet. Now, it was over.

"Yep, all taken care of," Meredith said. "I have saved us all."

"Sorry I wasn't more helpful," Britta said.

"We didn't expect you to be," Spider said, then regretted it.

"It's fine," Meredith said. "More people would have scared him. It."

"Well, thank you for being so brave." Britta giggled.

Spider started to say that they hadn't really been brave, but she stopped herself. "So brave!" she echoed, and was rewarded when Meredith laughed.

"Meredith was flirting with that boy," Kate issued from her room.

Ruthie's bedroom door squeaked, and she stepped out. Once she, too, had ascertained that the coast was clear, she said, "All right. To the store!"

"To the store!" Britta echoed.

"Wait—all of us?" Spider looked at Britta. She'd missed the memo on the group shopping expedition. Cooking lessons from Britta were bad enough. "We're *all* going?"

"Certainly," Ruthie said. "You didn't think I was going to do all the shopping, did you?"

Had Spider taken the time to consider it, she probably would have thought exactly that. After all, Ruthie had always done that when the family came while Spider read at the lake. Still, Spider said, "I'm guessing no?"

"No." Ruthie smiled when she said it, but her eyes said she meant business.

"So we all have to go?" Spider glanced at Britta again. "Together, in the same car?"

"We only have one car, silly." Ruthie clapped her hands. "Let's go."

They did, Britta gushing about how it sounded "so fun" to shop and cook together. "I can't wait to make my grandmother's *arroz con pollo* for you guys—oh!" Britta jerked down several steps, then collapsed at the bottom. "My ankle!"

All turned. Britta was sitting, clutching her foot. At first, Spider thought maybe she was faking. Her siblings were huge fakers. But then, she saw the tears in Britta's eyes and was ashamed of herself. She hated when people thought she was faking.

"Oh!" she moaned. "I twisted it."

"My goodness!" Ruthie rushed down to Britta faster than Spider would have thought an old lady could run. "Do you think it's broken?"

"No, I . . ." Britta tried to stand up. "I think I can—ouch!" She winced as her ankle collapsed under her.

"Let me help you." Meredith offered her a hand.

"It's okay. Oh, I'm such a dork." Britta pulled herself up on the banister, her face screwed up. "I'm fine. I'm fine." But she sat down again.

"Oh, you poor thing," Ruthie cooed. "Perhaps you should lie down."

"But I wanted to do my part." Britta tried, again, to stand. She succeeded this time, but she put no weight on the foot. She glanced at Spider. "I don't want people to judge me."

That was when Spider realized that Britta not going was almost as good as not having to go herself. "Oh, poor Britta! Ruthie's right. You shouldn't go!"

Ruthie was looking at her weird, but Spider went on. "Did you make a list of ingredients we need, before the bat?"

"Actually, I worked on my list upstairs." Britta reached into her pocket and pulled out a sheet of paper. "This should be enough for three recipes. I tried to organize it with all the veggies in one place, then all the dairy, and so on."

Spider examined the list. Britta's handwriting was super neat, unlike her own cramped penmanship. The list was neat and had what looked like ingredients for a whole chicken, a stir-fry, and a pasta dish. She had to admit she was a little impressed.

"I can give you money too," Britta said.

"Later's fine, dear," Ruthie said. "Can I get you an ice pack?"

"That would be sooooo nice," Britta said in a gushy voice that made Spider forget her moment of admiration. Britta started to pull herself up the stairs.

"Can I help you?" Spider asked, because Ruthie was looking at her like she should.

"Oh, it's fine." Britta heaved herself up the stairs, using the banister for balance. She reminded Spider of herself. Stairs were always hard because of the pressure on her joints.

Meredith and Ruthie went to get ice while Spider wandered off in search of Kate. She still suspected Britta might be faking. Still, those tears were pretty convincing. She couldn't be that good an actress.

16

Britta

NEVER LET IT be said that Britta Rodriguez wasn't a good actress. If the judges at the District 8 Thespian conference had seen her powerful performance as Teen Girl Injured on Staircase, she'd have won Critic's Choice. Now that everyone had scattered, she strode into the bedroom, flopped onto the bed, and propped her uninjured foot on the pillow, ready to writhe in pain when anyone came to check on her.

She couldn't say why she'd faked it. Yes, she could. Because of Spider. When she'd been up in her room, making the list, she'd been excited about cooking together. It seemed like such a sisterly thing to do, and she'd wanted to show off her skills to the other girls. But she'd caught the look of dread on Spider's face when Ruthie had said they were all going together. The way she'd kept looking at Britta and asking if all of them had to go, *Together, in the same car?* She didn't know what Spider's problem with her was, but she didn't want to deal with it. She'd come here to relax, impossible with that girl hating on her.

There was a light knock on the already open door. Kate stepped in.

"Heard you were under the weather." Her voice was soft. She held up an ice pack with pictures of yellow ducks on a blue background. "Ruthie said to bring you this."

Britta searched her face for signs of skepticism, but found none. "Oh, thanks." She straightened up, wincing as she did. "Thought Meredith would bring it."

"She had to finish her shopping list, and Spider's hip hurt, and Ruthie's old, so there's just me." She smiled. She had possibly the most beautiful teeth Britta had ever seen.

"You're in a good mood," Britta said.

"Well, I'm not in a bad one anymore," Kate said. "I have decided it's best to concentrate on the task at hand."

Britta wasn't sure what that meant, exactly, but she nodded. "Good idea. When I'm upset, I tend to get a little flighty, and then I get in trouble. I guess you probably know that's a problem of mine." Kate had, after all, heard the whole saga of Rick's car, because Britta had been so stupidly loud on the bus. "Well, that and being too talkative."

Kate winced. "I'm sorry I got so mad about that. I'm usually nicer."

"We all have those days," Britta said.

"I have the opposite problem. When something's bothering me, I can't let go of it. It shakes me awake in the morning and whispers in my ear at night."

"Oh." Britta nestled the ice pack under her ankle. Britta knew Kate had been awake late last night, early this morning too. Britta wanted to ask what was wrong, but she was sure Kate wouldn't like her asking. "Do you ever jog?" she asked instead.

"What?"

"Jog? Exercise? Running real fast gets your mind off everything. It's pretty out here. We should go later." Too late, she realized she was supposed to be grievously injured. Britta saw Kate's eyes flicker to the ice pack. "I mean, when my ankle's better."

"That's a good idea." She gave a short, forced smile, then started to leave. "But first, I'm off to see a man about a chicken. That's what my father says—except he says it about a horse."

Britta laughed. "My dad says that too." She adjusted the ice pack. "See, that's something we have in common."

After Kate left, Britta listened to the noises downstairs. Spider and Ruthie argued about who would drive. Finally, the door shut. Britta waited until she heard the car's engine turn over and wheels rolling down the road. Then she got up.

Alone now, she wasn't sure what to do. She decided to explore. The bedrooms were off-limits, of course. She headed downstairs.

Ruthie had given them a perfunctory tour when they'd arrived, but now, Britta really took everything in. One of the end tables was a trunk, which she opened to reveal board games: Life, Monopoly, and Pictionary boxes held together with yellowing tape. There was a drawer filled with magazines and, on one table, a well-used book called *Guide to Adirondack*

Trails. The family had obviously hiked a lot, and there were notes like "Nice view!" or "Trailhead is eight miles down a dirt road—don't give up!" and speckles of dirt and maybe ice cream on the pages. The photo albums held years of photos of the same family, wearing similar clothes, with lakes or mountains in the background. Sometimes, they showed off a fish, sometimes not. Sometimes Spider was with them, at first as a cute, if awkward, little girl in an assortment of Disney princess attire, later dressed in black, a sullen expression on her face. But half the time, she was missing. Britta wondered why.

Finally, Britta got bored. It had been almost an hour since they left. They'd be back soon.

Just as she started upstairs, she noticed two big, brown scrapbooks on a bookshelf near the stairs. Both were bulging with photos and clippings. She turned and slid them out, holding them shut to keep the contents from falling out.

The first was labeled "Ruth, Theater." The second, "Summer Stock, 1961–1964." Ruthie's. She pulled them out.

She started to look through one, the summer stock one, then thought better of it. She put the "Ruth, Theater" one back on the shelf but took the other with her, so she'd remember to ask Ruthie about it later.

She went upstairs, weighted down under the giant scrapbook. It would be pretty ironic if she actually fell down the stairs under its weight. Was that irony? Meredith would know.

Finally, she reached her bed. The ice pack had melted slightly, but still she nestled it against her ankle and lay down.

17

Kate

KATE DIDN'T REALLY understand why they all had to shop together, but she was glad of it. There was something so relaxing about the neat, colorful displays of apples, strawberries, and string beans that made her forget home, forget her parents, almost forget Colin's fading voice.

Before she left, she had stuck her phone into her nightstand drawer. Then, she ran outside before she could change her mind.

Kate glanced around at the piles of cucumbers and summer squash, rows of moist lettuce. "Nice."

"What is?" That was Meredith, and Kate realized it had been a dumb thing to say. It was just a supermarket, probably a shabbier-than-average one at that. She couldn't be sure. She hadn't spent a lot of time marketing. But this one looked small and unimpressive, one that would serve a community that was underpopulated most of the year.

But she improvised. She wasn't an extemporaneous speaker for nothing.

"I mean, it's so quiet. The supermarkets at home are always crowded."

"Tourists usually come on weekends," Ruthie said, clearly putting herself in another category. "We'll have the lake to ourselves too."

The produce section was by the cash registers, divided by a display of bouncy balls and a pyramid of canned pineapple with a sign that said "Taste of the Tropics." A little boy was playing with a red bouncy ball he'd pulled from the larger display.

"Stop that, Ray-Ray!" the cashier, a girl around Kate's age, said.

"We'll only get a few vegetables here," Ruthie said. "There's a farmers market Thursday at the church, so we can get more then." She checked Britta's list and grabbed onions and two peppers. Kate was happy she didn't have to cook but worried that Britta would set a high bar.

Ruthie gestured for them to move on. Kate started to, noticing that the little boy had taken the ball out anyway and was bounding around the checkout area, bouncing it.

"Ray-Ray, cut that out!" the cashier said.

"No!" Ray-Ray bounced the ball off a display of newspapers. Kate wondered if there was anything in the newspapers about Daddy. Unlikely. They lived in a small town, even if it was a suburb of Atlanta. No one would have heard of it here, much less care about some small-time public servant. Her life seemed so big to her, yet it was insignificant to others. Everyone's life was like that, when you thought about it.

Beside her, Meredith was saying something. She didn't respond, and Meredith waved her hand before Kate's eyes.

"What? I'm sorry, I didn't hear you."

"Grab the green beans."

"Sure." Kate didn't know anything about cooking green beans. She hoped Meredith did.

"Do you know how to . . . ?" Meredith stopped, possibly seeing from Kate's expression that, no, she didn't. She tossed the bag into the cart. "I'll teach you. Come on."

They squeezed past an elderly couple, who were choosing a watermelon.

"Put that ball away!" the cashier said to the little boy. "We can't afford it." Kate knew there was nothing about her father in those papers, not here. But he was in the papers at home. That was how Colin knew about it. All her friends knew.

"Come on, Kate." Meredith was gesturing her up the aisle to the salad dressings. Poor Meredith, having to lead her around like she was some feebleminded old aunt. Still, Kate felt drawn to the *New York Times*. She walked over toward it, gesturing to Meredith that she would be a second. She pulled out the paper and started to look.

"Are you going to buy that?" the young cashier asked. "The paper is for paying customers only."

Well. Kate could certainly afford a newspaper, so far, but

something about the cashier's voice made her throw it back like a guilty child. "Sorry."

But she stood there a minute more, staring at the cover.

Boom! A ball hit her in the head.

"Oh!" She whirled. "Excuse me!"

"Sorry!" The little boy breathed deeply. "Sorry, lady."

"It's fine." She looked at the cashier. "It's fine."

"Ray-Ray, put that back!" the girl said again.

Kate started to follow Meredith. She wondered if they could be friends. It hadn't escaped her attention that, out of all the missed calls on her phone, none had been from her friends. She was an outcast, a pariah. They'd probably only liked her because she was pretty and her father was a councilman. They were rooting for her to fail. Now, she had. She'd made up with Britta. Would Meredith like her?

Not if she kept acting like an idiot.

Meredith had disappeared up the aisle of spices and condiments. Kate looked for her.

Suddenly, there was a sound. Not exactly a crash, but a thud, a series of thuds, and something wet and squishy hit Kate's bare leg.

She turned around. The pineapple pyramid, or at least a large part of it, was on the floor with cans of pineapple rolling in every direction. Some of the cans had bounced and burst. That was apparently what had hit Kate's leg.

She heard a small voice yelling, "Sorry! Sorry!"

"Ray-Ray, I am going to get in trouble!" The cashier ran

toward the rolling cans and started picking them up, attempting simultaneously to do that, keep an eye on the register, watch the little boy, whose ball had hit the display, and warn Kate of the rolling cans. "PUT THAT BALL DOWN RIGHT NOW! Watch out for the cans! Hold on, I'll be right there!"

The little boy started sobbing.

Kate ran up to her, avoiding the rolling cans. "Let me help. How can I help you?"

"No, I don't . . ." The girl dropped one of the cans she was holding. "I can't . . . can you get someone from customer service?"

The little boy ran through the cans and slipped on some pineapple juice.

"Oh, God!" the girl said. "Or watch him maybe?"

Kate could do both. "Come here!" she commanded the boy. "Is that your sister? She is very busy with this mess you just made, so we are going to go get someone to bring a mop."

She didn't know if he would listen to her. She'd never babysat and had no experience with young children. So she was surprised when he held out his hand. Kate took it. She marched him over to the window that said "Customer Service," avoiding the still-rolling cans. "Excuse me," she told the man there. "The cashier out there needs some help cleaning up a big mess."

She expected him to ask for details, and she didn't want to say the little boy caused the mess, so she was glad when he said "Okay" just as Ray-Ray was making a break for it.

"Whoops!" Kate grabbed his arm. "Hey, come on, let's . . ."

She looked around. Let's what? He was still clutching the ball. "Let's go outside and play with that ball while your sister— Is that your sister?"

He nodded yes.

"While your sister cleans up."

The boy looked up at Kate. Then, without a second glance back, he walked out with her.

Kate was glad. She wanted to help, but she also wanted not to be in the way. The boy wriggled in her grip. She hadn't really noticed him, except to see he was a boy. He was about five, with brown hair cut in bangs that spiked over his forehead, deep-blue eyes, and a shiny, slightly runny nose that was somehow more endearing than disgusting. With the hand not in hers, he clutched a red ball.

"I'm Kate," she said, tightening her grip on his hand. "And you're . . . Ray . . . Raymond?"

"Racecar," he said.

"Racecar?" He must be getting it wrong.

He nodded. "Jupiter is the biggest planet."

"Why . . . yes." She thought that was true. "It is." She tapped the ball. She would buy it for him after all this was over. Who knew if she'd have money in the future, but for now, she could afford a bouncy ball. "Do you know what planet is that color?"

"Mars!" he said.

"That's right. You are going to have to hold very tightly to that ball and make sure it doesn't roll away in the parking lot. Can you do that, or should I?"

"Me." He clutched it closer.

"Okay, but if you drop it, even for a second, it's mine." This wasn't going to be hard.

"Okay." He squeezed it even harder. "Lizzie will be mad at me."

Lizzie must be the girl, his sister. "I did hear her tell you not to throw that ball."

"It's boring," the boy said.

Kate wondered why he was here in the first place. Didn't they have parents? But there must be some good reason.

He said, "I had to come here because Mommy is sick in bed."

"Well, that was nice of Lizzie to watch you then. Maybe you should bring something to play with next time, like crayons."

"I always have to come."

"That's tough." The boy nodded. Maybe she should move him away from the traffic whizzing along Route 9. On the side of the parking lot was a scraggly area with weeds and wildflowers. "Do you know all the planets? Tell me while we walk over here."

"Mars," he said. "And Venus. And Jupiter, and . . ." He stopped.

Kate remembered a mnemonic. My Very Elegant Mother Just Sat Upon Nine Pins. But she wasn't sure it would work if he couldn't read. Could kids that age read? Also, it included Pluto, which had been a planet when the mnemonic was made up but wasn't anymore. Unless you asked her dad. Pluto not being a planet got him almost as upset as tilapia.

"Where are we now?" she asked, as a hint.

"Earth!"

"Right! And the one with the rings?"

He threw the ball to her. "Saturn."

"Good. And . . . Nnnnn . . . ?"

"Neptune."

"Two more."

Lizzie came out, looking a little sweaty and a lot disheveled, her uniform shirt covered in pineapple juice. Again, Kate noticed she was around Kate's own age, maybe younger.

She walked over to them. "Hey, Ray-Ray." She pointed to the ball in Kate's hand. "We're going to have to put that back. I'll get it Friday."

"Oh, I was going to buy it for him," Kate said.

"No, thank you," the girl said.

"But I want to," Kate said. "He was really good. He knew most of the planets."

"He's supposed to be good," the girl said, "and he can learn to wait a few days in life. He's going to have to. Some of us have to. We aren't a charity."

"I didn't say . . ." But the girl had turned away. "Okay. Sorry." Kate started back toward the door, a warm flush spreading across her cheeks. Had she been inappropriate? She didn't like to think so.

Kate remembered once, when she was a little girl, her mother had given some old clothes to the housekeeper. The woman had refused. "Wrong size," which made sense, because the housekeeper was tiny and Kate's mom had an athletic build.

Her mother had pressed, "Give them to your friends," but the housekeeper had still refused. It had been dropped, but a few weeks later, the housekeeper was gone, and there was a new maid. Kate hadn't thought about it. But now she wondered, was it because the woman had embarrassed her mother by refusing to accept the old clothes? Had her mother been inappropriate to offer them? The woman wasn't a charity any more than this cashier was.

That was silly. Kate just wanted to give the kid a ball because he'd been good. She'd have done it for a rich kid too.

Wouldn't she?

Would people be treating her like a charity case if her father went to jail? Would she hate it? Or would she be grateful?

She'd hate it.

She didn't look toward the cashier as she tossed the ball into the holder by the register. She fairly flew up the aisle, searching for the others, glad they hadn't seen.

She finally found them by the cereal.

"Oh good, you're here," Ruthie said. "You can settle it."

"Me?" She hoped it wasn't anything important. "Settle what?"

"What's your stand on multipacks?" Meredith said. "I think they're a waste of money, not to mention too much packaging being bad for the environment."

"And I think we can't all be expected to eat the same kind of cereal," Spider said.

Okay, nothing serious. She looked at the cereal aisle. Not much variety.

"Could we just get two kinds?" Kate said. "After all, there are five of us."

"We could get a healthy kind and a less-healthy kind, like one for breakfast and one for snacks," Spider said.

"We should get some grits for Kate too." Ruthie sought the round container.

"Oh, I . . ." Kate was about to say she didn't know how to cook grits, then thought better of it. Surely there were instructions on the box. She had this. "That sounds great. Do we have butter?" Because even someone who couldn't cook knew that grits needed plenty of that.

They picked out a few more items, then headed for the register.

When they arrived, Lizzie was holding Ray-Ray's hand, facing away from them, but even from behind, Kate could tell she was in tears. Her shoulders trembled. Kate edged closer to hear what they were saying. The manager said, "Go home now. Come back tomorrow without him, or don't come back."

The cashier said something Kate couldn't hear, and the manager's face softened. "I know. I know all about your mother, but this is a business."

Ruthie motioned them toward a stern-looking older woman who was ensconced by the register now. They started to follow her. Kate heard the girl say, "Please. You know I need this."

The manager began to repeat what he'd just said, and Kate could stand it no longer.

"Excuse me. The boy didn't knock over the cans. I did. I

132

knocked into the display with my cart." Behind her, she heard someone—maybe Spider—start to say something, then stop. "She was really helpful. She should be Employee of the Month."

The girl said, "You don't have to say that. Please."

But Kate continued in her best debate-team voice. "This seemed like such a nice, friendly business." She noticed Ray-Ray was now swinging from his sister's hand. "But if you'd turn out a nice young woman like this, we might have to take our business to that other store we passed along the way. What was it called?"

"Price Chopper?" Spider said.

Ruthie and Meredith were putting the groceries onto the belt. Kate knew she should keep her mouth shut and help. Was she embarrassing them? Spider stood beside her.

"We can't have unsupervised children here," the manager said.

"I'm sorry," the girl said. "My dad had a job today. I'm looking for a sitter."

"Oh, is that the only problem?" Kate asked, and then, realizing even as she said it that it was stupid, she said, "I can sit. He can come stay with me while you're working."

"What?" the cashier said.

"What?" Spider said beside her.

"Don't worry. I won't let him get in your hair," she said to Spider. To the girl, she said, "We have a beautiful lake. Can he swim?"

"I can swim!" Ray-Ray said. "There's water on Mars!"

"You can't swim," the cashier snapped. "And there's no water on Mars."

"There is!" Ray-Ray protested. "It said on TV."

"Well, then I'll have to teach you. I have my lifeguard certification." True. She'd gotten it at sleepaway camp, but she'd never used it. "Doesn't that sound more fun than hanging around this"—Kate glanced at the manager—"nice but not exactly kid-friendly store?"

"Yay!" Ray-Ray said. "I want to swim in a lake!"

The cashier started to shush him, and Kate knew she didn't want to accept the favor, just as she hadn't wanted to accept the five dollars for the ball. Yet, was she supposed to let the girl lose her job? The manager said, "That would solve your problem, Liz."

"I love kids." It wasn't a lie, Kate told herself. She had enjoyed playing with her brother in that brief, radiant moment when he'd looked up to her. "Sometimes, you just have to let someone help."

"Okay, yeah, maybe." The girl held out her hand to Ray-Ray. "Come on." She started toward the door.

"Don't forget what I said," the manager said.

"How could I forget that," Lizzie replied.

The cashier was still checking them out, extra slowly, hanging on every word. Kate followed the girl out the door and into the parking lot. She was trying to walk quickly toward a beat-up blue Corolla, but Ray-Ray slowed her down.

"Hey! Wait! Ray-Ray!" Kate caught up with them. "Let me give you my number."

Lizzie turned on her. "I told you, I'm not a charity."

"It's not charity." Kate squished her shoes around on the tiny red-flecked bits of gravel. "I really want to watch him. It will be fun."

"Are you a pedo or something? Why would you want to watch someone else's kid?"

"Why would you?"

"I have no choice. My dad's working, and my mom's sick. I'm the only one he has."

"Okay." Kate nodded. "I have some problems in my family too. I came up here to try and forget, but so far, that's not happening. Maybe watching your brother would distract me."

"So you're the charity now?"

"Isn't that your preference?" Kate noticed that Spider had followed her out and was standing a few feet away, probably to prevent her from doing anything crazy. Too late! "I'm offering to help as a fellow human being." The girl avoided eye contact, staring longingly at the Toyota. Kate knew she should just walk away and enjoy the lake. Yet seeing this girl doing something useful with her life made Kate want . . . something. Something. Maybe if she did, she would feel less helpless than she felt right now.

"I want to swim in a lake, Lizzie. Can we go tomorrow?"

"No. Maybe Sunday, when I'm off. Because I never get a single minute to myself."

Maybe from debate, maybe from watching her father's political maneuverings, Kate sensed that this wasn't the time to dig in. It was the time to walk back.

"Look," she said. "It sounds like you're super busy. I realize I'm being intrusive. If you don't want my help, fine." She started to turn around.

"I WANT. TO GO. IN A LAKE!" Ray-Ray bellowed.

"Shush!" Lizzie said.

Kate turned back. "But let me just give you my phone number just in case you change your mind." She fumbled in her purse for some paper and came up with a receipt for her checked bag. She turned toward Spider, who was still tailing her. "What's the phone number?"

Scowling, Spider provided it, and scowling some more, Lizzie took the paper from her.

Kate knelt down beside Ray-Ray. "Maybe I'll see you again one day." She stood and walked toward the car where Meredith and Ruthie were already waiting.

18

Meredith

Essay topic: So where is Waldo, really?

NOT HERE. NO one else was here, and that was wonderful. Meredith inhaled deeply, smelling the scent of pines. She was walking to the lake for the first time, with Ruthie and Kate, even though she'd rather have gone by herself. At least the other two weren't there. Britta was still nursing her dubious injury while Spider claimed to be tired. So 40 percent less noise.

The three who remained were all intent upon being quiet, making their way down a trail blazed by generations of feet. The only sounds were the crunch of pine needles beneath Meredith's flip-flops, Ruthie's Birkenstocks, and Kate's Tory Burch sandals, which even Meredith knew were too expensive to wear to the lake, plus the occasional crow's caw. It was cool in the shade, and the slight breeze made Meredith shiver a bit.

Ruthie was lagging behind. Kate gestured that they should wait for her.

"No, no," Ruthie said. "You young ladies go ahead. I have old knees."

Still, Kate slowed, and Meredith did too. She didn't mind, caring more about the journey. She wanted to look at the lake more than swim in it, and mostly (it was hard to admit this), she hoped to see Harmon. This was more likely to happen in the woods than at the lake. She wanted to ask him about the picture he'd taken, the one of her. But they'd walked quite a distance, and so far, they'd seen no one.

Suddenly, a branch snapped behind them. Meredith whirled. Was it him?

No. Ruthie pointed to the culprit, a dazed-looking squirrel, struggling by a fallen pine branch. Ruthie laughed. "Poor thing!"

But Kate was looking at Meredith. "Your face! Did you think it was a bear?"

No, a boy, Meredith thought, a bit ashamed. She had come to relax, not to flirt like some girl in a Jane Austen novel waiting to sprain her ankle so a man could rescue her in the rain.

But she laughed. "I didn't know what it was! Guess I'm just a city girl."

"No bears around here," Ruthie said.

"Good," Meredith said.

"We sometimes see deer, but perhaps it wasn't wildlife you were looking for."

Meredith shrugged. "I was just in a daze. It's beautiful here." Old people always thought girls her age were boy crazy.

"It is," Kate said, and they continued downhill, walking a bit sideways against the steepness until they finally saw the lake.

It was everything Meredith had imagined, or perhaps it just resembled the photograph in the ad, vast and blue with clouds, trees, and sky reflected in its depths, making it seem like a blue-and-white orb. Black-necked geese—Canada geese—explored the shores. It was quiet, as Ruthie had promised it would be during the week. They were completely alone, except . . .

A girl's laughter pierced the silence. "Oh my God! You are such an idiot!"

"Like you never thought that! You think you're so smart because you're in college!"

It was Harmon. Harmon in a tank top. And a girl, a pretty girl from what Meredith could see, with long, blond braids down her back. They were in the water, fishing.

"Show me again," the girl said.

"I thought you knew everything."

"I know nothing about fishing. You were supposed to teach me."

Harmon took the pole from her and proceeded, Meredith assumed (she didn't fish either), to demonstrate how to cast.

Meredith turned away. She gestured toward some old, wooden Adirondack chairs on the opposite side of the waterfront. "Let's sit over there."

"There are lounge chairs on this side," Kate said.

But Ruthie glanced at Harmon. "Yes, let's." She started to

where Meredith had pointed. The others followed. They settled in on the chairs, and Meredith took out her book, *Vanity Fair*, by Thackeray, a book Britta had called a doorstop when she'd seen it on the plane. But it was light reading, the story of Becky (who was a bit like Britta, cute and flirty) and Amelia, two schoolmates searching for husbands, and, um, the Napoleonic Wars. And, yes, it was eight hundred pages long, but it wasn't assigned for class. Meredith settled in, skimming the chapter headed "Vauxhall," listening to Kate talking to Ruthie, until finally, her eyes were at half-mast and she could barely see the page, the sky, the birds . . .

"Hey! Look!"

Meredith's eyes flew open.

"You caught one!" Harmon's voice. "Can you reel it in?"

"I think so!" The girl's voice was excited. She stepped back, pulling up the rod and trying to fight what was on the other end of it. Suddenly, she stumbled in the water. "Oh!"

Harmon caught her, just like he'd caught Meredith the night before. "Gotcha!"

"Take my pole!" the girl yelled.

Meredith imagined what boys at school would say to such a sentence, but Harmon behaved, grabbing the fishing rod and reeling with an expert hand while the girl struggled to stand. She and the fish both came up at the same time. The fish was big and green, wiggling angrily at the end of the line. "Dinner!" Harmon exclaimed.

"Really?" the girl asked.

"Sure." Harmon gestured at some bags at the shore. His precious camera, Meredith guessed. She was proved right an instant later when he said, "Want me to take your picture?"

"Uck, no. I'm gross. But can we really eat it?"

"Don't see why not. It's big enough. My mom will make me clean it." But he seemed proud, the hunter-gatherer.

"Let's show her," the girl said.

"Okay." Harmon unhooked the fish and threw it, still struggling, into a bucket he'd brought. He started to gather their gear.

Meredith tried to go back to reading about Amelia and Dobbin and Becky and Jos. If she pictured Becky as Britta, did that make her Amelia, quiet, boring Amelia? But their chatter and the girl's high-pitched voice, "Oh, I'm so dirty!" got in her ears and made it hard to concentrate. She changed position.

"I wonder how that chicken will be," Kate said.

"I hope Britta can cook," Ruthie replied. "Alicia certainly can't."

Finally, the couple had gathered their belongings and started up the hill. When they passed by, Harmon said, "Hi, Ruthie. Hi, Meredith." At Kate, he paused. "Hi . . ."

"Kate," she supplied.

"Nice day for fishing," Ruthie said.

"Always nice when you catch something," Harmon agreed. To Meredith, he said, "The mountain folk can eat today!"

Then, without further words, he continued uphill. A moment later, Meredith heard the girl say, "You didn't introduce me."

Harmon replied, "Oh, they're just . . ." But his voice faded into the trees before Meredith could hear who they were. She went back to Becky flirting with buffoonish Jos Sedley.

When they were out of sight, Kate said, "Hmm, wonder who that girl was. His sister?"

"No," Ruthie said. "The Dickinsons only have boys."

Meredith realized she'd been holding her breath, waiting for Ruthie's answer. Stupid. She stared at her book. She didn't need to wonder who that girl was. Obviously, Harmon Dickinson had no interest in her, Meredith. Which was okay, because she had no interest in Harmon Dickinson and his dimple and his camera and his stupid muscles in his stupid tank top. If only she didn't keep running into him.

19

Britta

WHEN THE OTHERS came home from shopping, Britta pretended to sleep. Anyone who knew Britta would know this was unlikely. If Britta was asleep during the day, a doctor should be alerted. But they didn't know Britta.

Still, she was sorry when she heard Meredith say they were going to the lake. Britta wanted to go to the lake! But instead, she waited for them to leave. Then, she opened the borrowed scrapbook. Ruthie had already said she'd show it to her. But Ruthie was on her way to the lake too, and Britta was bored. She'd just take a peek.

The first page was a letter on yellowed paper, typed on an old-fashioned typewriter.

★ ★ ★

Dear Miss Green:

I am writing to invite you to participate
in our Green Pines summer stock program.
We were very impressed with your audition
and references, and while we cannot offer
you a paying position, we hope that you will
consider this internship for the opportunity
it is.

The program begins June 15, 1962.

The letter went on to list details of bus transportation and
how Ruthie might go about accepting this opportunity.

How exciting! Ruthie must have been around Britta's age.
To have the opportunity to be in a real theater company like a
grown-up! Her mom must not have been so overprotective!

And the return address on the letter was from the very town
they were in.

The next page was a program from a play called *Babes in the
Woods*. Britta scanned the cast list and saw that Ruth Green
was listed in the role of Arcadian Shepherdess. At the bottom
of the page, stuck on with white mounting corners, was one
of those old, square black-and-white photos like the ones her
grandmother had. It showed a young Ruthie dressed in panta-
lets and carrying a shepherd's crook. Even in the tiny picture,
Britta could see Ruthie was smiling and just Britta's age. She

looked like a girl Britta might have been friends with.

Britta remembered Ruthie's story about going to the March on Washington. What year was that? If she'd had her phone, she'd have googled it, but definitely early 1960s.

The next page was a program from a play Britta had never heard of, and Ruth Green was listed as crew. The third page was from a play called *Peter Out of the Frying Pan*, and it listed Ruthie as a mermaid, but a slip of paper in the program stated, "At tonight's performance, the role of Wendy will be played by Ruth Green."

She got the lead—every understudy's dream! As Britta flipped through the pages, something fell out from between them. A note.

Break a leg, my golden-voiced girl!
Or, at least, be glad Susan did!
Love, Janet

A quick glance at the program revealed that someone named Susan Malone had been playing Wendy. Britta wondered if she was some big star of the time. A broken leg must have ended her run. Janet Calisti, the only Janet, was listed as "Slightly," one of the Lost Boys.

This must be the Janet that Ruthie had meant, her friend from the picture!

There was a knock on the door. Instinctively, Britta shut the scrapbook. "Who is it?"

"Me." Spider's voice sounded sullen. Well, there was a surprise. Britta shoved the scrapbook under the bed. She didn't know why, only that it seemed weird to be snooping.

"I brought you some ice," Spider said.

Britta lay down on the bed. "Oh, come in."

Spider opened the door. She was such a strange girl, with her dark hair and long-limbed, slightly stooped build. Her pale-blue eyes took in the room as if she knew Britta was hiding something. They flicked toward the floor, and Britta wondered if the dust ruffle wasn't covering the scrapbook. No. It was the discarded ice bag. It had fallen onto the floor.

"I guess we're supposed to make dinner," Spider said. "Maybe we should put off our night to cook since you're so badly hurt."

She emphasized *so badly* and smirked. Britta knew Spider thought she was faking. Britta hated to give her the satisfaction, but she wanted to make dinner, wanted to impress the others with her prowess in the kitchen.

"Actually, I guess it was just a charley horse."

Spider's eyes twitched like she was trying not to roll them. But she said, "Are you sure? You took quite a tumble. I saw you." She walked over. "Let me check if it's still swollen."

So weird that she was being all nice now. Britta stiffened as Spider touched her ankle.

"I'm sure if you gave me the recipe, I could slog through it."

Unlikely. More like Ruthie would slog through it.

"My grandmother could help."

Bingo. "Yeah, no. It's fine. Ruthie said you'd be my *sous* chef

146

or whatever, so I guess I could sit while you cut things up." Britta examined her ankle. "Even though it still hurts a little, I should be able to manage. You are so sweet and helpful." Spider was anything but.

"Oh, not really."

"This way, you could learn to do it yourself, for future reference." Britta grinned. "I've been looking forward to cooking with you."

Because lying in bed was really boring.

20

Spider

INT. CABIN, KITCHEN — DAY

Britta and Spider are starting dinner.
Britta, completely uninjured by the way, is
surprisingly competent. Spider is standing
there with her, looking stupid.

"DO YOU HAVE poultry shears?"

Spider gave Britta a blank look. "Poultry shears?"

"They're like big scissors for chicken."

Spider had hoped Britta would be "too injured" to cook. That was a pleasant thought. But Britta had clearly been faking, so now, she and Britta were at the kitchen table, and Britta was teaching Spider to cut up a chicken.

"No poultry shears?" Britta asked. At Spider's confused look, she said, "Okay, guess not. It'll just be a little harder, but get a firm grip on the chicken."

Spider grimaced as she took the chicken's cold, slimy hand, um, talon, um, drumstick. She squeezed hard enough to make her own hand ache.

"You've really never touched a chicken?" Britta asked.

"I'm doing it now! You don't have to be so condescending." She hated that Britta was the authority in this situation. It wasn't Spider's fault that her mother didn't teach her to cook.

Britta looked like she wanted to say something but didn't. "Oooookay, then. So if you're left-handed, pull the chicken with your right hand, and with your left . . ." She mimed slicing through the chicken's flesh.

Spider did as instructed, trying not to show her distaste. The stupid chicken fought back as if it wasn't already dead. Who knew cooking required brute strength? But eventually, the knife sliced through, and she held the severed limb in her left hand. "Done!"

"Great!" Britta clapped as if encouraging a child. "Now the other."

Spider obeyed, sighing, then turned the chicken over to remove its wings under Britta's watchful eye. She felt like a med student, something she'd never aspired to be. Still, she guessed she was learning a skill.

"This could be useful in filmmaking," Britta said.

"Huh?"

"You said you wanted to be a filmmaker. If you did some kind of *Silence of the Lambs* thing, where a killer dismembers his victims, it would be useful to know how to do it."

"The killer in *Silence of the Lambs* skinned his victims." Spider didn't try to hide the haughtiness from her voice, even though Britta was sort of right. "He didn't dismember them."

"What about disposing of them—didn't he cut them up then?" Britta said, then shrugged. "Okay then, I guess it's useful to know how to feed yourself. Whole chickens are way cheaper than cut-up pieces from the grocery store, and they're supposed to be healthier too."

Spider separated the breast from the back. It was satisfying—not that she'd admit that.

"So, how long has your family had this place?" Britta asked.

"I don't know. Since before I was born. When my dad was little, maybe."

"Did Ruthie and your grandfather buy it together?" Britta pointed to the chicken. "You're going to want to cut the breast into quarters. But cut down the bone first."

"Cut *through* the bone?"

"I can do it if you want. It's my ankle that's injured—nothing wrong with my hands."

Nothing wrong with her ankle either. But Spider blocked Britta's way. She wasn't going to let a chicken—or Britta—defeat her, although her right hand ached as she pressed down on the knife. She tried not to grimace.

150

Britta noticed. "I can finish it. I do it all the time." She reached for the knife.

"I'm fine!" Spider pushed down until the bone snapped. "See?"

"Good job!" Britta gushed. "Can you gather the spices while I finish up? You know, since my ankle hurts?"

"Of course it does," Spider simpered, but was glad to abandon the chicken. She took the list of spices from Britta. "What's cumin?"

"Kyoo-min," Britta corrected. "It's sort of a yellowish-brownish spice."

Spider went to the cupboard and found the garlic powder, cayenne pepper, and oh yeah, there was the cumin. It was way in back, and she stood on tiptoe to get it.

"How did your grandparents know about this place?" Britta asked. "Had Ruthie been up here before?

"Why are you asking so many questions?" Spider said.

"Just making conversation," Britta said. "Like normal people."

"So I'm not normal?" It was an accusation with which she was not unfamiliar. But it hurt to hear it here, in this place she loved so much.

But Britta said, "I didn't say that. But you obviously don't like me. I don't know what I ever did to you. We're renting this place *from* you because you advertised for renters. But you've been rolling your eyes at me since I got here and I don't know why. I mean, maybe I don't watch old movies no one's heard of, but how many people do?"

Spider didn't know why either, except that she guessed Britta wasn't the type of girl she'd pictured in the place. Britta seemed more like her sister, a giggly, brash girl who, after all, didn't want to be here. Why did Britta? She didn't seem like she was into nature.

"You keep asking all these nosy questions, and you act like I'm stupid because I don't know how to pronounce cumin." Too late, she realized she'd said it wrong again. "Kyoo-min."

"*I* act like *you're* stupid? That's hilarious."

"Or have poultry shears. And I know you're faking that injury. I have real pain, so I know what it looks like." She stopped. She hadn't meant to say that.

"I faked it so I wouldn't have to be in the car with you!" Britta burst out.

"Ha! I knew it!" But considering what Britta had just said, it wasn't that satisfying. Spider was used to having people avoid her, even her own family.

"I thought it would be fun to make new friends this trip. People like me! I'm vice president of Thespians. I'm nice!" Britta stood on completely uninjured feet. "I even thought it would be fun to cook together. I mean, I know it's not a hugely intellectual activity, but human beings require food to sustain life. So maybe you could, I don't know, chop an onion?"

She picked up an onion off the counter and hurled it at Spider.

Okay, she didn't actually hurl it. She tossed it. But it surprised Spider as much as hurling would have, and she reached up to protect her face. The onion hit her hand, and she grabbed it. She caught it. Which was a big surprise.

"Cut it?" she said to Britta.

"Like in rings, thin if you can?" Britta looked exasperated at having to explain this.

Spider walked over to the cutting board and picked up a knife. She wasn't sure what kind of knife you used for an onion, but she chose a long one. Holding the onion with one hand, she sliced through it, top to bottom. The slice was lopsided, and the peel got in the way. Was she supposed to peel it? And it was definitely not thin.

When she tried again, the whole onion slipped from her klutzy hand, bounced to the floor, and rolled away. She leaned to get it. When she stood, she saw Britta staring at her.

Britta held out her hand. "Never mind."

"What? I'll wash it."

"Yeah, no. It's fine. You win. I'll cook the chicken myself." She reached for the onion.

Spider held it away. "That's not what I meant." God, what would Ruthie say?

"It's fine," Britta said. "I'll tell Ruthie you helped." She reached for the cumin.

"I can do it." She didn't want to let something like an onion defeat her.

"Just let me work. It's fine. I'll have it in the oven before they get back. I'll tell everyone what a great job you did."

Britta flipped the oven to 350, then went back to the cupboard. Spider handed her the onion. Britta put it in the sink, then started to pour the various spices into a large plastic bag, seeming to know the amounts without consulting a recipe or even using a spoon. She shook the bag angrily. No, probably Spider was just imagining that. She was shaking the bag to mix the spices. Then she started adding the chicken parts— the chicken Spider had cut up. After a few pieces, she closed the bag and shook it. Yes, it was definitely angrily, considering the chicken bag sounded like a punching bag. Poom, poom! Poom! She dumped the spice-coated chicken onto the counter and added new pieces to the bag.

Spider didn't know what she wanted to do. She hadn't really tried cooking, but it would be nice to be able to make something that wasn't canned soup. It wasn't Britta's fault that Spider was defective, wasn't Britta's fault that she didn't admit it. But Britta was concentrating on covering each piece of chicken with spices, as if it was fascinating.

Finally, Spider turned and started upstairs.

She turned back. "I won't tell them you faked your injury since you're not telling that I didn't cook."

"Deal!" Probably glad to be rid of her, Britta started shaking the bag again. Poom! Poom! Poom!

21

Kate

KEEPING BUSY WAS the best way to stop worrying. That was why Kate had suggested the lake, had made lively (for her) conversation with Ruthie, and had tried to engage Meredith, whose attention seemed to alternate between a brick of a novel and mooning over the townie who'd helped with the bat. Meredith probably thought she didn't notice this part, but she did. Now Meredith had been silent for thirty minutes, staring at her book but not once turning a page.

Finally, Kate went swimming, using cutting, efficient strokes to reach a point so deep she couldn't even imagine the bottom. She contemplated continuing across the whole lake. It wasn't that big, barely more than a pond. But she didn't want to freak the others out. Maybe next time.

She returned to her uncomfortable wooden chair. Meredith

looked up. Was she giving her side-eye? Girls her age always did, and it irked her. She couldn't help how she looked. Was she supposed to wear a granny suit with a skirt? But no, Meredith just smiled.

"You went so far," she said. "I was worried about you."

Kate said, "You should go swimming. We could swim out to the dock and jump off." She'd done that once, actually, and it had made her feel like a kid, but a luckier kid than she'd actually been, a kid who got to jump and frolic instead of taking polite swimming lessons at camp or staying in the shallow end at the country club.

"Maybe tomorrow. I'm at an exciting part."

Judging from the fact that the book's cover had a picture of a girl in a Victorian dress sniffing a flower, Kate doubted that. But she said, "Yeah, it looks it."

"No, really," Meredith protested. "They made it into a movie."

"Was it any good?" Kate asked.

"I haven't seen it," Meredith admitted. "I wanted to read the book first."

"So you can complain about how they ruined it with the movie?" Her friend Philippa had once spent a solid hour complaining about how Hermione's dress in one of the Harry Potter movies was blue when it was supposed to be pink or pink when it was supposed to be blue. Kate couldn't remember which.

"Maybe they won't ruin it," Meredith said.

"Judging from the length of that book, I'm guessing the movie will leave out some details," Kate said. But she liked that

Meredith seemed as weird and sheltered and quirky as Kate was, as Kate *felt*. But, unlike Kate, she'd been encouraged to be that way. No one told her not to be a know-it-all, which was the same as saying not to show that she was smarter than her mother's friends. But she was. It wasn't hard.

Kate realized all these girls were strange in their own way. Maybe everyone was.

"Okay, can I borrow that book when you're finished?" Kate realized that, in three suitcases, she hadn't packed a single book.

"Sure." Meredith looked pleased. "I'll try to read more quickly."

Meredith got back to it, and silence reigned again, silence so complete that Kate could hear the drip-drip of the water off her hair, and the silence made her think of Dad and Colin and Mom. Maybe she could find a book at the house to read.

Finally, Ruthie glanced at her old-lady watch. "It's almost six!"

The sun was still bright, and the day had flown, though they'd done little. One day down, twenty-nine to go. Would she regret when it was over or be happy?

22
Britta

BRITTA TOOK SPECIAL care with dinner, being sure to mince, rather than simply chop, the garlic and slice each piece of onion thin as paper. Her Cuban ancestors would have been proud. When the others came back from the lake, she was chopping parsley to sprinkle on top. She called out, "Dinner's almost ready!"

"Oh, good. Swimming makes me so hungry," said Kate.

Ruthie glanced around suspiciously. "Alicia isn't helping?"

"She went upstairs to rest, I think. I just came down to check on the chicken." Britta flicked a piece of parsley off the cutting board.

"I hope she didn't bamboozle you out of helping," Ruthie said.

"No, she was really helpful. She's going to be a great chef someday. Don't know what I'd have done without her." Britta laid it on thick.

Ruthie raised an eyebrow. "Great chef?"

Oops. Maybe too thick. "I mean, if she works on it. If you'll excuse me." She started to rise. "I have to take this out."

At that moment, Spider came back downstairs, and Britta said, "Spider, would you mind helping me with this?" Britta wanted to see her squirm. "I was just telling Ruthie how extremely helpful you've been."

"Oh. Great. So what do you want me to do?"

Britta instructed Spider, making sure she knew where the potholders were before she burned her hands up in the oven, and eventually, dinner was on the table.

"This is really good," Meredith said, taking the first bite. "You made this?"

"Well, Britta did. I just helped," Spider said.

"You're being too modest," Britta said. "She cut it up, and she blended the spices and—"

"What kind of spices are in this?" Ruthie interrupted, looking at Spider.

Spider took a bite and chewed with great concentration before answering, "Um, salt and pepper. Two kinds of pepper." She glanced at Britta, who fluffed the rice on her plate with her fork, seeming not to notice Spider's distress.

Finally, Britta said, "Cayenne pepper, right?"

"Oh, right. Cayenne pepper."

"But there's something more interesting in here." Ruthie took a forkful. "What is it?"

Britta suspected Ruthie knew exactly what it was. After all, it was in her kitchen. Cumin. She was testing Spider to see if Spider knew. Spider should know. "Come. On," Britta enunciated. "Come. On. You know. Come on."

"Cumin!" Spider burst out. "There's cumin and salt and two kinds of pepper, and I put all the spices in a bag and put the chicken in and shook it up. So—ha!"

Ruthie looked a bit taken aback. "Ha?"

"You didn't believe I was helpful. Admit it."

"Of course I believed you were helpful." Ruthie raised an eyebrow. "Why would you lie?"

"I wouldn't," Spider lied. "I wouldn't."

"So what does everyone want to do tomorrow?" Meredith changed the subject.

"I want to go hiking," Spider said. "There are so many mountains around here. My family has a book of great day hikes."

"I saw it!" Britta said before remembering she'd seen it when she was supposed to have been upstairs, writhing in pain. "It looked fun, sort of like that movie."

"*The Revenant*?" Spider quipped. "Or *127 Hours*?" These were survival movies about hikes gone very wrong.

"The Reese Witherspoon one," Britta said.

"I know. *Wild*."

"I loved that movie," Britta said. "It should have won an Oscar." She wanted to ask Spider why she wasn't in so many of the photos of her family's outdoor adventures.

Spider seemed surprised, but nodded. "Hollywood sexism. Anyway, some of the highest peaks have fire towers on top of them. They're these towers they put up so someone could sit up and see . . . um . . ."

"Fires?" Britta asked, she hoped helpfully.

"Right. There's a fire-tower challenge. Hike to twenty-three towers in the Adirondacks, and more in the Catskills, but they're kind of far. Once you get to the top, you can climb the tower. It's really high, and you can see all the mountains and lakes and take pictures."

"It sounds beautiful," Kate said.

"It is." Spider seemed excited for the first time since Britta had met her. "I climbed one with my family once, but I want to climb all of them this summer."

"Twenty-three towers sounds ambitious," Ruthie said. "Especially with your—"

"I want to try," Spider snapped.

"Fine." Ruthie held her hands up, offended, and even Britta was surprised how Spider had cut her off. They seemed really close. When Ruthie saw Britta looking at her, she said, "Too strenuous for my old hips."

"Oh." Spider looked disappointed. "Okay. How about the rest of you?"

"My ankle is feeling better," Britta volunteered.

The rest all wanted to go, and Ruthie offered to clear the table and do the dishes so they could plan their trip. They walked to the living room to get the book Britta had seen. On the way there, she nudged Spider's arm. "Hey. Thanks for including me."

Spider looked startled, then smiled at her. "Sure. Just don't throw any onions at me."

"I won't," Britta said. Then, after a second, added, "On a hike, it would be rocks."

23

Meredith

Essay topic: When you daydream, who do you hope to become in the future?

NOT SOME SILLY girl who goes around chasing boys.

Not that Meredith was doing that. Of course not. What would be the point, since Harmon obviously had a girlfriend? She'd been stupid to think he'd been flirting with her. She knew about lots of things, but not about boys. Besides, he was clearly a rugged outdoorsman, not an intellectual. Meredith hated rough, coarse boys, the type of boys who thought the outcome of a football game was more important than the outcome of an election.

She'd come out to look at the stars.

The night was cool and dark. Meredith settled into an Adirondack chair. Alone by design. She liked the other girls, but she loved the silent loneliness of the night, loved standing still as her eyes became acclimated to the darkness. Then, each star appeared. She shivered a delicious shiver and found the Big Dipper.

The only sound was the crickets.

And a giggle.

A giggle?

Yes, a giggle. And a voice. Voices.

"I don't believe you saw an owl here."

Oh no. It was a girl. The girl from the lake.

"You don't have to believe me." Harmon. "If you'd be quiet and walk softer, we could find it."

"Are you telling me to shut up?"

"Yes."

Were they coming here? Would they see her? Maybe. Maybe not. Would they make a ton of noise and ruin her enjoyment of the evening with their chattering? Absolutely. But maybe if she was quiet, they'd move on.

"Harmon Dickinson, I cannot believe you're—"

"Shhh!"

". . . shushing me! I'm going to tell your mother."

A loud whisper. "If you want to see wildlife, you need to shush."

"Fine!" the girl said loudly enough to scare away any bird in a five-mile radius.

Even their footsteps were loud. Actually, it was probably only the girl's footsteps that were loud, and the good news was that they were stomping away from Meredith into the woods. For a few minutes, they were actually quiet.

Then, "Harmon! Harmon! Where are you?"

Why would Harmon like such a loud girl?

Oh yeah, she was pretty. Hot. He would probably say hot.

"Harmon?" Running footsteps.

"I'm over here. Hold on a sec."

Weirdly, his voice came not from where the girl was, the woods where he'd been the night before, but from behind Meredith, closer to the house.

What was he doing by their house?

Meredith was pretty sure he didn't know she was there. Should she say something? Or just sink down in her chair and hope he didn't see her, hope he'd leave so she could enjoy the quiet night with its lace coverlet of stars.

"Harmon!"

"Oh, for God's sake, Hope, no owl would come within half a mile of you, even if you were covered in dead mice. Let's go inside."

His voice was right by Meredith, and she realized there was no way he wasn't going to see her. If she sat still, he might trip over her.

She stood.

"You should do that," she said, kind of smirking when he started at her voice. "Some of us are trying to enjoy the quiet."

He recovered himself enough to put his smarmy voice back on. "Some *tourists* are the ones who ruin the quiet for everyone else."

"I wasn't noisy. You obviously didn't even know I was there. If you had, you wouldn't have acted like such a buffoon."

"A buffoon, huh?" In the darkness, she saw him glance toward the house, then back at her. Finally, he said, "Anyway, we were just leaving." He walked toward the woods and yelled, probably louder than necessary, "Come on, Hope! Let's leave!"

Meredith lasted about five more minutes in the beautiful silence, enjoying the stars, until finally it got too cold and she had to go inside.

When she did, she noticed something stuck into the frame between the screen door and the solid one, paper, an envelope. She picked it up and turned it over.

It had her name on it, misspelled, Merideth, in messy, boy handwriting.

What was it? What did he want of her? Was it hate mail? Or, the opposite, a love letter?

Stupid. Of course it wasn't a love letter. They'd spoken twice. And this was the twenty-first century. If a guy liked a girl, he said, "Hey, let's hang out." And he hadn't said that either. He had a girlfriend. Meredith read too many books.

Meredith opened the envelope. It was a photograph Harmon had taken earlier, the one of her face as she saw the bat fly up. She didn't know if he had used some type of filter or technique, but in it, she looked beautiful, like an angel.

But why had he left it there?

Meredith looked off in the direction the pair had disappeared in, but they were long gone.

24

Spider

INT/EXT. SPIDER'S CAR — DAY

The four girls are driving down a rural
route, without much else in sight. Spider
is driving. Britta is shotgun, the others
in back. They are lost, and it is obvious
they are getting antsy.

SPIDER HAD HOPED to impress everyone with her knowledge of the fire towers. She'd spent the winter and all of June
researching them in *Adirondack Life* magazine, online, and in
stacks of books from the library to supplement those her family
had already owned. It wasn't enough. She should have predriven
all the routes to the trailheads. She'd made a wrong turn somewhere, and they were lost. She'd gotten on a dirt road, then

turned back and headed the other way, going around in a circle like the family in the old *Vacation* movies.

"Can we ask Siri?" Britta said.

"It doesn't work," Meredith said. "I already tried. The service is bad."

"Besides, you can't ask for directions to a trailhead." Even from the driver's seat, Spider could tell that Kate was rolling her giant blue eyes. "I thought you knew your way."

"I'll find it," Spider snapped. She was just barely holding it together. Also, she wanted to scream at Britta that cuh-min was an accepted alternative pronunciation of cumin. She'd looked it up.

The truth was, she hadn't been on any of these trails since she was a kid in the back seat. Her siblings had stopped asking her along, deeming her too slow to keep up, saying, "We knew you wouldn't want to go anyway," when questioned. And she hadn't, not really. But now she did. Adulting, though, was a bit overwhelming, especially in front of a bunch of strangers.

"There was a town that way." Meredith pointed toward the back of the car. "Maybe we could ask for directions."

Spider ignored her, driving forward.

"This is really charming," Britta said as they passed a dilapidated farmhouse with a lone spotted cow outside. She leaned back to address the others. "Isn't it charming?"

"It really is," Meredith agreed.

They sat in silence for another minute until they saw a yellow house with a hand-painted sign advertising quilts for sale.

"Maybe we should stop here and ask," Britta said.

"It's not a store," Spider said as they whizzed past the house. Two dogs—one maybe a hybrid wolf—barked from behind a fence. "It's a lady selling a few quilts. They're not in the directions business."

"Maybe I want to buy a quilt," Britta said.

Only Kate didn't speak, but Spider heard judgement in that silence too. She decided that maybe they were right or, if they were wrong, at least she could prove them wrong and be done with the whole stupid conversation. She slammed on the brakes. "Okay, okay, we can go back." She pulled off the road to make a U-turn.

Boom! The car lurched down the shoulder of the road.

"Ooh!" All three girls yelled at once.

"It's fine, it's fine," Spider assured them.

But when she tried to back the car up, it wouldn't budge. She floored the gas and tried again. It made a loud "Vroom!" but stayed put.

"It's stuck." Britta stated the obvious.

"You think?" Spider kept trying, but the car was, indeed, stuck.

"Maybe if Britta moves to the back seat," Meredith said.

"What would that do?" Britta said.

"Change the weight so it's not so front-heavy. Or maybe we should all get out."

"Are you calling me fat?" Britta said.

"But what if opening the door makes it worse?" Spider said.

So Britta climbed between the seats to get into the back. Spider tried again.

Nothing.

"What if we get out on this side?" Meredith gestured to the side closer to the road.

"Are we sure it's safe?" Kate said.

"There's no traffic," Meredith said. "I'm going to try it."

Meredith unlocked her door and pushed it gingerly. It didn't budge.

"Ugh, stupid gravity," she said.

"Let me help," Britta said.

So they both shoved themselves against it. This time, it opened enough to let them out.

"Try now!" Meredith yelled.

Spider tried. The Subaru made loud, frustrated noises, like her great-uncle Stanley coughing into a handkerchief, and like Great-Uncle Stanley, it didn't budge an inch.

Britta was knocking on the window, probably to gloat. No, that wasn't fair. She hadn't gloated. Still, Spider took her time opening the window.

"Should we try to push it?"

Spider shook her head. She'd thought of that already. "It might run you over."

"I think we're going to have to call a tow truck," Meredith said.

Spider nodded. But when she tried her phone, it didn't work.

So they were, after all, going to the quilt lady's house.

25

Britta

OKAY, SO IT was a little bit of poetic justice that, after Spider acted like they were all so stupid to want to ask for directions, they were going to have to. Not that Britta was thrilled about driving off the road. And she could tell Spider was embarrassed.

"Don't worry about it," Britta said as they trudged down a road bordered in lady slippers and Queen Anne's lace. "It's about the journey, not the destination."

"I sort of wanted the destination," Kate said.

Britta didn't think they'd gone that far past the quilt house, but the road was winding and it was out of sight. Fifteen minutes later, they were still walking. "Maybe it was a mirage," she said. "Like when people in the desert think they see water."

"That's caused by a gradient in the reflective index of the air from the varying temperature between the air on the road's surface and the cooler air above," Meredith said.

"Obviously," Britta said, even though she had no idea what Meredith had just said or if it was even English.

"That wouldn't apply here," Meredith said.

"It was a joke," Britta said.

"So was mine," Meredith said.

"Of course it was," Britta said. But Britta didn't believe her for a moment. Meredith was still a big know-it-all like she had been in fourth grade.

Finally, though, they saw the yellow house in the distance and heard the dogs barking to greet them. Britta quickened her step, almost to a skip. She wanted to see quilts and pet dogs and, mostly, call a tow truck. She was supremely grateful that she hadn't been the one to drive into a ditch. It was definitely the type of thing that happened to her.

"Come on!" she called back to the others. "It's an adventure!"

But they kept walking at the same leisurely pace.

Britta crossed over. The dogs were yipping and baying. One of them looked wolfish. Britta hesitated. "Hello? Hello?"

Now the dogs were jubilant. The little one sounded like a machine gun, but the bigger one put his paws up on the fence, craning to be petted.

"Good boy!" Britta said. "Who's a good boy?"

"Oh, I see you've met the doggies."

The woman just materialized. She had long, gray hair and wore a floor-length denim skirt and a flowing blouse, possibly her own design. Her un-made-up skin glowed like a pearl. Britta's mother would say that came from living where there was no harsh sun.

"They like you," she said as the wolfy one licked Britta's hand. "And they are excellent judges of character. I'm Jacey. You here for quilts?"

Britta shifted in her sneakers. "Well, yes and no. I have a strong interest in quilts and definitely planned to stop. But there's sort of a—ah—more immediate problem." She glanced back to see if the others were close. "My friend drove into a ditch." The dog tried to flip Britta's hand onto his head. Britta didn't fight it.

"A ditch, huh? Must be city drivers."

"She's from Long Island, I think. She acts like she knows her way around. I'm Britta."

"Well, Britta." Jacey opened the door wider. "Why don't you come inside? You can use the phone and look at the quilts."

Britta was reminded of her mother's constant admonishments not to go into strangers' houses. That was how you got kidnapped. Still, the old lady seemed nice. And it was either that or flag down some rando who passed them, or just leave their car in a ditch. Besides, the other girls were close behind.

Britta walked through the door. No chains in the wall or dirty mattresses on the floor. Instead, it was a homey room with rag rugs, family photos, and about a dozen quilts on racks, in patterns of stars, pine trees, and grizzly bears.

"Pretty." Britta brushed against a green-and-white one. She glanced at the photos on the end table. One was an eight by ten, obviously from the 1950s based upon the hairstyle, and showed a woman who looked weirdly familiar.

"Joan Fontaine," Jacey said.

"Huh?"

"That's Joan Fontaine, the actress—*Rebecca, Jane Eyre, Suspicion.*"

Britta realized these were the names of old movies. "Oh."

"She bought a quilt from my grandmother decades ago. You've probably never heard of her, though."

Britta squinted at the photo, with its faint autograph. "I bet my friend has." *Where was Spider?* "She likes old movies. I mean, not that you're—"

"I *am* old. A lot of famous people used to come here back then. Now, they've all moved on to South Beach."

Britta thought of Ruthie's summer stock photos. Maybe the famous people had acted in the plays. She hadn't recognized any of the names in the programs, but it was a long time ago. "I'm from Miami."

"Oh, my condolences. I like the peace and quiet here."

Britta picked up a quilted pillow with an appliqué of a chipmunk on it. "Me too."

"Do you want to use the phone? There's only one tow operator around here," Jacey said. "And he comes for all the people who drive into a ditch. I'm sure he'll treat you right—he's an old friend."

Jacey already had the phone in her hand and was dialing. Just as she said, "Hey, Randall, I have a customer for you," there was a knock on the door. Jacey gestured to Britta to get it.

The other three girls came in just as Jacey hung up.

"He's coming," she said. "He always jokes that I keep him in business because people make a U-turn to come see my quilts, then run into a ditch and have to call him."

Spider started, "Oh, we weren't—"

Britta gave her a sharp look. So she finished, "I guess we weren't very careful."

"We really wanted to see the quilts, me especially." Britta walked over and showed Spider the photo of Joan Fontaine. "Do you know her? Jacey was telling me that famous people have bought her quilts."

"Really?" Spider looked dubious. "Joan Fontaine was here?"

"Not lately," Jacey said, and laughed.

"Well, yeah, she's kinda dead," Spider said.

Jacey continued. "Actually, that's from my mother's house when I was a little girl in North Creek. And once, there was a film director shooting a commercial. He stopped by our house with his whole crew, saying they wanted to use the bathroom. They just came trooping through there like they owned the place and tried to give my mother two bucks. Can you believe that?"

"Pretty big nerve," Meredith agreed, flipping over one quilt to look at something embroidered on the back.

"She took it, of course, since it was clear they weren't going to buy anything. I was ten then, small for my age, and I was singing and dancing around the house, trying to impress the big director. My mother told me to shush, but he said it was fine. Then he left, and I thought, 'Well, that's our excitement for the month.'"

"Funny," Britta said. "When's the tow truck driver coming?"

"Maybe half an hour," Jacey said, "if you're lucky. Maybe longer."

"Wow." Britta looked at her watch, then the others.

"I'm sorry, okay?" Spider said.

The girls sat down, and Jacey went on. "But it turned out, the excitement wasn't over, because the next day, the same gentleman showed up again.

"My mother was ready for him that time. 'We are not a public toilet,' she said. But he said they wanted me to be in the commercial. The girl who was in it had had a meltdown and wouldn't work. They offered me twenty bucks to take her place.

"'Make it fifty, and we've got a deal,' my mother said without even asking me. I couldn't believe it. Fifty dollars was more money than I'd ever seen. Even twenty would have paid for a month's groceries.

"So they paid me fifty dollars to run through a field hollering, 'It's so creamy, Mama!' I guess it was a commercial for butter. We didn't even have a television set. No one did. But my father took that money and bought one and a huge antenna so we could watch the commercial when it aired. I was all starry-eyed and wanted to be on television."

"Were you ever?" The showbiz stuff piqued Britta's interest.

"I'm here, aren't I? I got married, like everyone expected,

and now I'm making quilts like my mother before me."

Britta was going to ask her questions, but there was a knock on the door.

"That'll be Randall, I bet!"

"That was quick," Britta said.

"Yes, thanks," Spider said.

"Well, I was enjoying myself," Britta said.

"It was a lovely story," Kate agreed.

"Hey, Randall." Jacey opened the door and let in a large man about her age with a close-clipped gray beard and a vest that said "Randall's Towing."

"Little distracted driving?" he asked.

"That would be us," Britta said, not wanting to implicate Spider specifically.

"It's over that way." Spider jerked her hand in the direction of the car.

"Yeah, I saw it. The Subaru." Randall gestured for them to follow him to a red tow truck. "That's where they usually are. I think you girls can all squeeze in."

"Not with seat belts," Meredith said. "We'll walk." Meredith gestured to herself and Kate. Britta and Spider got into the truck. Spider waited for Britta to slide over, then took the spot by the door.

Randall started the truck. "So what brings you girls to these parts?" he asked.

"Vacation," Britta said.

"She's on vacation. My family are summer residents. Been

coming here my whole life, and my dad and grandparents before that."

Britta waited for Randall to comment that he was surprised Spider couldn't drive on the roads if she was such an old hand. Instead he said, "What's your family's name? Mine's been here a while too."

"Webster. We're in Warrensburg."

"Don't know any Websters in Warrensburg."

"Guess they haven't needed a tow," Britta joked.

"My family used to run a restaurant near there," Randall said. "It's still in business—the one with the giant chicken outside. And I waited tables."

"I've seen it!" Spider's face lit up. "My grandmother told me she went there when she was young. Her maiden name was Green."

"Ruthie Green?" Randall slowed down the truck. He gazed at Spider. "Ruthie Green has grandchildren. My, my."

"You knew her?" Spider sat a bit straighter.

"I had the biggest crush on your grandmother. She used to come in there with a big group of her friends from the theater company that was around there."

"It was?" Spider said at the same time Britta said, "Green Pines?"

"That's it—Green Pines. They brought in famous actors like, like . . . well, people you wouldn't have heard of anyway, and they had young folks like your grandma in the chorus."

They approached the Subaru. Randall kept talking as he

pulled over. "Ruthie Green. That little blondie was the prettiest thing with the bluest eyes I ever saw. She's your grandma?" He shook his head.

"I look more like my mother's side," Spider said.

Britta nudged her to get out. She wanted to hear the rest of this. "So did you two date?"

Randall scoffed. "Me and Ruthie? No, it was a crush from afar on my part. She wasn't dating any townies. She had other interests."

"Other interests?" That was a weird way of putting it.

Spider must have thought so too because she said, "You mean like a boyfriend? Was it my grandfather?"

"Oh no, no boyfriend. She was . . ." He seemed to think about it as he walked toward the lift at the back of the truck. "She was serious about her art. That's why I'm surprised she got married. She didn't seem the type. Didn't seem like she'd be happy."

Britta remembered the photos of Ruthie's friend Janet. But before she could ask Randall about her, Spider said, "She was married for forty years and had two children."

Randall hooked the truck up to the car and pulled the car from the ditch. Britta applauded, as did Kate and Meredith, who had just arrived on the scene.

"Perfect timing!" Meredith said.

But Spider looked perturbed. "So what do we owe you?" she asked.

"For Ruthie Green's granddaughter—no charge. Just say hi to your grandma, from Randall."

He pulled a grubby card from his work pants. Britta grabbed it. "I'll tell her we met you."

"She probably won't remember me."

"I bet she will," Britta said. "I bet you were cute."

"You know how to flatter an old man," Randall said.

"I'd be happy to pay," Spider persisted. "I don't have much on me, but if you take a debit card . . . Or send a bill to our place. Ruthie would want—"

"If your grandmother wants to contact me, she has the card," Randall said. "It was a pleasure meeting you young ladies."

"Thank you," Britta said, gesturing to the other girls to get into the car before Spider could protest anymore. "Thank you so much!"

26

Meredith

Essay topic: Recount a time when you majored in "unafraid."

IT WAS NEARLY two when they'd finally dragged the car from the ditch and were on their way. Meredith was driving. At least she'd drive straight. "So are we still climbing the mountain today, or is it too late?" she asked, hoping for the latter.

Spider shrugged. "It's a little late. Maybe we could just start a little earlier tomorrow."

"And not drive into a ditch this time." Britta patted the chipmunk pillow she'd insisted on returning to purchase.

"Britta . . . ," Meredith said, but she agreed this was a good plan.

After some discussion, they decided to find a spot along the

Hudson River and picnic there. They passed fields of wildflowers and signs advertising chainsaw-carved bears. They passed a "Hudson River Display" sign but saw it too late, and Meredith wasn't about to make a U-turn. "There'll be another one," Spider said.

But there wasn't another for a while, and eventually, they reached a building with a sign that said "North Creek Railroad Station."

"Should we just stop here?" Meredith asked. "It looks interesting."

"I'm really hungreeee." Britta's voice was a squeaky door. "Pleeeeze can we stop?"

"Y'all, let's stop before she busts something," Kate agreed. So Meredith pulled over.

It turned out the railroad station was a museum, but the museum part was closed on Wednesdays. They parked and walked toward the picnic tables.

"What's that?" Britta pointed to a small metal sign on the railing.

The sign said, "North Creek Railroad Station. At this site early in the morning of September 14, 1901, Theodore Roosevelt received the message that President McKinley had died in Buffalo and that he had become president of the United States."

"Oh, I remember this," Spider said. "Roosevelt was vice president. He was climbing Mount Marcy when McKinley was shot. They thought he'd be okay, so Roosevelt kept on with his vacation, but when McKinley got worse, Roosevelt went to the train in North Creek. And when he got here, they said they had to swear him in as president."

"Wow." Britta placed the cooler atop the picnic table and opened it. "Talk about life changing. He just went on a trip, thinking everything was normal; then he was president?"

"Well, he was already vice president." Meredith helped Britta unload the sandwiches.

"But most vice presidents don't become president, do they?" She looked at Meredith like it was an actual question. Considering they'd just finished American history, Britta should have known the answer to that herself.

"Not many," Meredith conceded. "How many presidents have died in office?"

"Well, McKinley," Britta said. "And Lincoln."

"McKinley, Lincoln, Kennedy, and Garfield were assassinated," Meredith said, not wanting to watch Britta struggle. "And one resigned." She looked at Britta.

"Nixon resigned," Spider said. "And four more died of natural causes."

"Right." Meredith nodded approvingly at Spider's knowledge of American history. "But some of those were after Roosevelt, so it wasn't unheard of, but it was a surprise. She counted on her fingers. "Four before Roosevelt became president because someone died."

"Still would be weird." Britta unwrapped her sandwich with great concentration. "Like how often do you have a moment when your life changes, and you know it at the time?"

"I had that." Meredith was surprised at Britta's insight. "In third grade. I was sitting doing my homework at aftercare, waiting for my father to pick me up to take me to dance. I remember I was mad at him because he'd been late the week before, and the teacher, Miss Kim, was super mean about it. She said I couldn't expect to get into intermediate acro if I wasn't on time."

"You took acro-jazz?" Britta said. "So did I. Where?"

So not the point. "Oh, we lived in a different neighborhood then. That's what I'm saying. That day, my biggest problem was getting into a dance class. Everything changed after that."

"Oh. Sorry." Britta clapped her hand over her mouth, as if she was physically forcing herself to shut up.

"Anyway, I was getting upset because it was after five, and my class started at five thirty, and he'd promised to be early this time, and he wasn't. That's when this woman Teri, a paralegal from my mom's office, showed up to get me."

"Uh-oh," Kate said.

Meredith pictured the moment like it was yesterday. Teri, a woman she didn't know, who was wearing a weird dress printed with dachshunds, showed up at the door of aftercare. "They didn't want to let me go with her because she wasn't on the list. But, finally, they called my mom, and she said something that made them let me go with her. I was so upset because Dad had my dance clothes. But she said we had to go to her house instead, and then I started crying until she said she'd personally call Miss Kim and explain what happened. That calmed me down enough that I let her drive me through McDonald's and take me back to her condo to watch *Simpsons* reruns, which my mother never let me watch. It was the one where Homer gets them a dog for Christmas."

"I remember that one." Britta moved closer to Meredith.

"Yeah. It wasn't until later that night that I found out the reason Dad hadn't picked me up was because he was in an accident on the way there." Meredith felt a little short of breath, like she always did when she remembered that day, though she never talked about it. She wasn't sure why she was now, except that she knew Britta thought she was a snot, and she wanted her to know something else about her. "And while I was sitting on Teri's sofa eating chicken nuggets and watching the Simpsons celebrate Christmas, my own father was dying in the hospital. That was what my mother had told the aftercare lady so they'd let Teri pick me up. And I always wondered if it was because he left early for my dance class. Like maybe traffic would have been slower if he'd left at five." She stopped talking. Her throat hurt.

"That's awful," Britta said. "I never knew your dad died, Meredith."

"No one did," Meredith said. "We moved to a new neighborhood, closer to my grandparents, so they could watch me after school. No one ever knew me when I had a dad."

"I remember you that year," Britta said. "When you first came to school, you barely talked to anyone. We just thought you were weird." She looked down at her Doritos. "Sorry."

"No, I was weird," Meredith agreed, despite the sinking feeling. "I changed that year when we moved, with no friends or anything. All I had was school. If I'd stayed where I was, I might have been . . ." She looked at Britta. "I could've been you."

Britta laughed. "That would be awful, I guess."

Meredith thought about it. Britta was nice. And well-liked, the type of person who didn't constantly worry about saying or doing something wrong, even if she did, because she was confident in her social abilities. In a way, Britta was smarter than she was. "No," she said finally. "Just different."

She didn't want to talk about herself anymore. She never did. "How about you?" She passed the buck to Britta. "You ever have an experience like that?"

"Yeah." Britta hesitated. "I mean, it's not as bad. No one died. But yeah, it changed me. My parents got divorced when I was little. They were having problems my whole life. I'm five years younger than my brother, and I feel like they probably had me to, like, save their marriage or something. But it didn't work. They split up when I was five. We visited my father Wednesdays and every other weekend, the usual routine, I guess. Anyway, my mother always said she would be a mother and a father to me, because she was all I had."

"So your parents' divorce was a life-changing event?" Meredith asked.

"No. I mean, yes, but that wasn't the day everything changed. A lot of people's parents get divorced. The day it changed was this time we were all out at the park together, me, my mom, my brother, and my grandparents. We went for a picnic. There's this little pond with lots of turtles in it, so my brother brought dog food to give them."

"The wayside park on US 1?" Meredith said. When Britta nodded, Meredith said, "I used to go there with my grandparents too, when my mom was at work."

"Okay, so you know how deep and scary that pond is. We walked down the rocks to get closer to the turtles, and we were throwing dog food. I was six, and I could dog-paddle, but I wasn't a good swimmer. My brother, Lukas, took this big hand-ful of dog food, and I tried to grab some from him. Then, next thing I knew, I was launching face-first into the water. I plunged deep down, and it was all black and murky, and I couldn't catch my breath. I heard Lukas screaming, but it seemed really far away, like I was hearing him through a wall."

"That must have been so scary," Meredith said, picturing it.

"Yeah. I can still feel the cold, murky water closing in on me." She held her hands to her face. "I don't know how long I was in there. I remember my hands scraping the rocks on the sides, like I was instinctively trying to pull myself up but couldn't. Then, suddenly, someone was there beside me, hoist-ing me out of the water." Britta gulped in a breath.

"It was my grandmother. She'd been sitting way far back from where we were, like I said, at a picnic table. When she saw me fall in, she ran over and jumped into the pond in her dress, to get me. She didn't hesitate. Like, it was just maternal instinct to try and save me."

Meredith nodded. She got it. "But your mother didn't."

"Exactly. She was there. My grandmother was farther. And my mother was younger and dressed more appropriately, and she was my *mother*, who's supposed to have that instinct. But she didn't jump in. Like, she had to decide whether to get her hair wet or something."

"Maybe that wasn't it?" Meredith said. "I thought you said she was overprotective."

"I've thought about that. I feel like she acts overprotective because that's how she's supposed to act, how her friends act. But when she had the opportunity to actually protect me, she didn't. Like, now, she's more concerned with her skeezy boyfriend than with me. Last year, we were making plans to go on a cruise together, like this girl-bonding thing. Then, she met Rick, and she went on a cruise with him for Christmas break and left me home with my grandmother and the cat."

"Wow," Meredith said. "That's so the opposite of my helicopter mom." Not that her mom ever did anything fun like a cruise. They mostly took trips to see colleges.

"Pick your poison, right? But anyway, it really did change everything, everything about me and about how I thought about myself. From then on, I knew I was sort of on my own. And now that she's with Rick . . . God, he's so awful. Sometimes, I think he's just with her because she has a daughter. Like, it's creepy."

The other two girls were silent. Those two didn't talk. The half-mile-or-so walk to that woman's house had been excruciating. Britta had sprinted ahead, so Meredith was stuck with Spider, who walked slowly and wouldn't speak, and Kate, who seemed to be in her own private Idaho. It wasn't like she and Britta were besties, just two people who valued conversation over stony silence.

Should Meredith say something? Just to fill the silence?

Then Britta said, "Did either of you guys have an experience like that?" at the same moment Spider said, "I sort of had an experience like that too."

She speaks. But that would be obnoxious to say, so Meredith said, "When was that?"

Now, despite volunteering, Spider squirmed and looked down.

Finally, Britta broke the silence again. "We're being depressing, guys. How about this topic I saw online the other day: If you discovered a fountain like the one in *Tuck Everlasting* that gave you eternal youth, would you be able to drink when your driver's license said you were twenty-one, or would you always be, like, seventeen?"

They all looked at each other, and Kate said, "I don't know, but I loved that book."

"Me too," Meredith agreed.

27

Spider

EXT. NORTH CREEK RAILWAY STATION, A HISTORIC
RAILROAD STATION, PICNIC TABLES — DAY

Spider, Britta, Meredith, and Kate are
enjoying some really incredible chicken
sandwiches and sharing not-so-incredible
personal stories. Spider is trying to act
casual to hide her internal cringing.

"I LOVED IT too," Spider said. "I saw the movie at least ten
times." She looked over at Britta, grateful to her for giving her
a way out of embarrassing self-revelation. But did she want it?
It was so weird, these girls pouring their hearts out. Her first
instinct was to say nothing, to joke, "Yeah, these chicken sand-

wiches I made are life changing," because, by the way, she'd made them. No big deal. And she hadn't just put meat on bread either. She'd sliced up red onions and stuff.

But they were looking at her, and she wanted to be friends with them, she realized. But was that more likely to happen if she revealed something about herself, or if she didn't?

Too late to back out without them thinking she was weird. Everyone always did anyway.

She said, "You know, Theodore Roosevelt was my favorite president. He was really into conservation, and he established national forests like this one." The other girls were nodding like, *What does this have to do with anything?* "So yeah, I like nature, so I like Roosevelt."

Silence. Britta finished the bite she was chewing, examined her sandwich, and said, "These are really good. What's in here, red onion?"

"Yeah. Red onion."

Meredith opened her sandwich to look at it. "Very good."

Spider had never been one of those people who talked just because she feared silence. But, on the other hand, they had a month left of this. They couldn't just not talk.

So she said, "The thing about Teddy Roosevelt that not everyone knows is, he was a really sickly kid. He had asthma." Meredith was nodding, like she knew that. "His father was disappointed because he couldn't do all the normal boy things, so, to make his father proud, he started hiking and doing all the stuff he was famous for."

"Like killing bears?" Britta said.

"Actually, he is famous for not killing a bear," Meredith said. "That's where they got teddy bears from, because he wouldn't shoot this little bear."

"True," Spider said. "But he shot lots of other things. He was a big hunter, and his house on Long Island is full of his trophies. But he did it to work through his health problems."

"Not so healthy for the animals," Meredith said.

"Did that actually work?" Britta asked.

"Apparently. He climbed the Matterhorn and led a two-year expedition to the Amazon." The other girls were leaning forward like they were actually interested in what she had to say. Even Britta was paying attention. Maybe they were just being polite, but on the other hand, that was more than Spider's own family, except Ruthie, would do. She could do this.

"Anyway, this is really significant to me not only because Roosevelt lived in the town I'm from but also because I have health problems. When I was little, I was always hurting in some way, my legs or my hands or something." She looked to see if they were still with her. People tended to roll their eyes if you said you had a health problem and it wasn't cancer or being in a wheelchair. A girl in her class had a peanut allergy, and some people said it was just for attention. Like, why would anyone lie about that? "Sometimes I'd cry myself to sleep."

"You don't look sick," Kate said, and Spider tried not to show her annoyance.

"Yeah, people always say that. I look fine. My family thought I was faking. They're athletic, so they played tennis or soccer, and they thought I was making excuses because I didn't want to do those things. I was a whiner, or it was psychosomatic." She looked at Britta. "That means in your head."

"I know what it means." Britta straightened her shoulders. "My mom thought my middle school stomachaches were psychosomatic. It was, like, her favorite word."

"I think we all had those stomachaches in seventh grade," Meredith said.

"Seventh grade was the worst," Kate agreed.

Wow. Had seventh grade sucked for everyone? She hadn't realized. "I'll write a movie about seventh grade someday. Anyway, this went on for a while. I wouldn't participate in something, so everyone would get mad, and my mother would say, 'I'm taking you to the doctor,' like it was a threat, because what kid wants to go to the doctor. But I was like, 'Yes! Take me to the doctor!' because I really wanted not to be in pain. She never did. Then, one day, my sister came in my room because I was taking forever to get dressed and Mom sent her to hurry me. But when Emily saw me, trying to step into my shorts without bending over, she told my mom, 'I think there's something really wrong with her. She can't even get her shorts on.' So that was when my mom actually did take me to a doctor, and they did tests and blood work, and they found I had an actual condition with a name, juvenile idiopathic arthritis. I thought arthritis was something only old people got, but apparently, there is a juvenile version, and I hit the lottery. One of my mom's friends said she knew a girl who had it and died."

"Died?" Britta's mouth was wide-open. But Spider didn't want sympathy. In fact, it was the opposite of what she wanted.

"Oh, don't worry. My doctor said that's very, very rare. I'm not going to turn this trip into *The Fault in Our Stars* or something. My doctor said not to worry about it."

"But I bet you did worry," Britta said. *"Pobrecita."*

"Yeah, what a thing to tell a kid," Meredith said.

"I know," Spider said. "But I'm fine. I mean, pretty fine. I take a lot of ibuprofen for the pain, and my mom makes me exercise sometimes. She thinks yoga is the answer to everything, and she doesn't want me to take anything that could be addictive. I'm not athletic. I don't think I would have been anyway, but it's hard to hit a tennis ball with stiff joints."

"So why did you want to climb a mountain?" Britta asked.

"As a challenge. I have good days, and I can go at my own pace, and maybe twenty-three mountains is a lot, but I want to do things. I don't want to be the sick girl. I always set goals for myself, to learn things, even to cut up a chicken." She looked at Britta. "I hate to think there's one big subset of things, the physical part, that eludes me, that I absolutely can't do. I'm not quite Stephen Hawking."

"The smartest man of our time?" Meredith said.

"He said, 'Look up at the stars and not down at your feet.' But, my point is, if you're hella smart, like Hawking or the other Roosevelt, maybe you can get away with not being able to use your body. But I'm not that smart . . . yet."

"I would have guessed you thought you were that smart," Britta said.

Spider wondered if she came off that elitist. "Anyway, finding out there actually was something wrong with me was the day everything changed, because I knew I wasn't just complaining, even though people still think I am. I knew I had a real problem."

They were silent for a while, listening to the birds and the breeze, and finally, Britta said, "We'll do it. We'll definitely do it."

"Do what?" Kate said, looking up from her phone for once.

"Help Spider. Do whatever it takes so she can climb these towers, or at least some of them. Or one of them."

Silence. Britta looked around. "I mean, you don't have to. I just thought . . ."

"No, I want to," Spider said. "I just figured you'd think it was a stupid idea and I was a pathetic person to want to do it."

"I absolutely don't think that." Britta looked at the other two. "I think you're brave."

"Me too," Meredith said.

Only Kate didn't say anything. She was back to her phone.

28

Kate

SO THEY WERE bonding again. Fabulous. All sharing their life experiences and getting closer. Except Kate. She didn't want to share with a bunch of strangers.

Kate didn't tell anyone, but as soon as they hit the train station, her phone had exploded, buzzing with texts and calls during Meredith's and Spider's sad stories and Britta's original oratory on motherly duty.

It sounded mean to think that about Britta, even to Kate. Britta actually seemed really nice. All the girls did, but especially Britta, who was sweetly trying to encourage Spider even though Spider was being a jerk. She wondered what it would be like to have friends like these girls, normal girls who probably had never heard of a debutante cotillion, much less thought it was a reasonable thing to spend money on, never stepped foot in a country club or gone skiing in Jackson Hole, girls who'd never heard of Peach Springs or her father.

She tried to participate in the conversation. But now their eyes were on her like they expected her to tell a story. The only one she could think of to tell was the one told by the dozen articles her mother had sent her about her father's fall from grace.

Would they all hate her if they knew about that?

Kate wasn't ready to out her family. Nothing the other girls had said was really that self-revelatory. Spider was obviously sick. Kate had noticed her hobbling upstairs the first day. Meredith's father was properly dead, at least, which was better than being a crook.

No, that was horrible. She didn't even like herself for thinking these things.

Finally, she said, "This trip is when everything changed for me."

She took a bite of her sandwich and watched their reactions. Spider raised an eyebrow. Britta looked genuinely confused.

Meredith was the first to speak. "Really?"

Then Britta. "But you've barely talked to us, and when you have, it was to get mad."

That made Kate cringe a bit. Was Britta afraid of her?

"I'm sorry. I guess I'm a little . . . shy." She hated that word. Ugly girls were allowed to be shy. When you were pretty and shy, people thought you were a snob. "I'm not good around strangers, but I wanted to come here." She looked around. "Anyone ever hear of Peach Springs, Georgia?"

Blank stares all around.

"Is that a . . . body of water?" Britta asked.

"Sorry. I don't think I have," Meredith said, and Spider shook her head.

Kate shrugged. "No, it's fine. That's the name of the town I'm from. It's forty-five minutes from Atlanta, about ten thousand residents, and my father is on the town council."

"That's cool," Britta said, a little too quickly, and they all agreed.

"No, it's really not. All my life, my father's been obsessed with local politics. We can't go out to dinner or even to the drugstore without someone cornering him about their drainage problems, and my brother and I are expected to go to all these community events, ribbon cuttings and veterans' picnics. Even a turkey pardoning at Thanksgiving."

"Do you enjoy that?" Meredith asked.

"Would you?" Kate countered. "We had to worry about what we wore and how we spoke and being nice to old ladies. And lately, my mother's been pressuring me to prepare for my debutante year."

Now, all their eyebrows were up. "Debutante year?" Spider said.

"It's a tradition. They have these balls." In Peach Springs, no one thought twice about saying *balls*, but Spider smirked. "Dances. They have them in New York too, by the way. It's not just a dumb southern thing. They raise money for charity. But the main reason is to 'introduce young ladies to society,' as my mother would say, which really means to parade me around like a prized Holstein in front of men I'm supposed to marry one day."

"What, like an arranged marriage?" Meredith said.

"Well, not exactly like that," Kate said. "But sort of. They want to make sure I meet the right kind of guy—rich, from a good family, with a couple of ancestors who fought in the American Revolution and a few more who fought for the Confederacy."

"There are still people who care about that sort of thing?" Spider asked.

"Everyone I know does. My mother volunteers at the art museum and for the Junior League and for the Daughters of the American Revolution, all so I can be sure to be invited to walk around in a white dress at the country club in Atlanta."

"So it's sort of like a *quinceañera*," Britta said.

"I'm afraid I don't know what that is," Kate said, thinking probably not.

"It's like that, a party Latina girls have on their fifteenth birthday. They wear a big white dress like a wedding dress, and the girl gets presented by her father. Some of them are outrageous—with the girl showing up in a Cinderella coach or coming out of a clamshell—and some of them are classier. But yeah, you're supposed to be introduced to society, I guess, so same type of thing."

"I didn't have one. I told my mother to spend the money on a car instead. My cousin's *quinces* cost as much as a new Accord with leather seats. I said I'd be happy with a Civic, so it was a bargain." She laughed.

"I wish I could do that," Kate said, even though she already had a car. "And yes, I guess my parents expect me to get a job, for a while. I'll go to a good college where I'll meet someone rich and work, maybe at a museum or a charitable foundation, but I'll quit to have a baby, and I'll never go back. And then, if my husband leaves me or . . ." She hesitated, realizing what her father's disgrace meant to her mother. "Or gets in trouble or can't work, I'll have no meaningful experience, no skills. But, that's the dream."

"And you're okay with that?" Meredith looked skeptical.

Kate shook her head. "It's what was always expected of me." As she said this, she realized it was the first time she'd said it aloud. Her teachers didn't really talk to her about her dreams, not even her debate coach. Oh, sure, they talked about college, but never about what she wanted to do after that. They were used to families like hers. She didn't even know what she wanted to do. "I have to play by my parents' rules, go along with the stupid ball, spend six months of my life talking about the dress, the menu, the flowers, the band, my escort."

She stopped again, thinking of Colin. The one text that hadn't been from Mother had been from him.

It said, **Remember Tybee Island?**

Kate did remember, too well. One night Colin had texted her telling her to bring her bathing suit and meet him outside at six the next morning. They'd skipped school and driven four hours until they reached the ocean. Close to midnight, they rolled back home, sunburned and stuffed full of local shrimp. It had been maybe the best day of her life.

Now Kate took a deep breath. Forget Colin. "Anyway, I told my parents that if I was going to do all that, I needed a break, so I came here. It's the first time I ever stood up to them."

Except it was a lie. She hadn't. It had all been her father's idea.

"But you're still having the party?" Spider asked.

Kate paused, staring at the frilly green lettuce leaf in her sandwich. "I have to. I mean, unless they change their minds." As she said it, she realized for the first time that could happen. Who knew if her mother was even planning the party anymore. Maybe her grandmother would offer to pay, but maybe she wouldn't be invited if they were laughingstocks.

And suddenly, she felt soothed.

"It's a tradition," she said.

"Like the rebel flag," Spider muttered under her breath.

"It's not like that," Kate said, even though she'd never thought about it. But she made her best debate team argument for being a debutante. "It's not like they actually expect me to get married at eighteen. But my mother was a debutante, and my aunt. My grandmother has their pictures hanging in her house. It's just a way to make the old people happy."

"I get it," Britta said. "My grandmother wanted me to have the *quinces.*"

"It's pretty expensive for something you don't really care about," Meredith said.

Kate nodded. She wondered if her father was in trouble because he needed money for her to be a deb. "Anyway, I have to do what my parents want next year. But this summer is all for me, a real adventure."

"So let's do it," Meredith said. "Let's have a great summer, climb mountains, stand up to challenges."

"Agreed," Spider said.

"Agreed," Kate said.

"Agreed." Britta raised her Diet Coke in a toast. "To . . . we should have a name for our group."

Meredith raised her bottled water. "To the Girls of July!" she said.

The others raised their drinks. "Girls of July!"

29

Meredith

Essay topic: Reflect on a time when you questioned or challenged a belief or idea.

WHEN THEY RETURNED, since they hadn't hiked a single step, Meredith told the others she was taking a walk. She wanted to go someplace where she wouldn't run into Harmon and that girl, but where was that? He was somehow everywhere, like a stalker, only one who didn't like her.

So she decided to go to the only place she hadn't seen him, Service Hill. She'd text her mother from there too.

She started uphill, feeling slightly breathless from the thin mountain air. More than slightly. Was she that out of shape? By the time she reached the top, she felt so tired she had to sit down on a giant lichen-covered boulder. Then she leaned back, fairly panting, closing her eyes against the sheer blueness of the sky. She felt the riffle of breeze across her arms.

And someone watching her.

She opened her eyes.

No one there. Only a hawk making languid circles above. She drew out her phone. She'd photograph the hawk and send it to her mother, possibly with a note about how she was reaching for the sky in her college essays. Her mother loved stuff like that.

As she held the phone up, she heard the open-close of a camera shutter.

She felt a frisson of . . . something. Excitement? Maybe fear. No, neither of those. She knew who it was, knew the emotion he caused in her.

It was annoyance.

Couldn't she get a moment by herself?

Why did she even care? He was just a boy, an overgrown, stupid boy with eyes the color of a sun-dappled river. Stop it! Since when did she care so much about boys?

There was no reason Harmon Dickinson should prevent her enjoyment of this beautiful place. She raised the phone, waited for the bird to circle again, then quickly snapped the photo.

As she did, she heard a flurry of the shutter, a burst of photos. She checked her own. The hawk was missing a wing. She raised the phone again.

"You'd do better up here," a voice said.

Meredith started, dropping the phone. It bounced—bounced—off the rock and fell downhill. With an expletive, she scrambled to get it.

"Language!" He was up in a tree!

"Oh, who asked you?" Meredith yelled back, picking up her phone. Fortunately, it wasn't cracked. "Why are you always wherever I am?"

"I could ask you the same thing." He was climbing down the tree now, a giant maple. He had on jeans and a green T-shirt that blended with the leaves and sky. He reached the lowest branch and dropped down with a light thud. "Are you following me?"

"Why would I do that?"

He smiled. Meredith looked down. "Maybe you want photography tips. Or maybe you think I'm cute."

"Unlikely." She was still looking down.

"Of course not." He walked around to get into her field of vision. "A serious girl like you doesn't look at guys."

"I'm not that serious."

"So?"

"You're not that cute." Though she wondered if he thought she was cute.

He chuckled. "I've been told I'm cute."

"Who told you that? Your mother?"

"Absolutely. I have five brothers, and she says I'm the cutest. It caused controversy at Christmas last year."

Meredith suppressed a smile. "How about your girlfriend?"

"What girlfriend?"

Meredith examined her phone, pretending to check if it was broken. She was so stupid. Mentioning a girlfriend was akin to asking him if he had one, which in turn was akin to admitting she'd been watching him. Which she hadn't.

"I just figured a cute guy like you had a girlfriend," she said.

"Oh!" He clapped, and his eyes lit up. "You mean Hope!"

"That's your girlfriend's name?"

"That is my cousin's name—the girl I was with at the lake yesterday."

The girl was his cousin. Meredith's concentration on her phone became more immersive, but she said, "Cousin?"

"My cousin, Hope Ann Bradford, just finished her freshman year at SUNY New Paltz. She is here for a few days, ostensibly to enjoy the lovely scenery."

"Ostensibly?" She was surprised he knew such a big word. Most people—even some of her AP class friends—wouldn't. Or they'd make fun of her for using it, even if they did.

"Yeah." Harmon started clicking through the photos in his camera. "Really, though, she's here as a good example. Hope struggled in school, but dammit, she kept her nose to the grindstone so hard she practically has a snout. So now, as a reward, she gets to study more. She is here to convince me that college is a good idea."

"Of course it is." Meredith didn't know anyone who thought otherwise. "What would you do without college?"

"Save a lot of money. Become a nature photographer. I've already sold some photos."

"To whom?" Probably some local magazine with a circulation of fifty.

But he said, "Tourists. I showed my photos to the manager of Telly's Diner in town. He displayed them, and people wanted to buy them. I took the money I got, bought some framing supplies, and talked this touristy store in Bolton Landing into taking them on consignment. They sold three in June—June, before the real tourist season even began!—and they want more."

"Wow. I'd never have the nerve to do something like that."

"It's good money, and I'm entering a photography contest in *Adirondack Life* magazine. First prize is tuition at a photography workshop, but it'd be a good way to get my name out there. And by the way, sure you would."

"Would what?"

"Have the nerve. I've seen you be brave. You were brave with that bat."

Meredith thought about it, and about what Kate had said about standing up to her parents and taking the trip. She'd been brave to come here too. She straightened her shoulders. She wanted to ask him more about why he didn't want to go to college, but she realized it would come off as snobby. So instead she said, "That picture you left for me . . ."

"Yeah?"

"I liked it. But why'd you take it?"

"Why do you think?"

She thought he'd taken it to flirt with her. But she couldn't say that. Could she?

She could not.

"I guess I thought you were being nice," she said.

"Oh." He looked disappointed. "Yeah. I was being nice. I should go. The hawk's gone."

He started down the hill. So much for that. She started to send the hawk photo to Mom.

"You know what?" he said, turning back.

"What?"

"I'm not that nice. I took the photo because I thought you looked beautiful."

"Oh, sure." He was making fun of her. No one had ever called Meredith beautiful. Her mother would actively disapprove of the idea, the same way she disapproved of Disney princesses. She was smart, not beautiful.

But Harmon went on. "The look on your face when you saw that bat—same as when you saw the hawk just now—you looked so fascinated by it all, like you'd been living in a box all your life like Skinner's daughter, and suddenly you got out."

"I hadn't seen one before." He knew Skinner too. Who was this guy?

"Sure you have. Hawks are common."

She looked into his eyes. "Maybe I never noticed one before."

He said, "Maybe. This place has that effect on people. That's why I never want to leave." He showed her the photo he'd taken of the hawk. Unlike Meredith's, it was perfectly centered, the hawk's wings spread wide as it glided downward against the clouds.

"Incredible. Can you teach me to take better photos?" She wanted to see through his eyes.

He pointed to her phone and scoffed. "With that?"

"I got the one that was supposed to have the better camera." Meredith turned away, embarrassed. "A simple no would have been nicer."

He touched her shoulder. "I'm not saying no."

"What are you saying?"

"I gave you the picture because I hoped maybe you'd go out with me."

"Out? Like on a date?" She felt a chill. She didn't know if it was because it was cool out or because he had asked. Her. Out. On. A. Date. People in Miami didn't go out on dates. They "hung out." And Meredith didn't even do that. She was serious. Focused. She didn't have time for things like dating.

He laughed. "Yes. Like on a date."

And yet, wouldn't going on a date be a new experience? Wouldn't it—as the essay prompt said—question or challenge the idea or belief that she didn't date or didn't care about boys? Wasn't that the point of traveling? It wasn't like she had to settle down and have five kids with the guy. Also, she was sup-posed to be on vacation.

"Let me cut to the chase," Harmon said. "Movie? Tonight? Pick you up at seven thirty?"

She looked at her watch. It was five, plenty of time to have dinner and be ready by seven thirty if she didn't spend too long getting ready. Meredith never did.

"Yes, I'd like that," she said.

They made plans. Harmon offered to pick her up at the house, but Meredith didn't want to discuss it with the others. She had a feeling Spider would have some things to say about Harmon. "Why don't we just meet at the bottom of the hill?"

He shrugged. "Suit yourself."

"I have to go now," she told him. "For dinner."

He nodded. "Hurry back."

She started down the hill. "I will!"

She waited to be out of his sight, even checking the trees to make sure he wasn't up in one, before she broke into a run.

30

Britta

BRITTA HAD VOLUNTEERED to cook again, though it wasn't her night. So she was surprised when Spider showed up at the kitchen doorway.

"Can I help?" she asked.

"I'm just making meat sauce," Britta said. "It's pretty easy."

"Easy's good." Spider looked around. "But if you got it . . ."

"No." Britta recognized the peace offering. Britta also realized that Spider might be so pathetic around the house because she'd never tried due to her health issues. Maybe she wanted to try now. "I'm just adding some ground beef and onions to a jar of sauce. I could show you how to brown the meat."

She suggested it with the tentativeness of someone approaching a feral cat. But Spider didn't scratch, so Britta opened up the package of beef. "Put the burner on medium high, then in a minute, add the meat."

"Okay."

"This was actually one of the first cooking things I learned. When my mom went back to work, she wanted me to be able to start dinner." She gestured toward the beef. "Okay, so you put it in and break it up with a fork."

"Like this?" Spider cut it up with the tines.

"Right." Britta got out a pot and filled it with water. "I remember I was really proud because we went on a Girl Scout campout that year, and I was the only one who knew how to make taco meat."

Spider kept stirring.

"Now you add the onions when it's almost brown, and be sure to stir that too."

Spider picked up the cutting board with the onion. Fortunately, it was already cut up this time, so they didn't fight over it. She added it to the pan.

Britta had returned Ruthie's scrapbooks to the bookshelf. Now, to make conversation, she asked Spider, "So, when I was in Ruthie's room the other day, I noticed she had some photos of a friend of hers from summer stock, Janet. Does she ever talk about her?"

"Why do you ask?"

Britta shrugged. "It's just weird when you think about it, how you know someone so well, and then, you might never see them again. She had a framed photo of just her, and then one of the two of them."

Spider paused, stirring the onions with the meat. "That is

weird. I don't think she ever mentioned Janet to me. But you seem to have bonded more with my grandmother in a few days than I have in my whole life."

She was letting the onions get too crisp. "I doubt that's true—keep stirring it. I'm probably more interested in the theater stories than you are, but you're an artist too. She'd probably rather talk to her granddaughter."

"So you're saying I'm not being nice to Ruthie?"

"I didn't—can you mix that, please?"

"I'm the one hanging out with her, here when my brother and sister and cousins all can't be bothered, all have better things to do."

"I didn't say you weren't being nice." Britta got another spoon from the drawer, pushed past Spider, and stirred the meat and onions, then took it off the burner. Talking to this girl was like being on social media when people seem to *want* to misunderstand you. "You're great."

Spider didn't answer, and Britta drained the fat off the meat into the garbage can, then added a jar of sauce. She returned it to the burner.

"Can you turn it to low when it boils?" she asked.

"Sure. I guess I'm competent to do that. I might even be able to boil pasta. I've made Kraft mac and cheese before."

Britta tried not to look surprised at that. "Great. Be sure to stir it when you put it in so it doesn't stick together."

"Duh." Spider rolled her eyes.

"And use a wooden spoon."

"Okay."

"And set the timer for ten minutes." Britta wondered if this was how her mother felt when she said it was easier to do something herself.

"I know that!"

"It's just that it's whole-wheat pasta, so it takes longer than regular."

"So it'll be *al dente*. That's a thing, right?" Spider made a big deal of peering into the pot.

Britta left then and started to set the table for five. She didn't bother to check back. She knew Spider would do it right, to spite her. Or maybe she'd burn the house down.

31

Spider

```
INT. CABIN, DINING ROOM — EVENING

Spider, Meredith, Ruthie, Kate, and Britta,
sitting in that order, are eating dinner.
Spider and Britta are studiously avoiding
one another.
```

THEY ATE HER pasta, and nobody died. Something to be proud of on a day when she'd failed at mountain climbing, driven her car into a ditch, and argued with Britta. Again. Over nothing.

Truth was, she didn't know you had to stir the pasta when you added it. The box didn't say anything about it, and she'd wondered why the macaroni always stuck together when she made mac and cheese. Not that she was going to tell Britta that.

But now they were finishing up, and Ruthie looked around the table. "Does anyone want to play Rummikub?" She said it to the table at large but looked only at Britta. Spider found her lip curling up again. She clapped her hand over her mouth, but not before Britta noticed.

"Oh, I'm really tired," Kate said. "Big day. But thanks."

"I'm going out." Meredith looked around, Spider would almost say guiltily, but she had no reason to think that. "For a walk. I want to go up the hill and call my mom." They'd promised to let the others know if they went out.

"What about you two?" Again, Ruthie mostly looked at Britta.

Britta yawned. If it was a fake one, it was convincing enough to make Spider yawn herself. "I am just so, so tired. I bet Spider would play with you." She fixed Spider with a look. Great. So now she was being instructed on how to interact with her own grandmother.

Still, Spider said, "That would be nice. We haven't played in a while."

"I'll clear the table, so you can play sooner," Kate said. Spider started to object, but Kate was already picking up plates. Spider and Ruthie adjourned to Ruthie's bedroom.

Spider hadn't been in Ruthie's room in a long time. She scanned the family photos, her eyes landing on Ruthie's wedding photo, in which Ruthie wore some kind of hippie 1960s knit gown and carried a bouquet of daisies. Her grandfather wore a regular suit.

Ruthie noticed Spider looking at it. "My dress looked like a bathrobe, I know. I knit it myself. It was my *Barefoot in the Park* look."

Spider knew *Barefoot in the Park*. She'd seen the movie, starring Robert Redford and Jane Fonda. "But you didn't dress Grandpa like Austin Powers."

"He was Robert Redford in *Barefoot in the Park*," Ruthie said. "Very straitlaced. He said I gave him life."

"He was handsome."

"He was." Ruthie started to unfold a card table near the bed. "I have such fond memories of you coming into my room to play when you were little."

"You mean of all of us coming here?"

Ruthie hesitated. "Well, yes. That too. But you especially. You were a sweet girl."

Spider remembered herself as a prickly little girl who never liked being touched. "I don't think I was ever sweet."

"You were to me. One night, when you were six or seven, there was a terrible storm. All the others slept through it, but the noise kept me awake. Every time I started to drift off, another flash started me. After a particularly large clap, there was a knock on my door."

"Me?"

"Do you remember what you said?" Ruthie opened the box.

Spider noticed a 1960s-style poster for the Peace Corps, an

American flag where the stars were doves. It had been there that night too. The monsoon-like rains here had frightened her as a kid. Even now, she wouldn't drive in them.

"I think . . . was it something about swimming?"

"Exactly right!" Ruthie spread the tiles around. "You said, 'The rain's trying to get inside the house, and I'm not a good swimmer!'"

Spider laughed, though it reminded her a bit of Britta's story about almost drowning. "And do you remember what you did?" she asked, remembering it well.

"I asked if you wanted to sing about your favorite things, like in *The Sound of Music.*"

"Because of course you did," Spider said.

"Why write your own script when you have Richard Rodgers?" Ruthie said.

"At least you didn't make lederhosen out of the curtains." But Spider felt an incredible urge to hug Ruthie right then. She didn't. She wasn't a hugger, so it would be weird. Confiding in the girls at the train station was quite enough sharing for one day.

"You were a girl. It would have been a dirndl," Ruthie corrected. "From then on, you came to my room every time it rained, and we always sang, until one day, you didn't anymore."

Spider remembered that. She didn't know why she'd stopped coming to Ruthie's room. She guessed it had something to do with wanting to be seen as a big girl instead of running to her grandmother any time it rained. It wasn't like her older siblings had seen her as one of them. She'd just been alone, reading or, lately, watching a movie when the rain woke her. She looked at her tiles. Three sevens. "I'm sorry I stopped coming."

"You're here now."

Ruthie drew a tile, then Spider. She looked at the old photographs clustered on a little cherrywood shelf in the corner by the bed. "Tell me about the people in those photographs."

"You always used to ask me that when you were little too."

"I don't remember. I mean, I know those are your parents." She gestured to a pink-framed photo. "But who's that one there, in the silver frame?"

It was a photo of a young woman in a dropped-waist dress, obviously very fashionable.

"That was my aunt, Lieselotte, my mother's sister. She was a great beauty in her day. She never married."

"What happened to her?" Though she knew. It was starting to come back.

"She died in the camps. My mother had come here by then, and they wanted to bring her over, but . . ." She butterflied her hands. "Too late."

"That's sad."

Ruthie selected a tile. "Yes. Next to that is my brother, Stanley, and me when we were little." The girl wore a huge hair bow and carried a beagle puppy.

Spider took a tile. She wasn't really concentrating on the game. "And who's the next one?" In this one, a young Ruthie was wearing an old-fashioned dress. She met eyes with a similarly costumed taller young woman.

"That was me in summer stock."

"And the other girl?"

Ruthie smiled, the smile reaching her eyes. "That was Janet. We were . . ." She hesitated, looking down at her tiles. "Best friends. We were together both summers I was here, and we planned to go to New York City and have exciting careers."

"And did you? I mean, I know you did, but did Janet?"

Ruthie put down three fours. "Do you still not have enough points to begin?" she demanded. "Do you need help like when you were little?"

"No." Spider examined her tiles. In addition to the three sevens, she had a run—eight, nine, ten—and three threes, more than enough to start. She put down just the run and the sevens so Ruthie wouldn't suspect she hadn't been paying attention. "Here."

"About time." Ruthie looked at her own tiles and added an eleven to the run.

Spider took a tile. Another three. "So what happened to Janet?"

Ruthie shook her head. "Her parents sent her away to college—in Florida, of all places. I never saw her again." She gazed pointedly at Spider's tile rack until Spider put down the threes.

"Really? Never?" Spider was sure there must be something else to this story.

"Yes. It wasn't like now, with Facebook and the internet. Back then, even your dearest friends . . ." Her throat caught, and she cleared it. "Sorry. Once someone left, they were gone forever." She gestured to Spider as to whether she was done. Spider nodded. Ruthie fixed her attention on the tiles.

"*Was* Janet your dearest friend?" Spider had lived in the same neighborhood all her life, with the same people. Sure, someone occasionally moved, but for the most part, you couldn't lose someone, even if you wanted to. Everyone was so connected. "That's so sad."

"Actually . . ." Ruthie added a seven to Spider's group, then sat up as if making a decision. "We were in love." It came out a sigh.

Spider sucked in her breath. Could that really be true? If it was, it meant Ruthie was not quite who she had thought, not who anyone in her family had thought. Did her father know? Or Aunt Laura? What would they think if they did? Spider remembered to breathe. Ruthie was still speaking, still telling her this secret she'd told no one.

"We spent summers together and wrote to one another all winter. We made plans. We planned to get an apartment together in New York, attend college, and become actresses. But her parents must have found my letters and forbade her to see me. I never knew what happened. I sent so many letters, and I ran home from school each day, hoping for a reply. Nothing. Finally, I got a letter from her mother, telling me not to contact her again."

Spider had given up any pretense of playing the game. She could picture Ruthie as if it were an old-time silent movie, the Ruthie in the photograph, pretty and blond, arriving home to check the mailbox, only to find this. She must have been devastated. The Ruthie in her vision clutched her heart and sobbed.

"You never heard from her again?"

Ruthie shook her head. "She sent me one letter the following fall from someplace called Gainesville. She said she was studying nursing and that her parents had made her realize our relationship was wrong. She sounded different, like she'd been brainwashed. Your generation would say reprogrammed. She concluded the letter, 'May you find the same happiness I have.' I still have it."

Ruthie became interested in her tiles again. She flipped the egg timer, as one did when one was going to make an elaborate move, then began to move first one group of tiles, then another. She started by moving apart one of the runs and inserting a seven in the middle of it.

"And then what?" Spider felt a chill that went from her upper arms across her torso.

"And then nothing." Ruthie put another of the sevens with her own eight and nine. "You know the rest. I did move to New York, became an actress—of sorts—met your grandfather—"

"But you loved . . . ?"

"I loved your grandfather, I did. And my children. Of course I did. It was different in those times. People expected certain things."

"But . . ." Spider couldn't believe it. Her grandmother was so cool and liberal. She had a Peace Corps poster. And she was going to run around naked onstage. She didn't do things just because they were expected. "But you loved Janet first?"

"I guess I wasn't as brave as your generation. I realized Janet was right. If my parents found out, they'd have disowned me." She made a few more moves, then added two more tiles to the result. "Your turn."

Spider stared at the board, then at her own tiles. "So was your entire life a lie?"

Ruthie shook her head. "I've had a happy life, children, grand-children. Back then, one had to choose. It wasn't like today. I chose your grandfather."

It was like that old movie, *It's a Wonderful Life*, where George Bailey chose one life over another, and it affected everything. But George Bailey had been happy. Was Ruthie? Spider divided a big run, then inserted a nine in the middle. "And you never wondered . . . ?"

"When your grandfather passed, I looked for her. And, a few years later, when Facebook started, I looked there too. But I didn't find her. She must have gotten married. Or died." She said this matter-of-factly, used to the idea. Yet, she still had Janet's photo on display, so many years later. Ruthie turned over the egg timer and started moving pieces again, beginning with the ten Spider had just put down. After about a minute of shuf-fling and adding, shuffling and adding, she flipped her empty tile stand. "I win!"

Spider showed her leftover tiles. When she was little, the losers used to pay a penny for every point showing on the tiles. "I owe you seventeen cents. Another game?"

"Oh, I don't think so. Maybe tomorrow. Let's clean up."

They were silent as they gathered the tiles and stands and returned them to their box. Ruthie left it on her nightstand. "For another day."

Spider started for the door, then turned back. "I love you, Ruthie."

"I love you too, *bubbeleh*."

Spider closed the door. She wanted to talk to someone, to Britta, she realized. But Britta's door was closed, lights off. Spider wondered if she was awake. She hadn't heard Meredith come in. Perhaps she was outside again. Spider was too tired to check.

Yet when she lay down in bed, she couldn't sleep. Her knees ached, but that wasn't why. She was used to that. No, it was the whirring, whirring, whirring in her brain that kept her awake, the anger at herself for not realizing and the sadness for Ruthie, having lost maybe the love of her life.

32

Kate

AFTER KATE FINISHED the dishes, she went to her room to check her phone. She had successfully kept herself from checking her texts all afternoon, but they needled her like a small, unavoidable mosquito. She couldn't stop thinking about them.

But did she really want to read all those articles about her father?

She did. She would walk up the hill to look. Based on yesterday, she guessed there was at least an hour of daylight. Also, maybe she could call her father.

When she went outside, she saw Meredith, leaving at the same time.

Meredith looked none too happy to see her. She wondered why. Still, she said, "Where are you off to?"

"I was, um, just going to check my phone on the hill, maybe walk around a little."

"Oh." Kate didn't want company for this particular errand, though she liked Meredith. From the looks of it, Meredith didn't want company either. "I was doing the same thing. But—"

"I'm lying, okay?" Meredith looked around, as if sharing a confidence. She lowered her voice. "I just didn't want Spider to know. I have a date."

"A date?" The word, like everything else, made her think of Colin. "With that cute guy from the lake?"

Meredith looked down, but she couldn't stop herself from smiling. "Yeah. Spider hates him, so I figured it was easier not to bring it up."

"I could see that," Kate agreed. "Spider's a little, um, opinionated."

"Right. So I'm walking to the hill to meet him. I wouldn't listen in on your call if we walked together."

"Oh, that wasn't . . ." It was obvious she was lying. "Okay, let's go together."

Just as she started down the steps, the door flew open. It was Britta. "Oh, good, you're there," she said to Kate. "Someone's on the phone for you."

Someone on the phone? Kate guessed her father had the phone number here. But his calling couldn't be a good thing. What if there was some terrible emergency? What if she had to come home? What if the texts were more than simply sharing the bad news?

"Oh, thank you!" Kate said to Britta. Then she hurried inside.

She hadn't realized she was holding her breath until she picked up the phone and heard not her father's voice, nor even her mother's.

Instead, it was a girl's voice. "Hi, um, this is Liz. From Best."

"Best?" She didn't know a Liz.

"The supermarket, yesterday?"

"Oh!" Kate exhaled. This may well be an emergency, but it was someone else's emergency, an emergency she might be able to help with. "Yes. Hi. I remember."

"This is kind of awk. You said you could watch my brother, Racecar, while I was at work, and I know I said I didn't need you to. I may even have been a little rude about it, but I was wondering—"

"Yes," Kate said, throwing any thought of home out like yesterday's coffee grounds. "I'd be happy to."

33

Meredith

Essay topic: Please briefly elaborate on one of your extracurricular activities or work experiences that was particularly meaningful to you.

SHE REALLY SHOULDN'T have to lie about meeting Harmon. She didn't owe Spider anything. She could do what she liked here. That was the whole point of here, actually.

If she could only figure out what it was she liked.

When she reached the hill, he was already there in an older white Dodge pickup that looked like it had been through some stuff. The truck had a bumper sticker on the left side of the window, with a picture of a moose and a quote from Tolkien, "Not all who wander are lost."

He got out of the car, his grin bringing light to the dusk. He wore a blue school hoodie, and his hair was damp. He walked around the passenger side to let her in. "You made it!"

"Did you think I wouldn't?"

He laughed. "Next time, I'll pick you up on my motorcycle. Will you go?"

A week ago, Meredith would have said no. But now, she said, "I don't know."

"Don't know if you want to go on a bike with a bad boy?"

He was already planning their second date when they'd barely started their first. This was actually Meredith's first date ever. Oh, she'd told herself that going to homecoming with Alaric McHugh, because neither of them had a date, counted. But it so didn't. Alaric had brought his SAT printout, so they could go over the questions he missed. And she hadn't felt excited. That evening had had a sense of inevitability to it. This date had an element of uncertainty. She liked it.

"Meredith?"

She jumped. Had he been speaking to her before?

"Sorry!"

"Nah, it's okay. You looked sort of dreamy. I was just asking what movie we should see."

She realized she had no idea. "I don't know. What are the choices?"

He pulled onto the interstate. "Glad you phrased it that way. Choices are sort of limited up here. When I went to Long Island last year, they had a theater with twelve different movies and another with twelve more. I'm betting it's like that where you're from too."

"Yeah, we have a lot of movies. But I don't really care what I see."

"That's good, because you only have two choices, two double features." He mentioned two kid cartoons, one a sequel to something Meredith had seen, and two superhero films.

"You won't mind if I choose the kids' movies?"

"Nah. In fact, I'm kind of nostalgic about that. I saw the first one when I was, like, ten."

"Then it's settled," she said as he turned on his headlights. "You drive very carefully."

"There's deer around twilight, which is now. Also, I got a ticket last month, and my mother's still on my back about it. Most of the money I got for the first photo I sold went to pay it, close to two hundred dollars."

"Two hundred dollars for a photo, wow," she said, remembering he'd sold three.

"I know, right? It was actually two fifty, minus the frame I bought. The manager at Telly's said, 'Price 'em high so people think they're worth something,' and she was right. I'd have sold it for forty dollars or something."

"What were the pictures of?"

"It sounds dumb. Just a sunrise over Schroon Lake with a canoe. But I took them in fall, so there were a lot of colors."

"It sounds beautiful." Meredith wondered what she ever did that was beautiful. "It must be nice, sitting someplace pretty and setting up the perfect shot. One time, when I was little, my dad took me out to Shark Valley in the Everglades. We went in the morning. It was so dark and quiet." Meredith remembered holding her dad's hand, afraid that she might stumble over an alligator in the blackness. "We thought we were all alone. But when the sun rose, there were maybe a dozen photographers, snapping pictures right near where we were." She remembered being there with Daddy. It must have been just a few months before he died.

"That would never happen here. It's never crowded."

They drove in silence. Harmon pulled off at an exit. Then, Meredith saw the theater sign.

Glen Drive-in

"A drive-in?" she asked. "That's still a thing?"

"Guess we're a little retro here." Harmon drove up to the yellow-painted ticket booth.

"Isn't the drive-in where people go to . . ." She trailed off.

"Make out? Yes, I have also seen *Grease*. But there's a bunch of little kids and old people here, so I think you're pretty safe." He pulled forward and reached for his wallet.

"Oh, let me pay for myself."

But she wasn't quick enough, and he handed the old woman cashier a twenty.

"Who you with, Harmon?" the cashier asked. "Girlfriend?"

"We'll see." He took the ticket she handed him. To Meredith, he said, "I'm feeling flush with my photography sales. You can get the popcorn."

He drove into a patchy field with a giant screen at the front. It was still light out, but people were already lounging on lawn chairs or walking with pajama-clad kids to a brown building, apparently a snack bar. Harmon was right. It didn't look like a den of iniquity. He backed into an empty parking spot. "We can sit in the truck bed."

So now she was going to be a girl who sat in truck beds. Who even was she?

"I think even a city girl like you will be okay with the arrangement," Harmon said. "But check it out, and if you don't like it, I'll turn the truck around, and we can sit in the cab."

"Okay." She started to get out of the car only to find him there a second later. Was he going to open the door for her every time? And was that gentlemanly? Or sexist? In any case, she let him shut it behind her and followed him to the truck bed, which was lined with patio chair cushions. A small cooler perched in the center. He also had a Frisbee, a football, an old-fashioned big radio, a giant can of Off, and some fishing poles.

He saw her eyeing the fishing poles. "I'm prepared for any-thing," he said, grinning. "Should we head to the snack bar?"

Meredith glanced at the cooler, wondering if it was full of worms, but she followed him.

"I used to come here every week in the summer, growing up," he said. "There were so many of us we took two cars, and we'd park near other friends from school and tailgate."

"How many of you?"

"Six of us boys. I'm the youngest. After me, they stopped trying to have a girl, and my mother taught me to knit and bake."

"You knit?"

"Should I make you a scarf? I do bake. In fact, I made the blondies in the cooler."

The boy was full of surprises. They reached the old building. Some people their age were crowded there. Harmon introduced them and said, "Guys, this is Meredith. She's from Miami."

"Ooh, city girl," a guy he'd introduced as Nick said.

"Miami," a girl named Kelly said. "You ever see a drug bust?"

Meredith shrugged. "Some girl at school got busted selling her ADD pills, but I didn't really know her."

"You don't look very tan either," Kelly said.

Harmon turned to Meredith. "What do you want? I recommend the Slush Puppie. That's what I've always gotten since I was a kid."

Meredith ordered two blue Slush Puppies and insisted on paying.

"So do you know everyone here?" Meredith asked as they walked back to the car.

"Pretty much. That's how it is in a small town. Don't you know people in Miami?"

Meredith laughed. "Hardly anyone. Just the drug dealers."

"Really?"

"No, not really." Meredith took a swig of her Slush Puppie. "It may surprise you to know that I have not seen a single shoot-out in Miami."

"Not even a little one?" Harmon feigned shock. "Yeah, Kelly watches too much TV."

"Uncle Harmon! Uncle Harmon!" a tiny voice yelled as they passed.

"Are you Uncle Harmon?" Meredith asked.

"I might be. Depends who's asking." Harmon turned toward the voice. "I am!"

A little girl with red pigtails ran up. "Uncle Harmon, I lost a tooth!" She lifted her lip.

"So you did." Harmon scooped her up. "And have you won any spelling bees lately?"

"No, silly. It's summer."

"Daisy is the spelling champion of her grade," Harmon told Meredith.

"Wow! What grade is that?"

"Second. But I'm going into third." To Harmon, she said, "Give me a word to spell."

"Maybe Meredith has a word." He started to carry her toward her parents' car.

"Um . . ." Meredith thought back to her own spelling bee days. "How about gleam?"

"Easy. G-L-E-A-M. Gleam. Give me a harder one."

"Okay." Meredith thought. "Together. That one was hard for me when I was your age."

"Together," Daisy repeated. "T-O-G-E-T-H-E-R. Together."

"Great!" Meredith clapped. "I can see why you won."

"Ask me another." Daisy kicked Harmon in the ribs as he carried her.

"Ouch! No, sweetie. She's done for now. You stumped her." Harmon put her down.

"Aw!" Daisy ran to a man who looked like an older, bearded version of Harmon, who was with a little boy. "Daddy, ask me more words!"

"Meredith, this is my nephew, Noah, and my *oldest* brother, Colt."

"Be careful around him," Colt said. "And have his blondie, if he made them."

Harmon took Meredith's hand. "Come on."

They continued through the crowd. The setting sun turned the sky pink. Harmon pulled Meredith toward him. "Watch out!" She realized it was to avoid an oncoming Frisbee.

"Hey, buddy." It was Nick from before. He walked ahead of them, sort of getting in their way. "So tell me about yourself, Melissa."

"Meredith," Harmon said.

"Meredith. Meredith from Miami. What do you do in Miami, Meredith?"

This guy was weird. He seemed like he was purposely trying to waste their time.

"She trains alligators to be lifeguards," Harmon said. "Why are you messing with her?" To Meredith, he said, "Sorry. Nick's a little clueless. It's what happens when siblings marry."

They walked about five feet before another guy was in their way. "Hey, Harmon, Coach Palermo wants to know if you're going out for football this year."

"Still no." He smiled and tried to steer Meredith around the guy.

"Who's your girlfriend?" the guy asked. "Are you new in town?"

"Not exactly," Meredith said.

"Well, Harmon here is a great guy, no matter what people say. I'm Zack, by the way."

"What do people say?" It was so weird having all these people talk to them.

"That he's a wimp who won't go out for football. Can you talk him into it?"

"I don't know. He seems pretty stubborn." A lot of her friends played soccer or lacrosse to make themselves look well-rounded for college. Football seemed really violent. "He's probably just aware of the risk of neurodegenerative disease from repeated head trauma."

Zack looked a little surprised, which made Meredith pause. Too late, she realized he'd obviously just been teasing Harmon about football. She was being too serious and saying this guy had a head injury. Why was she such a nerd? "I mean . . ."

"Good point," Harmon said. "My mother would agree with you."

They were almost at the truck, and even more people were talking to Harmon. Meredith wondered if this was what it was

236

like to be popular. "Is your whole school here?"

"It's a summer tradition."

"It's so different here." In Miami, there was no place where everyone was. She'd lived there eight years now, and even at school, most people were still strangers. When Britta had spoken to her that day in the library, it was the first time in five years she'd talked to someone outside her little clique of AP class friends. Yet she didn't feel close to those people either.

"They don't get many new people here, so you're different and exotic."

"So exotic."

"Well, you do have blue lips."

"You do too. I guess it's a new style." She looked at him, grinning with his blue lips, and she wondered what it would be like to kiss him. Not that she'd kissed anyone before. She wondered if he would try. And, if so, would she let him?

Probably, she realized. Probably.

They reached the truck, and he offered his hand. "Help you up?"

"Oh, I can . . ." She looked at the truck bed. She had no idea how people got in. "Okay."

"Just hold here." He gestured at the side next to the open tailgate. "And put your other hand on my shoulder. That's it." He helped her hoist herself up.

She heard a pop as she got off the tailgate and wondered if she'd broken something. But she felt okay and stumbled onto the cushions. Harmon followed. There was another pop, then another. And an even bigger pop as she sat down. "Oh!"

"Those guys!" Harmon was laughing. He sat and there was a huge burst. Someone had put balloons under the cushions. Harmon stood and stepped on another one. "Real funny!" he yelled into the night.

"You know we love you, or we'd have put water balloons!" a girl's voice said. Kelly. Suddenly, everyone they'd run into surrounded them, laughing, offering popcorn.

"Guy can't just leave his truck unattended," Colt said.

"You got the kids in on this?" Harmon said.

Meredith looked at Daisy, who was with her father. "And I thought you really wanted to impress me with your spelling!" she said in mock outrage.

"I did!" To Harmon, she said, "Tell her I did want to I-M-P-R-E-S-S her."

"I believe you." Meredith laughed. "I'll even think of words for next time I see you."

"Aha!" Colt said. "There's gonna be a next time."

"I noticed that too," Harmon said. "I think the movie's about to start."

"You want us to leave?" Colt asked.

"Kind of. I don't want you to scare her away," Harmon said.

After they left, Meredith settled into her place and Harmon started unpacking the food.

"I'm sorry about the balloons," Harmon said. "Did they startle you?"

"It was funny." No one had ever played any kind of prank

on Meredith or included her in on one either. She knew they pranked other girls. Last year, the football team had moved—actually lifted—a cheerleader's Mini Cooper out of its parking space and into the courtyard of the school. And one of the history classes had barricaded the classroom with signs that said "Vive la réforme" when the class studied the French Revolution. Lots of people got their houses toilet papered. She bet Britta had. But people took Meredith seriously. "You have nice friends."

Harmon placed the blondies between them. It was dusk, so the movie would start soon. "How about you? I don't know anything about you except you're kind to animals and look cute in a bathing suit."

Meredith felt her face warm. No one said things like that to her.

"What do you like to do?" he asked. "Like, if a job application asked for your hobbies, what would you say? Three things."

"Oh, that's easy." She'd been working on her resume practically since birth. "I'm on—"

"Not stuff you think sounds impressive to colleges. What do you actually *like* to do?"

That was harder, and Meredith hesitated. "Three things, huh?"

"I'd settle for two good ones."

Meredith thought about it. "Okay, well, first off—and this is going to sound super nerdy, but—I'm on the bowling team." Harmon started to speak, but she interrupted him. "Now, I know what you're going to say. It started out as a resume thing.

My mother thought I should be on a team, and my freshman English teacher coached bowling, so I did that. But I'm actually good at it. Also, if I'm mad at someone, I can think about them when I'm throwing the ball."

"Ha. Good thing you don't know Krav Maga." He mimed a right hook.

"Krav Maga would look really good on my college applications, though."

"I never think about that stuff."

"Everyone I know thinks about that kind of thing all the time."

Harmon nodded. "We are very different. So what's your high score?"

"I broke two hundred once, two oh two." Meredith found it hard to keep the pride out of her voice. "But usually, in the low one fifties. I was second team all-county last year. But the funniest thing is, when I was in grade school, I went to a bowling birthday party, and I got the highest score of anyone there."

Meredith smiled, remembering. It was in fifth grade, the last year people invited the whole class, which was why she'd been invited. She'd barely known the birthday girl.

"I only got an eighty-five. I was probably the only one taking it seriously. So the bowling alley gave me a bowling pin as, like, a trophy to take home. The birthday girl was mad. She said, 'Eighty-five's not even that high a score.' I said, 'It's higher than you got.' So that ruined my social life for the rest of fifth grade. I didn't care, though. I'm a little competitive."

"You?" Harmon looked pretend shocked.

"Is it that obvious?"

"Well, yeah. You only noticed me when you thought I had a girlfriend."

"That's not true exactly." She had definitely noticed Harmon before that. How could she not? But she probably wouldn't have looked at him in Miami. Why was that?

"Exactly?" he asked.

"It would be hard not to notice you, the way you were stalking me."

"I was not stalking you. I had a perfect right to—"

"Okay, but you showed up a lot," she said.

"Coincidence."

Meredith gave up. "You're not the type of person who's usually interested in me."

"How so?"

Of course he'd ask. How could she say that handsome, popular, fun guys usually thought she was a boring nerd without sounding like a boring nerd? Or, even worse, like she thought he was dumb, which, she was starting to realize, he wasn't at all.

Finally, she said, "I guess I don't really know anyone like you."

"What am I like?"

Busted. "Can I have a blondie?" *Or buy a vowel?*

"Absolutely." He handed her the container, and she chose a big, fat one.

She took a bite. "Wow. It lives up to the hype." She hoped maybe he'd forget his question. He'd been right about the drive-in not being a particularly intimate date. In the car next to them, two little boys were fighting, and one of them was trying to climb onto the roof.

"So what am I like?" He hadn't forgotten.

"You just seem like you have a lot of fun."

"Don't you?"

"I guess. But all my friends are obsessed with the future, and I've gotten that way too. Like I thought coming up here would be a good opportunity to work on college essays. You can't just write about something normal, like volunteer work or your favorite teacher. You have to be 'unique' and 'interesting,' like write an essay about Target. Or maybe do it in the viewpoint of a squirrel or in the form of interpretive dance, something like that. My friend Lindsay said I was lucky that my dad was dead because I could write about it."

"Sheesh." He looked down. "Sorry about your dad."

"I know. But on the other end of the spectrum, a lot of people at my school don't seem to *care* about anything. Like they take videos and selfies and work out and watch *Real Housewives*. Those people don't like me."

"Maybe you just think they're like that because you don't know them."

Meredith took another bite of blondie. She'd probably thought Britta was like that before she knew her. But she wasn't. Maybe everyone had an inner life. Some people were just jerks about it. Finally, she said, "Maybe." The kid in the next car had ascended the roof.

"So you figured I was shallow?" he asked.

"I don't know. Maybe I'm shallow." She breathed deeply, enjoying the cool night air.

"Shallow people probably don't think they're shallow. They don't worry about it at all."

"True." She'd never thought about it that way.

"I totally get what you're saying about being good at something you're not usually good at. When we learned to read, I was in the bluebirds group, when all the smart kids were redbirds. And I wasn't even the smartest bluebird. Turned out I had dyslexia, but the school didn't figure it out right away, and even when I got help, reading wasn't my favorite. Like, I wouldn't read if I could do something else, like playing with my dogs or collecting rocks or, you know, staring blankly into space, because that was still more fun to me than reading."

Meredith laughed even though she loved reading. "That's how I felt about PE."

"But then, in fourth grade, my teacher gave me this book about a kid named Hank Zipzer. He had dyslexia too, but he was smart, and he was always doing silly things like putting his report card in the meat grinder. I was obsessed with those books. Even though it still took me longer than it took other people, I read all of them. They made me feel less dumb about reading—the same way bowling makes you feel less dumb about sports."

"Exactly." Meredith felt a little guilty because, in elementary school, she'd always judged those bad-at-reading kids. But now, some of them were in AP Calculus. "Is being dyslexic why you're so good at photography? Like, do you see things differently?" She finished the last bite of her blondie. She kind of wanted another one.

"Maybe. They say people with dyslexia make good photographers. But I don't know if what I see is different than what you see."

"I'd love to see your photography."

"I'll have you over and show you."

The movie was starting. Harmon took another blondie and offered the container to Meredith. When she started to take one, he said, "Oh good, I was worried you'd think I was a pig if I had two."

"I wouldn't even think you were a pig if you had three," she whispered.

"Done." Harmon took a third. As he did, his hand brushed hers. Everything was quiet now, even the kids in the next car, except for the big radio Harmon had brought to hear the movie, which was about a gang of animals who get lost (as gangs of animated animals tend to do). The air was cool, and Meredith shivered.

"Need a blanket?" Harmon whispered. "I brought one. I just didn't want you to think I was . . ." His voice trailed off.

"I'm okay for now." She wasn't about to lie down in a truck bed with a boy with blankets. She resolved not to shiver. It was July! But the more she thought about not shivering, the colder she felt, until she was shivering from the effort of not shivering.

She tried to watch the movie. Someone was chasing the animal gang down a street.

She shivered, then tried to turn the movement into a laugh.

Beside her, Harmon laughed too. "You like this movie?"

"It makes me nostalgic." As she said it, she realized she hadn't seen the previous movie with a friend or even her mother. She'd watched it at school, after some standardized test. She was actually nostalgic for school. What a weirdo!

Harmon nudged her. When she turned, she saw that he was holding out his hoodie.

"Oh, no, I don't—"

"You're shivering so much I can't concentrate."

The cartoon lion was pretending to be fierce. Meredith pulled the hoodie over her head. It was feather-soft and smelled of air and pine needles and some sort of masculine deodorant. She inhaled deeply, then side-eyed Harmon to see if he'd noticed. He didn't seem to have. She was wearing a guy's sweatshirt. She'd have to give it back. Spider would freak if she saw it. It had the name of Harmon's school on it. Besides, it wasn't like he was her boyfriend.

Still, it was very warm.

Suddenly, a woman's scream ripped through the night air. Then, crying. The kid in the next car! He'd fallen off the roof!

Before Meredith could even say it, Harmon had jumped out of the truck bed and was rushing over. Meredith heard him ask if the boy was okay, heard the boy yell, "My leg!" Meredith ran to join them. She saw the boy's leg was strangely bent out of place.

"We need a doctor!" the mother said.

Harmon looked at Meredith. "Go get my brother! Do you remember where he was?"

"He's a doctor?" Meredith said, surprised.

"Yeah, a pediatrician. The blue CR-V." He pointed.

Meredith hustled toward the car. When she got there, she knocked on the window.

"Hi. I'm Meredith, Harmon's friend. There's a little boy who might have a broken leg."

Colt was out of the car. "I'll come look. Can you stay with the kids?"

Meredith nodded and took his spot in the driver's seat. Daisy was beside her, and Noah in the back seat. "Hi," Daisy whispered.

Meredith had lost the thread of the movie, but she tried to watch it anyway. Noah leaned his face between her and Daisy. "I get to be in front for the second movie," he said.

"Got it." Meredith wondered if Harmon was coming back soon.

"Is that Harmon's sweatshirt?" Daisy asked, a little accusingly.

"Um, yeah. He let me wear it. I was cold."

"Isn't he cold?"

"He said he wasn't." He probably was cold, out in the night air with his brother.

Daisy quieted down and watched the movie, nestled against Meredith's arm. The movie was short, so it was almost over when Harmon came back and knocked on the window.

"Hey, sorry. Colt's helping take the boy to the hospital," Harmon whispered. "He asked if we could bring the kids home."

"Sure."

"I know it's sort of a bust. We could just stay for the first movie, and—"

"No, we can't!" Noah yelled. "I get to sit in front for the second one!"

"It's fine," Meredith reassured him. "We can stay."

"I'll make it up to you." Harmon took his seat in the back with Noah.

Both kids were asleep by the time the second movie started. Harmon scooped Daisy up and carried her to the back seat. Meredith waited until Daisy was safely in back before saying, "Look at you, uncle-ing. That's so cute."

"That's me, Mr. Cute." He pulled the car out slowly, careful of people on lawn chairs.

"So your brother's a doctor?" she asked.

"Yeah, we have those up here, hospitals too."

"I wasn't saying you didn't. I just thought it must be hard to have six kids and send one through med school."

"Colt was always the smartest one. He was in college when I was a kid, got a full ride to SUNY Albany. Teachers always asked my older brothers if they were related to Colt, but by the time I came around, they knew I was one of those wild Dickinsons— my brother Brodie once rode a motorcycle down the hallway at school—so I was neither the smartest nor the craziest."

247

"That's nice, though." Meredith wondered if her teachers would remember her when she was gone. Probably not. In a big school like hers, there was always another Meredith coming up behind her. She wondered what it would be like to have people know her for her.

They pulled into the driveway of a colonial-style house. Harmon's sister-in-law came out, and together, they carried the kids inside. When Harmon returned, he said, "Okay, so this wasn't the most fun date you've ever been on. Can I have another chance?"

"It was fun." It was her most fun date considering it was her first date that didn't include Alaric and his SAT printout. Also, Harmon was nice. "Yes, I'd like that."

Harmon pulled out of the driveway. It was dark and quiet.

"Friday night, then?" he asked. "Same time, same place?"

Meredith listened to the sound of tires on the empty road. "The other movie?"

"Nah. Maybe next week. Friday's a new moon." He said this like it meant something.

"Are you going to tell me what the plans are?"

"I'd rather surprise you."

Meredith supposed if he'd intended to murder her, he wouldn't have introduced her to his extended family, so she said, "I like surprises, nice surprises."

"It'll be nice. Bring my hoodie. It might get cold."

Meredith touched the hoodie. "Oh, I'm sorry. I can give it back."

"No, keep it. That way, you can't cancel on me." He pulled onto the street that led to the house. "Do I get to drive you all the way back, or is Spider staying up to call you out for dating me?"

He'd known why she had wanted to meet at the hill.

"You can drive me back. I don't care what she thinks."

"You cared earlier."

"I didn't know you earlier."

"If you did, you'd know my mother didn't raise me to dump girls off half a mile from their door—or pick them up there either."

"I could tell that." Finally, they reached the house, and he came around to open the car door. She waited this time until he got there and offered his hand. It felt big and a little rough, a man's hand, and as she squeezed it, Meredith wondered if he was going to kiss her.

Instead, he said, "Look up."

She did and saw what he meant—so many stars, even more than the first day they'd met.

"Wow." She realized she'd been holding her breath. Also, she could hear his breathing.

"There'll be even more Friday, darkest night of the month."

He put his arm around her shoulder and led her to the door. What was she supposed to say? Thank him for the date? Tell him she'd had a nice time? She'd never been at a loss for words before, but now, alone with Harmon under a circus tent of stars, they failed her, and she almost wanted to burst out in a chorus of "Twinkle, Twinkle, Little Star" or something. She wanted to say *something* to make the evening last longer.

"I'm really . . ." She felt his side pressed against hers. She thought she could feel his heartbeat. Then, she realized he was shivering. "You're freezing, aren't you?"

He laughed. "Just a little."

"You're freezing, and you're too polite to ask for your hoodie back, but you want me to go inside so you can run to the car."

"Run makes me sound like a wuss. But otherwise, yeah."

"Okay." She slipped out from under his arm and hurried up the steps. "What time?"

"Same time."

He waited for her to open the door, go inside, and close it. The house was dark and, once inside, she hurried to the living room window. Despite the darkness, she could barely make out his silhouette. He stood there a moment longer. Finally, he turned and walked to the car. Meredith watched, nose buried in his hoodie, until his taillights disappeared into the night.

34

Britta

BRITTA HAD GONE to bed at eight and pretended to be asleep in broad daylight, to avoid Spider. But really, she'd been awake, sitting up on the quilted chipmunk pillow she'd purchased at that lady's house, reading the old hiking book and listening to the click of Rummikub tiles. She wanted to play too. But she didn't want to deal with Spider and her mood swings. This was supposed to be a vacation, not a sentence.

She had also stayed up late enough to realize that Meredith had done more than take a walk last night. Unless she'd walked to Albany. Britta bet she was out with that guy!

She'd finally fallen asleep close to midnight.

Britta wasn't someone who held grudges. She could have a fight with a friend and, the next day, embrace her and let her borrow her favorite top, as if nothing had happened. But she knew most people weren't like that.

That was why it surprised her when Spider greeted her with, "Hey, Britta, do you like blueberries or chocolate chips in your waffles?"

"Um, chocolate chips. Why?"

"Ruthie and I are making waffles. Hold on. I'll tell her."

Then, after she sat down to a perfect Belgian waffle, which she was sure Ruthie mostly made, Spider said, "Are we going hiking today?"

Depends. Are you going to make me want to hurl myself from the mountain?

But Britta didn't say that. She wanted to go hiking. She needed the exercise and, besides, what was the point of coming here if she was only going to sit in the house?

So she said, "I guess," because she wasn't going to give in that easily.

"Come on." Which was what people said when they didn't want to say please. "Meredith's still sleeping. She came in at, like, midnight from her 'walk.'" She made air quotes around the word *walk.*

"Yeah, I noticed." Britta went into gossip mode. "You think she was out with Bat Boy?"

"Ugh, I hope not. Anyway, she's asleep. And Kate's babysitting, and I can't go alone."

"So what you're saying is, you don't want *me* to go and talk or anything; you want *somebody* to go in case you break your leg?"

"Yes." Spider hesitated. "No. Okay, I want whatever you want. If you want to be there in case one of us falls off a cliff, that's fine, but if you want to chitchat, I'll do that."

People only said *chitchat* if they found her annoying. "Politely?"

"Sure. Of course. Why would I go out hiking and argue with you?"

"You've been arguing this whole time. What would we talk about?"

Spider shrugged. "Hiking things."

Britta waited.

Spider acted out, "It sure is beautiful weather. How much farther do you think it is to the top? Did you see that rock or tree that looked like an animal?"

Despite herself, Britta laughed.

Spider said, "My sister always thought she saw a mountain lion, but it never was one. Also, we could talk about actual animals we see."

"Will we see any actual animals?" Britta's interest was piqued.

Spider shrugged. "Chipmunks. Some birds. But I've never seen a moose or a bear, if that's what you mean."

That was what Britta meant. She was thinking about the Abercrombie and Fitch logo, a moose. "We don't have chipmunks in Miami. That sounds cute."

"There's a hundred-percent chance we'll see cute chipmunks," Spider said. "Please?"

She was saying *please*. Britta had bargaining power. "Okay, but . . ." How to put this? After what Spider had said about her arthritis, Britta was worried that Spider was overestimating her own abilities, wanting to hike such a tall, difficult mountain. What if she hurt herself with only Britta there? "Could we maybe try an easier hike? There are no hills in Miami, and I'm kind of out of shape." Britta was lying. Sure, there were no hills in Miami. But there were treadmills, and she could run an eight-minute mile on an incline on one of those. But Spider didn't know that. "I was looking at this guidebook and found this great trail."

She slid the book across the table. It was open to a page about Buck Mountain, a trail the guidebook said was a little easier, and which looked close by. "There's a waterfall."

"No fire tower." Spider flipped to another page. "How about this one?"

Someone had made notations such as "sheer rock" and "straight uphill." They'd definitely end up hanging from a cliff, surrounded by buzzards, like in a cartoon.

"I've never seen a waterfall," Britta said.

Spider hesitated, so Britta added, "Please."

Finally, Spider conceded. "I guess so." She picked up the plates. "There was actually something I wanted to talk to you about too."

Now it was time for Britta to wonder what that might be. But she didn't ask.

35

Kate

HOW HARD COULD it be? That was what Kate had thought when she'd offered to take care of Ray, Ray-Ray, Racecar? How hard could watching one little kid for a few hours a day be? Play a few games, maybe read the kid a book. Then, down for nap time.

Turned out five-year-olds didn't take naps. At least, not willingly and not naps that lasted more than two minutes at a time, which wasn't even worth the effort it took to make that happen. Better to let the kid run around in circles until he dropped from exhaustion. At Kate's suggestion, they were playing "the floor is made of lava," hopping from the half-sectional sofa (the other half was missing) to an ottoman to a sort of precarious-looking rocking chair over and over and over. At this rate, it might be Kate who collapsed.

Ray-Ray jumped onto the rocking chair, catching the seat with only half his flip-flopped foot but managing not to fall.

This time.

"Careful!" Kate said. "Maybe flip-flops aren't the best shoes for this!"

"Can't change 'em."

"Why not?"

"The floor's made of lava!"

It felt like lava. The wall-unit air conditioner had tape over the controls and a sign that said "Don't even think of turning on if temp is under 85 degrees." The temperature, per Kate's phone, was eighty-four. It didn't seem to bother Ray-Ray. Lizzie didn't "feel comfortable" with bringing Ray-Ray to the cabin, as Kate had suggested, so they were in this tiny house with an assortment of broken baby items, a hutch with no rabbit, and a weedy backyard. Kate wondered why she'd thought it was a good idea to spend her vacation here.

Oh yeah, to be nice, maybe out of some weird sense of guilt over Daddy.

At least it wouldn't be that long. Since it was Independence Day, Ray-Ray's father was working a half day. He'd be home by two. Kate glanced at her watch.

Nine twenty-five.

Ray-Ray skipped past her on the sofa, again barely making the leap to the rocker.

"Let's play a different game," Kate said.

"The floor's lava!" Ray-Ray leaped to the coffee table.

Why hadn't she remembered how difficult boys could be? Oh yeah, because they'd had a nanny. Any romantic imaginings she'd had about watching her brother were just that.

Kate caught him before he made the next jump. "Oh, I just realized the floor solidified. You can walk on it now. See?" She took a few teetering steps.

"Awww."

"Hey, you won!" He struggled against her. "Now stop before you split your head open. Let's play hide-and-seek."

"Okay." He stared at her, and she realized he'd never played before.

"I'll hide. And you count to . . ." She thought. "How high can you count?"

"A hundred."

Kate doubted that. "Maybe we should just count to twenty."

"A hundred!"

"Okay, a hundred." Because why discourage him, and at least she'd get a break. Kate established the oven as base, chose an easy spot behind his bedroom door, and waited.

It did not take long (he didn't get close to a hundred). In fact, Kate had barely managed to catch her breath when he was at her knee, yelling, "Caught you!"

"You did! Now, you hide." She only had to do this about five hundred more times.

In light of this, she decided she actually was going to count to a hundred. Maybe he'd learn from it. She used the opportunity to wash the dishes Lizzie had left soaking in the sink. It couldn't be healthy for a child to grow up in such depressing clutter. She took her time finding him, looking first in the master bedroom, saying, "I wonder where Ray-Ray could be!" so he could feel like he'd accomplished something. Then, she tried the bathroom. She was rewarded when he dashed past her, giggling, on the way to the kitchen, yelling, "Yah! I'm a rocket!"

"Guess I'll have to be 'it' again!" She'd count even more slowly this time.

The second time, she'd finished about half the dishes when her phone rang. She'd kept it on in case Britta or Spider fell off a mountain, hiking. Kate glanced at it.

It was Mother. She ignored it. She didn't know what to say.

It was harder to find Ray-Ray this time. She looked under his bed and in the closet, then under Lizzie's bed, behind all the doors, and in the master bedroom, which was even messier, even in the garage. It was there, in the garage, that she heard something, pounding on the roof.

She opened the door that went to the backyard. "Ray-Ray?"

A tiny giggle from above. "Ray-Ray!"

She spied a ladder leaning against the house. "Ray-Ray? Are you up there?"

She glanced up. He was lying on his back on the roof. Fortunately, the roof was not that high-pitched, but he could still fall. "Ray-Ray, don't move." She grabbed a ladder rung.

He rose. "I'm a rocket!"

She pictured him swan-diving to the lawn. "Don't move." Hand over hand, she climbed the ladder. "Stay right there.

Stay . . ." She tried to remember where rockets sat. They'd been to the Kennedy Space Center in Florida once, when her brother, Blake, had wanted to be an astronaut. "Stay on your launchpad. We haven't counted down yet."

"Count down!" he yelled.

"Do you know how to count down?" She figured he wouldn't, but he started.

"Ten . . . nine . . ."

She scrambled up the ladder as he was saying, "Eight!"

"Got you!"

"No!" He screamed in mock terror. She'd forgotten what fun hide-and-seek was.

"That's where I used to hide from Mommy!" he said. "To see the stars."

"Oh, I thought you never played hide-and-seek before."

"I just hided."

That was weird. Or not weird. Maybe his mom was scary sometimes or yelled. Poor kid.

"Don't go on the roof anymore. You can't see stars during the day."

The phone buzzed three more times while she was hiding. Finally, when it was her turn to be "it" again, she picked up.

"Hello?"

"Do you know what people are saying about us?" Her mother's voice.

Kate was about to say she didn't care, but that wasn't true. She did care. Caring was ingrained in her, like a dog who can always find the way home at sundown.

She sighed. "What are they saying?"

"What?" As if she hadn't expected Kate to ask. Kate wondered how many times Mother had called when she had no service. "Well, some of them are saying you were in on it."

"In on it?"

"Your father's . . . activities. They're saying you were some sort of a . . . conduit."

Kate stood silent, stunned. Then, she didn't know why she was surprised. She knew these people, knew they loved gossip and thrived on schadenfreude, pleasure at the misery of others.

"You know that's not true." She hoped her mother would say of course she did. That's what mothers were supposed to say.

Instead, she said, "I don't know what to believe, Kate. I believed in your father. And now, people are being so awful." Kate tried not to notice the catch in her mother's voice.

"What people?" She didn't really have to ask. She knew all their friends were awful.

"Well, the Davises, and the Olivers. Betsy Oliver called the night of bunco to let me know she could get a sub if I didn't feel up to attending."

Kate frowned. Greer Oliver had been one of her close friends. She hadn't called since the news broke. Kate looked around at the filthy, depressing kitchen. Her mother was saying, "Colin Blackwell's come by a few times."

"Colin? What does he want?"

"He wants to see you, know where you've gone. He says to

tell you he cares about you. And he said something else, something I didn't understand."

"What was that?" Kate walked over to the sink and swirled a scrub brush against a pot with cooked-on mac and cheese.

"I wrote it down. He said, 'Add astera for aspera.'"

Ad astra per aspera. They'd learned that in Latin class, "To the stars, through difficulties." Kate brushed harder. It was the perfect thing to say. But he was just trying to get her to call him. He just wanted gossip. She remembered her mother laughing at the Linds. People loved awful rumors. Everyone was just waiting for someone's kid to get a DUI or get kicked out of prep school, so their screwup kid would look good in comparison.

Suddenly, she felt a snap and droplets of water flew up over her. "Oh!"

She looked down. She'd broken off the scrub brush.

"Kate? Are you still there?" Kate had no idea what Mother had been saying.

"What?" she said, looking around for the other half of the brush.

"You should come home. I miss you so much!"

"How would that help? I'd just be afraid to go out because everyone's talking about me." It was true. Even this disgusting, filthy house seemed better than Peach Springs.

The house! Ray-Ray! Kate realized she hadn't heard a peep out of him in quite a while.

She glanced around. "I have to go, Mother."

"Don't hang up on me."

"I'm sorry." She left her phone on the counter. She checked all around. "Ray?"

Nothing. She headed back to the kitchen, hoping he'd reached base.

He hadn't. Panic rising, she checked each bathroom, then yelled, "Come out, Ray-Ray! You win!" Nothing.

She went to the garage. He must be on the roof again. She stopped, staring. The garage door to outside was open. So he wasn't in the backyard, which he had accessed through a side door before.

A thousand swear words rose in her ears even as she heard her mother's voice telling her not to use such language. You can't stop me, Mother, she thought, grimly jubilant.

"Ray-Ray, are you out there? Please come out!" She tried to yell, but her voice shook. Lizzie had been right not to bring him to their place. He might have drowned in the lake.

Instead, they were near Route 9, with its speeding cars.

Kate ran to the front yard, yelling, "Ray-Ray! Ray-Ray!"

No answer. She dashed toward the road.

36

Spider

INT. WAY-TOO-SMALL CAR — DAY

Britta and Spider are in the car. Spider is
driving, while Britta is absorbed in her
phone, or pretending to be.

IT WASN'T AS bad as Spider had feared. Maybe because
the other two girls weren't there, or maybe because Britta had
sworn silence, she was pretty quiet. Once they reached an area
with service, she became absorbed in her phone, texting and
posting photographs.

Britta must have a lot of friends. Her phone buzzed contin-
uously.

After half an hour of silence, Britta said, "Can I ask how much farther?"

"Not far. Maybe another ten minutes. That's a good thing about it."

"I'm sorry we're not doing the fire tower."

"It's fine." The more Spider thought about it, the happier she was that they were hiking Buck Mountain instead. It would be her first hike of the summer, and she should work up to higher trails. She wouldn't admit that to Britta, but she could be charitable. "I think this will be a good first mountain for you."

"I'm looking forward to it."

Spider couldn't shake the idea that Britta was also being charitable to her. But she had no reason to think that, so she said nothing. Neither did Britta. It was longer than she'd thought, but finally they saw the brown-and-yellow sign that said "Buck Mountain Trailhead."

"Yay! I feel like we've already accomplished something," Britta said as Spider pulled into one of the few remaining parking spaces. Spider felt a little stiff from driving, so it took her a moment to get out of the car.

"Everything okay?" Britta asked.

"Perfect." Spider stretched her legs. She hated to admit that some of her mother's yoga moves of old actually helped. Stretching was essential. She just preferred to call it "lunging" rather than "warrior one."

"Oh, good idea." Britta started to stretch too. "Warrior one."

Spider winced. "Yep."

"Can you do dancer pose?" Britta balanced on one leg, the other bent high behind her.

"Um, no. I'll just stick with this." She bent her knees and thrust her arms out.

"Ooh, chair pose." Britta copied it. "My drama teacher starts every class with yoga."

"Oh, well, this isn't really . . . you're right. Terrific." Spider did a few perfunctory reps, then said, "Let's get going." She opened the trunk and removed her backpack, which contained water and a sandwich. She also took out a long stick she'd brought, one she'd found on a family hike years ago. She used it for balance and to reduce the stress on her knees. There were also special hiking poles made for that, but that would make her look like an old lady.

She saw Britta notice it, but she didn't remark.

"I could carry something," Britta said. "I mean, if you—"

"I'm not an invalid!"

"Sorry." Britta slung her backpack over her shoulder and strode toward the trailhead.

Spider hurried after her, but Britta was going very fast. She yelled, "You have to sign in."

Britta returned to the trailhead register, a wooden box containing a binder where hikers wrote down their plans.

"It's so they can look for your mangled corpse if you fall off a cliff," Spider tried to joke.

"Would that really happen?" Britta looked worried.

"No, it's not Mount Everest. And if it was Everest, they'd

just leave you there, frozen, if you didn't make it."

"You sure are pleasant."

"It's true," Spider protested. "I saw a documentary about it. There are over two hundred dead bodies on Mount Everest. It's too dangerous to—"

"Just stop. Stop talking about dead bodies." Britta opened the binder. "Awww."

Spider finally caught up to her. "What?"

"Look."

In the Comments section of the visitor log, someone had written, "I said yes!" The person below had written, "Congratulations!"

"Aw," Britta repeated. "I hope someday, someone proposes to me someplace cute."

Spider could have said something sharp about not waiting around for a man to make your dreams come true or, at least, point out that the engaged couple would never see the comment below theirs. But she didn't. It *was* cute, and she didn't want to ruin their day from the start. "Wonder if they're big hikers."

Britta wrote her name, the number of people in their party, and the time. In the Comments section she wrote, "First hike with a new friend!" and added a smiley face. Was she for real?

"Let's go," Spider said.

They started out on the trail. At first, it was pretty easy, almost flat, actually, and Spider regretted bringing the stick. Just something else to carry. Having the right shoes helped, and Spider had looked long and hard for hiking boots that didn't look orthopedic. But soon, it became a lot steeper and rockier, with places where it was hard to find a foothold. She dug the stick in to keep from slipping as they crossed a stream.

"Pretty hard, huh?" Britta was having no trouble. She had hopped across the stream and generally was like a fricking mountain goat. If anything, she was struggling to slow down for Spider. "Let's stop for water."

"I don't need to."

Britta plunked down on a flat rock. "I'm thirsty. Besides, if we drink the water, it's less to carry." She unscrewed the top. "But you can go ahead if you like. I'll catch up."

Spider was sure she would, but she said, "No, you're right. You should never leave a man behind." She took a big swig and stretched her legs. Beside her, Britta was doing the same thing. She had been blessedly silent most of the hike so far, only once pointing out a rock that looked like a T. rex. Spider was silent too, thinking about Ruthie. Britta had been right about hiking the easier trail, and she'd been right about Ruthie too. Spider didn't know which was harder for her to admit, but it was definitely hard to admit both of them at the same time. So, when Britta started to say something, Spider said, "Okay, we should go now." She stood.

"I was about to say I could use another minute."

Spider was pretty certain Britta could sprint up the entire mountain, so she said, "Take your time. I want to keep going."

"What happened to never leaving a man behind?" But Spider pretended not to hear.

Another little stream, another rocky place, another fall on her butt averted by grabbing a branch, another time Britta politely pretended not to notice. Britta had stayed behind for several minutes after Spider started. But soon, she was waiting as Spider struggled uphill. Spider realized Britta had been lying about being out of shape. The girl definitely worked out.

When Spider caught up, she whispered, "Listen."

"What?"

Britta cupped her hand and gestured toward her ear.

Spider listened. From above, she heard lapping, percolating water. The waterfall. Was Britta worried the waterfall would hear them and get scared away?

"It sounds pretty close," Britta said. "Let's go!"

"Go ahead." Spider surveyed a collection of rocks ahead, trying to figure out which route offered the safest passage, like Buttercup and Westley in the Fire Swamp in one of her favorite movies, *The Princess Bride*. Spider chose a log that didn't look too wet, then waited for Britta's perky ponytail to be far enough away that she wouldn't notice if Spider slid on her ass. She took a step. Fine. Another. Fine. Using the stick for balance. It was useful now, but when she planted it in a third spot, it slipped in the mucky brown leaves and Spider felt her foot slide out from under her. She landed on her rear and tobogganed down the mountainside. "Oh!"

"Are you okay?" Britta was already running (running!) toward her. Plus a family of two red-haired parents, three kids, and a dog, all (except the dog) wearing matching T-shirts that said "The McCoys," all (especially the dog, who didn't care about ending up in a puddle) more agile than she was, all saying, "Are you okay? Are you okay? Are you okay?"

"I'm fine!" It didn't come out as cheery as she'd intended. She pushed herself up.

"Are you sure you can get up okay?" Britta asked.

"I said I could," she snarled, then regretted her brusqueness, especially in the face of the three little red-haired children. "I mean, it's okay. It looks worse than it is."

Britta offered her hand, but Spider ignored it. "I'm fine. I'm fine."

She got to her feet with all of them staring at her. She hated this, hated pity of any kind, hated looking weak and pathetic. She wasn't. It sucked that her body made it seem that way sometimes, but in her mind, she was strong, stronger than anyone.

The McCoys' dog came over and licked her leg, and she realized she was bleeding. Great.

37

Kate

WHEN KATE WAS little, she'd had a Siamese cat named Rama, after a Siamese king. He wasn't allowed outside. Mother had him declawed, so he wouldn't destroy the antique Chippendale chairs Mother's grandmother had brought over from England, and Kate had to clean out his litterbox daily. But it was worth it when Rama curled between her legs at night and purred and purred until Kate fell asleep to the soothing sound.

Then, one day, Kate had awakened to find him gone. She checked the kitchen, the living room, even the Chippendale chairs. After a frantic hour, her father broke the news to her: Rama must have gotten out, and he'd found him on the street. "He looked real peaceful, honey. I'm sure it was quick."

Kate had never gotten another pet. Daddy had offered. Even Mother had told her about a friend whose dog had puppies, and her brother, Blake, had gotten one. But, to Kate, it wasn't worth the heartbreak.

That memory, Daddy's stricken face, her kitty—though she hadn't seen him—in the road, was what went through Kate's head as she dashed toward Route 9. How would she explain to Lizzie or their father that she hadn't watched Ray-Ray, that she'd been on the phone?

"Ray! Ray!" Her throat was raw, and she must look weird, especially as a stranger in a neighborhood that seemed to have few, if any, strangers. To add to the wild look, she ran first in one direction, then in the other, before realizing with some relief that he wasn't there. He was a little boy with short legs. He couldn't have gotten that far. She herself was winded. She jogged next door to check there.

That was when she saw a red spot up in the green-leafed tree, his T-shirt! He was in a treehouse behind the neighbor's house.

"Ray-Ray!" she screamed. "Ray-Ray, you get down from there!"

As soon as she said it, she realized her mistake. He started visibly at her voice, then disappeared. Had he jumped—or tumbled—to the ground? Kate searched for an opening in the fence, all the while screaming, "Ray-Ray! Ray-Ray!" in an unlady-like manner. Finally, she scrambled over the fence, something she hadn't done since she was maybe eight years old, and ran toward the tree.

He was still up there, but hiding, secure in the childish belief that, if he couldn't see her, she couldn't see him either. With a relieved sigh, Kate clambered up the wood-slatted ladder. She grabbed his arm. "Gotcha!"

He shrieked, leading her to wonder, for the first time, if anyone next door was home, if they'd yell at her or, more to the point, if they had any dogs.

"Come on, Ray," she whispered. "Get down."

"No!" He wasn't whispering.

"You can't stay here. It's not your treehouse."

"No!" he screamed, and struggled against her. Kate let go, fearing he'd fall. Up close, she realized the treehouse was old, dilapidated. With every move, the railing slats creaked, and she could see they were close to coming unmoored, despite the nails. She climbed the rest of the way up the ladder and grabbed Ray-Ray around the waist. He screamed and held tight to the railing as she pulled him out of the treehouse. "NO! NO! NOOOOOO!"

"Need some help?"

38

Britta

BRITTA KNEW EXACTLY how Spider felt. Sometimes she was clumsy too, and she wanted nothing more than to pretend no one had noticed. But was Britta supposed to let Spider bleed out to save her embarrassment? Still, she moved on, walking at a snail's pace, so Spider, now limping, could catch up to her.

When she finally did, Britta said, "I have some Band-Aids."

"I don't need Band-Aids."

"You do. It looks gross. You're scaring those kids." She gestured toward the McCoys, whom she'd let go ahead.

"They're way past us."

"We'll see them on the way down. We'll see other people. Plus you'll see me." She held the baggie that was serving as a first aid kit out to Spider.

Spider made no move toward her. "I'm fine."

Britta knew she should just move on, but she said, "What's the big deal?"

"I'll get it when we reach the top. Go ahead."

"God!" Britta moved as if to toss it to her, then thought better of it. "Why can't we just walk together? Why do you keep trying to lose me?"

Spider took another step, avoiding some slick leaves that Britta had almost slipped on a moment before. She planted her feet and her stick. It had been smart, bringing the stick. Britta had been looking for a good one the whole time.

Finally, she said, "I don't want you to see me fall, okay?"

Britta couldn't help rolling her eyes. "But we all fall, Spider. It's not that big a deal."

Spider reached the path where it was level. She caught up with Britta. "You don't."

"I don't fall? Of course I fall. I fall all the time."

Spider didn't answer and kept walking. Britta knew she didn't believe her.

Britta continued. "I literally fell in front of the whole school last semester."

"God, I hate when people say *literally* for emphasis."

"I didn't say it for emphasis, though I literally hate when people are snobby about that. But in this case, I did literally fall in front of the whole school—or, at least, all the people who fit in the auditorium. We were doing *Little Women*, and I was playing the youngest sister, Amy, who's sort of silly."

"Perfect casting."

"Shut up." Britta kept walking. "There's this scene where she comes downstairs in an old ballgown that doesn't fit, and when I did it, I tripped over the long skirt. I rolled down and face-planted center stage. People laughed so hard. Some of them thought it was part of the show, but all my friends knew it wasn't. And, for a minute, I couldn't breathe. I thought my nose was broken. But everyone just went on with the play, so I had to. Then, when I went backstage, instead of offering me an ice pack or some help, people made fun of me."

"That sounds really embarrassing," Spider admitted. She was managing to keep up now.

"It was. And as far as nonliterally . . ."

"Figuratively," Spider said.

"Figuratively, I've fallen a lot too. I flunked math. I'm going to have to take two math classes next year to graduate, and I don't want to tell my mother about it because she only cares about her stupid, pervy boyfriend who hits on me one minute, then acts like I'm annoying the rest of the time. So I'm so not perfect, but I'm also not someone who doesn't understand anything. I'm an actress. I have empathy for people. I . . . hey, look." She pointed ahead.

There it was. The waterfall, or at least a rushing river, ahead of them.

"We made it," Spider said.

"Yeah, we did! We did it." Britta felt a flood of pride and camaraderie, and also, the urge to take selfies and post them on Instagram. She'd set it so her mother couldn't see it. "Do you

275

want to stop for lunch here?"

Spider checked her watch. "I don't know. Maybe we should stop for a drink, definitely take some pictures. But I want to have lunch at the top. I mean, if that's okay."

Britta nodded. "It's okay." She kept walking. Spider followed until they reached the water. Then she started washing her bloody leg with water from the waterfall.

"I brought a towel." Britta offered it to her.

"Oh, thanks." Spider took it.

Britta removed her hiking shoes and dangled her feet in the water. Her toenails were painted blue. Suddenly, she felt a splash of cold water on her face. Spider!

"Hey!" Britta yelled. "Hey!"

Spider concentrated on applying a second Band-Aid to her leg.

"No big," Britta said, then splashed her back. The day was so beautiful and peaceful. She heard the flowing water and the wind in the trees.

"Hey, thanks for coming with me. I . . ." Spider looked down. "I appreciate that you came when no one else did."

"I wanted to come. We'll still do the fire towers."

"We can work up to them." Spider trailed her fingers in the water. "I talked to Ruthie."

Britta didn't answer, staring up at the filtered light coming through the trees.

"She and Janet, they were . . . you were right. They were special to each other. They were . . ."

The light hurt Britta's eyes, and she looked down. "They were in love?"

"Right. Their parents kept them apart. Janet's parents. They haven't seen each other since then."

"Wow." Britta had suspected it, but it was still so strange to think about. Britta breathed in through her nose. "That's tragic."

"I know. I guess that's how it was back then, but yeah." She shook her head.

Britta thought about it, the way she did when she was playing a role. Sometimes, she got caught up in the characters' emotions. At Thespian conference the year before, she'd done a monologue from *The Diary of Anne Frank*, and when it came to the line "I still believe, in spite of everything, that people are really good at heart," she couldn't keep from sobbing, even when Ms. Barfield said she was being melodramatic, because she was just so consumed with the sadness of it all. Now, thinking of Ruthie, she felt the same ache behind her eyes. She drew in a breath before saying, "And there's no way to find her now?"

"Ruthie said she tried."

"That's so sad."

They sat there another minute. Britta took a few selfies in front of the waterfall. She put her shoes back on. "Hey, do you mind if I take a picture of the two of us together?"

She was worried Spider would think it was silly, the way adults thought it was stupid to take selfies and post on Instagram. But Spider said, "Why don't we wait until we get to the

277

top? Then we can get someone there to take one of us with the whole valley in the background."

"Good idea," Britta agreed.

It was maybe half an hour to the summit, and they walked it together. When they reached an area where they had to use their hands, Spider held Britta's backpack while she did it, then tossed her own to Britta for her final ascent.

Then, they were there, atop the rocks, the clouds, above the entire world, below only the round, blue sky, above the aching beauty of July.

"I never want to leave," Britta said.

Spider said, "I never want to walk down those rocks."

Britta wanted to say she'd help her, but she knew that wasn't what Spider wanted to hear. Instead, she said, "We can stay awhile, anyway."

39

Kate

"NEED SOME HELP?" It was a lady's voice. Kate, startled, loosened her grip on Ray-Ray's waist. He scrambled to the other side of the treehouse.

"Oh!" Kate looked down. It was an older woman, at least in her sixties, with a face like a pink pincushion. "I'm so sorry. I turned my back for a second, and he ran into your yard. Come on, Ray-Ray." She tried to make her voice firm.

"No!" he said.

"We can't just stay in this lady's yard."

"Mind if I give it a try?" the woman said.

Kate shrugged like, *Do I have a choice*, and came down the ladder.

The lady replaced her. "Racecar—you must get down from the tree."

Ray-Ray seemed unimpressed, clinging more stubbornly to the far side of the treehouse.

"Don't you ignore me, young man. That is *my* tree, and I am telling you to come out of it. Your father will be very angry when he comes home."

"My mother's asleep!" Ray-Ray said.

The woman nodded. "I know. And this nice young lady who is watching you was very worried when you ran away. I heard her yelling, and that's what brought me outside."

Ray-Ray didn't seem to care.

"Well, stay if you like then. But I have some lovely brownies I just baked, and if you come down, you can help me eat them."

Ray-Ray squished his lips together. Kate said, "You can't stay up there, Ray-Ray. Those boards are old. You could fall."

"That's true," the woman said. "The treehouse is from when my children were young."

"Come on, Ray-Ray." Kate wasn't sure it was a good idea to tell him to go inside a strange lady's home, but she obviously knew his name, Racecar. Also, it was better than trying to drag him out of the tree. "Your father will be home soon, and he'll wonder where you went."

"If you come down, you may have two brownies after lunch," the woman said.

This seemed to persuade Ray-Ray. At least, he started for the ladder.

"Hold on tight." Was this what it was like for mothers, always worried something bad could happen to their offspring?

Kate had a new appreciation for her own mother. For about a second. Her mother worried only because she viewed Kate as an extension of herself.

Finally, he was able to scramble down the ladder, and, to Kate's surprise, ran right to the lady. "Mimi!" Kate watched as they hugged. The woman looked at Kate. "I'm Mimi Steele."

"Kate. Nice to meet you, Mrs. Steele." Kate reluctantly followed the pair into the house.

The house was small but very neat. A man about twenty watched *SpongeBob SquarePants* on television while doing a maze from a book. He was short and blond and had Down syndrome. "Hello?" he said when they entered.

"Robert, we have visitors. You remember Racecar from next door, Lizzie's brother." To Kate, she said, "Robert works at the supermarket with Lizzie some days."

"Hi!" Robert waved, but he looked in a hurry to get back to his puzzle and show.

"And this is Kate," Mrs. Steele said.

Robert waved his hand in annoyance and gestured toward the television.

"Yes, you can go back to that. Maybe Racecar would like to watch with you."

Ray-Ray said, "Brownies!"

"I'm sorry," Kate said. "I was about to make lunch when he ran away." She'd actually forgotten all about it, but now Mrs. Steele had already offered the brownie as a bribe.

Mrs. Steele smiled at Ray-Ray. "We'll have a nice sandwich

and *then* the brownies."

Ray-Ray agreed to take a grilled cheese sandwich, and Mrs. Steele set out to making it while Ray-Ray settled down by Robert. One episode of *SpongeBob* had ended, and another started, with both Ray-Ray and Robert chanting "AYE-AYE, CAPTAIN!" along with the television. Television! Why hadn't Kate thought of that?

"So how do you know the Bittels?" Mrs. Steele was asking her.

"Oh, we just met, actually. I offered to watch Ray . . . Racecar, since Lizzie was having a hard time."

Mrs. Steele raised an eyebrow. "And she agreed?"

Kate laughed. "She said no at first. I think she only agreed because they were going to fire her from her job if she brought him again."

"Still more than I've been able to do." Mrs. Steele turned on the stove and added the butter. "I used to watch Ray-Ray all the time when his mother . . ." Her voice trailed off.

That piqued Kate's curiosity. "What did happen with his mother?" She kept her voice low. "He keeps saying she's asleep. I don't know what that means."

Mrs. Steele added the sandwiches to the pan. She looked over at Ray-Ray. In a low voice, she said, "I guess that's what they told him. His mother overdosed. This was a few weeks ago, maybe a month now. When they found her, she was unresponsive."

Kate felt her mouth form an O. "Overdosed on what?"

Mrs. Steele paused, as if trying to decide whether to say anything. She checked the bottom of one sandwich for doneness, then another. "Did you want a sandwich too?"

Kate nodded. "Thanks." She didn't know if Mrs. Steele was going to tell her more about Ray-Ray's mother. In fact, she respected Mrs. Steele if she didn't want to talk about it. She was so used to gossips. "You don't have to tell me if you don't want to. It's fine."

Mrs. Steele turned over the sandwiches that were on the stove. Then she started making another one for Kate. "He came over here because he was used to it, I suppose. I used to watch him all the time when Lizzie was at school and his mother was having trouble."

Kate thought she saw. "Oh, so that's why he ran over here to go in the treehouse." It also explained his easy way with Robert. "So his dad won't mind."

Mrs. Steele shook her head. "Oh, he'll mind."

"Why?"

Mrs. Steele took the two sandwiches she'd started off the grill, cut them in half, and brought them over to Ray-Ray and Robert. "Feet off the table! You know the rules!"

They both sat straight so Mrs. Steele could put down the plates.

"What do you say?"

"Thankoo," Ray-Ray said.

"Thanks," Robert muttered, waving his mother away from the television again. "Squidward sucks," he said to Ray-Ray before chomping his sandwich.

"Sucks," Ray-Ray agreed, then chomped his own.

Mrs. Steele walked back to the stove and started to grill the other sandwiches. She glanced at Robert and Ray-Ray. Still engrossed. To Kate, she whispered, "Someone reported Angie, that's Racecar's mother, to child protection. The police came to look for drugs, but they didn't find any. Angie accused me, and I wasn't able to have Racecar over after that." She sighed. "He was like my own little boy. All my children are grown now. Robert is my youngest."

"I can understand why you'd report it. You were just trying to keep Ray-Ray safe."

"But I wasn't the one." Mrs. Steele flipped both sandwiches. "I tried to mind my own business and watch him. Though considering the situation she's in now, she might have been better off if someone had done more."

Like everything else, this made Kate think of her family's friends, her old neighborhood. Had people covered up for Daddy? Were they right to do that, or had it made things worse?

Mrs. Steele finished the sandwiches. She gave one to Kate and gestured to sit at the kitchen table. Kate recognized the episode Ray-Ray and Robert were watching, where Pearl gets the Krusty Krab to sell salads. They were repeating "Saaaaa-laaad" behind her and giggling.

"Will his mother get better?" Kate asked in a whisper.

"I don't know. I heard from someone at the market that she came out of her coma, but I gather she's in bad shape." She looked back at Ray-Ray. "It's a sad situation."

"Yeah." Kate was amazed that people in such a small, beautiful town would have such bad problems. Then again, her small town was a regular reality show. Maybe everyplace was.

"I wish I could help. I love that little boy." Mrs. Steele took a bite of her sandwich and chewed. "If you're going to be babysitting, maybe you could bring him over to visit."

Kate ate her own cheese sandwich. Her mother never bought processed cheese. Clearly she'd missed out. Mrs. Steele seemed like a nice lady who just wanted to help. Also, she was going to be around after Kate had gone back to Georgia. "I'm not sure I can do that, if his dad doesn't want him over here. In fact, I should bring him back to the house soon."

Mrs. Steele shook her head. "I know you're right. It's a shame, though. Neighbors should help each other."

Kate nodded. She knew it was true. And she was helping, she realized. She was an actually good person. Sort of.

After lunch, Kate let Ray-Ray watch the rest of the episode before telling him they had to leave. Ray-Ray gave Mrs. Steele an extra-long hug, and she said, "You know you can come over whenever you want. Just be sure to *tell* someone before you leave." To Kate, she said, "Think about it."

Kate knew she would.

Kate got Ray-Ray settled onto the sofa at his own house, watching *SpongeBob* (the cable worked, thank God), and Kate texted Colin.

> You can tell everyone I'm fine. I'm up in the mountains trying to get away at this awful time. That doesn't mean I'm a criminal. Thank them for their concern.

She sent it, along with a photo of the Websters' house, to Colin. Then, she muted the conversation.

40

Britta

BRITTA LOVED CROWDS. Her middle school drama teacher told them to use the opportunity to people-watch, and Britta always tried to imagine people's stories. Despite the long walk from their parking space at a church to Canada Street in Lake George, where they'd gone to see fireworks, most people seemed happy, with little kids waving flags, old people shuffling along with their families, couples holding hands, dogs. Britta wondered if the dogs would freak out from the noise. She petted quite a few dogs, hoping it would help.

Spider trailed behind, shooting footage of the crowd with her camera, which Britta guessed was her own way of people-watching. In honor of the holiday, she was wearing blue instead of black jeans and a T-shirt that said "Meet me in Montauk" with red hearts.

"I miss the Fourth of July in Miami," Britta said to Meredith as they waited on line for takeout pizza. "Every year, we get together at my grandmother's house, all fourteen of us cousins. We watch the fireworks at the Biltmore."

"Fourteen cousins?" Meredith said.

"Some of them are second cousins. My grandmother roasts a pig and makes the Cuban stuff, and we have apple pie and hot dogs too."

"That sounds nice." Meredith didn't elaborate on what she usually did.

Britta didn't ask, in case it was nothing. "I guess when you grow up, you stop doing some stuff. It's sad, though."

They started back toward Shepard Park, where a band was playing. Ruthie had saved seats. Lake George was probably more "American" than Miami, but it was also a little tacky. Okay, a lot tacky. Thousands of tourists milled around in front of T-shirt shops and the House of Frankenstein Wax Museum. Britta studied the Jack and Sally tattoos on a couple ahead of them.

"Can you hurry her up?" Kate gestured at Spider, who was crawling along, still peering at her camera.

Britta shook her head no. No, she wouldn't piss off Spider at the beginning of a long evening when she was finally being pleasant. "We should wait for her."

Kate sighed. "The pizza will get cold."

Britta fell back beside Spider. "Whatcha doing?"

Spider waved her hand to silence Britta. She panned down

the street. Finally, she turned off the camera. "Just taking some crowd footage. Never know when I might need it."

"You're very serious about filmmaking."

Spider actually perked up. "Yeah. I won a contest online for a suicide prevention video I made. And I just entered a short-film contest. I should hear soon."

"That's so cool." Britta hoped she didn't get bad news. It would ruin her slightly improved mood. "You should put me in a movie."

Uncharacteristically, Spider laughed. "Okay. What would it be about?"

Ahead of them, Kate and Meredith were gesturing for them to hurry up. Britta ignored them. "Well, someone very beautiful, of course." She stepped over two Chihuahuas, resisting the urge to pet them. "And talented and funny."

"And a little full of herself," Spider said.

"Oh, definitely. Hey, they could be in this too." Britta looked for Kate. "Hey, Kate! Meredith! Control your FOMO and come back!"

Kate looked back. "Shush!" She waited for them to reach the crosswalk. "Didn't your mothers tell you it's rude to yell a lady's name in public?"

Britta looked at Spider, who nodded that, yeah, that was nuts. Britta said, "Nope. That must be a Georgia thing. As is calling people 'ladies.'"

"Well, I'm from Georgia, so don't do it, please." Kate sailed across the street.

Britta followed. "Kate, don't you want to be in Spider's movie? You could be the mysterious young maiden."

Kate began to answer, then stopped, a stunned expression on her face, like Britta's cat, Scooby, when Britta sang a high note too close. She backed up a bit, crouched down behind Meredith, and held the pizza box closer to her face.

"What's wrong?" Meredith said.

"Just walk faster," Kate said.

They did. And Kate got ahead of them when they finished crossing, walking in the opposite direction of Shepard Park, taking the pizza with her. Britta started to say something, but she felt Spider's elbow in her ribs. They kept going in their original direction.

When they reached the park, they found Ruthie, ensconced in the perfect location at the top of the hill in sight of the band and with an unobstructed view of the lake.

"How'd you manage this?" Spider asked. "We weren't that early."

Ruthie patted the ground beside her. "I am a woman of considerable charms. These young men . . ." She gestured toward a group of college boys nearby. "They were more than willing to share their space with me, especially once I told them I had four young ladies with me."

"Good job!" Britta held up her hand for Ruthie to high-five.

Ruthie did even as Spider said, "You didn't, did you?"

"No, I didn't," Ruthie said. "They were just being nice. Where's the pizza?" She surveyed the bags the girls had brought, full of canned soda and garlic rolls.

"Kate absconded with it," Meredith said.

"That doesn't sound like her," Ruthie said.

Just then, Kate showed up. "There she is," Spider said.

"And the pizza," Britta said, "not necessarily in order of importance."

Kate was still holding the pizza close to her face. She gestured to Britta's Miami Heat cap. "Can I borrow that?"

"Sure. My hair looks bad, though." Britta took off the cap and fluffed her hair.

"It's fine." Kate tucked her hair up inside the cap as best she could and glanced around.

"Is everything all right, Kate?" Ruthie asked.

Kate must have decided the coast was clear, because she calmed down. "I'm sorry. I thought I saw someone from home."

"Is that a bad thing?"

Kate glanced around again as Britta cracked open the pizza box. "It might be. See, no one knows I'm here, and the woman I saw was one of my mother's friends, Mrs. Scott. She's a huge blabbermouth who always brags about her daughter who lives in New York City."

"You mean you lied to your parents about coming here?" Britta asked. How weird if they both had.

"No. No, of course my parents know where I am. It was my father's idea, actually, to get me away from Peach Springs." She lowered her voice more. "I left town because of a scandal."

A scandal! Britta's ears perked up. "Are you pregnant? Is it a political opponent's son?"

"No!" Kate looked so sad that Britta abandoned hope of it being anything juicy. "It's my father. He took some money he shouldn't have."

Spider and Ruthie both said, "Like Bernie Madoff?" at the same moment Britta said, "Like Caroline's father on *2 Broke Girls*?" She used to love that show. Kate even sort of looked like Caroline, all classy and blond.

"Oh, no." Kate glanced around again. "Nothing as big as that. He didn't steal from people. They say he took a bribe, and it's in the papers, so he sent me away for the summer so I wouldn't have to deal with the whispers or be hounded by reporters. No one knows where I am, unless Mrs. Scott tells them." She stopped speaking and sat a little awkwardly.

"That sucks," Spider said. "I hate people."

So she'd sort of lied when she said it was her decision to come here. No wonder she'd been so cranky when they met. Britta wanted to reach over and give Kate a hug, but she worried Kate would rebuff her. "Yeah. That does suck."

Ruthie had no such compunction, for she reached over and wrapped her arms around Kate. Kate hugged her back, saying, "It's all right. I'll be fine." But Britta heard a catch in her voice. "It probably wasn't even her. Let's have the pizza before it gets cold."

She slipped away from Ruthie and fumbled for the pizza box.

"Good idea." Britta looked around for the paper plates. "It's getting dark. Uh, anyone do anything interesting today? Spider and I went hiking. It was beautiful."

"I went to the lake," Meredith volunteered.

"Um . . ." Kate took a slice of pizza. "The little boy I babysat for scared me to death today. He went on the roof because he likes to pretend he's a rocket."

"That's crazy," Britta said, appreciating the change of subject. "What if he fell?"

Spider was silent, pushing herself up to her feet to pan the crowd with her camera again. Britta tapped Spider's leg and gestured to the pizza, so as not to annoy her by talking.

Spider turned off the camera. "Oh yeah, thanks."

They sat, eating pizza, listening to the cries of children mixed with the strains of the marching band playing John Philip Sousa. Britta again tried to figure out the stories around her. Was the young couple nearby, him with a long, red ponytail, her with a punk haircut dyed blue on the sides, on their first date, about to become engaged, or on the verge of a breakup? She wondered what people thought about them, an old woman with four clearly unrelated girls.

"This music is so cheesy," the punk-rocker girl said to her boyfriend.

The red-haired boy answered, "Of course it's cheesy. That's what the Fourth of July in Lake George is about. I like it."

Finally, the band struck up "The Stars and Stripes Forever" (exactly as the band in Miami would have) and the first red, white, and blue fireworks filled the night sky.

41

Kate

KATE CLOSED HER eyes, hearing the silence of the night. Back home in Georgia, there would still be fireworks, homemade or store-bought, going off all night, set off by neighborhood boys, riling up the dog. Here, it seemed like that one display was enough for people. Now, it was silent, fireworks still dancing under her closed eyelids.

She'd confessed her deep, dark secret to girls she'd known less than a week—and they hadn't cared. Or, if they did care, they hadn't blamed her for it. Why had she told them?

She thought of poor Ray-Ray, whose mother was a drug addict. He'd suffer for that, as Kate would suffer for her father's conduct. Yet there, too, people wanted to help. Kate did. And Mrs. Steele next door. Spider had said she hated people, but they weren't *all* bad.

Maybe when the thing you dreaded most actually happened, it was a relief because it meant things could start getting better. It felt good, telling them the truth.

Kate decided to call her mother back tomorrow and find out what was happening with Dad, what she could do. Weirdly, she missed her mother.

With fireworks still behind her eyes, she fell asleep.

The next morning, she woke early, walked up the hill, and called her mother.

Her brother, Blake, answered the phone.

"Wait, why are you home? I thought you were at your computer thing." Her brother had left days before her for some fancy "program" at a college in Boston.

"Yeah, I ditched that."

"Oh, wow. Was that a mistake!"

"Nah." Hearing his voice, Kate could picture him lying on the floor, feet up on his labradoodle, Simon, in his mess of a room—he chased the maid off when she tried to clean it. Who knew if they had a maid anymore? "It was super boring, all these kids who thought they were geniuses. What kind of weirdo wants to go to school in the summer? It was just something for Mom to brag about me doing, and now, that's sort of shot, right?"

Good point.

"So, what are you doing at home?" she asked, feeling guilty that she wasn't there suffering with him. "And is Simon there?" For some reason, she wanted to make sure.

"Of course Simon's here," he said, and then, clearly talking to the dog, he added, "Aren't you, boy? Aren't you?" In his normal voice, he said, "The usual. Gaming, and I went to the Springs with Hamill and Trey yesterday."

Kate stretched her calves. "Mom let you? Their moms let them?"

"Yeah, Mom let me. If anything, she's happy they aren't kicking me out of their houses, with Dad being a criminal and all."

"Don't say that!" Kate stopped stretching. "So, should I come home?"

A pause, and she heard Simon moving around. "Quit it, boy." Finally, Blake said, "Why?"

"I don't know, because our family's in crisis, and our parents are suffering?"

"And you coming home would somehow make it suck less?"

He was such a jerk. "Make me feel better?"

"Or make everyone else feel more guilty. God, Kate, Dad screwed up, maybe Mom did too. Why should you suffer?"

Which totally pointed up the difference between older and younger siblings, Kate thought. Younger ones felt like everyone owed them. Older sibs felt responsible. But Blake wasn't wrong. If she couldn't do anything, why suffer, especially since Dad had paid for her to be here?

"Mother says people think I had something to do with it."

Another pause, and Blake muttered something Kate couldn't understand. Kate tried to take a deep breath. The air was cool and smelled like pine trees.

"People are gonna think stupid things no matter what you do. Better to live your life."

"Yeah, you're probably right." Kate did some lunges to keep warm. "Good talk, Blake."

"Don't sound so surprised."

"Tell Mom I'm good."

"Okay."

Kate hung up and jogged down the hill before she was tempted to call Colin.

42

Spider

```
INT. SPIDER'S BEDROOM — MORNING

Spider is lying in bed, unable to will
herself to move. If she died, would anyone
notice?
```

STIFF. LEGS STRETCHED out ahead of her in place, not because she wanted them there but because they wouldn't go anywhere else. They felt like they were bound by a kidnapper's rope.

Arms, slightly better. Slightly. Sitting on the ground last night—or, rather, going hiking on a day when she knew she'd be sitting on the ground at night—had been a rookie move. Now, she lay still one minute, two, rotating her ankles, stretching her shoulders, preparatory to rolling out of bed. At home, she'd have texted Mom to bring ibuprofen. As it was . . .

"Alicia!" Ruthie, overly cheerful, knocked on the door. "Are you awake? What do you want in your omelet?"

Ruthie had boundless energy for someone in her seventies. Omelets. What was next, running a marathon?

But Spider tried to keep her voice level. She didn't want to sound pathetic. "Ruthie, hi. I'm not hungry yet. Can you bring me my pills? And some water? Please?"

Ruthie cracked open the door. "Too much hiking?"

Spider waffled between saying she was okay and the truth. "I'm okay."

"Do you need help?"

Spider reached over to her nightstand and tried to push herself up even though she couldn't bend at the waist. "Drugs will help." But not enough. They just dulled it.

"I can bring up breakfast if you want."

"I'll come down later." Though she dreaded the stairs. Walking down stairs wasn't bad, a controlled fall. But then she'd have to walk up. Probably she should have taken the downstairs bedroom but, she realized, she didn't want to be isolated no matter how much she complained about the noise.

Speaking of noise . . . two minutes later, Britta was at the door. She didn't knock. She held out water and a bottle of pills. "Ruthie says should you take this with food?" Britta's voice was uncharacteristically soft, like someone visiting a cancer patient.

"It's fine." She held out her hand. Screw Ruthie for sending

Britta up to feel sorry for her when she'd just wanted a few minutes to herself.

"Sure." Britta placed the glass on Spider's nightstand. "Should I open the bottle?"

"I can do it." Some days, childproof caps were difficult, but today, her hands were okay. It was knees and back, mostly. She opened the bottle with what she hoped was a normal amount of effort. But, probably because Britta was watching, she took twice as long as usual.

Britta turned away. "I can leave. I just wanted to ask you something. It's about Ruthie."

Spider shook out the pill and dry-swallowed it, one of her talents. She wanted Britta to go. But it seemed even more pathetic to send her away.

"Shoot," she said, which was a Ruthie thing to say.

"Every time I'm in a crowd, like last night, I think about who else is there. There are so many people. Anyone could be there, like how Kate saw that woman from Georgia."

"Thought she saw."

"Thought she saw. But she might have seen her, all the way from Georgia. For all I know, the love of my life could have been there last night, like dragged by his parents."

"Uh-huh." Trying really hard not to tell her to go away. Britta had been nice yesterday. Spider could be nice for two more minutes.

"Or the love of *your* life," Britta continued.

"I guess." Spider sipped some water.

"And then, I started thinking, the love of Ruthie's life could have been there too."

Spider swallowed and waited for Britta to finish blahblah-blah. "Wait . . . what?"

"Janet. Ruthie doesn't know what happened to her. She could be anywhere, right? And you have the exact tool to find her."

"I repeat, what?"

"Your filmmaking." Britta gestured at the camera on the dresser. "Did you ever see the thing where the kid made a viral video to get his mother a boyfriend? Maybe you could make a video about Ruthie and Janet, to help them find each other."

"Um, how would that work?" She'd taken the pill, but now Britta's enthusiasm was giving Spider a headache. "I mean, how would anyone see it?"

"You made that suicide prevention video, right?"

Spider nodded, then twisted her neck.

"So how many views did that get on YouTube?"

"Um, I'm not sure." Spider knew exactly how many it had gotten, at least up until she'd left Long Island and Wi-Fi, seven hundred twenty-seven, which she thought was pretty good. But maybe Britta was one of those social media types with thousands of followers, who'd think seven hundred was nothing. "A few hundred?"

"Shut your mouth—you know it's more than that. I looked it up last night, and it had close to a thousand. And the video was incredible, by the way. I can see why you won."

"Oh . . . ." Britta watched her video? She'd had on headphones in the car on the drive back, and Spider had been enjoying the peace and quiet. If she'd known Britta was watching, judging her, she'd have freaked out. "So you liked it?"

"It literally made me cry. I shared it too."

"It made you cry?"

"Is that not what you were going for?"

The video had been teenage girls reflecting on their suicide attempts and how their lives had improved since then. She'd interviewed dozens of survivors for the script, and the girls in the scout troop her mother had forced her to stay in had acted it out. "Actually, I was going for people not killing themselves, but crying is also good."

"Anyway, it was *so* good, and if you got that many views, imagine what you'd get for a cool topic like true love."

Spider was just putting together what Britta was saying. "So you want me to make a video about my grandmother to help her find Janet?"

"Isn't that such a great idea?"

"But how would we get people to watch it?" Despite herself, despite the fact that it was Britta's idea and therefore bad, Spider was kind of excited. She could use her filmmaking to help Ruthie. "We'd have to tell Ruthie before we post it. I mean, she might not like it."

"Agreed. But let's make it first, so she can judge. You worry about the video, I'll research how to make it go viral. Can we go to town today and use the internet, maybe the library?"

Spider arched her back. Maybe. Like, maybe she'd get out

of bed today. The library seemed like a stretch. "Sure. Maybe tomorrow, though?"

"Okay. And hey, do you think they'd have any yoga DVDs we could watch on your computer? I'm really messed up from climbing yesterday, so I was thinking I'd start on a monthlong program of self-improvement, eat healthy, yoga in the morning, fresh air."

"I guess."

"And . . . you could join me if you wanted?"

Now Spider saw Britta's game. She was trying to help her without letting Spider know that's what she was doing. Spider had done enough yoga to know it wasn't going to cure her. Yet, somehow, she didn't mind that much.

"Yeah. We can probably do that. Just let me think. Maybe you can ask Ruthie to pretty please make me an omelet with cheese and onions? And, actually, I think we have yoga DVDs somewhere. My mom does yoga."

Possibly, a little happy baby would help her lower back, not that she'd admit it.

43

Meredith

Essay topic: What is your favorite recording?

A NEW MOON. Meredith had wondered why that was important in the days since Harmon had said it. Now, it was almost time to find out.

"Got a date?" Spider asked when she saw Meredith leaving that evening.

Meredith sucked in her breath through her teeth. Might as well just deal with it. "Yes, I do." Then, before Spider could pitch a fit, she added, "I like him. He's nice."

Spider shrugged. "No accounting for taste. Just thought it would be nice to all hang together."

"That would be nice. We will definitely all go hiking. But now . . ." There was a knock. "Oh, gotta go." Meredith opened the door and slipped out. Harmon stood there grinning.

"Perfect timing," she said. "I was just admitting I knew you."

"Maybe someday I'll get inside," he said.

Meredith laughed. "You were there when you caught the bat."

"As a guest, not an exterminator."

Meredith carried Harmon's hoodie. She'd worn a long-sleeved shirt in case he asked for it back. But he didn't ask. He wore a green fleece jacket that brought out the greenish flecks in his hazel eyes. When they reached the car, she said, "Where are we going?"

"See some fireworks." Harmon started the engine.

"Oh. The Fourth of July is over."

"Not that kind of fireworks," Harmon said.

Meredith had no idea what he meant, but after the other day, she decided to let the evening unfold. She trusted him.

At least, she thought she did. When he pulled onto Route 9, he turned north to an area even more secluded than where they were. "I was thinking, we should go bowling sometime," he said.

She laughed. "I'd kick your butt."

"I'm counting on it. I think I'd like to see you in your natural habitat."

Meredith thought that her natural habitat was more likely the library, but Harmon didn't have to know that.

"Besides," he said. "I bet you could kick some other people's butts if we played as a team. Sort of a secret weapon."

"I'd enjoy that very much," Meredith said.

They drove through a town smaller than the one where they'd gone to the supermarket, passing a group of teens clustered outside the lone pizza place. Harmon turned onto another rural route. Meredith saw nothing in the distance but road, trees, and hills. She wanted to ask where they were going but decided not to. She needed to take more risks in her life. Or some risks, at least.

After another five minutes, during which they saw few houses, Harmon turned onto a road that said "Farmer's Hill." The sun had begun to set, the sky to pinken. Harmon turned on his headlights and drove uphill. When they reached the top, he said, "Get out. Have a look around while it's still light. I'll set up my equipment." He took out his camera bag.

"Tell me if you see any stars," he added.

Meredith trotted to an open spot where no trees blocked her view. The clouds were turning red, and there were two mountains in the distance. She wondered how tall they were, how far. She surveyed the horizon for stars, like Harmon had said, though it seemed too early. Then, one appeared. Or maybe it had always been there, and she'd just noticed it, low in the sky between the two mountains.

She turned back and found Harmon right behind her. "Oh!"

"Sorry. Did I startle you?" He held the camera bag and tripod.

"I didn't hear you. I was so engrossed in looking for stars." She pointed at the sky. "I think I found one."

"That's actually Jupiter." He took a few steps back and put down the tripod. "It's out early this time of year. I'm going to set up a little farther back, but I thought I could take a picture of us before it gets too dark—if you don't mind."

He gestured that she should stand where she was, between the two mountains. Then he set up his camera a few feet away, explaining that there was a timer. He stood beside her and they smiled. At the last minute, she thought she should put her arm around him. Would that be weird? Instead, she leaned her head close in. The shutter clicked.

He went to look at it. "Perfect. I'll send it to you later."

"So now are you going to tell me what we're doing up here?" It hadn't escaped her attention that it was going to be pitch-dark soon.

"I forgot I hadn't told you." He picked up the tripod and moved it closer to where they'd been standing. Then he crouched down to its level and looked into the camera. "I'm photographing star trails."

"You say that as if I know what that means."

"You will soon." He adjusted the angle of the camera. "It's a sort of time-lapse technique where you take a bunch of photos of the stars at short intervals so you can see them change position. Then, you use a computer to stack the images." He rummaged in his backpack.

"This is like a foreign language," Meredith said.

He held out a photo. "It ends up looking like this."

The photo showed the night sky over a farmhouse. It looked

like a real version of Van Gogh's *Starry Night*, with swirls of white light filling the blue sky.

"You took that? It's beautiful." It was. Breathtaking. Meredith could do many things, but nothing artistic like this, and she was in awe of it.

Harmon straightened his shoulders. "I wanted to try tonight because you can see the most stars when there's no moon. Now, if you can help me . . ."

"How?"

He took her by the shoulder and led her close to where they'd stood before. "Stand right there and hold your head up."

She obeyed, and he trained the camera on her face.

"Why?" she asked.

"That's where the North Star will be. I came out here last night to check." He gestured that she could move. "Take a look through the lens."

She did. Through the lens, she could see two pines and a rock in the foreground, a mountain farther away. It all served as a frame for the red canvas of the sky. The sun was almost fully set, the stars beginning to appear.

"It looks cool," Meredith said. "But will you be able to see the trees and stuff?"

"Good question." Harmon pulled a flashlight, the big lantern kind, from his backpack. He propped it up, then turned it on so it shone up on the trees. Then, he went to his truck and brought out two folding chairs. He set them up behind his camera. "Have a seat, milady."

"You are quite the Boy Scout, aren't you? Always prepared."

"I brought a thermos of hot chocolate, in case you get cold."

"I think I'm okay for now." Meredith stuck her hands into the pockets of his hoodie, which she'd donned in the car.

"I see that. I came prepared anyway."

Meredith looked out at the trees, swaying in the sinking sun. "What do we do now?"

"We wait. Maybe I put on some music?"

"That would be nice."

Next thing she knew, Coldplay's "A Sky Full of Stars" filled the night air, wafting out over the darkling, fading world and out to the mountains, like the soundtrack of a movie.

Darkling. She'd actually thought that. No one, not even Meredith, used words like *darkling*, but the moment was so beautiful that it made her wax poetic, even in her mind.

"I'm gonna give you my heart," the Coldplay singer (Meredith didn't know his name; she was pretty proud of herself for knowing it was even Coldplay) sang against the setting sun.

"This is sublime." Meredith sighed.

"I love that you use words like sublime," Harmon said.

Meredith laughed out loud.

"What?" He sounded a little offended.

"It's silly. A minute ago, I was thinking that it was darkling. Then, I thought no one uses a word like darkling."

"No one but you." He laughed. "What does it mean, exactly? I mean, I think I can guess from context."

"It's basically a fancy word for 'getting dark.'"

"Darkling," he repeated. "Darkling. I'll have to think up reasons to say it. Hey, Mom, when's dinner? I see it's darkling outside."

She knew he was making fun of her a little, but she didn't mind. "The music is a nice touch," she said.

"I made a themed playlist." And sure enough, the next song was about counting stars.

He was wooing her, she thought, another crazy, old-fashioned word. And, because she was pessimistic, Meredith questioned it. Why? Why would he work so hard? For her? She couldn't imagine.

Unless he was just weird in a way that matched her weird.

She decided to draw in a deep breath and enjoy it, enjoy watching the sky fill with stars like a roomful of people gradually showing up for a meeting.

The next song was an old one, the one that began, "Starry, starry night."

"I know this is the theme of every middle school dance on the planet," he said. "But I thought it was cool."

"I never went to a middle school dance." She wasn't even sure they'd had any, other than the eighth-grade dance. If they'd had one, she'd probably have been in charge of it.

"Me neither," he said.

"Is that true? You seem like the type of guy who'd go to a dance."

"Maybe one. But my mother made me go."

The sun sank below the mountains as more and more stars

became visible. Harmon stood to press a button to start his camera. Meredith heard it click, and Harmon returned to his seat as the singer sang, "How you suffered for your sanity . . ."

"This is so dark," Meredith said. "The song. I never listened to the lyrics before." She'd always thought it was a romantic song. Now, she realized it was about Van Gogh's suicide.

Harmon nodded, and a few feet away, the shutter clicked again. "I know. That's why I like it. He was a dark guy, Van Gogh. An artist."

"Do you have a dark side?" Meredith said.

"I guess everyone does, right? Maybe artists most of all. It's hard to find the right balance where you're happy with what you're doing and still striving to do better."

Meredith settled back into her chair, listening and looking at the starry sky.

"Do you have a dark side?" Harmon asked after a moment.

She didn't answer, not right away. Harmon had been right. The sky was darker than dark, no moon at all, no lights in the distance like at home, and only the flashlight illuminating a short way ahead of them. But behind and all around them was blackness, and up in the sky were millions of stars. Every time Meredith thought she'd seen them all, she noticed something— hundreds of somethings—new. But she couldn't see Harmon's face in the darkness, and maybe that made it easier to talk, as if she was speaking to herself.

Finally, she spoke into the darkness. "Of course I have a dark side. My father died when I was little, and I guess when something like that happens, when someone says they're coming to get you at five and then they never come, that really messes with your trust. You know?"

He nodded. She could barely make out his outline inches away, but he didn't speak, waiting for her to go on. An electronic-sounding song came on. Its lyrics were about being made of stars.

She continued. "I don't mean trust people but, you know, trust the world. Trust that things will work out for the best, you know? Like, be an optimist. I don't know if everyone has a dark side. My friend, Britta—I don't think you met her—she seems like she just sees the best in people, assumes everything will be fine. And she's probably right. But me, I lie awake at night worrying. That's why I work my butt off in school and in activities, so I won't mess up. And when something goes right, I wonder, what's the catch? How will it fail?"

"What would happen if you didn't? Like, if you just did what you wanted?"

Violins filled the air and then, a soft voice. Nat King Cole. "Stardust." Man, he had really thought this out.

"I love this song," she whispered as Nat King Cole sang,

Now my consolation
Is in the stardust of a song.

"I'm glad," he said.

After a moment, she said, "But I was optimistic coming here this summer. Or, at least, I stopped being cautious."

"And how'd that work out?" His voice floated through the pitch-darkness.

She stared out at the sky filled with so many stars. "I'm up here, at the top of a hill, looking at stars with a handsome guy. Maybe I'll write that if a college application asks what I did the past two summers." Several of them actually did.

"Will you write that I'm handsome?" Meredith heard laughter in Harmon's voice.

"Probably not."

"What do you think of the guy?" he asked as an old big-band song came on. Meredith thought it was something about moonlight.

"I like the guy," Meredith said. "I like him a lot."

"Do you?" He leaned closer to her as the mournful clarinet filled the starry sky.

"I do." She leaned in toward him.

Their lips brushed. He pulled her closer, the trombones wah-wahed, the camera shutter clicked, the stars shone, and they kissed, standing simultaneously and embracing, enveloped in the music.

Out of the corner of her eye, Meredith saw a flash of red and blue behind them.

She twisted to look just as a white chrysanthemum shape erupted in the sky. "Wow. Literal fireworks when you kissed me." They must be left over from the Fourth.

"You see them too? I thought maybe they were just in my head."

"Then they're in my head too." But it was, Meredith had to admit, ridiculously perfect.

Harmon must have read her thoughts because he said, "Remember this moment the next time you think nothing works out."

"I will," she said as he kissed her again under the sky full of stars and the fireworks and the music of the darkness, and for that moment, she gave in to it, gave in to the sublimity of it all and didn't wonder, didn't question if there was a catch. There was no catch. For once, everything was perfect.

And Meredith thought, maybe this is the girl I'm meant to be, not the drone who does nothing but study, but a girl who kisses a handsome, funny guy on a perfect, starlit night.

44

Britta

IT HAD BEEN a week since Britta had suggested she and Spider make the video together, and they had become, if not friends, *friendly*. They got into a routine together. Each morning, they woke early and Britta did yoga (yes, DVDs still existed up in the boonies!) before breakfast. Spider joined her most days. Britta had initially suggested it to help with Spider's obvious but unspoken aches and pains. But Britta found that yoga relaxed her too.

Some days, Kate and Meredith joined them for yoga. Other days, Kate was off on some mysterious mission, and Meredith was out—even more mysteriously—with a boy. Knowing Meredith, Harmon was probably an SAT prep tutor or knew someone on the Harvard admissions committee. That was all she cared about.

After breakfast, if they weren't hiking, she and Spider planned their video, going through footage Spider had taken of Ruthie over the years. She had hours, days of it. She also had similar amounts of coverage of her siblings, kids at school, and her cat.

"Are any of the cat videos funny?" Britta asked Spider one day, sitting on Britta's bed, watching Spider's laptop. "Like, maybe you could build up a following with a funny cat video, then get those same people to watch your video about Ruthie."

Spider stretched out her fingers and grimaced. "That's your marketing plan? Cute cat videos?"

"Not my entire plan." Though she was still working on her plan.

"That's good, because Ilse mostly just lies there."

"Then why do you film her so much?"

Spider raised an eyebrow. "Duh. Because she's my kitty!"

It was pretty funny to hear her refer to "my kitty" while wearing a T-shirt depicting the *Psycho* shower-stabbing scene, but Britta said, "Oh, yeah, that is actually a pretty good reason. I miss my cat. You should have brought Ilse up here."

"She pukes in the car, or I would have."

"Another good reason. You're crazy logical today."

Spider hit Britta with the chipmunk pillow she'd bought from the quilt lady.

"That was completely unprovoked!" Britta said.

Late mornings, they did more of that, or they went to the old, mildew-smelling town library to use the internet and research how to make a video go viral. Some ways were easy (release it on a Monday or Tuesday! Make it short!). Others were harder (give it a viral title). Others were harder still, like figuring out who would want to share their video.

"It says, figure out products that might tie in with your video," Britta said, looking up from her laptop. "What products tie in with true love?"

"Can't think of any products," Spider said. "Maybe theaters, theater blogs. And LGBTQIA bloggers, though that's not a product. But maybe they'd think it's a compelling story. They were separated because of society's disapproval. But now they can be reunited." Spider glanced around at the library shelves, which held books that looked like they were from Ruthie's summer stock days. The windows were stuck together with layers of white paint. "You think Ruthie will like it, right?"

Britta paused in her reading. "I hope so. We were going to show it to her first, remember?" She realized that posting the video would out Ruthie (and maybe Janet) to her family and friends. They absolutely needed to get her approval first.

"Of course we are," Spider said. "As soon as we're finished."

Relieved, Britta wrote down some key words she thought should be in the YouTube description, another tip. "Is star-crossed one word or two?"

"Maybe two with a hyphen. Definitely not one."

Britta wrote down all three. She could use all of them as tags, just in case, and figure out which was the most popular for the actual description.

"I wish we had some film of them together," Spider said. "Or, at least, some more photos instead of just that one."

"Um . . ." Oh. Britta hadn't mentioned the scrapbook to Spider, since that would mean also admitting she'd snuck around. And snooped. She and Spider were getting along really well, which was good since the other two girls kept disappearing. But Britta wasn't sure how Spider would react to her snooping and sneaking. "Do you think there might be some film? Or, I think she mentioned a scrapbook? Can you ask her about that?"

Spider looked down. "You should ask. You're outgoing and talkative. I'm the one who hasn't asked my own grandmother about this in seventeen years of life. And she loves you. You're like a little mini-me with all the theater stuff."

Wow. It almost seemed like Spider admired Britta. Britta didn't say that though. "She likes me. She loves you. It would be more meaningful coming from her granddaughter."

Spider seemed to accept this, and that night, when the girls were making dinner (a simple stir-fry that didn't require dis-membering a chicken), Spider walked over to the kitchen table where Ruthie was reading.

"So, Ruthie?" Britta heard Spider say. "Do you have any pho-tos or scrapbooks of you when you did summer stock around here? It sounds so cool."

"You never seemed interested before."

"Yeah, well, Britta . . ."

"You two are spending a lot of time together. You've gotten over your initial animosity."

She'd told Ruthie she disliked Britta? Britta felt betrayed.

"Yeah, well . . ." Spider lowered her voice, and Britta strained to hear. "She's not that bad, I guess."

Britta couldn't hear the rest of the conversation over the sound of angels singing. To have Spider actually acknowledge that she was "not that bad" was incredible. She'd live on this for the next week.

"What are you smiling about?" Spider asked over dinner.

"Nothing. Just happy."

Later that evening, Spider knocked on Britta's door.

"Come in."

Spider tossed two scrapbooks onto Britta's bed. One, Britta had seen before. The other, she hadn't. "Jackpot."

They looked through them. The first, of course, was photos, programs, theater stuff.

The other was full of handwritten letters.

October 23, 1963

My dearest, darling Ruthie,

No, I can't tell either. Our love will have to
be our secret, yours and mine alone, always.
Always. My family would disown me if they
knew, so they must never know. I have to
admit that having a secret like this, though
sad, is also delicious. I don't have to share you
with anyone! We will be together soon, and we
will be so happy! As for my family, they will
just have to believe that I am an unfortunate
spinster who lives a very mundane existence in
the city—but for the presence of my platonic
roommate, who is a star on Broadway. I know
that you will be, my darling. I must be
content to bask in your light. But bask I will,
and soon.

I've put in my applications to the colleges we
discussed. Hunter seems like the best bet. I
will keep you posted.

I miss and love you, but I am making plans.

Love, JC

45

Spider

INT. SPIDER'S ROOM — DAY

Spider is sitting at her computer, wearing a T-shirt that says "I speak fluent movie quotes," poring over Janet's letters. A voice-over of YOUNG JANET reads excerpts from each of them, her voice overlapping itself in places.

YOUNG JANET (VO)
Remember when we went to the Italian restaurant?
Remember when we tried to pierce each other's ears, but I chickened out?

I was just thinking about that day with
the champagne!
I can't wait until we can be together again!

THE LETTERS OPENED up whole new vistas to Spider.
Before she'd seen them, Ruthie and Janet were like girls in a
novel. Now they were real girls who wrote prose that was a
little too purple. But reading about their shared experiences
and shared plans, the fact that Ruthie had priced apartments
and was practicing her typing while Janet worked in a five-
and-dime store to save money, made it all so real, and in the
end, so poignant. All the letters were in Janet's handwriting,
so when Spider reached the final letter she understood how
hard it had been for Ruthie to receive it—and for Janet to
write it.

The filmmaker in her wanted to tell the entire story from
start to finish. But Britta's tips (keep it SHORT!) rang in her
head and made her focus her vision. And she'd been obsessing
over the title. The working title was "Help My Grandmother
Find Her True Love."

"Do you think that's too long?" she asked Britta a few days
later when they attempted Mount Prospect near Lake George.
It required walking on a scary bridge over the expressway. It
was also possible to drive all the way up by car, but they were
climbing.

"I thought we were taking a break from the movie today,"
Britta said.

"I know, but I get obsessed," Spider said.

"Yeah, me too," Britta admitted. "I think the title's catchy, but I wonder if we should mention that they're two women."

"I thought about that too. Do you think it would be less viral because of haters?"

"Haters gonna hate, hate, hate," Britta sang.

"Okay, Taylor." Spider laughed and stepped over a branch. The good thing was, with her mind on something else, the climbing was easy. Spider knew that getting into a rhythm was the trick. After this, she'd try to persuade Britta to climb one of the fire tower mountains.

"Or maybe star-crossed love? Lost love for sure."

"Help My Grandmother Find Her Lost Love? Help My Grandmother Find the Girl She Lost?" Spider suggested.

"They're both good."

Spider had written the script. It would begin with her, in a voice-over, saying that Ruthie had met Janet in 1962, and they'd fallen in love. In the background, Britta (as Janet) would read poignant passages from her letters, talking about all their plans. Visually, it would show the beautiful woods where the theater had been, photos of the girls, scrapbook pages. The last seconds would focus on Ruthie alone, filled with memories and wondering what happened to Janet. Then, it would appeal to people to help find Janet, if they knew her.

"Do you think it's too schmaltzy?" Spider asked Britta.

"It depends. What's schmaltzy?"

"I keep forgetting you don't have a Jewish grandmother. It's like cheesy."

"Ah. My grandmother would say *picuo*. Or sometimes, *es como una de mis telenovelas*." At Spider's questioning look, she added, "Like one of my soap operas. I'm thinking Cuban grandmothers and Jewish grandmothers are similar."

"Probably. They're probably so alike they'd hate each other." Spider turned sideways to go up some rocks. "But I bet yours doesn't talk about getting naked onstage."

Britta laughed. "Only from lack of opportunity." They were almost to the top. Almost there. Britta stopped climbing and looked thoughtful. "Your video's going to be so good. I wish it could be longer, tell the whole story."

"I was thinking about writing a full-length script," Spider admitted, catching up to Britta. "After I know how it ends."

"Shut your mouth! That would be so great. I wish I could see it. I wish I could be in it."

"Maybe . . ." Spider stopped. She was about to say maybe Britta could be in it, but that was stupid. She wasn't going to make a whole movie over the summer, and Britta would be gone after that. Her thighs suddenly ached with the effort of climbing.

"What were you going to say?" Britta stopped climbing.

"Nothing. It's dumb."

"I'm going to be in New York for college auditions next year, and maybe for college after that. I have to talk my mother into it, but I will. So we can still see each other after this summer."

Spider gestured to Britta to keep climbing. "We're almost there." She felt good, mostly, but she also felt like if she stopped, she wouldn't want to start again. She also wasn't quite ready to admit she'd miss Britta when she was gone. But weirdly, she felt like she might. It was almost like Britta was some kind of annoying little muse.

They continued trudging uphill, Britta talking to hikers who were coming down, asking how much farther it was, stopping to pet every single dog. Finally, they reached the summit. It was crowded with people, people who'd driven there, mostly, people climbing on rocks, clustering around binoculars that cost a quarter to use.

"I don't have a quarter," Britta said. "Do you?"

Spider shook her head. "It doesn't matter. The sky is so cloudless." She remembered a line from a song in a Barbra Streisand movie. "I feel like I can see forever."

46

Meredith

Essay topic: Please tell us how you spent the last two summers.

RIGHT NOW, IF Meredith had to write an essay about what she had done this summer, it would be a total fail. What would she say: I fell in love? Yeah, that would get her into Princeton. And yet, it was true, with all the movie-montage connotations that went with it. Someone who knew how to make movies, someone like Spider, would cut her whole summer together to a Coldplay song. Her and Harmon hiking and caught in the summer rain, goofing around in the river, kayaking until the boat tipped over (okay, the boat never tipped, but in the movie version, it would), looking at the beautiful star photos Harmon took, kissing under the night sky.

God, what would she say? That she liked the way she felt when she was around this guy? Yeah, that made her sound like a serious student. But she did.

She also liked the person she was when she was around him, the person who wasn't stressed out and competitive all the time, the person who didn't have panic attacks.

She kept waiting for Harmon to mess up in some way, for some reason other than his not being a book or an essay or an activity she had to do. But he stubbornly refused to be anything less than a wish-fulfillment boyfriend.

Still, she kept searching for the catch. There was always a catch. You can have a great father, but you can only keep him until you're nine. You can have a 5.2 GPA, but you have to be willing, on occasion, to feel like you're having a heart attack. What was the catch here? Harmon was too good to be true. He was nice, and for someone so determined not to be educated, he seemed smarter than most of the boys she knew in her AP classes at school.

"Why don't you want to go to college?" she asked him one day as they were driving through the mountains. They were on a field trip to Vermont, because they couldn't go to Canada without parental permission, and Meredith wanted to go somewhere. It was only an hour away by ferry, but they were taking the long way, wandering, but not lost, as Harmon's bumper sticker said.

"I feel like that question has been asked and answered, as they say in the lawyer shows. I hate school, and I suck at it."

"College isn't like high school. They don't make you take English every year." She knew English class and reading books by "dead guys" was a big sticking point with Harmon. "You take a few required courses, then you take what you're interested in."

"Have you been talking to my mother?"

"Maybe," Meredith admitted.

"Why do you want to go to college, and not just any college, but the hardest college?"

Meredith stared out the window at the rocky gray mountainsides whizzing by. They'd passed an exit for State University of New York at Plattsburgh. The next exit was for Vermont. It was like she'd reached a crossroads, like Frost's two roads diverging in a narrow wood, and she had to decide which one to take.

"I want to be a lawyer. You need to go to school for that."

"But why do you want to be a lawyer? You want to help people in trouble? You want to make a buttload of money? You've just watched that many episodes of *Law and Order SVU*?"

"I don't think I've watched any," Meredith said. "I don't know. My mom's a lawyer, and my father was too. They started my college fund when I was in utero, and after my dad died, my mom put in the Social Security checks I got too. It's always been . . ." Meredith stopped. She'd been about to say a dream. Her mother's? Her father's? Or her own? "I'm smart in school, and everyone's always known I'd go to a top college and then law school."

"What would happen if you didn't go to a school like that?"

She imagined what her friends, what Hannah or Lindsay,

would say if she suddenly announced she wasn't going to college or, more likely, was just going to stay home and attend the University of Miami (a perfectly good school where they'd probably give her a full ride) instead of applying to Harvard or Princeton. They'd think she'd lost it. And they'd be happy because she wouldn't be competition for them. Plus, they could point to her and tell their parents at least they weren't like flaky Meredith. God, did she even like her friends?

"Meredith?" Harmon had been talking, and she hadn't heard him.

"Sorry, what?"

"I said what would happen if you didn't go to some fancy school?"

She shrugged. "Everyone would know I didn't get in, and I'd be a cautionary tale. Like, they'd say, 'Don't slack or you could end up like Meredith.' And my mother would flip out."

"Okay, so we know what your mother and your friends want. What do you want?"

She thought a second, and she realized she did know something. "Well, I don't want to stay home. A lot of the colleges I'm thinking about are pretty close to here, actually. Cornell's in Ithaca. Dartmouth's less than two hours away." She had looked that up on Google Maps. Dartmouth was the closest, even though it was in New Hampshire.

Harmon pumped his fist. "Well, go, Dartmouth . . . what's their team called?"

"The Big Green." Meredith could run a *Jeopardy* category

on Ivy League mascots. Everyone knew Yale's bulldog, but how many people knew Penn had the Quakers?

"The Big Green? Is that what dances on the sidelines at football games?"

"It's not a big football school. But I think their mascot is an anthropomorphic keg."

"Anthropomorphic?"

"Having human qualities, like a keg with arms and legs."

"Okay, A, I know what anthropomorphic means. I just don't know anyone who would use that word in conversation."

"Then you don't know any of my friends."

"Clearly. And B, a school that has an anthropomorphic keg mascot doesn't really sound like you."

"Are you saying I can't party?" Meredith demanded.

"I haven't seen any signs of it."

"You could visit me on weekends if I get in. I probably won't get in." Meredith believed in not jinxing things.

"I bet you get in, and you wouldn't have time to talk to me on weekends because you'd be spending most of your time studying and the rest, talking about smart stuff with guys with anthropomorphic keg T-shirts. The question is, do you want to go there?"

And the answer was, she hadn't really thought much about it beyond the elation of getting a letter from one of those schools and showing it to her mother and Instagramming it for all her friends to see and die of envy, GREEN envy. She hadn't thought much about the part where she would work really, really hard until she was old and this summer was a dim memory. She wondered how SUNY Albany would be. Harmon's brother went there, and he was a doctor.

"How many times have you taken the SAT?" he asked.

"Truth? I've taken the SAT five times and the ACT three times," Meredith said.

"What'd you get?" Harmon asked.

Too late, Meredith regretted saying anything, for the first time ashamed of her near-perfect scores. They meant she had no life, had time on her hands to take two full courses and a few dozen practice tests. "I'd rather not say."

He smirked. "If I said that, it would be because my scores were bad. I'm guessing that's not the case with you."

"You know, if you have a learning disability, you can get extra time, even double." It was a topic that had been well discussed among her friends. Kayla Feinstein, who took honors and AP classes despite her ADHD, had bragged about getting double time. Her friends had thought that was so unfair, practically cheating. But now Meredith got it. The extra time was so smart people like Harmon wouldn't give up on college just because of some dumb test.

"Yeah, my mom mentioned that two or three hundred times." Harmon didn't conceal his irritation. "And I'll tell you what I told her: I'll think about it."

There was really only one time left to take the SAT for a senior, October. But Meredith guessed Harmon's mother knew that too, so she kept her mouth shut.

She changed the subject. "So when we get to Vermont, do you think I'll be able to kiss you in two states at once?"

He laughed. "I will pull over right by the sign, so we can do that."

Ten minutes later, they did. They kissed on a shoulder full of wildflowers, in full view of several cows, and they bought maple syrup and visited the Ben & Jerry's factory and Harmon bought her a shirt that said "Love comes in all flavors," so she would have it to remember this day, to remember him. She wished she could capture the day and keep it forever, not in a college essay, but in a snow globe on the shelf of her college dorm, to see whenever she wanted, whenever she wanted to give up.

On the way back, Meredith drove and, watching Harmon half dozing in the passenger seat under the pitch-dark sky, Meredith finally realized what the catch was with Harmon.

She couldn't keep him.

47

Kate

IN THE WEEK after she talked to Blake, Kate relaxed some. Her brother might be a little turd, but he was also right. People would say stupid things no matter what she did. Also, she couldn't do much for her parents. Her mother had Blake to fuss over, and it didn't sound like she was even doing that.

So she went to the lake with Meredith on days when Meredith's time wasn't consumed by that townie boy she was seeing, took long walks on the other days. She discovered a house to the north where a woman sold fresh eggs and homemade jam off her porch, another to the south where they sold doughnuts, starting at five a.m. She brought some back one morning, which made her popular. But mostly, she spent time with Ray-Ray.

The kid was starting to grow on her. After the first day with Mrs. Steele, Ray-Ray had begged to go back there.

"You can watch *SpongeBob* here," she told him at first.

"I want to go in the treehouse."

"It's not safe. It will break, and you'll fall and break your arm."

"I want to see Robert."

"He's probably working." She had no idea how much Robert worked, but it sounded better than just saying no for no reason.

"I want a grilled cheese sandwich."

"I'll make you a grilled cheese sandwich," she said, hoping they had cheese and bread and butter, and that she could manage not to burn it. She had never made one, but she had watched Mrs. Steele that day.

They did. Kate made two sandwiches and only burned one, which she ate. She sat Ray-Ray down in front of Nickelodeon. *Thomas & Friends* was on, but *SpongeBob* was next. Kate was sort of getting into that show, to be honest. "Patrick's so funny," she told Ray-Ray.

"*Now* can we go next door?"

Kate suppressed a sigh. "Why do you want to go there? I already said Robert's probably not home, and you can't go in the treehouse."

"I like it there. Mommy used to let me go all the time. You're boring."

"Feeling's mutual, kid." Kate gave up. The kid wanted to hang with the cute, grandmotherly-type woman instead of being stuck inside with her all day. He had mad logic skills. Lizzie wasn't coming home until five. "Okay, but you have to leave when I say." Kate felt bad lying to Ray-Ray's dad. But, on the other hand, they hadn't specifically told her not to go next door, and she was going to stay there the whole time, to watch him. And what were they going to do, fire her from her free babysitting job?

She hurried Ray-Ray over before she changed her mind.

Mrs. Steele looked surprised but also happy to see them. "Oh, my goodness! Look who's here, Robert!"

Ray-Ray gave Kate a reproachful look before following Mrs. Steele into the house. He was soon settled down with clay and a bunch of cookie cutters.

They came the next day and made actual cookies, and the day after to play with Legos. That third day, Kate had an idea. "Hey, if I bought you some wood, do you think we could fix that tree house?"

48

Spider

INT. SPIDER'S ROOM — DAY

Britta has entered Spider's room and
stands in the doorway. Their friendship
has progressed to the point where Spider
doesn't throw something at her for doing
this. Also, her fingers hurt (as evidenced
by the fact that she is bending and flexing
them in front of her laptop), so throwing
something would be difficult.

"CAN YOU HELP me with some of this?" Spider asked Britta
the day after their hike at Mount Prospect. She hated asking
for help, hated to admit that her legs ached too much to stand
right away and her fingers ached too much even to type. But

she'd completed all the filming on her video, so now there was only editing. She couldn't wait to see the finished product—and show Ruthie.

"Sure." Britta pulled the desk chair up near Spider's bed. "What do you need me to do? Are we doing yoga today?"

"I don't want to do stupid yoga!"

"Okay, okay." Britta looked offended. "A simple no would also have worked."

"My mom made me do yoga long before you thought it was the solution to all my problems."

"I didn't say it was. I like doing yoga. My thighs hurt from yesterday. But I'll do it by myself. Or I'll ask Meredith, if she's around. Let's work on this now."

"That's what I wanted to do." Spider tried to push herself up, but it hurt.

With Spider's instruction, Britta opened the file, and Spider showed her how to start making the edits. It was way slower to show someone else how to do it than just to do it herself, but fortunately, Britta wasn't as completely incompetent as Spider had originally thought, so she was able to do a lot of it. But finally, Spider got tired of Britta leaning over her, tired of having to explain things to her, tired of having Britta in her room at all. So she said, "It's fine. I'll finish the rest later."

"I don't mind doing it."

"That's not the problem. Go do yoga."

"Fine." Britta stood and started toward the door. She turned back. "You know, I know I'm not perfect at everything like you are. But I am trying to help." She started to leave again.

Great. Now she was casting herself as the victim. Why was Spider always so mean? But was it mean to want to be able to do things on her own like everyone else, not wanting constant, often begrudging help?

Britta's help wasn't begrudging. She was just a genuinely helpful person. But Spider begrudged her the ability to help.

"I know you're just trying to help. It's just that sometimes, I want to do my thing *myself* even if I'm slower. I don't want to be pathetic."

Britta nodded. "I get it. Can I bring you something, an Advil or a heating pad? Or I froze these wet towels in the freezer. My dance teacher taught me that."

"Frozen towel sounds good," Spider admitted.

When Britta returned, she said, "I'm sorry. I'm just really excited to see it."

"Me too," Spider said.

She ended up not working on it all day. But the next day, she finished it. She showed it to Britta, who pronounced it perfect. Then, together, they brought it to Ruthie and told her their plan. They waited for her reaction as she watched it. When the last strain of poignant, royalty-free music came to a close, they looked at her.

"You're putting this on the internet? For everyone to see?"

Spider hesitated, but Britta said, "We've been researching how to make it go viral."

"Is it up there now?" Ruthie's voice sounded strained.

"Not yet, but—"

"Well, good," Ruthie said, then added, "I don't want it to be. It's very pretty. I see you worked hard. But—"

"You don't want a bunch of strangers to see it." Spider thought she understood. She liked her privacy too. Why hadn't she thought of that?

"Not strangers. Strangers are fine. I click on videos like this all the time—someone's baby, someone's father, someone's kitten trapped in a tree. You never think of the real lives involved. But I'm not a kitten. I'm a person with a family, a family who will get hurt. And if they see this video—your father, Alicia, or your aunt—they'll think my whole life was a lie. You said it yourself."

Wasn't it? But Spider didn't say it, nor, thankfully, did big-mouthed Britta. What *would* her father think? Or her siblings? How had she been so insensitive?

"I'm sorry." Britta's voice was soft. "We were just trying to help."

Spider found her voice. "I think Dad would understand."

"I'm glad you think so," Ruthie said. "I'm not so sure. I can't just come out on the internet like a teenager. That's not how my generation did things. This is my decision to make—or not make. It's my choice."

Spider saw that now. She had never known her grandfather. Her only loyalty was to Ruthie. Had she betrayed it? "I'm sorry. We didn't mean to do anything against your will. Come on, Britta."

She wanted to destroy the video. In the days of film, she could have ripped it to shreds. Now, what could she do? Hit Delete on a computer file? Not very dramatic or satisfying. Still, she would. As soon as she watched it one last time. She'd been so stupidly proud of it.

Britta followed her out. "I'm sorry," she told Spider. "It was my bad idea. I should have realized."

"No, I thought it was a good idea too. It's not your fault." She felt really bad for Ruthie. Her grandmother was so brave and outspoken, an inspiration. If it was difficult for her in the twenty-first century, Spider could only imagine how much harder it had been back then, and for others. She often worried about not being able to be who she wanted to be, because of her aches and pains. But what if you couldn't be who you wanted to be simply because someone else didn't like it?

49

Meredith

IN THE DAYS after she and Harmon kissed in Vermont, they drove to Massachusetts and went to an outdoor concert. They planned to drive to New Hampshire to see how far it actually was to Dartmouth, but first, they went fishing at the lake. "I've never been fishing before," Meredith said as they set off down the hill early in the morning.

"Don't they have fish in Miami?" Harmon asked.

"Yeah, we're kind of known for our fish, I think. But I don't exactly come from a fishing family. I'm kind of culturally illiterate that way. If we catch one, can we cook and eat it?"

"That's sort of the point of fishing. A bass makes a crummy pet. Is that okay?"

Meredith knew the right answer, the answer that would keep her from looking like a prissy city girl. "I eat fish all the time."

But she added, "I just don't want to touch any worms."

"Well, you have to. Otherwise, you're not really fishing."

"Ew," Meredith said. "I just don't want to hurt them. Or have them squirm away."

They reached the lake and Harmon set down the gear. He pulled something from his tackle box. "I don't think this guy's very fast." He tossed it to her.

"Oh!" She shrieked and jumped away, evading the worm. It fell to the ground, where it lay unmoving.

"Can you get that?" he said.

"I can't believe you." She looked down and realized it was a bright-orange rubber worm.

"Fish like them better than real worms," Harmon said.

"Aw, you don't want to put a hook in a worm either," Meredith said.

"That's not true. I'm a big, tough man."

"You are a friend to all living creatures." Meredith held out the worm to him.

"I'm telling you, the rubber ones are just better." He took it from Meredith and showed her how to thread it onto the hook. Then, he demonstrated how to cast, standing behind her and holding her in his arms.

"I'll miss you so much when summer's over," she said. It was a little more than a week.

"We can still see each other. Maybe I'll come down and photograph the Everglades next summer, or when my college goes on spring break."

"The College of Hard Knocks?" Meredith asked, because that was where Harmon kept insisting he was going to get his education.

"Nah. I don't know. I've been thinking about what you said about being able to take mostly classes I want. So I looked it up and, if I went to Adirondack, I could major in media arts and only take two semesters of English. Or maybe I could go to SUNY Albany like my brothers."

"You looked it up?" Meredith turned her reel, trying not to react, but she was surprised.

"My mother's been leaving their catalogs sitting around the house for the past year. But you're the one who inspired me." He helped her cast again. This time, it landed far away. "A girl like you doesn't want some uneducated hick."

He let go of her and watched as she turned the reel over and over. A month, even a week ago, Meredith would have assumed she wouldn't have been interested in a guy like Harmon, a guy who would laugh at the idea of being in German Club or reading a nonrequired novel. Now, she knew that wasn't the case. But she also knew she wasn't ready. Ready for what? To leave him? Or to think about changing her life for him?

But before she could say anything, she felt a tug on the line. "Oh!"

"You got one!" Harmon yelled. Meredith struggled against whatever it was. "Reel it in!"

"I'm trying!" It was like trying to pull Spider's car out of the ditch. "You're sure it's not hooked on a rock?"

"Nah. You can feel the difference." Harmon didn't say how, but she believed him. "Want me to help you?"

Meredith simultaneously tried to hold the rod up and turn the reel. Slowly, gradually, it moved. "I think I . . . can." Another little bit. Then, suddenly, she had her momentum, and she was pulling it up.

"Come on, Meredith!" Harmon said. "You can do it! Think of it as bowling in reverse."

She laughed then and almost released the pole. But that gave her some more energy, and she kept going until finally, the fish was flying out of the water.

"You did it!" Harmon yelled.

"I did!" The struggling fish was green and over half the length of her arm.

"Huge bass!" Harmon caught it up in his hands. "You want me to take it off?"

"Yeah, is it a good one?" It was bigger than the fish Hope had caught that day.

"It's dinner if you want it to be."

"I want it to be." Meredith imagined what her friends at school would think if they saw her now, Meredith Daly, fisherwoman.

When Harmon stowed the fish in the cooler he'd brought, Meredith put her arms around him. He smelled of the lake, but she imagined she did too. "You've opened up new worlds to me."

It was true. Before Harmon, she'd been on one path, her mother's path, which had started before she was born. But she was on it only because she knew no other. She was like a show dog or a racehorse or any other creature that wins not due to motivation but because of what they are. Now, even if she stayed on that path, it would be a choice. And making that choice would mean giving up other choices, the choices that involved fishing or stargazing or chilling out or kissing a cute guy in various geographical locations.

Harmon kissed her now. "You're the best at fishing too. I don't know if anyone ever caught such a big fish here. You can put it on your college resume."

"Oh, sure."

"We can look. My mom has an archive of every decent-sized fish a Dickinson boy has caught over the years. I'm not just saying it because I love you."

"We'll have to look at . . ." Meredith realized what he'd just said. "You what?"

Harmon caught his breath. Then he turned away from her, hands in pockets. "I thought it was pretty obvious how I felt."

It was. But him saying it was changing the rules, like a teacher giving a test on material they'd barely discussed. It wasn't fair. Without him saying it, she could always pretend it was no big deal, a temporary summer fling. Now that she knew it was more to him, she had to acknowledge that it was more to her too. Was it more to her?

Then, he made it worse. He turned back and said, "Yeah. It's so weird. At first, I only asked you out because I knew it would bug Spider. But now, I . . ." He stopped, seeing her face.

"What?"

"I mean . . ." He stepped back. "When I first saw you, that's how I happened to notice you. But now, wow, you've really—"

"That's why you liked me?" She could barely keep her voice from trembling. "I've been wondering what would make someone like you notice me, and the answer is that you didn't?"

"Someone like me? What's someone like me?"

Someone handsome. Someone obviously popular. Someone with people skills. But she couldn't say any of that, not after what he'd just unloaded on her. She sucked in her breath. "Nothing. You're obviously not an intellectual."

"If intellectual means obsessed with books and nothing else, then no, I'm not."

She couldn't speak. She threw down the fishing pole and started away, thoughts swirling. She'd thought he was different from the boys at school, not shallow, sort of profound, like Henry David Thoreau or something. Now she saw it was all a put-on. Him and his stupid playlists. He'd probably made that playlist for another girl, for Kelly at the drive-in.

"Meredith, wait up!" He was trying to gather up the gear and follow her. "Meredith! What about the fish?"

The fish? She reached the stairs that went up the hill. She looked back at him. He had dropped one pole and leaned back to pick it up. "Eat it!"

She left him there fumbling and stormed up the hill, her anger making her step faster. She'd hoped maybe he hadn't realized she was a huge nerd, that she'd been able to reinvent herself, just for a summer, into the type of girl someone like him would like. If that wasn't the case, she had at least hoped that he liked her because of, rather than despite, that. As it was, her romantic summer adventure was a lie.

She knew he'd show up, and he did, an hour later. She saw him from the window, cleaner and without the fishing poles. She'd told Spider about their fight as soon as she'd gotten home. So when she saw him approaching, she said, "Can you get it, Spider?"

"Gladly," Spider said. A moment later, she yelled up the stairs, "Meredith, there's a person here for you. Should I tell him to screw off?"

"Aw, come on." She heard Harmon's voice.

"Yes, please do," Meredith yelled down.

"God, Meredith!" he yelled up. "I said I loved you!"

Before Meredith could reply, Spider said, "She doesn't want to speak to you."

Meredith couldn't hear the rest. Finally, he must have left, because she heard Spider close the door.

50

Kate

ONCE, WHEN KATE was little, her mother got a flat tire with both Kate and her brother in the car. Though Mother called the service number, they took too long. Finally, Mother opened the door, declaring, "I'll change the tire myself!"

"Do you know how to change a tire?" Kate asked dubiously.

"You wait for Daddy to change a wightbulb," Blake added.

"Of course I can't change it," her mother said. "But if an attractive woman appears in distress, some man is bound to come along and offer to help!"

Kate had rolled her eyes. Her mother always thought they lived some kind of *Gone with the Wind* existence and would likely start reciting the "As God is my witness" speech if this didn't work. But before her mother even got the tire out of the trunk, a guy pulled over.

Kate didn't know if it was because she was pretty, because people in this town were friendly, or maybe because building treehouses was fun enough for Tom Sawyer value. In any case, that was how it went with her project.

The first day, when she went to the lumberyard to buy boards, the older man working there quizzed her about her project. "What kind of saw are you going to use?"

"I don't know." Mrs. Steele had said she owned a saw. "Just a regular saw, I guess."

"Not a table saw?"

Kate had no idea what that even was, but considering Mrs. Steele wasn't a carpenter, Kate guessed she didn't have one. "No."

"How about a circular saw?"

"I don't think so."

The man shook his head. "You sure you measured these right?"

I can count. But, by this point, Kate wasn't sure at all. "I think I did."

"I better go with you and check." He yelled to his helper. "I'll be back in an hour."

He followed Kate back to the house, took measurements, cut the boards to order at no charge, then brought them back to Kate.

Then, when she and Robert started actually working on the house, neighbors began showing up. They showed up with sandwiches. They showed up with hammers. They showed up with suggestions.

"Nah, you don't want to use those nails," one neighbor, Don, who said he was a carpenter, told Kate. "Let me get you some better nails."

Then, he spent an hour ripping out the old boards and building an entirely new floor while Kate handed nails up to him and Robert.

"Are you going to paint it?" Tracy, who lived on the other side of Mrs. Steele, asked Kate. "We just painted our back fence. We had almost a whole can left."

"Thank you!"

"I'll bring Evie over to play with Ray-Ray," Tracy said. "And I can bring some brushes and help you paint too. Will you be finished building it tomorrow?"

Kate glanced at Don, who said, "We should be finished today."

"Thank you. You've all been so kind," Kate said.

Tracy shrugged. "We've all been wanting to do something for the family, but they won't take any help."

"It's true," Don said, reaching for another nail.

Kate grabbed him one. "But why won't they?"

"Pride, I suppose. Or shame." Don started hammering again.

"Which is silly," Tracy yelled above it. "I mean, it's terrible that Angie had that problem, but every family has problems. And neighbors should help, not judge."

"You're absolutely right." Kate thought of her own family, her own neighbors. What if she had woefully misjudged them? Maybe they wouldn't all ostracize Kate. After all, Blake was apparently still friends with them. What if her mother was the only one who was awful to people, so Mother just assumed others would judge?

"What happened exactly?" Kate asked Tracy. "I never got the whole story."

Tracy looked around, as if to make sure no one was listening. "The girl came home from school and found her mother on the floor. Thankfully, Ray-Ray was all right. She called an ambulance, but they couldn't revive her."

"That's why Ray-Ray said his mother was asleep," Kate said.

"Right. She was in a coma for a week, and now . . ."

"Brain damage," Robert said, even though Kate hadn't thought he was listening.

"I feel so bad for that girl," Tracy said. "At first, no one knew what to do. I didn't contact them because I didn't want to seem nosy. Maybe that's why they're mad at us."

"True." Don had stopped hammering.

Kate thought about how her friends hadn't texted those first days. Since then, she'd gotten some texts on her phone, one from Marlowe asking how she was, another from Greer saying to call her, inviting her to a barbecue she was having. But she'd ignored them, assuming it was just gawking. Or schadenfreude. Was she judging them too harshly?

"Look!" Robert said.

Kate got out of her thoughts and looked. The treehouse was finished, except the paint.

"Racecar, look!" Robert yelled.

Ray-Ray came running up to them. "Is it done? Can I go in?"

Kate was about to say no, they still had to paint it. Then she thought better of it. "Okay, but we still have to paint it, and once we start, you can't go in until tomorrow, when it's dry."

"Can I paint it?" he asked.

Kate hesitated, but Tracy said, "I have some old clothes for him. He could do a little."

"Okay," Kate said.

"Yay!" Ray-Ray scrambled up the ladder. Kate tried to take his hand, but he said, "I don't need help!"

He and Tracy's daughter played for a while as Tracy went next door and got the paint. Kate guided Ray-Ray's hand while he helped apply the first coat.

That was when Lizzie showed up.

"Kate? What are you doing here?" She looked at Kate, who had some green paint on her hands. "Ray-Ray, what—?"

"Lizzie! Lookit my treehouse!" Ray-Ray yelled.

Lizzie ran over to him and grabbed his hand. "Ray-Ray, let's go home. And you . . ." She gestured toward Kate. "You need to leave and not come back."

"But—"

"I trusted you. I trusted you with my little brother. I shouldn't have."

She tugged on Ray-Ray's arm. "Come on!"

Ray-Ray started to cry, but Lizzie led him away.

"Darn," Tracy said. "I feel really bad."

Kate watched them go. "Me too." Kate wondered what Lizzie was going to do for childcare now. Part of her said she shouldn't care. After all, Lizzie and her father were rejecting help. But she knew from personal experience it was hard to admit you needed people.

51

Meredith

AN HOUR AFTER Meredith's fight with Harmon, Ruthie knocked on the door.

"Someone brought this." She held out an envelope. "It was stuck in the screen door."

Meredith opened the envelope. In it were two photographs, the one Harmon had taken of them with the timer and another, the swirling star-filled sky from that night.

With it, he'd left a note. It said:

GO ON AND TEAR ME APART. JUST GIVE ME ANOTHER CHANCE.

It took Meredith a second to recognize the lyric from the Coldplay song he'd had on that night. She didn't tear the photos apart. But she didn't give him another chance either. She tucked the photos into the lining of her suitcase, deep inside her closet.

Then, half an hour later, she took them out and looked at them again.

She put them back, deeper inside her closet, farther down inside the suitcase.

She looked at them again.

She did that five more times before she left the room and found Britta. "Maybe we should all do something together tonight."

Weirdly, Britta threw her arms around Meredith.

Then she said, "Good idea."

52

Britta

EVERYONE WAS IN a bad mood. Britta knew the reason for her own bad mood, the usual reason: because she had done something without considering all the consequences and now, someone was mad at her. Maybe everyone was.

Ruthie was mad about her stupid, thoughtless idea of making the video.

Spider was mad that she'd wasted her time. Of course, she was always mad. Still, Britta thought they were becoming friends. So much for that now that Britta had wrecked Spider's relationship with Ruthie. Stupid, stupid, stupid.

Britta snuggled against the chipmunk pillow on her bed and thought about what Meredith had said. They should all do something together. But what?

Meredith was also in a bad mood. Probably because of Bat

355

Boy. But, with Meredith, it could also be something like not having gotten perfect scores on all her AP exams.

Downstairs, a door slammed so hard that Britta jumped. Then another slam. Kate's bedroom door. Kate was back and, from the sound of it, her day hadn't gone well either.

Britta put down the pillow. She went downstairs and knocked on Kate's door.

No answer. Had Britta been mistaken about Kate being back? She knocked again and yelled, "Hello?"

Still nothing. She started to walk away when a small voice came from inside. "Yes?"

Now it was Britta's turn to hesitate. She didn't know Kate as well as she knew the other two, and approaching her was a bit like touching a pot on the stove if you weren't sure if it was hot. Still, she'd knocked. She turned the doorknob.

Kate was sitting on the bed, reading a magazine. But something told Britta she wasn't really reading, probably the fact that she was staring at a perfume ad with a picture of Rihanna.

"Hey," Britta said.

"Hey." Kate stared at the ad some more. What was wrong? At the beginning of the summer, Kate had seemed distant, almost sullen. But lately, she'd been in a good mood. Britta had even heard her singing that morning.

"Can I help you?" Kate asked.

"I just . . . are you okay? I heard the door."

"Oh, sorry. It slipped."

"Sure." Britta didn't know what to say. She barely knew Kate.

What would make her think Kate would confide in her? Just another example of Britta acting rashly.

"Um . . ." She remembered Meredith's request. "Meredith thought it would be fun if we all did something together tonight. I mean, if you're available."

Kate frowned. "Of course I'm available. What did you want to do?"

Good question. Britta glanced around the room for something to give her an idea. She found one. It was a photo of a family around a campfire, parents and two kids. The photo was too old, and the shorts too unfashionably long, to be Spider's family. Maybe it was her dad, which meant the mom in the photo was Ruthie.

Ruthie.

Britta said, "We're having a campfire tonight at eight."

Kate seemed to accept this. "Sounds fun."

Britta started to close the door, then thought of something else. "Bring something to burn."

Kate squinted. "Something to burn? Like . . . wood?"

"No. I'll take care of the wood. Bring something you want to forget."

Then, before Kate could ask any more questions Britta couldn't answer, Britta closed the door and ran upstairs to tell Spider her plan and borrow the car keys.

53

Spider

EXT. CABIN — DAY

Spider is fighting a pile of brambles that
have grown around what used to be a fire
pit. The branches are winning and threaten
to drag Spider down to their hell.

"SHIT!" THE BRANCH Spider was wrestling with wouldn't
budge.

They hadn't used the fire pit since they were little kids. Half
of the rocks had rolled down the hill. Spider thought reviving
it sounded like fun, so she tried to unearth it from its branchy
crypt. Britta was buying marshmallows or something. Spider

knew she should wait for her to come back, but she wanted something to take her mind off things. So she tugged and pulled and, lacking a saw, tried to break the branches. They weren't too cooperative, though.

Just as she was struggling with that, a voice called from the road. "Need help?"

She jumped. Harmon. "Go away!"

To Harmon's credit and Spider's surprise, he did. He must just have been asking to be polite. Or to bug her. The branches fought back until she was covered with dirt and pine needles and little scratches all over. And, just as she was dying this death of a million paper cuts, stupid Harmon returned to witness her humiliation. This time, he got out of his truck.

"I said go away!" she yelled.

He didn't answer. He walked around to the truck bed and pulled out pruning shears, gloves, and a long, skinny electric saw of some kind.

He stalked over and offered her the gloves. "Are you sure you don't want help?"

"I'm fine. Get off my property!"

He surveyed the area. "Planning a campfire?"

"None of your business!"

"When? September? October? That's how long it's going to take to clear this without tools. People have been using tools since the stone age."

Spider scowled and dug her toes into the dirt. She tugged on the branch, which snapped, finally, sending her soaring back.

God, why did she suck at life?

Harmon suppressed a laugh. "Maybe don't think of it as help? Think of it as the country folk doing their country work so that your city mind is free to solve the world's problems."

"You're such a douche canoe."

He donned the gloves, walked over to an as-yet-unmolested section of brambles, far from where she was standing, and started up his power tool.

"Stop it! That's so loud!"

"What?" he yelled. "I can't hear you over this! It's loud!"

"I said it's loud! Stop it! Stop it!"

She gave up and walked away. She wasn't about to get near an idiot with a chain saw. Okay, not exactly a chain saw in the *Texas Chain Saw Massacre* sense of the word, but still, a scary electric tool. He could murder her and say it was an accident.

He didn't murder her. Within minutes, the section was all cut. Harmon stopped, and the silence was as bright as the light between the trees. "If you want, you could make a pile to use for kindling." He moved on to another area.

Begrudgingly, Spider started to do that. "You're not invited to our campfire."

"I figured it was a girl thing." He pulled aside some branches. "Is Meredith going?"

Spider shrugged but said, "Yeah. But she doesn't want to see you."

"So she told me."

Spider walked away. Harmon went back to his cutting. When

all the branches around the firepit were cut down, he started moving the rocks into the circle.

"You don't have to do that! I can . . ." She stopped. He was actually being really helpful.

"You could just say thank you, you know," he said, putting down a rock.

"Thank you."

He turned away to find another rock, then turned back. "Look, I know you don't . . . is there any way, could you just *ask* Meredith to talk to me?" His face was all sad and scrunched up, like a blown-apart dandelion. "Please."

Spider knelt to pick up some of the branches. "So let me get this straight: You only asked her out to annoy me, and you *told* her that, but I'm supposed to take your side?"

"Yes." He drew in a breath. "I shouldn't have said that, but . . ." He shook his head.

"What?"

"Nothing. I know it's hard for you to feel empathy."

"I need to feel empathy for you? Why, when you hate me so much?"

"You hated me first," he said. "Ever since we were little kids, that day you made such a big stink about our dog."

"It ate my cover-up." She dropped half the sticks she'd picked up.

"And my mom made me buy you a new one with money I earned from, like, a solid week of pulling weeds, which I think was just a chore my mom invented to punish me, considering we don't usually pull out wildflowers. *And* we had to keep the dogs inside for the rest of the summer, so they wouldn't bother the little city girl."

Spider scoffed. But she'd forgotten they'd bought her a new cover-up, and she hadn't known Harmon had paid for it himself.

"From day one, you always acted like you thought you were so much better than us."

Spider laughed in disbelief. "Thought I was better than you? You thought you were better than me. The rugged outdoorsmen."

"What? You said we were hicks. You hated us."

"I wanted to *be* you. You and your brothers, all of you. You ran all over the place and had so much fun. You knew all the secret places where animals hid, and you got to stay here all year long, every year." She was rambling. And as she said it, she realized it was true. "I wanted to swim in the lake in summer, then be here when it hardened to skate in the winter." It was painful to admit this, painful to admit envying one's enemies. And yet, didn't most hate stem from envy, when you came right down to it? Could you really hate someone with all your heart if you didn't secretly love them with some of it?

Harmon was stammering. "I . . . I didn't . . . I never stopped you from doing that."

"And your one brother, the one that's older than you but just a little, the tall, dark-haired one, Brodie, I think. He has some kind of health problem?" She could picture the boy, panting up the hill behind Harmon, even though Harmon was younger.

"Brodie? He's got asthma. That's why we don't have the dogs anymore."

Spider nodded. "One time, he had an asthma attack or something, and you all ran to help him. You found his inhaler, and your other brother, he looked really concerned."

"He'd been in the hospital, and we were worried he'd have to go back. You hate us because of that?"

"No. I liked you because of that. My brother and sister always acted like I was faking when I said I didn't feel well." It was a betrayal of her family to say that. But it was also true.

"That sucks." Harmon shook his head. "Brodie swims faster than any of us. Mom put him on the swim team because it's supposed to be okay for people with asthma. He's teaching swimming at YMCA camp this summer."

"I wanted to swim with you guys too," Spider said.

"I didn't know," Harmon said. "You could have. You still could. Gibb's coming home for Mom's birthday in August. He lives in Florida, and Brodie and Tanner and Jackson will be around then too, before college starts. And Colt, but he's old and boring with kids of his own. It's sort of a family reunion."

"I'm not part of your family," Spider said.

He thinned his lips, thinking. "Sure you are. What's a family without that annoying little sister who gets in the way but everyone still loves? You've been around my whole life, every summer."

Spider thought about it, then said, "Maybe." It was nice to think of them that way.

"It would be fun. Your friends would be gone by then?"

She didn't want to think about that yet. Her friends. "Yeah. They'll leave at the end of the month." She looked back at the circle of rocks on the cleared land, his handiwork. "That was so stupid, what you said to Meredith. She really liked you. I have no idea why." She kind of had an idea why. She had eyes, after all, but Meredith seemed too smart for it to be just that.

"I know. I liked her. I *like* her."

Spider could tell. He looked really destroyed. Like, if she saw an actor in a movie looking like him, she'd think he was overdoing it. And she knew Meredith had been crying about him earlier, but she couldn't tell him that. Even she knew it would violate Girl Code to do so.

"You're kind of like Lloyd Dobler," she said.

"Who's that? Some guy from Long Island?"

Spider scoffed. "I forgot most people are basically ignorant about movies. Lloyd Dobler's this guy in a movie, *Say Anything*. He's kind of a regular lowbrow guy, and he falls for this really smart girl, Diane Court."

"So I remind you of him because he's stupid?"

The guy was very perceptive. "He's not stupid; he's just . . . normal, and she's a super-genius, like Meredith. He's exactly what she needs, but she breaks up with him, and he tries to get her back by standing outside her window and playing 'In Your Eyes' on a boom box."

His eyes lit up in recognition. Everyone knew that part. It had been parodied on *The Simpsons*. "The trench coat guy.

Does it work? Should I do that?"

Spider thought about it. "Not really. I mean, she doesn't come back to him because of the grand gesture, but she does come back to him in the end."

It was maybe her favorite "teen" movie, and she smiled thinking about it. She picked up some twigs to use as kindling. Harmon started to get his tools. "Can you talk to her for me?"

She shrugged. "I don't think it would help. But I can see if there's an opportunity."

"That's all I'm asking." He started to walk toward his truck with the tools.

"Some kind of gesture probably wouldn't hurt."

He nodded. "What kind of gesture?"

"I don't know. Something that shows you understand her."

"That's easy," he said in a voice that indicated it wasn't. He started to walk away again.

"Harmon!"

He turned back again, and she said, "Thanks for helping with this."

"Think about coming over next month. It'd be fun to catch up."

She smiled. "I will. Thanks."

When he reached the truck he said, "Spider? About your family?" When she looked up, he said, "Sometimes, I think people are in denial about how bad you're feeling because they hope it's not really that bad, for your sake. That's how it was for us with Brodie."

Spider wasn't sure if she believed that. It would be nice to think that was true.

She waved as he drove away. Strange, talking to him after all these years of hating him and his family. She wanted to talk to someone about it. But, she realized, the person she wanted to talk to was Ruthie.

54

Britta

"WHAT ARE YOU doing?" Kate asked when she saw Britta rooting through the laundry room garbage.

"Getting lint for a fire starter. Weren't you ever in Girl Scouts?"

Kate shook her head. "My parents aren't real into female empowerment."

Britta laughed. "My mom's idea of camping was staying at a Hilton instead of a Hyatt, but our Girl Scout leader, Nancy, taught us to make fire starters out of dryer lint."

Kate seemed to have no response to this, so Britta headed to the kitchen.

Meredith looked at her quizzically when she started taking the paper towels off the roll.

"I guess you weren't in Girl Scouts either?" Britta said.

"Nope." Meredith waved her hand. "My mother said learning to make a fire was a waste of time. No offense."

"None taken. I'll be ready for a hurricane, and you'll be in the dark."

Spider, to her credit, didn't have anything negative to say about Britta's fire starters. But Britta suspected it was just because she was too sad to be sarcastic.

Finally, they were ready, as the sky was darkening, gathered around the fire.

"Wow, this looks really good," Britta said. "I can't believe you did all this."

"I may have had some help," Spider said, looking at Meredith. "From Harmon."

Meredith was silent, so Britta said, "Okay, well, we should get started." She threw one of the fire starters onto the sticks and lit the end. "I brought lighter fluid, just in case."

But when she lit it, it blazed to life.

"Whoo!" Kate yelled, impressed.

"Should we tell ghost stories?" Meredith asked a few minutes later as they bobbed their marshmallows over the fire.

"Does anyone know any?" Kate asked.

"Ruthie used to tell one about a play she was in, Shakespeare's *Henry VI*," Spider said.

"Which part?" Meredith asked. "*Henry VI* is in three parts."

Spider said, "I have no idea. But one of the characters, Suffolk, gets killed in the play, and one of the other characters carries around his severed head."

"Part two," Meredith said. "That's part two."

Britta cleared her throat. "You're being weird," she whispered.

"ANYWAY," Spider said. "It was opening night, and the actor playing Suffolk didn't show up. They called his phone number, and he wasn't there. Finally, they sent his understudy on. That was when bizarre things started to happen."

"Whoooooo!" Britta said, getting into the mood. It was starting to get dark.

"First, someone heard a knocking on a dressing room door. Then one of the empty balcony seats started rattling, nonstop. They took an intermission. As soon as the lights came up, the rattling stopped, but when they went down, it started again."

The firelight flickered on their faces, and Britta felt a chill.

"Then, when the prop master went to get out the severed head for Margaret to carry around, he screamed. It was a real head!"

"Oh!" Kate shrieked.

"Yes, a real head, the head of the actor who played Suffolk." Spider was getting into the story now. She stood to finish. "Still slightly warm and *dripping* with blood. He was murdered, possibly by his understudy! No one knew what had happened to his body. No one ever found it, but from that day on, the theater was always haunted by his ghost!"

She grabbed Meredith's shoulder. Meredith shrieked. "You guys!"

Britta shivered slightly. "That was so scary." She looked at the marshmallow she was holding over the flame. It was on fire. "Oh!" She rushed to blow it out.

Kate handed Britta her skewer. "Here, take mine. I like the burned ones."

Britta hesitated. "That is unusually nice of you."

Kate waggled it. "Take it before I change my mind."

Britta swapped with her. "Does anyone else have any stories?"

No one did, so Britta said, "I think we should move on to the ritual part of the evening, but people can still make more s'mores if they like."

"Maybe later," Spider said. "I don't like to muck up my rituals with a lot of chocolate."

"Fair enough." Britta licked the chocolate off her fingers and tried to remember things Nancy had said around campfires. She always said they were ancient ceremonies, but Britta suspected she made them up on the spot. "The ancient people believed in cleansing by fire. Fire is a destroyer and a purifier. Its light can bring us closer to the divine."

"Oh boy," Britta heard someone, maybe Kate, whisper under her breath.

Britta ignored her. "I have asked each of you to bring something to burn, to sacrifice, something you want to forget, to move past. Who wants to start?"

When no one volunteered, she said, "Okay, I'll start."

She held up a sheet of paper. Her grade report. She'd gone to the library to print it out. "These are my grades. I failed math.

So I'm going to have to spend all next month and part of the fall making it up online so I can graduate. But the thing is, it's part of a general pattern of behavior. I do thoughtless things that make people think I'm stupid." She looked at Spider when she said *thoughtless.* "Anyway, I'm burning it as a symbol that I am going to think about my actions more. I want to put that thoughtless part of my life behind me."

Britta stood and walked to the fire. She held up the paper. She said, "I offer this report card up to the fire, so that it may be cleansed, so that it may be destroyed, so that it may be forgotten and I can move on to the future. Accept it into the fire."

She threw the paper onto the fire. It lit up and sparked in the wind. In seconds, it was gone. Britta turned and went back to where she'd been sitting.

Spider patted her arm. "I don't think you're stupid," she whispered.

"Really?" Britta's eyes got big. "You used to."

"I changed my mind. Don't make a big deal about it."

"Okay." Britta tried not to smile. "Who's next?"

"I'll go." Kate stood.

Beside her, Meredith whispered, "I'll help you with the math when we get home."

"Really?" Britta said. "I thought you had to do college stuff."

"I'll put it down as peer tutoring or something. Shh!"

"I'm her peer!" Britta said.

Kate cleared her throat.

"Oh, sorry." Britta and Meredith both turned to look at her.

She was standing over the fire, her blond hair rippling slightly in the wind. She held up a sheath of papers. "This is the list of all the debutante stuff my mother needs me to do—choose three escorts, find a white dress that's modest enough but doesn't make me look like the cast of *The Handmaid's Tale*, and ten other outfits for parties, think of a theme for the party they'll throw for me."

"A theme?" Spider said.

"Yeah, like pirates or *The Great Gatsby*."

That actually sounded pretty cool, but Britta realized that was not the point.

"Anyway, I've decided I'm not doing it. When I get back, I'm telling my parents it's a waste of money."

"Won't they be mad?" Britta leaned forward, eyes wide with admiration.

"Sure. My mother, at least. My father might be relieved about the money."

"Will they still pay for your college?" Spider asked.

Kate shrugged. "I don't think they'll disown me or anything. I mean, it's embarrassing to have a daughter who's not a debutante. But it's way worse to have one you don't speak to. If they disown me, I'll just get a job . . . at Hooters."

"Ha!" Britta laughed.

Kate stuck out her chest. "But, more importantly, I'm done worrying what people think of me. I see now that a lot of problems come from worrying about people's stupid opinions. My dad got in trouble because he spent money he didn't have, to impress people. And this family I've been sitting for won't accept any help cause they're too proud to admit that they need it. Being a debutante is worrying about what other people think, on an epic level. So I'm done." She held the packet close to the fire. She turned to Britta. "Am I supposed to say something?"

"Oh!" Britta remembered. "Yes. Say, 'I offer this paper up to the fire . . .'"

"I remember. I offer this paper up to the fire so that it may be cleansed," Kate repeated. "So that it may be destroyed. So that it may be forgotten and I can move on to the future."

"Accept it into the fire," Britta said.

"Accept it into the fire," Kate repeated, dropping the papers. They flamed up, higher and brighter than Britta's report card had. Kate watched them burn, standing until it was gone.

"Whooo! I feel strangely better!" She turned and sat.

"I'll go next." Meredith stood and held up a paper. She looked at Britta. "Mine's kind of the opposite of yours. These are my AP scores."

Britta rolled her eyes. "Oh, Meredith. Are they not perfect?"

"They are perfect." Meredith held out the paper, a printout of all Meredith's AP scores, eight in all, subjects like German and statistics. Next to each subject was a number, five. Britta guessed that was the highest. The girl was a robot!

"I've been so stressed out and miserable," Meredith continued. "When school is the only thing you have, it's scary. I've worked so hard, and now . . . what if I don't get into Princeton or Harvard? Will my friends gloat? Will my mother be ashamed of me?"

"Oh, Meredith, of course she won't." Britta hoped that was true.

Meredith shook her head "Sometimes, I think I wouldn't want to live if that happened."

She said it matter-of-factly, but Britta was horrified. "Oh, Meredith."

"It's true." Meredith wiped at her eyes. "I have no friends, not real friends."

"I'm your friend." Britta stood and held out her arms.

"You don't think I'm a weirdo who's obsessed with school?"

"No." Britta hesitated, knowing Meredith could spot a lie. "Not anymore."

"I don't know if I even want to go to a school like that," Meredith said. "I feel panicky just thinking about it, four more years of competing. I just don't want to be a failure."

Kate stood and walked toward her. "Me neither."

"Me neither," Spider said.

"Me neither," Britta agreed. "I worry about that all the time."

"How to make my parents happy but still be myself," Kate said.

"How to be myself without chasing everyone else away." Spider added herself to the group hug.

"Whoo-whoo-whoo-whoo!" A wailing noise came from the trees.

Meredith sniffed and looked around. "Harmon, is that you?"

"Whoo-whoo-whoo-whoo. Whoo-whoo-whoo-whoo!"

Meredith yelled, "Harmon, quit it! It's not—"

"Whoo-whoo-whoo-whoo. Whoo-whoo-whoo-whoo!"

"I think it's an owl!" Britta shrieked as something swooped through the air behind them.

"Oh, God!" Meredith tossed the paper onto the fire. "What do I say? I offer this up to the fire, so that it may be cleansed, so that it may be destroyed, so that it may be forgotten and I can move on to the future. Accept it into the fire!" She scurried to a tree.

"Should we go inside?" Spider said.

"You haven't burned anything," Britta said. "Besides, I think the owl's gone."

They listened. Crickets. The wind. No other sounds in the starlit night.

Spider stood. Britta could tell from the way she lurched up that she was in pain, probably from clearing all the brush away. Britta felt a stab of guilt for not helping.

"It's largely symbolic." Spider held up a paperback book about living with arthritis. "I've memorized this, and my problems aren't going away anyway. But like Meredith, like Britta, I guess maybe like all of you, I'm tired of letting this one thing define me. I want to—"

"Whoo-whoo-whoo-whoo. Whoo-whoo-whoo-whoo!"

"God!" Spider said.

"Maybe we should . . . ?" Britta ducked.

"Yeah!" Spider chucked the book onto the fire. "I offer this book up to the fire, so that it may be cleansed, so that it may be destroyed, so that it may be forgotten, and I can move on to the future. Accept it into the fire."

"Whoo-whoo-whoo-whoo. Whoo-whoo-whoo-whoo!"

"And run!" Britta said.

The girls scattered in different directions. When Britta came back with a bucket to put out the fire, she still heard the owl in the distance.

55

Kate

WHEN KATE CAME in from the fire, she felt cleansed. She wasn't going to debut. She was going to sit down with her parents and have a real conversation about the future.

Then she noticed a letter on the front table. Someone must have brought it in. It was addressed to her, and she recognized the handwriting.

She opened it with shaking fingers. The letter that fell out was written on notebook paper in that same familiar handwriting. In Latin.

Katarina carissima,

Quom tibi apud saltationem obveni, scivi me tecum in aeternum saltare voluisse.

Quom primum tibi in schola Latina locutus sum,
scivi te solam loqui linguam meam.

Scio hanc aetatem esse tibi perdifficilem. Scio
quoque te putare me non intellegere. Fortasse
putas me te amare tantum pecuniae tuae causa vel
familiae tuae causa, sed non est. Te amo, sine ulla
illius. Omnes vos estis.

Te exspectabo.
Colin

She took it to her bedroom. She wished she had her Latin–
English dictionary. It was the one thing she hadn't packed in
those three suitcases! But, after about an hour of trying to
remember what she'd learned in school, she thought she knew
what it said. It wasn't perfect, but she understood.

Dear Kate,

When I first met you at the dance, I knew I wanted
to dance with you forever.

When I first spoke to you in Latin class, I knew
you were the only person who spoke my language.

I know this is a hard time in your life. I know you
think I don't understand. I guess you think I only love
you for your money or family. But that's not true. I
love you without any of that, for all you are.

I will wait for you.
Colin

Kate read and reread the translation. She wanted to believe him, but could she? She folded the letter and slipped it under her pillow. Maybe her dreams would tell her what to do. Her conscious thoughts weren't pulling their weight.

56

Spider

INT. SPIDER'S BEDROOM — NIGHT

Spider is lying in bed.

SHE LOVED THESE girls. She loved this summer. She loved the smoky smell of the campfire on her "Save Ferris" T-shirt and even her hair as she lay in bed. She never wanted it to go away, ever. And yet, as sure as the scent of smoke would fade, soon Britta, Meredith, and Kate would leave. She'd be alone, as usual.

When Spider had thrown the book on the fire, she'd wanted to say more. But she hadn't known what. You couldn't throw your pain into a fire. People acted like it was that easy. Take a pill, do some yoga, get your mind off it, suck it up, buttercup. But, the truth was, she would probably never not be in pain. Some people did get over JIA as adults, but she wasn't counting on being one of those people. Some people got worse.

What she really wanted was not to have people define her by her pain. She wanted to be like these other girls, the one who was smart and applying to Ivy League schools, the one who did drama and was fun, the one who did debate and was pretty and was still trying to decide who she was. She could be the one who was obsessed with film, the one who was good at writing and wanted to make her own movies. She could be a friend, an ally, an advocate. She could be—what had Harmon said—the annoying little sister who gets in the way, but everyone still loves. She could be the one who told stories that changed the world.

That would be better than climbing Everest.

She wished she could discuss this with someone, someone who would understand. But Ruthie was the only one who'd ever understood her.

She had to make it right with Ruthie.

It was harder to get up than to stay up. Her hips ached, and her arms felt stiff as she pushed herself up. Yet she did. She turned on the bedside table light, hoisted herself from bed, and walked across the room. When she entered the hallway, someone was there.

"Oh!" they both screamed at once.

"I was coming to see . . . ," Spider started.

"I was looking to see if you were awake," Ruthie said. "But I thought you weren't."

"I was. I was sitting in the dark thinking about you."

"Me too, about you." Ruthie reached over and patted Spider's shoulder. "I loved the video. It was beautiful, and I know you worked very hard on it."

Spider shook her head. "It's fine. You don't have to say that. I'm not a child. I know it was a dumb idea." Making the video *was* like something a little kid would do, a child who thought all the world's problems could be solved easily. She saw that now.

"Your heart was in the right place. It's just more complicated. I have to think of the feelings involved with something so public."

"I know. I just wish you could do what you want. Or, rather . . ." She realized she wasn't sure what Ruthie wanted at this point. That was the whole problem. "I wish you could have done what you wanted fifty or sixty years ago."

Ruthie laughed. "If I had gotten what I wanted fifty or sixty years ago, you'd never have been born."

"True," Spider said. "I've just always thought of you as so brave. You've been like an inspiration to me."

"I hope I still am."

Spider thought of all the times she'd been here, to this place, with Ruthie, all the times she'd been hurting and her grandmother, despite her age, had taken care of her, been the only one who really understood. "You are."

"Maybe I'm just too old to change at this point," Ruthie said.

Spider didn't think so, but she had to respect Ruthie's space. She knew from experience that you could never fully understand how someone else was feeling. There would be other days to discuss it. "Do you want to play Rummikub?" she asked.

Ruthie smiled. "Yes. That's a great idea."

"Get out the game. I'll see if Britta's awake."

57

Britta

BRITTA CAME BACK from an hour of playing Rummi-kub with Spider and Ruthie. She was glad they were all getting along now, but she was wiped. She collapsed on the bed with the lights still on, smelling the campfire scent on her hair. It took her back to camping as a child. But the pine scent in the air, they didn't have that in Miami.

The campfire had been fun, but she had wanted to do more of a ceremony. She'd even written a song for them all to sing. But there would be other days.

As she lay there, her eyes found the little chipmunk pillow. It was green and white, and the chipmunk itself was brown. It held a lighter brown acorn. In the corner, something was embroidered in darker green. Britta noticed and read it for the first time.

Oh.

She remembered the woman who had made the pillow, her stories.

She had to go back there.

58

Essay topic: What would you contribute to SUNY Albany?

THE NEXT MORNING, on her walk, Meredith could still smell the burned branches in the air. She headed in the opposite direction of the hill, toward Route 9, which also meant she was going to pass the Dickinsons' street. She told herself she wasn't looking for Harmon.

But she wasn't really surprised to see him.

He wore the same green fleece jacket from the night they'd gone stargazing. She still had his hoodie. In fact, she was wearing it. She didn't want to give it back, but she should.

"Hey," he said.

"Hey." She slowed her step. "I have your hoodie."

"Yeah, I see that. Keep it."

She wanted to. But she said, "I should return it."

"It's better if you keep it. If I have it, I won't want to wash it because it'll still have the lingering smell of your hair on it, and eventually, people will be like, 'Dude, stop sniffing that jacket like a weirdo and wash it for God's sake—it's got mustard stains on it.' And I won't stop, and it'll ruin my life, so please keep it."

She laughed without thinking. "I could wash it before I give it back."

He mimed horror. "Nooooooo!"

"Okay." She'd put it in a box under her bed where she could look at it when she wanted.

"But, in exchange for the gift of this gorgeous high school hoodie with a picture of a guy with an ax on it, I wanted your help with something."

She raised an eyebrow. "What's that?"

He pulled some typewritten pages out of his pocket and presented them to her. "College admissions essay."

She started to laugh again, thinking he was messing with her. Then, she saw the look on his face and the essay title, "What I Would Contribute to SUNY Albany."

"You're serious?"

"As a heart attack. Why wouldn't I be?"

"I don't know. Because you've said five hundred times that

you weren't applying to college. You've said it to me and your mom and all your brothers and your cousin, Hope."

He shrugged. "I changed my mind." The papers fluttered in the morning breeze. "It's the least you could do, considering you're the one that made me feel like I wouldn't crash and burn and embarrass myself the first semester."

"Maybe not the *first* semester," she joked.

"Thanks." Awkward pause. "Will you look at it?"

When she nodded, he stuffed it in her hand. Then, he turned and strode away in the manner of Mr. Darcy in *Pride and Prejudice*, if Mr. Darcy wore Old Navy fleece. Meredith sort of expected his letter to start, "Be not alarmed, Madam, on receiving this letter, by the apprehension of its containing any repetition of those sentiments, or renewal of those offers, which were last night so disgusting to you." It didn't. It was actually a college essay. About her.

What I Would Contribute to SUNY Albany

I feel like I should be straight with you up front: 90 percent of the reason I'm applying to college at all is to impress a girl. That might seem bad. What if she broke up with me? Good news for you is she already did. I'm still applying.

I come from a family of smart people. One brother is a doctor. Another is an engineer, the other three are in college or grad school. My dad tries to be an invenntor and my mother illustrates childrens books. Most went to Albany except my mother who went to some art school in NYC and one brother who went to RPI for engineering. I'm like the mascot. But maybe their smartness has rubbed off on me. Maybe.

My talents are I make an awesome playlist (which would be something I would bring to campus, if I went). I can teach anyone to fish. Just ask. I make a decent omelette. I'm a good friend and a better brother.

What I'm really good at is photography. The newspaper teacher at school says I have an eye. I actually have two (Haha). I could probably take photos of the pep rallies or something if you have pep rallies. I just looked it up, and you do. Go Great Danes!

Honestly, 90 percent might be a low estimate. I really want to impress this girl. But like I said, it's too late. So what I want is to deserve a girl like this in the future. I mean, I get that she's out of my leage. So if I came there, I would work really hard and study, and be involved in alot of activities. Probably photography-related. I would try to better myself.

I would also make everyone omelettes if that would help. You provide the eggs.

It took her about a minute to read and, as with Mr. Darcy in every movie version of *Pride and Prejudice*, he was barely a speck in the distance by the time she finished. Probably for the best. Had he been there, she'd have told him 1) she absolutely would admit him to her college, if she was on the admissions committee (and if he fixed the spelling errors before he sent it) and 2) she loved him.

388

She wasn't sure she should tell him either thing. She had no experience with brutal honesty on college applications. These essays were, by their nature, BS. You said that this one school was the only place you'd really fit. Then, you sent similar essays to fifteen other colleges. Her friend Lindsay was planning on majoring in business if she got into Penn, agriculture if she got into Cornell, and folklore and mythology at Harvard—and she had great reasons for each. Meredith was pretty sure Mrs. Rose, the lady helping her with her essays, would tell him to keep the parts about his family, the part about photography, and *maybe* the part about the playlist, to make him sound interesting. Cut the candor and don't begin sentences with a conjunction. And yet, that was what made her like it so much, like *him* so much.

She didn't know how she was supposed to get this back to him. Throw it on the doorstep? Mail it? She didn't want to talk to him, but she so wanted to talk to him.

She hurried back to the house to read it three more times.

59

Kate

KATE WOKE THE next morning excited. For a second, she couldn't remember why.

Then she remembered. Today was the day Ray-Ray could finally play in the finished treehouse. Except he couldn't. Kate rolled over in her bed. Something crinkled.

Colin's letter. She read it over. Then she rose, dressed, and walked up Service Hill.

"Kate?" His voice sounded husky, as if he'd just woken up. "Is it really you?"

She took a deep breath of the cold, morning air. "You sent me that letter? In Latin?"

"Yeah." He cleared his throat, and Kate imagined him shifting onto his elbow on the blue sheets in his bedroom. "Did you like it?"

"Yeah. I think so."

"I couldn't say everything I wanted to say in Latin. But I miss you, Kate. If you hate me, I guess I have to deal with that. But if you broke up out of some idea of, I don't know, protecting me, you need to know I don't want to be protected. I want to protect you."

It was what she'd wanted him to say. "I don't want to be protected either." *I want to be loved.* She sat on a rock. "Are people being . . . awful?"

"Some people will always be douches," he admitted. "But I'd rather be with you than them—if I get a choice."

Was he telling the truth? She thought of how long it must have taken him to write that letter in Latin. He had struggled for a B in the class, and that was with her help. Finally, she said, "I'm not going to be a debutante." Then, she added, "Ainsi sera, groigne qui groigne," a quote attributed to Anne Boleyn.

A pause. Then he laughed. "Grumble all you like, this is how it's going to be, huh?"

He got it. "I miss you, Colin." She wished he was there. She wanted to touch him. "How did you find the address to send that letter?" She wondered if it was Mrs. Scott. Or the location on the photograph.

But he said, "I just asked your brother. And once he was sure I wasn't actually flying up here, he gave it to me."

"Blake!"

"Don't blame Blake. I was worried about you. A lot of people are."

Kate remembered the texts she'd gotten from her friends. "Greer invited me to a barbecue." It was hard to believe that she'd be going home soon.

"Yeah. I heard about that. And . . ." He stopped.

"What?"

"Nothing."

"Tell me," Kate insisted.

"Nothing." She waited until he said, "Caroline Harper said she wasn't going to go to the party if you were there, and Greer said she didn't even know if you were going, but if Caroline felt that way, she should stay home."

Kate didn't know what to say. It would be so much easier to ignore everyone. But was that the right way to go? Or was that being like Ray-Ray's family, running from people who really cared? A cool breeze rippled across her arms, and Kate shivered.

Finally, she said, "Tell Greer I'll go to the barbecue."

"Okay," Colin said. "With me?"

Kate made a decision. "Yeah, with you."

"I'll protect you from what they say," he said.

He was being sweet. And yet she didn't want protection. She wanted to hold her head up. "Don't protect me. Just be with me. *Amor omnia vincit.*" Love conquers all.

She could almost hear his smile when he repeated, "*Omnia vincit amor.*"

They stayed on the phone a little longer, her telling him about the place, the people she'd met, him filling her in on what was happening at home. When she glanced at her watch, it was close to nine. She said, "They're probably waiting for me for breakfast—my mountain friends. But I'll call you, maybe tomorrow."

"Okay," he said. And then once more, *"Omnia vincit amor."*

And suddenly, she knew she had to talk to Lizzie.

60

Spider

```
INT. SPIDER'S BEDROOM — MORNING

Spider blinks. There is thunder, or maybe
an earthquake, or someone trying to break
into  the  bedroom.  She  glances  around,
disoriented.
```

"STOP BANGING ON the door!"

Britta took this as an invitation to enter. It wasn't. "I'm barely tapping. Tapping!"

"Are you injured? Is Patty Jenkins here to offer me an internship? Is the house on fire?"

"Who's Patty Jenkins?"

"Oh, God!" People were so ignorant. "Patty Jenkins? The

greatest female director of our time, *Monster, Wonder Woman*."

Britta sighed. "No, I don't see her down there. Just me. I have to talk to you."

"You think you're funny." Spider cracked open her eyes. Britta stood there holding the stupid chipmunk pillow she'd bought the day of her humiliation. Spider closed her eyes again.

"Look!" Britta pushed the pillow into Spider's line of vision.

"It's a pillow." She actually felt pretty good today, for her. Other than the smoke inhalation and being rousted awake. "With a chipmunk. Very cute." She pushed it away.

"Not the chipmunk. Look at the embroidery on the side." Britta stuck her finger out at it.

Spider tried to focus her eyes on the tiny embroidery in a blue that almost blended with the green. When she did, she said, "Oh, God."

61

Kate

THERE WERE FEW cars in the parking lot. Kate didn't even know why she was there. What would she do, walk up to the cash register and browbeat Lizzie into talking?

She strolled past the neat tables of strawberries and cookies. Lizzie was at a register. Kate glanced at her, but Lizzie looked down at her phone, then up again.

Kate walked over to a table covered with boxes of giant green pistachio muffins. "These look good," she said aloud, though they looked like toxic waste. Kate tossed them into the basket, glancing at Lizzie before she went to look at hairspray.

Lizzie was scanning items. Kate didn't know why she cared so much. Maybe it was her father's instinct to want to help people, an instinct that had caused him to get into politics in the first place. Maybe she'd inherited it. Or learned it. She headed to the personal care aisle to look at hair products.

Once there, Kate examined the bottles of Suave and Final Net. Not that any supermarket hairspray had ever touched her hair, but if they were going to lose everything, maybe it would come to that soon. Kate selected the purple bottle of the Aussie stuff Britta liked. Lizzie was on her phone—again—when Kate reached the register. Kate just waited for her to finish.

"I'm sorry," she said when she finally got off. "There's been an emergency at home."

Emergency. What kind of emergency? "Is Ray-Ray okay?"

Lizzie scanned Kate's items. Her hands were shaking so she missed a few times.

"Lizzie, is Ray-Ray okay?" Kate wanted to reach out and grab the items out of Lizzie's hands to keep her from acting like everything was normal. "What's wrong?"

Lizzie shoved the items down to the bagging area. "Seven dollars and thirty-one cents. Do you have your loyalty card?"

"What happened to Ray-Ray?"

"He's disappeared!" Lizzie burst out. "He's run away! Daddy was thinking you kidnapped him, but I told him that was impossible because you're here. Maybe he went to look for you."

62

Meredith

Essay topic: Using a favorite quotation from an essay or book you have read in the last three years as a starting point, tell us about an event or experience that helped you define one of your values or changed how you approach the world.

AFTER HER THIRD read-through of Harmon's essay, Meredith decided that it was pretty humiliating to hand someone something like that and have her ignore it. She headed up the road to his house.

When she got there, he opened the door quickly, like he'd been waiting. "What'd you think?" She got the feeling he wasn't looking for a frank assessment of his writing ability.

But that was what she gave him. She sat right down next to him on the front porch bench, held out the essay, like the nerd she was. "It was great. It really showed your personality. I mean, I marked some misspellings and maybe don't begin sentences with conjunctions." He looked confused, so she said, "Like when you start with 'So,' or 'But,' or—"

"I know what a conjunction is." He sucked his lip. "I poured my heart out, and you're correcting my grammar. Really? Are you that angry about what I said?"

"I'm not mad about that," she admitted. "I was never mad about that. I'm not mad."

"You're sure doing a good imitation of it."

She sucked in her breath through her teeth. "I freaked because you said you loved me."

"Because you don't love me?" His eyes had flecks of green and orange in them, and he looked so sad, and in that moment, Meredith knew she did love him. Of course she did. But she also knew she couldn't tell him that.

She sighed. "I don't know if I love you. But at the end of this month, I'm getting on a plane and leaving, and I'm probably never coming back. I've worked my whole life to have all these opportunities. I'm not going to follow a guy to college. Everyone who does that ends up breaking up with the guy the second he meets some cheerleader, and then they're stuck at their fallback school." She felt her heart beating through his hoodie.

"I wasn't asking you to follow me. I'm not some Neanderthal who'd expect that."

No, but she'd been thinking about it. She'd been thinking she could go to Albany or Skidmore to be closer to him, to be closer to this place. She'd thought that his brother got to be a doctor, even though he went to a normal state school. Maybe that would be sensible. Maybe she could save money. Maybe she'd be less stressed. Or maybe she was following a guy.

"I know you aren't," she said.

"Maybe I could follow you," he said. "There's a million schools in Boston. Maybe I could just apply there. Maybe one of them has a scholarship for photography."

"It wouldn't work," she said. "You can't apply to every school near where I'm applying. We'd break up. So might as well just rip off the Band-Aid now. I'm taking the SAT again."

"For the tenth time?"

"Sixth." The wooden bench felt cold and hard under her. "And I've barely started on my college essays, and I need to get decent grades in my classes, and—"

"This is your mother talking. She's got you so programmed that you feel guilty if you have an independent thought."

"I have independent thoughts." Though even as she said it, she wondered if she did.

"Look, if you want to go to some fancy school, I support that. I'll even photograph it. But she's the one making you feel like you're some kind of failure if you don't."

"I have to leave." She stood and started down the steps. Then she remembered and handed him the paper. "I marked a few commas and places I thought you could tweak."

He took the paper and ripped it in half. He dropped it on the ground, and one part fluttered away.

"So you were never serious," she said, turning back to leave. "And you're littering."

"I was serious. I stayed up all night, writing an *essay*. But I was serious about us too."

She walked down the steps then.

"Meredith!"

She stopped. "What?"

"I'm leaving too. I'm going to go hiking in the high peaks, Whiteface Mountain. I'm camping, cooking outdoors, doing guy things. I figure I can get some good pictures."

"That's great," she said. She wished she could go with him.

He stared at her, his lips a thin line before saying, "Guess I won't see you again, then."

She shrugged, trying to pretend she didn't care. Then she nodded. "Goodbye then." She was down the driveway when she realized she still had on his hoodie. She didn't want it. It just made it too hard. She didn't want his dumb photos or anything to remember him by. She was making the right decision. He was a distraction, an unnecessary one, and now she'd have to work twice as hard to make up for the lost time this summer. Maybe she could go back to the cabin and start working on the essays right now. She knew them by heart. Think, Meredith, think. *Why* was it not easy being green?

That was easy. She looked around her at the blurred green trees, all green everywhere, and it was NOT EASY.

She stripped off his hoodie, balled it up, and stuffed it in the mailbox that said Dickinson.

Then she ran back to the house as fast as she could through the green blur from her tears.

63

Kate

"OH NO!" KATE heard Lizzie's words and remembered her panic the day she hadn't been able to find Ray-Ray. The house was right next to the highway. "Did you check the neighbors?"

"I told my dad to, but—"

"I'll help look for him!" Kate handed Lizzie twenty dollars and stuffed her items into a bag. If anything happened to Ray-Ray, she'd feel totally responsible. "Please let me!"

Lizzie took the twenty. "Yes, go! I'll tell my dad you're coming."

Kate ran toward the parking lot, then roared onto Route 9, her thoughts faster than the wheels of the Subaru. When she reached their street, she was almost certain she knew where Ray-Ray was. Don waved in the road. "Slow down! We got a lost kid here!"

Kate waved back as she ran toward the house.

"You're here!" It was Tracy, in the yard, going through the hedges. Robert was out in his yard, searching the shrubs. A few others were with Ray-Ray's dad, including Mrs. Steele.

Kate ran over to them. "Have you looked all over the house?" As she said it, she felt a raindrop on her arm.

Ray-Ray's dad looked annoyed. "Of course I have. Of course—"

"Do you mind if I look too? He's a really good hider. I've played hide-and-seek with him." If she was right, Ray-Ray was safe. If she was wrong, he might be one of those missing kids you hear about on the news.

Ray-Ray's dad made a gesture that Kate interpreted to mean "Do whatever you want." She ran to the open door, past the piles of junk and laundry. She dashed to the garage. "Ray-Ray! Ray-Ray!"

Nothing. She stood silent a moment. Then, she heard something moving on the roof. She opened the back door and saw the ladder. "Ray-Ray!"

It was raining now, and the ladder was slippery. Still, Kate grabbed it and started climbing. "Ray-Ray!"

He was there, wet and shivering. Kate climbed up.

"You have to come down, sweetie."

Ray-Ray looked around. "I don't want to!"

"My God, Ray-Ray, do you know how much you scared everyone! The whole neighborhood's out there."

"No! I'm a rocket. This is my launchpad."

"I have to tell your dad you're up here. Everyone is so worried about you, Daddy and Mrs. Steele and Robert and everyone."

"They're mad," he said.

"I bet they're not." She hoped they wouldn't be. It was raining harder, and she was worried he'd slip off the roof. She grabbed his arm just to hold him. "Come on, sweetie."

"I don't want to. They won't let me see Mrs. Steele or play in the treehouse."

Okay, the kid had a point. His family was mad. "Is that why you hid here?" She held on to Ray-Ray with one hand, the roof with the other. He was sort of red and juicy with tears. "It's okay. It will be okay. I bet they let you now." She thought of all the people looking for him. Surely Ray-Ray's dad had to realize these people were only trying to help.

Just then, Ray-Ray's dad and Mrs. Steele showed up. "He's up here! He's a very good hider," Kate said, praying Ray-Ray's dad wouldn't get mad at him.

He didn't. He rushed toward them. "Aw, God, Racecar, I was so scared! I can't lose you too. Why'd you leave?"

He was practically crying, and it made Kate think of her own father, how protective he'd always been of her, whether it was when she was little and her kitty had died or, more recently, when he'd sent her away so she wouldn't have to deal with this mess. Daddy!

Ray-Ray's dad ran to the ladder and climbed up. "You gotta stay with me, buddy."

Kate tried to move over, not wanting to interfere. "I should go."

"I want Kate to stay!" Ray-Ray said.

"I can't stay, baby," Kate said, though it tugged at her. She climbed down the ladder. A moment later, Ray-Ray's dad climbed down too, with Ray-Ray in his arms. Around them, the neighbors were cheering.

When they reached the ground, Kate gestured to all of them. "Look at them! You really need someone to watch him regularly, and there are so many people who care about him, not just me, but Mrs. Steele, and Robert, all these people who are helping you now."

He sighed, holding Ray-Ray tight. "I know you're right. It's just so hard. When Angie OD'd, people were talking, and—"

"I know what it's like to worry about people talking about you, but you can't let that stop you from accepting help. Now, I can come help you the next week. And I can help you make a schedule for the rest of the time, when Lizzie's back in school."

"We can work it out," Mrs. Steele said.

Within a few minutes, they had a schedule for the rest of the summer. They didn't even need her anymore, but Kate knew she'd be back. She also knew she couldn't wait to see her own friends back home, Colin and other people who wanted to reach out to her.

In her purse, her phone was buzzing. She picked it up.

It was Britta. "Kate, are you coming home soon? We need the car. It's important." Her voice sounded as if she'd been running, but you never knew with Britta. She could just have seen a cute chipmunk or something.

Kate looked around. It seemed to be in hand. "Yeah, I'll be back soon."

She'd call Lizzie from the car, to let her know it was okay. Her phone buzzed. Probably just Britta nagging her again. She ignored it.

64

SPiDER

MONTAGE

- Britta and Spider search Spider's room for Randall the tow truck driver's grubby business card.
- They take every object out of Spider's backpack and put it back in.
- They try to search the car, but Kate has driven off with it.
- They give up and make a list of pros and cons of telling Ruthie about Janet.

"WE SHOULD BE honest," Britta said. "Shouldn't we?"

"But what if she doesn't want to see her?" Spider said.

"True. We definitely learned from our mistakes. We'll tell her where we're going."

"And what if it's not her? Or what if she's married or something? We have to ask them both." Though it would be really cool to surprise her with a reunion, like something in a movie (the first Men in Black movie, where Tommy Lee Jones's character comes out of a thirty-five-year coma), but probably not the best or most sensitive idea. "Also, what if she has a heart attack?"

"What if both of them do?"

In the end, they told Ruthie where they were going and why. Once Kate brought back the car, Spider and Britta drove to try to find the house. Spider checked the map she'd used that day.

"Just don't go into a ditch a second time."

Spider gave her the finger.

"Nice," Britta said.

"Thank you."

But finally, they saw it. First it was the sign for quilts, then the hybrid wolf-dog at the window, barking at the car.

"Pull over! Pull over!" Britta shouted. "But carefully."

Spider slowed, then stopped a little down the road from the house. Britta was out the door before she'd even put the car in park. She ran toward the little house, the same one from that day. "Come on! Hurry!"

Spider hurried. She wanted to film the encounter. Michael Moore would have. But she wasn't sure she should. Probably Michael Moore pissed a lot of people off.

Britta reached the blue front door and waited. When Spider got there, she knocked.

Inside, another dog barked. Both girls held their breath. What if they were wrong? What if it had all been for nothing? What if some husband answered the door?

There was movement at the window curtain, someone looking out. Then, the door flew open, the dog flying out, the woman, Jacey—Janet—behind it.

"It's you! Oh my God, it's you girls!" She held her hands to her face.

65

Britta

"YOU KNOW WHO we are?" Britta asked.

The woman breathed in deeply, closing her eyes. She was tall with long, gray hair, and as Britta stared at her, the years seemed to fall off, and Britta recognized her from the photo on Ruthie's wall. Janet. Ruthie's Janet.

After a long moment, she said, "You're not here to buy quilts?"

Britta shook her head. Spider stood transfixed, like she was imagining how the movie version of this story would play out. Janet breathed another rattly breath, and Britta wondered if she was trying not to cry, like Britta was.

Finally, Janet said, "You were here a few weeks ago. You're . . ." She reached out and touched Spider's arm. "Ruthie—Ruth Green is your grandmother?"

Spider stared at her, stunned. "Yeah. But how did you . . . ?"

"Randall told me. Stupid old coot. He said, 'You wouldn't believe who that was.' He was right. I didn't believe he didn't think to get a phone number, didn't remember your last name."

"It's Webster." The woman really looked about to collapse with happiness and tears. It was probably better they hadn't brought Ruthie yet. Someone would definitely stroke out.

Spider must have thought the same thing. "Are you okay? Is there anything . . . ?"

"I might need a glass of water," she said.

"Let us get it for you." Britta gestured at Spider to lead Janet to the sofa. Britta went for water. When she returned, she noticed Spider holding the woman's gnarled hand in her own.

She accepted the water shakily. "So Ruthie . . . she's alive? Is she here?"

"She is alive. We thought we should check with you before we brought her. We didn't want to get her hopes up if you . . . I mean . . ."

"If it wasn't you," Spider said. "Or you didn't want to see her."

"She was the love of my life!" And then Jacey—now Janet—burst into tears.

It took a few more minutes to calm her. Britta explained that they'd been looking for her, about the video, Ruthie's refusal. Spider filmed a little of that. Then, she showed her the embroidered pillow, the one that said "Janet C. Pearce embroidery" in little blue letters. Janet C. Janet Calisti. "It said Janet Pearce. We didn't know if you were married."

Janet nodded. "I *was* married, not happily. After he was finally gone, I looked for Ruthie, but her name, Ruth Green, isn't exactly uncommon, and I didn't know her married name, or if she had one. I had followed her career in New York. But then she disappeared."

"When she married my grandfather," Spider said.

"Why did you stop talking to her in the first place?" Britta asked.

"Because I was afraid. What do you want me to say? My family didn't like who I was, and it seemed easier to get married like they expected. Times were different then."

It was exactly what Ruthie had said. How could they argue?

"I never knew anyone like her. We had such plans, such plans, and now . . ." She broke off, her hands working at the quilt on the sofa. "Can I see her?"

Britta hesitated. "We should ask her."

"I've waited so long. You coming that day was like a gift, like . . ." She looked down at her hands as if just now realizing how spotted and old they were. She shook her head.

"That's true," Britta said. "What were the odds you'd drive into a ditch right here?"

Finally Spider said, "Okay. But let's call her."

"That's fine," Janet said. "That's fine."

When they called Ruthie, Britta heard her say, "You're sure it's her?"

"Pretty sure," Spider said.

On the phone, Britta heard Ruthie ask something else.

Spider turned to Janet. "She wants to know, what did she do to Mayra?"

Janet laughed, a cackle. "Oh, Mayra! Mayra said I looked chubby in my costume. And Ruthie, she painted the phone in the dressing room black with shoe polish. Then, I called from the five-and-dime, and Ruthie told Mayra she had a phone call. Mayra went onstage with black shoe polish on her face and hands!" She laughed again. "It's like it happened yesterday."

Spider repeated this to Ruthie, listened again, then hung up the phone. "She says okay."

Janet smiled. "All right, then. I'll get my car keys." As she walked toward the door, she paused in front of a mirror hanging on the wall, its frame made out of rustic twigs. She peered into it. "I wonder if she'll know me."

66

Spider

INT/EXT. SPIDER'S CAR — DAY

Britta is driving along a rural route.
Spider keeps checking her phone for service.

"IT'S GOING TO be fine," Britta said. "Ruthie said she wanted to see her, right?"

"I know." Spider glanced back at Jacey—Janet—who was following in her car. "It's just so weird. Fifty years, and now, they're just going to see each other, like it's perfectly normal. It can't go this well."

"Sometimes things just go well, Spider."

Spider smiled. "Guess so. I'm starting to think this summer rental wasn't a terrible idea."

And then they were there. Spider had her camera rolling for

the reunion, even though she had no idea what to expect. Tears? Laughter? She wasn't sure if Ruthie would come out, or if they should knock. Jacey was taking her time getting out; then she reached the door.

It opened, and Ruthie stood there. Spider noticed she'd fluffed her hair or something. She stepped back to get Janet's reaction at seeing Ruthie. Janet didn't disappoint, obviously overcome with emotion. "Ruth! It's been so long."

Ruthie stepped toward Janet. "You bitch."

"What?" Her own voice.

"How could you?" Ruthie's face was stormy. "How could you just leave like that without saying anything, without even trying to call, without giving me a chance?"

"I wanted to. My parents kept their eyes on me all the time. They were worried I'd run away." Janet's voice was shaking.

"I wrote dozens of letters. I checked the mail every day. We had plans together. I needed you."

"I know. I know. If I could go back and change it, I would. But I can't." She walked toward Ruthie, hands out. "We've wasted so much time, but now you're here. Finally."

She was crying, and when Spider looked, she saw that Ruthie was crying too. It was amazing. These women were so connected, gone so long, reunited. But would Ruthie accept her? Was she really that angry?

"You broke my heart." Ruthie's voice collapsed. "I looked and looked for you."

"I was here. I'm here now." Again, Janet reached toward Ruthie.

This time, Ruthie met her halfway, and they embraced.

"Oh God," Britta said. "This is so adorable."

Spider had forgotten Britta was there. It seemed impossible that even she herself was there, as if the world had melted away, leaving only these two women. But she took a step toward Britta, touched her shoulder. "You did this," she whispered.

"We both did," Britta whispered back. "And maybe God or something. We should leave them alone a moment."

Spider nodded and turned off her camera. They went inside, where Meredith and Kate sat on the sofa.

"Should I ask what's going on?" Kate said.

Spider shut the door behind them. Britta said, "That woman, the woman from the quilt place, she was Ruthie's lost love, from when they were our age. They just found each other."

"How long has it been?" Meredith wanted to know.

"It was the 1960s," Spider said, "so fifty years—more than fifty years they weren't together when they could have been, if things were different."

"Wow, why?" Meredith asked, then she thought about it. "Never mind. I know why."

"They wanted to do what was expected of them, what their parents and society thought was the right thing," Spider said, and Britta nodded.

"Yeah, it's terrible to think of the time they wasted," Britta added.

"Wasted giving birth to my father, who had me, but still . . . ," Spider agreed.

"True, but what about Janet?" Britta said. "It seems like she was never happy, and all because she wanted to do what people

417

thought she was supposed to."

That's when the door opened. Ruthie and Janet were a little drier, but still red-eyed, and arm in arm. Ruthie said, "We're going to take a drive around, catch up . . . on everything."

And then they were out the door together.

Britta met Spider's eyes.

"Intense," Spider said.

"Our work is done."

Spider watched the two old women, one tall, one short, getting into Janet's silver Jeep.

They glanced back at the other two. "What now?" Britta asked.

Meredith looked at the door. "Actually, I have to go do . . . something. I'm sorry. It's something I just realized was important." And she sort of ran to the door.

"Okay, that was weird, right?" Britta said, and Spider agreed it was.

"I feel like I need to maybe lie down a bit, at the lake," Kate said.

"Well, then, I'm going to go up to work on my script." Spider started upstairs.

"Okay," Britta said. "I guess I'll find something to do."

Spider turned back. "Aren't you coming with me? This is our project."

Britta grinned. "I thought our project was . . ." She shook her head. "Never mind. Yeah."

Spider noticed Britta was skipping a little as she followed her to the stairs. That idiot.

67

Meredith

Essay topic: What makes you happy? Why?

YOU ALWAYS HEAR about people's lives flashing before their eyes when they're in danger. That was what just happened to Meredith. When she saw those two old ladies, who'd been apart their whole lives, her life flashed before her eyes. Only it flashed *forward*, and she was an old lady herself, on her deathbed, looking back on her life and thinking of everything she'd missed because she was too busy studying, working, stressing out.

She'd missed sunsets and baking cookies and hanging out with friends, real friends.

And she'd missed Harmon. Harmon and his playlists and star trails.

Even though she was wearing sandals, Meredith ran the half

mile or so to his house.

His truck wasn't outside. Had he left already? She went to the door and knocked. Inside, a vacuum cleaner turned off and after a long time, she heard footsteps. His mother opened the door.

"Meredith?" She wore a paint-splattered blue shirt, and something in her face let Meredith know that she knew what had happened. "What are you—?"

"Is Harmon here?" She tried hard to keep the edge of desperation from her voice.

"No, he just left. He was headed for the mountains to camp." She rolled her eyes. "That boy."

"Do you know where he was going?" She tried to remember what he'd said. Something about the high peaks. Lake Placid, maybe? It was about an hour north. But there were over forty high peaks, and people took years to climb them all. It was worse than Spider's fire tower challenge. She needed someone to narrow it down.

"Mount Marcy, maybe." His mother squinched up her face, thinking. "He's supposed to send his location when he gets there."

Mount Marcy sounded familiar. Or was that the mountain Spider had mentioned that day when they'd gone to the train station?

Did these people not know you were supposed to leave an itinerary with someone before hiking, in case you went missing? She bet Harmon also hadn't thought to pack a whistle and mirror, to signal to rescue teams in the event of an emergency. That would be so like him!

"Is Mount Marcy the one Theodore Roosevelt was climbing when McKinley was shot?" This was an insane question, and his mother's face showed that she thought so too.

"I really have no idea," she said. She thought again. "It might have been Whiteface he was going to."

Which also sounded familiar. How did people in New York keep track of all these mountains? To say nothing of lakes and rivers.

And a sky full of stars.

"I have to find him," Meredith said just as his mom said, "I thought you broke up."

"That's why I need to find him," Meredith said. "I think I made a huge mistake. Maybe I can just try to call him." Except her phone didn't work here.

She thanked her and ran back to the house to ask Spider for the car keys.

She felt a little like a heroine in a rom-com.

Except the rom-com might turn into a survival story if she had to find him in the mountains. She grabbed her hiking boots, jeans, and a water bottle just in case.

Five minutes later, she was ensconced in Spider's car. She'd tried Harmon three times from the Websters' landline, but it had gone straight to voice mail. She'd just drive north.

She felt wild and free, for the first time in her life. People at school were going to say Meredith Daly went crazy over the summer. They might be right.

She pulled onto Route 9. She would drive through town to the expressway and start calling him from there. Since deer were usually only out at dusk and dawn, she actually sped a little, ten miles above the posted speed limit.

Then she screeched to a stop. It was his truck! At least, a truck that looked a lot like his truck (which, too be fair, there were a lot of around there), an old, white Dodge pickup. As Meredith crept closer, she saw it had a bumper sticker on the left side of the window.

She could dimly make out a picture, maybe of a moose.

It was his truck!

She made a hard right into the supermarket parking lot, causing her wheels to shriek in a way that Meredith Daly's wheels did not shriek because Meredith Daly was a sensible driver, a sensible girl . . . woman. But she was not sensible today. They shrieked again as she made another right. The space beside the truck was empty, and she pulled into it.

The bumper sticker on the car definitely had a moose on it.

It said, "Not all who wander are lost." She hoped all was not lost.

She jumped from the car, not even bothering to lock the door. She dashed toward the grocery store. When she went through the door, she ran into a guy weighted down with reusable grocery bags. A loaf of bread fell out of one of the bags.

Harmon!

"Oh! Sorry!" he was saying, leaning down to retrieve the

bread. Then he realized it was her. "Meredith?"

She had leaned down at the same time. Their eyes met. "Harmon!"

He scooped it up and started to turn away. "Sorry."

"Wait!" she said.

He turned back toward her. "What?"

"*I'm* sorry. I was wrong. Please don't leave." This was so weird, standing in front of a supermarket, pouring her heart out, him looking at her like *Why should I stay here*, and she had to tell him why. "I love you. I do. I don't want you to leave. You make me happy. I want to spend every minute we can together and make plans. I want it to work out for us somehow. I at least want—"

He dropped the bags on the ground with a thud, and then they were in each other's arms, kissing. It was like that first kiss all over again, except this time, instead of fireworks, there were canned goods, rolling out of the bags on the ground beneath them. Meredith didn't even care.

"Excuse me!" A lady with a shopping cart nudged Meredith's thigh with it.

"Sorry!" Meredith tried to get out of the way, even though they were having a moment. She bent to pick up the bags, and he did too. They bumped heads, dropped the groceries again, stopped to rub their heads.

"I'll just go through the other door," the lady said.

"Thanks." Harmon saluted the woman. He held a finger up to Meredith. "I'm going in. Stay there."

He scooped up the canned chili and Gatorade into the two bags, then nudged her to follow him to his truck.

She did. When they reached the truck, he said, "What changed?"

"Nothing. Everything." She looked at his groceries, which he'd stuck in the passenger seat of his truck, and remembered what he'd said about never wanting to leave here. "I don't know if I want to stay here forever. I mean, I like it here, but it's over a half an hour drive to Target, and the supermarket only has ten kinds of cereal." She was making a mess of this.

His eyes were laughing. "We believe that's part of our quirky charm, but okay. I would consider moving closer to a Tarr-get in the future." He pronounced it like it was foreign to him. "That wouldn't be a deal breaker for me."

"My point is, I don't even know what I want yet. But you showed me that I don't. Before I met you, I thought I did. I guess I got scared because you seemed so sure of what you want."

He put his arm around her. "I want you. That's what I want. We'll be together somehow. I can take photographs anywhere. So far, they haven't managed to get rid of wildlife completely. I hear they even have some in Miami."

"Let's not get carried away."

He kissed the top of her head. "Well, listen, I've got a tank of gas and two bags of groceries. Want to come to the mountains with me?"

"I've got my boots," Meredith said, even as she wondered what she was getting herself into. Like, was she going to sleep in a tent? Did he even have a tent? "We should bring Spider's car back first. That might get her mad."

"Aw, don't worry. We're going to have to go back and get you some warmer clothes for overnight. It'll be cold. We'll pitch a tent under the stars. It's a waning gibbous tonight, but we should still be able to see them."

"How many nights are we talking about here?" she asked.

"How long are you staying? I'll be sure to get you back by then." At the panicked expression on her face, he said, "Kidding, kidding. Just one night, unless something goes wrong."

"I was all freaked out, and you were only leaving for *one* night?" she said.

He took her in his arms again. "I want to spend as much time together as possible, before I can't anymore."

68

Kate

KATE STARED AT the text. It was from Daddy.

Call me. Important.

As soon as she could escape unnoticed, Kate took her phone and ran up the hill at a speed that would make Ms. Pierpoint, her physical education teacher, unjustifiably proud. Her thighs hurt, and she was breathless. Finally, the call went through.

"Kate?"

"Daddy? It's so good to hear your voice!" She remembered Ray-Ray and his dad. She missed her father.

"Good news, Katy. They're going to drop the charges!"

"What?" The air at the top of the hill was thin. It made her light-headed. Her father's words didn't seem real.

"Edwin turned out to be, shall I say, not a very reliable witness. Seems like he has a drug habit. He was arrested trying to buy cocaine from a county commissioner's staffer."

Well, what do you know? Edwin was the informant who was testifying against Daddy. Kate felt legit dizzy. She backed into a boulder nearby and sat on it. Wait! "When did that happen?" She wondered if Colin had known about it when he wrote the letter, or when he spoke with her. Did her friends know? Was that why Greer had invited her to the barbecue?

"I've heard rumblings about it for a few days. But it just became public information this morning, when I texted you. It was on the noon news."

Noon. So Colin hadn't known.

Her father chortled. "Edwin's ruined. Remember what I told you about that female dog named karma?" It was a joke he made all the time.

"Daddy, that's not nice." Kate felt terrible for Lacey, Edwin's daughter. She would call her as soon as she got home. That would be a long enough cooling-off period that Lacey wouldn't assume she was gloating. Now she wondered if that was why her friends hadn't called right away.

"What'd I say about karma?" Daddy pressed.

Kate smiled. "Karma's a bitch. Ha ha." She pressed her hands against the rock, liking how solid it felt. Poor Lacey. But she also realized she now knew things about her own father that she couldn't unknow just because he wasn't going to jail. He wasn't blameless.

"You're right. I'll be nice. And you have a nice time the rest of the month. I can take back my position, and you can come home, and we can get back to normal again."

Normal? Kate dug her fingers into the rock, remembering the bonfire, what she'd said about her old life. Kate realized she'd meant it.

"Daddy?"

"Yes, Katy."

"I don't want things to be normal again."

"It'll be fine, Katy. I—"

"I'm not the same person I was." Kate felt like she had to scream, practically, to be heard with the bad reception. The thin air. "I can't go back to that. I can't be a debutante. I can't live the life people expect of me. I want different things. I might . . ." It was the first she'd thought of it, but she knew it was true. "I want to go to public school, meet different people."

Would Colin understand? Kate thought he would. And if he didn't, then Kate would have to deal with that.

"Oh, Katy, you don't have to change."

"I want to try." Then, worried he'd think she wasn't happy, she said, "I'm really looking forward to seeing you, Daddy." Despite his flaws, she was still Daddy's girl.

"We can talk about it when you get home."

"I won't change my mind," Kate said, knowing it was true. *Ainsi sera, groigne qui groigne.*

"Okay, Katy. I love you."

"I love you too, Daddy."

Kate sat up there a very long time, loving the realness of the stone against her hands, the smell of the pines. She wished she could stay up there forever. It would be hard to go to a new school senior year, no friends, no debate teacher who knew her. But not as hard as it was for Ray-Ray or Lizzie with no mother, and not as hard as pretending to be someone she wasn't.

That was all still weeks off. Kate gripped her fingers against the rock and breathed in the pine-scented mountain air and thanked God or karma or whatever for having choices.

69

Meredith

Essay topic: There is a Quaker saying: "Let your life speak." Describe the environment in which you were raised—your family, home, neighborhood, or community—and how it influenced the person you are today.

"YOU NEED TO call your mother," Harmon said later that day, when they were taking a break on Whiteface Mountain.

"About what?" Meredith asked evasively. But she knew he was right. She had to tell her mother her doubts about college. "It's just so scary."

"What's she going to do, disown you? You're, like, the perfect child. You probably drink eight glasses of water a day and ask for more homework."

"The water, yes, but I never ask for more homework," Meredith said. "The only people who ask for more homework are people who need more grades. If I have extra time, I just double-check my work, and try . . ." She looked over at Harmon. He was pretending to be asleep. At least, she thought he was pretending.

When he noticed she'd stopped talking, he shook awake. "Sorry, sorry. I fell asleep, listening to you talk about homework."

She swatted his shoulder. "What a jerk."

"So are you going to call her?" he asked.

"When I get back to the cabin." Meredith bought herself as much time as possible.

"Or you could call now, where there's still cell phone service." He tapped on her phone.

"Okay. But when she flies up here and tries to drag me home, it'll be your fault."

"I'm willing to take the risk."

Meredith dialed. It was Thursday, so maybe her mother was in a trial. Or a meeting. Or an elevator, anything to keep her from picking it up right away. She could leave her a voice mail.

"Hello?"

Leave it to her mother. "Mom, it's me, Meredith."

"I'm so glad you called. I've been telling myself that I shouldn't worry, that you're a really responsible girl, and—"

"I don't know how responsible I am." Meredith waited for her mother to stop talking, then repeated, "Mom, I'm not sure . . . I don't want to go to Princeton."

"That's okay. There are plenty of other schools, and even with an alumni connection, there's no guarantees that—"

"I'm not sure I want to apply to any of those schools, the Ivy League. In fact, I might want to take a gap year." This was an inspired idea she'd just had, or just admitted having. "To figure out what's right for me."

"Gap year?" Her mother's voice sounded far away, as if Meredith was hearing her across the mountains.

"I don't know, maybe work or volunteer. Or maybe just go to a state school or something, someplace"—she didn't want to say *easier*—"friendlier."

"Meredith, are you okay?" Her mother's voice was high and panicked. "Did something happen? Did someone do something to you or—?"

Jeez. Her mother thought it was body snatchers. "No, no, nothing like that. I just . . ." She felt Harmon's hand on her shoulder. "I've been having panic attacks for a long time. It wasn't just that once. Some days, it's hard for me even to go to school. Or I lie in bed at night and can't sleep."

Silence on Mom's end. Nearby, a bird cawed. Then, Meredith thought she could hear her mother breathing.

"Mom?"

"Why didn't you tell me this?" Meredith could tell her mother was gritting her teeth, the way she did when she was trying not to freak out. "I could have talked to your teachers, or you could have gone for counseling."

432

"I didn't want to disappoint you. I'm sorry." Meredith groped for Harmon's hand. This was a terrible idea. Her mother could have gone her whole life without knowing how messed up and crazy Meredith was, and they'd both have been happier. Was it too late to shout, "KIDDING!" into the phone?

"So that's why you ran away to New York? You were afraid of disappointing me?"

"No, I didn't run away." Seeing Harmon's face, she said, "Well, I guess I kind of did, but I planned to come back. I *am* coming back at the end of the month. I just needed a break."

Meredith squeezed Harmon's hand. If it was even possible, this was the hard part. Difficult to believe they hadn't even reached the hard part yet. Talking to her mother was like climbing up a mountain.

"It's just so much pressure, taking the SAT five hundred times and studying and doing volunteer work and activities and filling out applications and never getting a break."

"But I thought you wanted those things." Her mother's voice was soft, and Meredith wondered if someone else had walked in.

Instinctively, she lowered her own voice. "I do. I mean, I did. I thought I did. But then, I start thinking, what's it all for? Is it really going to make me happy to have to work so hard all the time, never to get a break?" She didn't add, *like you do.*

Harmon squeezed her hand. He whispered, "You're doing great."

"If you don't want this, why are you doing it?" her mother asked.

433

Her voice was weirdly calm. Meredith was surprised she wasn't screaming. Not that her mother was usually a screamer, but this was pretty shocking stuff Meredith was dropping on her right now. She felt like anyone would scream under the circumstances.

"For you . . . and . . . Dad. I thought I wanted it. And I thought you wanted it for me."

"I do. I mean, I did, but only if it's what you wanted. And now there's a new wrinkle."

Wait, what? Meredith sucked in her breath. What kind of new wrinkle?

"I lost my job," her mother continued. "It happened a few months ago, before you left. There were some changes at my firm, and I was a casualty. I have some possibilities, but they won't pay as much, and I was worried about paying for a school like that."

Meredith's thoughts were swirling. She could almost *see* them, moving around like physical objects in her head. They'd been saving since she was a baby—at least her mother said they were—had they just been trying to guilt trip her into doing well in school all this time? And why wouldn't her mother tell her she'd lost her job? Why would she let her get her hopes up like that, spend months applying, doing all this work, if they couldn't afford it? Why wouldn't she just treat Meredith like a grown-up and tell her that? Why would she let Meredith think she had a decision to make when it was made for her? Her vision started to blur as if she might faint.

". . . anyway, I figured you could apply and see what happens," her mother was concluding, and Meredith realized she hadn't heard a word she'd said.

"What?" she said. "So there's no money?"

"We have savings." Her mother was speaking carefully, as if pronouncing every word was somehow important. "I don't want you to think we're broke. But if you could apply some places that might give you a scholarship, that would be . . ."

Meredith felt herself nodding like a bobblehead, like her head wasn't completely attached to her body.

She said, "I think I have to go. I feel weird."

"Wait. So you're okay?"

"Yeah," Meredith said. "I'll be back the thirty-first. I'll give you my flight information. Or I can get a ride with Britta. I have to go."

"Britta? Who's Britta?"

"I'm climbing a mountain, Mom! Gotta go!" Meredith hung up the phone and turned it off.

She looked at Harmon. She felt like she'd been jogging uphill all day, which she sort of had, but she hadn't felt that way before the phone call.

"She said she can't afford to send me to one of those schools, even if I get in."

"Yeah, I heard." He rubbed her hand with his thumb. "How do you feel about it?"

"I built my entire identity around the idea that I was going to an Ivy League school. I was practically suicidal over a C on

435

a test. Was she secretly hoping I wouldn't get in? She let me write essays. She encouraged me. Everything's changed in a minute. I don't know how to feel."

But she realized part of her felt free. With her grades and scores and activities, there were hundreds of schools that would give her a full ride, or close to it, if she didn't want to get loans. She could get a great education and still learn how to be something other than a student, watch a sunset or climb a mountain and, for the first time in her life, not have to worry that it was taking away from something she *had* to do. She could even take a year off. She could get a job at the mall.

Well, maybe not at the mall.

Harmon was nodding supportively, squeezing her hand. She looked up at the trees and the sky and mountain still ahead, before they reached the cold, bare summit.

She said, "I feel like we should keep going."

70

Spider

INT/EXT SPIDER'S CAR AT PARKING LOT AT
MOUNT HADLEY TRAILHEAD

Spider, Britta, Kate, and Meredith pull
into a parking space on a glorious summer
day. Though they are talking and laughing,
there is an air of sadness too. Their days
together are numbered.

"SEE. WE DIDN'T get lost." Spider parked in the shade. It wasn't crowded that day, a weekday, three days before they were scheduled to leave.

"And no ditch," Meredith said.

"I'm so proud," Britta effused.

"I only drove into a ditch that once."

"And that really worked out," Kate said. "I mean, for Ruthie."

Kate and Meredith unloaded their gear and started for the trail. Britta lingered behind. When Spider got her backpack, Britta held out her hand. "Let me take your water. It's heavy."

"I'm fine." Spider hoisted her backpack up. "I rested yesterday."

"You have your heavy camera, which is cool because you're going to immortalize this experience for all of us, right?"

"Our one fire tower?" Spider laughed. "I know what old people mean when they say, 'Where did the time go?'"

"Besides . . ." Britta stuck her thumb into her shorts waistband. "I've gained weight from all the ice cream and pizza. Carrying more would be good exercise."

Spider kept the water bottle. "I don't want your pity help."

"It's not pity. Hey." Britta nudged Spider, and she turned back. "It's called being nice." She held her arms out, palms raised. "Please?"

Spider gave up the water bottle. "Okay, but only to help you exercise."

They joined the others, signing in at the trailhead register. Then they started to follow the red trail markers.

"So are we allowed to talk today?" Britta said, after walking in silence a few minutes. "And about real things or only cool rocks?"

"I do like to talk about rocks." Spider remembered telling Britta not to chitchat.

"There *are* some interesting rocks here." Meredith, long legged and determined, reached a boulder before the rest of them. "We don't have much variety in Miami, mostly lime-stone."

"It's true," Kate said. "Some of the rocks here seem to sparkle like jewels."

"There's lots of garnet around." Spider caught up. "You can even go to a garnet mine. We'll have to . . ." Her voice trailed off as she realized, again, that the month was nearly over.

"Next summer," Meredith said. "We'll do it next summer."

"Next summer," Britta agreed. "And we'll hike more trails too."

"Why not?" Kate said. "The rocks have been here for centuries. They'll wait a year."

"Meredith's coming back to see her boyfriend," Britta sing-songed, like a little kid.

Meredith smiled. "You know it."

"I'm coming back to see Ray-Ray," Kate said. "He called me 'Aunt Kate' the other day."

"So cute!" Britta said. "I want my brother to have a kid so I can be someone's aunt."

They shuffled forward over the steepening trail, across little rivers where they had to walk on logs. After one such log, Spider took out her camera, knowing that soon, it might be too difficult to climb and film at the same time. Britta noticed her filming and turned back to smile and wave like a tacky tourist. She nudged Meredith and Kate. Spider didn't mind, though. She wanted their faces in it. Spider filmed all of them climbing over some sheer rock, then turned off the camera so she could do it herself. Her knees ached, but she didn't say anything.

"Do you want me to hold the camera?" Meredith asked when they stopped to rest at another boulder. "I mean, I know I won't do as good a job as you, but you should be in it too."

"That's a good idea," Kate said. "You promised you'd send it to us, remember."

"Please," Meredith said.

Spider laughed. "I'm not sure I want my Frankenstein walk immortalized." But she handed Meredith the camera. "Okay, but be super careful. I actually babysat children to earn the money for this camera."

"I'm sure it was fun for the children, too," Britta said.

"What are you saying?"

Spider showed Meredith how to work the camera. They trudged uphill, over patches of bald rock where it was hard to find a foothold. Eventually, Meredith turned off the camera so she could use her hands. She packed it and its case into her own backpack, and Spider let her.

"Harmon says the bald patches are because of thin soil due to fires," Meredith said, and Spider didn't cringe at Harmon's name, though Meredith brought it up multiple times per day.

"I guess that's why they built the fire towers," Kate said.

Finally, they were within view of the summit. Spider stumbled a couple of times. Her coordination was already failing, and she sensed that the other three were hanging back to accommodate her pace. She didn't want them to, though. "It's okay," she said. "I'll catch up."

"Don't be silly." Kate stopped walking. "We're all going to summit this thing together." The others nodded in agreement.

Spider sighed, but they waited. Soon, Britta shouted, "Look!"

A patch of blue sky was visible between the pines. Then, they were there. They ran—even Spider, in a burst of adrenaline—to the overlook and gazed out at the purple, blue, and gray mountains, up at the white-marbled sky, down at dozens of towns, hundreds of houses, thousands of lives they'd never know. Spider breathed deeply through her nose, taking it all in, the view, the wonder of it. The wonder.

"This is so beautiful," Kate said. "It's hard to see so much beauty."

They all knew what she meant. The fire tower loomed scarily to one side. It had six flights of stairs and reached into the clouds.

"Let's eat lunch before we do . . ." Britta gestured at it.

Over sandwiches, Spider said, "I'm leaving the thirty-first too. So I can drive you guys to LaGuardia, if you don't want to take the bus."

"Oh, I don't know," Kate said. "I loved the bus."

"Yeah, no," Britta said. "I heard it was super loud."

"Well, just this one annoying girl. But surely she won't be there a second time."

"Why are you leaving so early?" Meredith tilted her head back to survey the sky. "I thought you and Ruthie were staying for August."

Spider shrugged. "I know. But my mom wants to look at colleges in New York that have good film schools. But mostly, I thought it would be nice to leave Ruthie some time to get to know Janet without me underfoot. I'm coming back for Harmon's family barbecue."

"That's so cool. I mean, about Ruthie. Well, the barbecue too." But Meredith looked sad.

"I know, right?" Britta stood and fairly skipped to the edge. "Hello, world!"

They all laughed, but it was beautiful with the summer sun and light breeze and four friends, real friends.

A cell phone buzzed. Britta's. "Your phone," Spider called to her.

"Guess there's reception here." Britta ran back to check.

"Just ignore it," Spider said.

"That's weird. It's Rick."

"Your mom's pervy boyfriend?" Kate said. "I'd ignore it."

"What if something happened to my mom?" Britta clicked to answer. "Hello?"

She paused, a weird look on her face. After a moment, she hung up, looking rattled.

"What was it?" Spider hoisted herself up. "Is everything okay? Britta? Is your mom okay?" Britta looked really freaked out.

"It was a pocket call," Britta said. "He was with a woman. Like *with* a woman."

"Your mother?" Meredith asked.

"Not unless my mom changed her name to Caitlin."

Britta's phone buzzed again. She started to pick up it. "It's him again."

"No, don't," Meredith said. "Let it take a message. For evidence."

"Good idea." Britta stuck the phone into her backpack. "But what do I do now?"

Spider shook her head. "Report the sleazeball."

"She'll feel so bad," Britta said.

"She probably sort of knows," Kate said.

"Maybe," Britta said. "I'm not going to think about it right now. I'm not even going to listen to it. It's too beautiful here."

"Good idea." Meredith patted Britta's shoulder.

"Let's climb the tower." Spider stretched her legs. She could do this. It wouldn't be that hard, at least no harder than you'd think climbing six flights of steep stairs over sheer rock when you've already walked over a mile uphill would be. She could rest tomorrow—and all of August.

Eventually, they made it.

"Wow, it's like flying." Britta held her hand up, as if testing the breeze.

"It's so blue," Kate said.

"Thank you for bringing us here," Meredith said to Spider.

"Yeah, we definitely have to do all of them," Britta said. "Even if it takes twenty years."

They stood there a long time, staring at the mountains below, the clouds all around them, not really wanting to come down, not really wanting the day or the month to end.

71

Kate

THE TOWN OF Hadley was, Kate thought, identical to every other sweet little town around here, identical welcome sign, town hall, post office, white-steepled church, like the Christmas village at her grandmother's house. But as Kate drove through, Britta yelled, "Look!"

Ahead, above them, painted on whitewashed slats with space between for the sky to show through, was a poem:

I took the Road
Less Traveled
By
And That Made
All the Difference

"Robert Frost," Meredith said.

"It's just there," Britta said. "Speaking to us."

"And to hundreds of other people." But Kate pulled over. Britta would want to photograph the moment and memorialize it, probably post on some kind of social media.

"It's like a prophecy," Kate said, realizing it was. She would take the road less traveled, not the road of her parents, grandparents, and every one of her classmates at Bradley Prep. Her own road. She was already on it. Would it make all the difference?

"So we have to get a picture." Britta opened her door. "And find someone to take a picture of all of us under it. And then ask them where Stewart's is so we can get ice cream."

"What happened to your diet?" Spider asked.

Britta took out her phone, glaring at Spider. "A, don't fat-shame me."

"I wasn't. You just said—"

"And B, where am I supposed to get mint cookie crumble in Miami? I have to have it while I still can."

Spider had no answer, so she followed Britta, though Kate could tell from her stiff gait that she was barely able to walk now. Kate had, at first, seen Spider as a fussbudget. She now realized she was a fighter.

Kate wanted to be a fighter. She got out too, to take a picture. She wanted to remember these girls, this moment, because she was pretty sure this was the month her life changed forever. But she couldn't keep up with Britta, who hopped toward the sign quick as a rabbit. Then, suddenly, Britta tripped and face-planted on the pavement.

"Britta!" Spider lurched toward her. Meredith followed.

Britta didn't move.

72

Meredith

Essay topic: The lessons we take from obstacles we encounter can be fundamental to future success. Recount a time when you experienced a challenge, setback, or failure. What did you learn?

HEAD INJURY.

Headinjuryheadinjuryheadinjuryheadinjuryheadinjuryhead-injuryheadinjuryheadinjury.

She was just lying there, eyes slightly open. But there was nothing behind them.

"Britta?" Spider's voice sounded like it was coming through water.

Nothing.

"Britta!" Meredith got down next to Britta and grabbed her wrist. There was a pulse.

Freshman year, when Meredith had still thought she wanted to be a doctor, she'd joined HOSA, the club for students interested in health professions. It hadn't gone well. She tried to remember what they'd said to do for a head injury. "Someone call 911," she told Spider and Kate.

Should she check Britta's airway? She wasn't choking, but Meredith guessed she might have been chewing gum. Meredith turned her over gingerly and checked. Nothing. She was breathing, which meant she didn't need mouth-to-mouth. But why wouldn't she blink? "Britta?"

"Maybe put something under her head?" Spider's voice was shaking.

"Yes!" Elevate the head, but don't move her. "Good. Can you . . . ?" But Spider looked rattled. Meredith decided to run to the car. Kate was on the phone, and Meredith grabbed Harmon's hoodie off the back seat. She ran back and wadded it up under Britta's head.

"They're coming!" Kate said. "Is she okay?"

Meredith didn't know. It was weird, how her eyes were still partly open. But she said, "I think so. God, I hope so." What would she do if something happened to Britta? What would she tell Britta's mother, who thought she was safe at some Girl Scout camp in North Florida?

This had been a terrible idea.

"She's still not moving?" Spider leaned closer. "Britta!"

A distant siren's wail broke through the perfect summer day.

"It'll be okay," Meredith said. "It has to be!"

"It has to be," Spider echoed.

Meredith spotted Britta's phone a few feet away, on the ground, still open to Instagram. She crawled over and grabbed it. She might need it if she had to call Britta's mother, which it seemed like she might have to. Oh boy. The siren came closer. Thank God!

Then it was there. Two paramedics rushed forward.

73

Britta

WHERE THE . . . ?

The last thing Britta remembered was a poem. "I took the road less traveled by." Then her ankle twisting as her toe met a rock.

Now she was lying on a bed with someone over her. A stranger. Her head felt foggy. It dimly occurred to her that she was in a truck . . . was she being kidnapped? No. It was too comfortable. People were speaking in soft voices, as if they were coming through a wall.

Somewhere in the distance, she heard a girl's voice, saying, "Is . . . coming out . . . ?" But in pieces, like a phone breaking up. The voice was familiar, though.

"Who is that?" she said. But she didn't think they could hear her, these weird, helpful kidnappers. "Who . . . ?"

"Please . . . Britta . . . okay?"

"Meredith . . . is it . . . ?" Britta could barely hear her own voice.

"She's awake." A woman's voice, a stranger. Louder. "Britta? Can you hear me?"

"Yeah."

Oh, shit. She was in an ambulance. Were they going to close the doors and keep her back here? Would they take her to a hospital? Would they tell her mother? It was all sort of coming back to her now, the hike, Meredith, Spider, and Kate.

She'd hiked uphill all day and then fell on a stupid pebble on the road. It was *Little Women* all over again. Shit. She heard the word *hospital*.

"Can I ride with her?" a voice was saying through the cotton stuffed in Britta's head.

"Only family."

"Oh, I'm her sister," the voice said.

Wait, what? Foggy as Britta was, she was pretty sure she didn't have a sister. Did she? But someone was sitting beside her, squeezing her hand. She could barely make out a "Vote for Pedro" T-shirt.

"Are you okay?" Spider. But her voice sounded weird. Britta couldn't really pay attention. She closed her eyes. "Is she going to be okay?" Spider asked.

Britta heard something about a concussion. They started moving. She tried to open her eyes, tried to speak. She had something she wanted to tell Spider. What was it?

"Spider?" She could barely hear her own voice.

But a second later, Spider whispered back. "Yeah?" Her voice broke.

Britta whispered, "I told you I fall all the time."

Silence. Then, a giggle. Maybe it wasn't Spider. Spider never giggled. Who was it then?

Then, "You did what Theodore Roosevelt said. You failed while daring greatly."

Theodore Roosevelt. Yeah, that was Spider.

They were on the road awhile, and the world became more real. That was good. Britta was pretty sure she was flaky enough without brain damage.

"What happened?" she asked Spider.

"You just . . . fell. Boom!" Spider mimed it. "And then you were lying there. Meredith tried to revive you, but . . . nothing."

Spider sounded normal now, but Britta remembered her weird voice before. "Were you, like, crying?"

"I thought you were dead! Or dying, at least. Would you want me not to be upset?"

It was true. If Meredith couldn't figure out how to fix Britta, things must have looked pretty grim. "No, it's just c—" Britta started to say *cute* then pictured herself getting another head injury if Spider punched her. "Sweet that you were so concerned."

"You really looked dead," Spider said.

At the hospital in Glens Falls, they put her in a room to await a CT scan. Meredith and Kate had followed them there.

"I, um, had to call your mother." Meredith handed Britta her phone. "They needed permission to treat you."

Britta had recovered enough to swear. "What did she say?"

"Well, I told her I was a friend from school, and I was sort of vague about where we were. But I'm guessing she'll figure it out when she sees New York on the form they send."

"Unless she's too engrossed in Rick to notice." Now that the emergency had passed, Britta realized her head hurt. A lot. She wasn't sure if it was hitting it or worry.

"Rick's not with her right now." Kate said. "Remember?"

It was starting to come back, the pocket call on the mountain. The climb seemed far in the past. Had it really been that day?

"You're going to have to tell her the truth at some point," Kate added. "Secrets only keep for so long, and they eat you up inside." She was talking about her father.

"Yeah, probably. My head just hurts so much. Don't they have any Advil here?"

As if on cue, Britta's phone buzzed. Mom. Britta looked around. "Anyone want to get it?"

No takers. Meredith said, "I'll go see if there's Advil."

"You can play the injury card better if you answer now," Kate said.

"And she's, like, ten states away, so she can't do much," Spider added.

Good points. Britta answered. "Mommy?" She tried to make her voice sound weak, not difficult because she really felt that way.

"Britta, where are you? Where is Glens Falls? Were you human trafficked?"

Oh God. Britta hadn't thought her mother would think that. But of course she'd go to the very worst-case scenario. Human traffickers didn't call your mother.

But Britta didn't say that. "No, I'm fine. At least, I think I'm fine. They're doing a CT scan. I just . . ." She tried to think of a good lie to explain how she got to New York from North Florida. Field trip from the Girl Scout camp? She came up empty.

"I lied about where I was going," she finally admitted. "I've been in New York . . . on vacation."

There were times when Britta wished she had one of those stereotypical television Latina mothers who let forth a string of Spanish when they were angry. Britta didn't speak or even understand much Spanish, so it would be easy to tune out. Unfortunately, Britta's mother also didn't speak much Spanish, not enough to come up with the eloquent stream of criticism that now issued from her throat. She let Britta know—in English— that she was the worst daughter in the world and it was a wonder she wasn't at the bottom of a ditch somewhere. But Britta noticed that a recurring refrain was how worried she was.

"I know, Mom," Britta said over and over. "I know it was stupid . . . No, I'm fine . . . I mean, my head hurts because I hit it, but . . ." She remembered what Kate had said about the injury card. They were looking at her with huge pity.

"Why did you do this?" her mother demanded.

"I'm sorry. I just had to get out of there. I couldn't stand it

454

with Rick." She remembered the pocket call, the phone message still waiting for her, someone saying that the best defense was a good offense. Britta had always wondered what that meant. Was that what it meant? Should she throw Rick under the bus to get attention off herself? But she felt bad doing that. Maybe her mother deserved to know, but would she want Britta to tell her? "He's just so gross, Mom. He bought me that bikini and kept asking when I was going to try it on."

Silence. Britta's head was pounding. Where was Meredith with that Advil? She'd almost died, and now, she couldn't get Advil.

"You didn't tell me he said that," her mother said.

"I didn't want to . . ." Britta tried to put the words together. "I wasn't sure you'd take my side." She remembered the story she'd told about the pond and realized it was true.

"You didn't . . . ? How could you think that?"

"I don't know. I just—"

"I think he's seeing someone else," her mother said.

He is. But Britta didn't say that. She said, "I'm sorry. About everything."

"Are you okay? I should come up and get you."

"You don't have to. I'll be home . . ." She looked around at her friends, trying to remember how much longer they had. "The thirty-first. It would cost a lot to change it."

"You're sure?" Her mother seemed calmer now.

"Yeah. You can talk to Meredith. She's, like, really responsible. Look at my yearbook, Meredith Daly. She's president of everything. And I'll send you my flight information."

"You're grounded the rest of the summer," her mother said.

"I know." She already had no car and had to do online math.

"And other things. I'll think of the things."

"I know. I'm sorry. But I'm fine. I'll send a photo to prove it—of my friends and me." She hoped she looked okay.

Finally, she got her mother to hang up. She looked up at the pitying faces of Spider, Kate, and Meredith.

"Wow, that sounded bad," Kate said.

"Brutal," Spider agreed.

"You know it was. I guess I shouldn't have done that."

Meredith smiled and handed her a cup of water. "It was worth it, though."

Britta laughed. "Yeah, it was. I don't suppose anyone got a shot of the poem?"

"You mean of you lying there under the poem, unconscious, while the ambulance came?" Spider said. "No."

"We'll just have to take one here, in the hospital," Britta said.

They did, and Britta sent it, along with a photo a hiker had taken of them at the summit of Mount Hadley, four friends in the waning days of summer, looking forward, the whole world ahead of them. Britta knew she was in huge trouble. She probably wouldn't drive until she was thirty. But, as Meredith said, it was worth it.

74

Spider

```
EXT. CABIN — NIGHT

The four girls plus Ruthie are gathered
around an open fire. They are happy and
laughing, but a somber air pervades the
scene.
```

"I CAN'T BELIEVE it's our last night," Meredith said.

"I didn't think I'd last this long with the bats and the owls." Kate's voice was high, imitating a southern belle, maybe Scarlett O'Hara, "And the company! My word, the company!"

"Yeah, this place gives a lousy Swedish massage," Britta joked. "And no room service."

Kate punched her in the shoulder.

Britta had suggested a final campfire with s'mores and

songs. They'd planned it for two days after the big hike, to give Spider, and all of them, a chance to recover. Spider had invited Harmon and Janet, but they'd declined, saying it should be a housemates' night. The last one. Spider shivered over the fire.

"I wrote a song about us, guys," Britta announced. "But you can't make fun of it."

"I'm not sure I can promise that," Spider kidded. Britta had on a T-shirt Spider had ordered for her. It was from the movie *Mean Girls* and it said "On Wednesdays, we wear pink." Spider's own shirt, from the same movie, said "Beware of plastics."

"I can," Kate said. "I am unfailingly polite. In fact, if a southerner doesn't like you, she just becomes *more* polite. I learned that from my mother."

"How about you, Meredith?" Britta asked.

Meredith shrugged. "I have to be nice, right? If you hadn't talked to me that day in the library, I wouldn't even be here. Neither of us would."

"If Spider hadn't gotten the idea to rent out rooms," Kate said, "none of us would be."

It was true, and they all looked around the circle, amazed at it, the roundness of time, rippling over all of them, changing all of them in this place that never changed.

"Okay. I'll sing it once. Then we'll all try it." Britta had a ukulele with a picture of a palm tree on it, because of course she did, and she strummed it with the confidence of someone who'd always been cute and popular, never laughed at or unsure of herself. But Spider knew better now. Still, her voice was loud and sweet, and Spider envied her bravado as she sang:

We are the Girls of July;
Sisters of summer weather.
Summer will live in our hearts
When we're no longer together.

Summer is always too short.
Winter days are long.
We will return to July
When we sing this song.

"Okay, now this is the bridge. Then, when I repeat, you guys try." And she sang, "We'll always be together. We'll be friends forever."

She started again from the beginning, and they all joined in, collapsing in giggles at their sad efforts at singing, except for Ruthie, whose voice was clear. When they finished, Kate said, "I love you guys, but that was really hokey."

"People like hokey things," Britta said. "That's why the Hall-mark Channel even exists."

"Truth," Kate agreed.

"Truth," Meredith said. "Or Netflix Christmas specials. I love those."

"Please don't let me be making Christmas specials ten years from now," Spider said, "but yeah."

"You are going to be an important filmmaker," Britta said. "That's why I'm keeping in touch with you. The only reason." But she laughed when she said it.

"I'm sorry I didn't really get to know you guys sooner," Kate said. "Was I awful at first?"

"Well, not awful," Britta said, "just a little frightening."

"I liked you," Meredith said, "the second you offered to help catch the bat."

"More likely the second I backed off and let you and Harmon catch it," Kate said.

"True," Meredith said. "But I still liked you."

"Are you guys really serious?" Spider asked Meredith. Now that she'd stopped hating Harmon, she'd noticed he was actually pretty nice.

"Probably," Meredith said. "We'll see how it survives the winter."

"How will *we* survive the winter?" Spider asked. "Do you think we'll still be friends a year from now?"

She was looking, especially, at Britta.

"Absolutely." Britta patted her shoulder. "I mean, if you want to be. And, as proof, I am going to tell you my deepest, darkest secret. Come closer. I don't want anyone else to hear."

Even though there was no one around, not even an owl this time, they all leaned in.

Britta said, "Okay, so I let people think that Britta is short for Brittany, the name on my birth certificate is actually . . . Bertha."

"I never knew that," Meredith said, laughing. "How did I not know that?"

"Well, first off, we never had any classes together after fifth grade, but also, any time a teacher starts to say my name, I just interrupt her and tell her it's pronounced *Britta*. Bertha is my great-grandmother's name."

"Well, I won't tell anyone," Meredith said. "My big secret is that Harmon is the first guy I ever kissed."

"Oh, thank God!" Britta said. "I thought for sure you kissed that creepy Alaric guy at homecoming. Do you know he told me my dress was too low-cut? Like, first off, it wasn't. Secondly, if it was okay with the *principal* and my mother, why would he care?"

"He's a jerk," Meredith agreed.

Kate said, "My big secret is, before I came here, I couldn't even make grits. That first day I made them, I followed the directions on the container, and I threw out the first two batches."

"I thought I smelled something burning," Ruthie said.

"Yeah, that was me. I took it all the way out to the trash can outside so you wouldn't notice. We've had a cook all my life. But I'm going to learn to cook at home now. My mother will be so ashamed!"

"I'm learning too," Spider said. "I'm going to make Britta's *arroz con pollo*, but I'll tell my mom to buy chicken already cut up." She looked at Britta. "They sell them that way, you know."

"You all know my big secret now," Ruthie said. "But what

461

you don't know is that I called my children last night and told them about Janet and me."

"Did you?" Spider thought Ruthie and Janet were such a cute old couple, like they'd never been apart. "What did Dad say?"

"He wasn't as surprised as I'd expected. Maybe there really aren't any secrets."

"I'm glad," Spider said.

Spider realized everyone had spilled a secret except her. She could take the easy way out and admit that she'd never been kissed either or that she couldn't cook. But she decided to be a little braver. She turned to Britta.

"My secret is that I couldn't stand you at the beginning of the summer. I tried to get Ruthie to put you downstairs because you were so annoying."

"What a cop-out!" Britta said. "I completely knew you hated me." She threw a marshmallow at Spider, though it sailed past her head and Kate caught it.

"Shut up. That's not the secret part," Spider said. "The secret part is, you are the best friend I've ever had." It was hard to say, hard to lay herself open like that, admitting she hadn't had a best friend since Lauren dumped her in fifth grade. But it was true.

There was an awkward silence, and Spider regretted saying anything. Britta was probably so popular at home. Literal crickets, and the crackling of the fire.

Then, Britta broke it. "I feel the exact same way!" She swiped at her eyes. "God, I'm tearing up. This really is like a Hallmark movie. I'm not crying; you're crying."

"We have to get together during the year," Spider said. "You have to get your mom to let you audition for schools in New York."

"I will," Britta said. "I will. This isn't the end of us."

They listened to the fire crackle and the music of crickets, enjoying the unspeakable beauty of a night in July, and when the logs had burned down to embers, Britta suggested they sing the song one more time before they went in. "Loud and clear this time."

They did.

> *We are the Girls of July;*
> *Sisters of summer weather.*
> *Summer will live in our hearts*
> *When we're no longer together.*
>
> *Summer is always too short.*
> *Winter days are long.*
> *We will return to July*
> *When we sing this song.*
>
> *We'll always be together.*
> *We'll be friends forever.*

The final ember died out, and the last ukulele chord faded, so they went inside.

75

Britta

BRITTA WOKE EARLY that last morning with an idea. She went into her suitcase and took out her favorite earrings, tiny gold hoops, and cleaned them off. She held them out to Spider at breakfast, which was Ruthie's chocolate chip waffles and Kate's now-famous grits.

Britta said, "We said that first morning that the one thing we all had in common was pierced ears. I think we've discovered some other things, but I'd like to give you these. My grandmother got them when she was a little girl in Cuba."

Spider looked touched but said, "I can't take these."

"It's a loan. You have to give them back next time we see each other. That way, we'll be sure to do it."

"Oh, cool." Spider felt her own earlobes. She wore the same earrings she'd had on that first day, the Big Dipper in one ear, a star in the other. "You can have these. I got them for my bat mitzvah."

"Thank you," Britta said. "But I'm wondering if maybe someone else should have them." She looked at Kate and Meredith. She hoped this would work.

"Oh, I get it." Meredith didn't always wear earrings, but she had some in today, tiny red stones. "So maybe Spider should give me her earrings, and I'll give mine to Kate? They're garnets, my birthstone." She started to remove them.

"That's my birthstone too," Kate said. "And I'll give mine to Britta. And then, next summer when we get together, we'll switch back?" She started to remove her earrings, which had a bunch of light-blue stones.

Britta nodded, but she looked at Spider just to make sure it was okay.

Spider smiled. "That's a great idea—just as long as you realize you and I are getting together way before next summer—when you come up to New York to audition."

"Absolutely," she said and meant it. She was going to have some work to do on her mother. Before she had come here, she'd thought she could be independent. Now, she knew she could—but only if she had the help of others and was able to help them in return.

This time, they made Kate sit in back with her suitcases. It wasn't as squooshed with only four people, though they almost left Meredith at Harmon's house when she took too long saying goodbye. They decided to take turns driving to the airport.

Meredith drove first, but Spider planned to drive when they got closer to the city, since she had experience. They pulled out of the driveway, leaving Ruthie and Janet waving at the door. It was sad, leaving behind this beautiful place, but Britta knew they'd be back. They'd be back.

Essay topic: Share a moment when you stepped out of your comfort zone, and describe how it helped you grow into who you are today.

By Meredith Daly

This past spring, I was sitting in the library when Britta, a girl I barely knew, suggested that she and I should rent a vacation home in the Adirondacks together this summer. Apparently, she thought I needed to relax. At first, I was shocked by her audacity. I needed to relax? Me, Meredith Daly, the coolest cucumber in town? What would relax me would be to finish my massive to-do list, which included twenty-seven college essays (Universal Application and various supplements), studying for five AP exams and the SAT, setting up interviews with local alumni, and researching scholarships, to say nothing of organizing the bowling team schedule, recruiting members for the Key Club, doing the minutes for the German Honor Society, and somehow getting dinner on the table because otherwise, my mom and I don't eat. If there was time, I also wanted to create world peace and organize my closets.

Also, no one I know has ever relaxed, ever.

Somehow, I decided she was right, and this summer, instead of going to a developing country to create a new drainage system and learn another foreign language, I escaped to the mountains, to a place with minimal internet service and wild animals in unexpected places (such as inside the house!). There, I learned to fish. I sat outside on a starry, starry night and listened to music. I hiked; I roasted marshmallows; I went outside without brushing my hair.

I fell in love.

This is no one's recommendation for the appropriate way to spend the last summer before college applications, and I know this may affect my chances of getting in. Nonetheless, I do not regret this decision.

Before this summer, the friends I had were more like coworkers. We chatted, but we didn't really know each other. We had common goals, but we competed. We also judged anyone who was different or less studious than we were. In New York, I made friends with three strangers who were nothing like anyone I'd ever met before: Britta, an aspiring actress from my hometown; Kate, an erstwhile debutante from Georgia; and Spider, an intellectual from New York who is dealing with an autoimmune disease. I describe them as if they were archetypes. I learned they were anything but. They are complex characters in the novel that is my life. It is a cliché to say we laughed and cried, but we did. I can call any of these women at two a.m., and they will answer.

It is hard to know how to save the world if one has never lived in it. Before this summer, I hadn't lived in the world. I'd only studied it in school. Now, I've lived in it. This experience is what I will bring to college. I recommend it.

Appendix B: Meredith and Harmon's Starry Night Playlist

"A Sky Full of Stars" by Coldplay

"Vincent (Starry Starry Night)" by Don McLean

"Counting Stars" by OneRepublic

"All of the Stars" by Ed Sheeran

"We Are All Made of Stars" by Moby

"Stardust" by Nat King Cole

"Moonlight Serenade" by Glenn Miller and His Orchestra

"City of Stars" from *La La Land*, recorded by Ryan Gosling

"Rhapsody in Blue" by George Gershwin (Leonard Bernstein and the New York Philharmonic)

Appendix C: Spider's Top Ten
Favorite Movies Ever

1. *The Piano*, written and directed by Jane Campion
2. *Rebecca*, screenplay by Robert Sherwood and Joan Harrison, directed by Alfred Hitchcock
3. *Inception*, written and directed by Christopher Nolan
4. *Back to the Future*, written by Robert Zemeckis and Bob Gale, directed by Robert Zemeckis
5. *Eternal Sunshine of the Spotless Mind*, written by Charlie Kaufman, Michel Gondry, and Pierre Bismuth, directed by Michel Gondry
6. *Pulp Fiction*, written and directed by Quentin Tarantino
7. *Mean Girls*, screenplay by Tina Fey, directed by Mark Waters
8. *Casablanca*, screenplay by Julius and Philip Epstein and Howard Koch, directed by Michael Curtiz
9. *Lady Bird*, written and directed by Greta Gerwig
10. *When Harry Met Sally*, written by Nora Ephron, directed by Rob Reiner

ACKNOWLEDGMENTS

Thanks always to my editor, Toni Markiet—I always feel so lucky to have such an experienced voice—and to her associate editor, Megan Ilnitzki, for all the day-to-day help.

Special thanks to Caitlin Greer for the sensitivity read and, also, for sharing her experiences with juvenile idiopathic arthritis, and to Jennifer Hartnett Wilson for sharing her family's experiences.

Thanks as well to:

My critique group, Alexandra Alessandri, Christina Diaz Gonzalez, Stephanie Hairston, Danielle Cohen Joseph, Silvia Lopez, Curtis Sponsler, and Gaby Triana.

Debbie Reed Fischer for reading my manuscript.

Bill Linney for providing a Latin translation.

My mother and late father for buying a vacation home at Green Mansions, a former theater colony in Chestertown, New York, when I was seven, and my two Girls of July, Kat and Meredith, for going there with me.